John

How to Farm Profitably

SALZWASSER
VERLAG

John Joseph Mechi

How to Farm Profitably

Reprint of the original, first published in 1859.

1st Edition 2022 | ISBN: 978-3-37512-908-8

Verlag (Publisher): Salzwasser Verlag GmbH, Zeilweg 44, 60439 Frankfurt, Deutschland
Vertretungsberechtigt (Authorized to represent): E. Roepke, Zeilweg 44, 60439 Frankfurt, Deutschland
Druck (Print): Books on Demand GmbH, In de Tarpen 42, 22848 Norderstedt, Deutschland

HOW TO FARM PROFITABLY:

OR, THE

SAYINGS & DOINGS

OF

MR. ALDERMAN MECHI.

With Illustrations,

FROM PHOTOGRAPHS BY MAYALL.

A NEW EDITION. WITH ADDITIONS.

LONDON:
ROUTLEDGE, WARNE, & ROUTLEDGE,
FARRINGDON STREET;
NEW YORK: 56, WALKER STREET.
1859.

INTRODUCTION.

A DESIRE having been expressed that I should collect my agricultural writings, for criticism and examination, I cheerfully undertake the task, hoping and believing that such a course may not be unacceptable or unprofitable to the agricultural public.

In the following pages, accordingly, will be found much that I have written and spoken on Agricultural subjects; and I have thought it right to reproduce these essays in precisely the form in which they originally appeared, notwithstanding those changes of opinion which they sometimes show to have arisen during the fifteen years which have elapsed since the first of them was published. Any alteration, indeed, which I have allowed myself—beyond the cancels (exceeding one-half) needed to bring the matter within the limits of this book—affects only the order of their appearance here. My latest publication has been placed first upon the list, as most nearly representing my present agricultural practice and opinions. The others have been, to some extent, classed according to their subjects, but they are, for the most part, arranged in the order of their original appearance; and a copious Index is provided, preventing the necessity of wading through the mass in search of any particular topic.

When I purchased land, and saw that it needed improvement, I laid down the theories on which that improvement should be effected, and while I admit that with my present improved practical knowledge and lengthened experience I could have worked out the details somewhat more economically, I am more and more convinced that the original principles on which I founded my operations have the full value which I then attached to them, and that it would have been good for the profit and honour of this great country had they been more generally adopted.

It is a sound principle, that all changes which take place in agriculture, if unattended by profit, are wrong, and are not improvements. It must, however, be borne in mind, that agricultural improvement is gradual, and progressively increased by time. Thus I have found it. Fortunately for me, and perhaps for agriculture, I have been spared long enough to witness the full development, and reap the reward of my improvements; but, better still, I have witnessed the gradual and more general acceptance and adoption of those changes for which I was once condemned, but for which I now get some credit.

Let us not, however, deceive ourselves by our self-esteem. The truth had better be spoken. We are, as it were, still only on the threshold of agricultural progress. As a whole, first-rate farming is the exception, and bad or moderate farming the rule of British agriculture. This is proved by our miserably low average agricultural produce, which is only £3 10*s*., or four rents per acre. Our whole system will yet undergo a mighty change by steam cultivation, by the economy of our town and farm manures, by the greater production of meat and manure, by the more general use of steam and machinery, by the economy of seed, by the eradication of weeds, and, above all, by the drainage and irrigation of lands not naturally filtrative: we shall not then, as we traverse our fields, probe the depth of cultivation with our walking-sticks, and have the mortification of finding an undisturbed, unmanured, and unaërated subsoil at the depth of a common wine-glass from the surface.

The subterranean glazed pan over which the plough has slid for a thousand years, will be torn up by steam-power, and the joyous roots of our plants will testify their exultation by a more vigorous surface vegetation, highly gratifying to the British stomach.

I. J. MECHI.

TIPTREE HALL, KELVEDON, ESSEX,

August, 1859.

PART I.

HOW TO FARM PROFITABLY, PARTICULARLY ON HEAVY CLAYS.

What will pay—Bad farming—Profitable farming—Land drainage—Shelter—Meat-making—Over-seeding — Covered yards — Education — Stiff clays—Implements—Labourers—Buying and selling—Corn and cake—Farm horses—Pigs—Iron as manure—Italian rye-grass—Beans—Weeds—Town sewage—Green crops—Cheap manuring—Artificial manures—Management—Crops—Prices—Conclusion.

ALTHOUGH I shall prove in these pages by unquestionable facts that numerous profitable things may be done in agriculture, I have no expectation that the generality of either landlords or tenants will practise them. The history of prejudice has always been the same, viz., resistance to innovation, and disbelief of progress: but that is no justification of despair; on the contrary, the evidence of all time shows that we must fight manfully against the old enemy, and that we shall overcome him by degrees.

We have hope to cheer us on, for can we forget that in our own time it was pronounced that gas was impossible, that steam-vessels would never cross an ocean, and that Stephenson's Express Train was an insane dream?—while, now, we hold converse through earth and water at lightning speed, defying time and distance.

That our lands might support all our population without foreign aid is not with me a matter of doubt, seeing by my own farm, as well as many others, practical illustrations of the fact. It is a common matter of figures. But I have no expectation that it will be done. Still, if my exertions in the cause of agricultural progression make some impression on agricultural lethargy and disbelief, my object will have been accomplished.

I have often been much amused by the compassionating look and manner in which my friends have inquired after my doings at Tiptree.

The translation of those sentiments is this:—"Mr. Mechi,

you are kindly losing money by your experiments, to oblige the country, and we ought to be grateful to you." But when I sternly ejaculate that whatever does not pay in agriculture is not an improvement, and when I demand categorical answers to these questions—

Does drainage pay?
Does deeper cultivation pay?
Does economy of manure pay?
Does efficient shelter for stock pay?
Do large, well-squared fields, good roads, and good buildings pay?
Do ample manuring and more cleanly cultivation pay?
Does a larger employment of labour pay?
Does the employment of steam-power, improved machinery, implements, &c., pay?—

I soon find how shallow and groundless are the objections to agricultural improvement.

The fact is, that for several years I have been deriving a most gratifying return for my expenditure, and it is of a very enduring and continuous character; but the world does not believe it.

In agriculture, as in other matters, you must invest a capital before you can get an interest or profit.

Whilst I am musing on the ignorance and prejudice that loses so many pounds per acre to the wretched tiller of undrained clays, I have no doubt that many such a man is chuckling at his own supposed pre-eminence, and congratulating himself that he does not throw away his money like that Mr. Mechi.

For **Evidence of the Backwardness of Agriculture** we have only to refer to the *Mark Lane Express*, the farmer's own paper. Annexed is a portion of its leading article of this day (Feb. 16, 1857). It is too true:—

"Upon a careful investigation, we safely assert that 20 per cent. of ordinary farm-yard manure is wasted. An examination of ten farm homesteads consecutively taken has fully established this supposition. In six of these the whole of the water from the roofs of the buildings fell directly into the yards.

"It is too much the fashion to look abroad for improvements, and forget that the first necessity for them exists at home. Year after year passes away regardless of consequences, and thus manure sufficient for the annual supply of the farm is lost once in every five years, and in some instances in a far less space of time. Whenever this subject has been individually adverted to, the answer is invariably 'My landlord will not do anything.' The same observation applies to the improvement of buildings, to drainage, and to every other point of recent introduction. Unless, perhaps, in the case of some few spirited individuals, things remain as they have done, and will probably continue to do so until the expiration of their occupation arrives."

Essential Preliminaries to Profitable Farming:—

A thorough knowledge of your business, practical and theoretical.

Ability to buy in the cheapest and sell in the dearest market.
To select the most able workmen of industrious and honest habits.
To choose as your bailiff a man of forethought, integrity, and firmness, combined with great industry and keen perceptive powers.
To apportion rightly your land and capital.
To maintain in economical efficiency the motive power, whether horse or steam.
Deep, frequent, and clean cultivation.
Drainage of land not naturally filtrative.
Shelter for stock.
Efficient machinery and farm implements.
Ample use of purchased food and manures.
Rigidly correct farm accounts, posted daily from the cash-book and journal.
Estimates of the cost and return of each crop in detail.

There has been so general an impression that my farming was my hobby for amusement, and not for profit, that I purpose to dispel what remains of this prejudice by a practical investigation of farm practice in a pecuniary point of view.

The real Test of Economy is the cost-price per quarter, per ton, or per lb., of the produce of the farm. The poor unimproving farmer is generally the producer of the dearest and most unremunerating food; whereas, on the contrary, the man who spends most per acre, and pays the highest rent, is the cheapest producer: therefore, I always ask, What does your corn cost you per quarter?—not, What do you spend per acre?

Let me illustrate this from actual facts.

PRODUCE OF UNDRAINED CLAY.

	£	s.	d.
First year, fallow—rent and expenses	5	0	0
Second year—oats, producing five quarters at 26s.	6	10	0

PRODUCE OF DRAINED CLAY.

	£	s.	d.
First year—tares, fed off by sheep eating rape-cake, beans, &c.	5	18	4
Second year—oats, producing ten quarters at 26s.	13	0	0

I quote this particular crop because I have watched it this year in comparison with my own, but we may carry out the comparison in almost all the others.

The Ruin is principally caused by Non-Drainage, for the more you disturb and pulverize undrained heavy land in fine dry weather, the more close and miry it will become during the rains of winter. There being no drains under it, the water accumulates and stagnates until the spring and summer, its only escape being upwards as steam, so that the heat of the sun is literally employed in evaporating the water instead of stimulating the plant to do this. The result of all this is, that such seeds as escape bursting and freezing in the mire of winter, vegetate slowly; the roots refusing to go into stagnant air and stagnant water, there is but little root formation, and consequently a miserably deficient surface growth, and an unprofitable crop. Contrast this with the drained land —there the roots roam freely and deeply, producing vigorous and branching shoots with broad and numerous leaves, passing through the plant under the influence of summer rays an immense amount of fluidity, the result of such elaboration being an abundant crop. The knowledge of vegetable physiology teaches us the value of drainage. A tree or plant will avoid stagnant water, but will seek out and multiply its roots in a running stream, the latter having a constant supply of fresh air. Water kept in motion becomes aërated. A small can of live fish in a gig or coach would travel from John O'Groats to the Land's End without injury, the water being in constant agitation; but stand the can quietly on a table and the fish would die, there being no change of air: roots of plants require change of air as much as fish or animals. Every shower on drained land leaves, by percolation and filtration, a new air and new fertility. Besides, it is well known that plants having one root in moisture, as in deeply-drained soils, will bring up to the dry surface, and diffuse by its other roots, a healthy humidity; and I suppose that it is the deep-rootedness of mangold wurzel that gives it, in our dry Eastern Counties, such a power of resisting drought.

Bad Farming is the Rule, and Good Farming the Exception.—It is impossible to travel through the various districts of this kingdom without coming to this sad conclusion, and that the bulk of the land is farmed in the least profitable manner. There are many causes for this, such as the poverty of landlords, the over-holding of tenants in proportion to their capital, the want of tenant valuations, or leases; but the greatest and most fatal cause is the comfortable belief in and self-satisfaction with the present state of farm practice. This remark applies equally to landlords and tenants.

I am aware that for many years a belief was entertained by agriculturists that Mr. Mechi was a visionary enthusiast; but I have seen enough to convince me that it would be happy for the bulk of our heavy-land agriculturists, if they could raise their produce at as low a cost as I do mine.

Living, as I do, in a district capable of immense progress, I am enabled to arrive at exact comparative results, and I have no hesitation in saying that the majority of heavy-land farmers would be in a far more advantageous position if they had to pay £2 to £3 more per acre for the advantages I have named.

In fact, the difference in my produce and that of many others is from £5 to £10 per acre—I mean at the recent liberal prices.

The great wants of our stiff clays are drainage, more manure, deeper cultivation, and covered yards for stock. I have watched attentively the most money-making farmers, and I find that they are those who practise as I have described.

The want of drainage on clays is ruinous. I have seen a clean summer fallow made on such land, and the whole in beautiful tilth; but what follows?—the rains of autumn and winter are absorbed and retained for want of filtration, and the fallow becomes a sea of mud, saturating, swelling, and rotting much of the seed, rendering the land most difficult and expensive to operate upon, and in the spring baking hard, and cracking like the mud bottom of a drained pond. The wretched and spindled plants struggle for an existence, and produce a miserable result. I have seen such fields adjoin my own, where the difference has been £10 per acre, principally owing to the absence of drainage.

You may always know undrained heavy land in dry weather: it is hard and knobby. The only seasons that suit the undrained heavy clays of England are a dry spring and a very hot summer. The wide and deep cracks answer the purpose of drainage to some extent, by an enormous and deep evaporation; but a wet spring is the ruin of such soils: and yet it is still difficult to make farmers believe that water will filtrate readily through the strongest clays to the drains.

The very best drainage in such soils would not cost more than £6 to £7 per acre, and I am sure that the loss arising from their absence has, in too many instances, been equal to the whole cost of the drainage in a single year. I am speaking now of wheat at 60*s*. per quarter, or oats at 28*s*. per quarter.

The question is not a disputable one, as the facts are patent wherever two adjoining fields are drained and undrained. I have watched the question closely during the last fifteen years, since I first drained my heavy soil.

In many seasons, a farmer who paid 9*s*., or 7½ per cent. on £6 per acre drainage, would find a difference of at least £5 in his corn crop; and still the great bulk of the heavy lands of England remain undrained!!! I believe at least fifty millions of money might be immediately and most advantageously so employed; it would add immensely to our home supply of food. The advantages of drainage have been so often and so largely explained by myself and others, that I will not dwell upon them.

Shelter for Stock.—This is the next important question. On clay farms your animals seldom do well on the land after October, and even if the weather is sufficiently favourable to permit their grazing, they should, during the long nights, be comfortably housed, and *lie dry*. To do this in a permanent manner would cost, at 5 per cent., an annual charge of 1*s*. 6*d*. per annum per sheep, or 12*s*. per annum for a bullock. Now, I have no hesitation in saying that it makes more than 1*d*. per sheep per week difference during the eighteen winter weeks, or, in other words, 3lbs. of mutton at 6*d*. per lb.

It is notorious that during wet and frosty weather whole fields of turnips have been consumed without making 1lb. of mutton; but it is easy to understand this by looking at the poor sheep at break of day, after lying for fourteen dark hours on a wet, cold soil, which absorbs the heat of their bodies, whilst their soaked and frosted fleeces complete their misery. The loss of sheep, by death, would pay for the shed-room. The value of a single sheep at 40*s*. would pay for the shelter of 480 sheep for one week. Practically, I have not lost one sheep per year on the average of the last fifteen years, although I fatten 300 to 400 annually.

The Quantity of Meat made on a Farm per Acre determines the quantity of corn grown. By asking a few questions of a farmer I can almost immediately arrive at a conclusion as to his position, without visiting his farm. The first question would be, "How much meat do you make per acre, over the whole acreage of your farm?" This question has been solved by Mr. Thomas Dyke Acland, in the Royal Agricultural Society's Journal, vol. xi. p. 666. There it will be seen that the largest corn-growing farmer in Norfolk, a most successful man, produces 4½ score of meat on *every acre* of his land: compare this with the general average of the farms of this kingdom, which certainly do not produce one score pounds of meat per acre. The more meat you make the more manure you produce, and the more corn you grow. The common labourer is the best evidence on this point: with his one-eighth of an acre of ground he knows that unless he keeps a pig to make manure, he cannot expect a crop. Therefore, he fattens one pig, which consumest hree sacks, or twelve bushels, of barley-meal, which, at 7lbs. of meal to 1lb. of meat, would be 84lbs. of meat, or four score on the one-eighth of an acre, or over 32 score per acre.

It has often been remarked that, amidst miserable land and wretched farming, the labourer's cottage-garden is like an oasis in the desert; but when I show that, independently of deeper cultivation, it receives in manure 32 times the farmer's quantity, the contrast needs no longer be a matter of surprise. Of course the farmer who makes the largest quantity of meat obtains a proportionate amount of manure, and of produce.

Some years ago, when good Danish barley could be had for 19*s*. per quarter, I fattened an immense quantity of pork and other meat, equal to at least 20 score per acre. The farm has never forgotten it, and as I made so much manure when corn was cheap, I have been enabled to grow large crops during the late high prices; thus justifying the calculations I made in my celebrated balance-sheet. I seldom make less than 10 to 13 score pounds of meat per acre over the whole farm; it is the key to good crops.

It would pay a Farmer well to sell his Beans to his Sheep at 40*s*. per quarter, because that price is about one penny per pound, and mutton at 7*d*. per lb. would pay for the seven pounds of beans required to make it. The beans thus remain on the farm. But, even supposing that you give to your sheep four quarters of beans per acre, and that you lose 10 per cent. by them, or 16*s*. per acre, I am prepared to prove that in the corn crop that follows the increase will be at least £3 per acre beyond the sum that would otherwise be realized.

I know a farmer within a few miles of me, who always allows his 1,500 fattening sheep 1lb. of beans per diem when feeding in the field; the consequence is a general and progressive enrichment of the soil, which almost compels him to take an extra corn crop to *tame* the land. In my own case I generally on one field, annually, which has become saucy, take five or six quarters of Rivett wheat per acre after a similar crop of ordinary wheat. The farmer to whom I allude takes green rye after oats, rye fed off with sheep eating beans; then turnips, put into little mounds, and fed off in February and March with sheep eating beans; then barley with seeds; then clover once mowed, and then fed off with sheep eating beans; then wheat followed by oats, which completes the rotation—thus growing three corn crops, one root crop, and two green crops in a course of five years, with an increasing fertility. The fact is, the poverty-stricken principle of a lot of hungry, half-starved sheep, *growing* into money, and exhausting the land, is a miserable and ruinous plan; and the time will soon come when our Welch and Irish friends will fatten more at home, rather than supply us with the heart of their land in the shape of lean stock.

There are certain fixed expenses on land, whether we grow a large crop or a poor one: rent, tithe, taxes, manual and horse labour, and seed, become a very heavy per-centage of charge on a minimum crop, whilst on a maximum one the expenses are proportionately diminished.

On well laid out land, with few fences, good drainage, and good roads, there is actually much less cost of labour than on a poor, undrained farm, with wide and irregular hedges, green lanes, and choked-up ditches: as most of my work is done by piece, I can estimate the difference with accuracy.

Evils of Over-seeding.—One of the crying evils of the day is the over quantity of seed drilled. In former times, when broad-casting was the practice, many seeds never vegetated, being consumed by birds; but now, with the accuracy of deposit by drills, a much smaller quantity is required, and the system of high farming positively demands a reduced quantity of seed, otherwise the crops run up densely, and are laid prematurely. This remark applies particularly to barley after turnips, fed off with oil-cake

My usual quantity of seed per acre is—

WHEAT	1 bushel.
BARLEY	6 to 8 pecks.
OATS	2 bushels.

and I feel that, with high cultivation, I still sow too thickly.

We do not half manure or cultivate for our Root Crops.—It may be said—Why, if we manure so highly we shall get our crops ruined. I reply—Who ever heard of over-manuring for a root, a green, or a pulse crop? Plough your manure in deeper, mix with it more of the subsoil, and follow, if you can, the example of our market-gardeners. I remember once saving £5 on a root crop, and lost, in consequence, 13 tons of mangold wurzel, which I was then selling at £1 per ton. The field, only dug one spit and once manured, produced 30 tons per acre; the other, double dug and twice manured, grew 43 tons. But see what a difference is felt in the subsequent corn and other crops. The effects are spread over many years. I am convinced that, for rapid summer growth, the manure should have reached the subsoil, either by solution or admixture, for during the dry hot months the roots go *down* deeply in search of moisture, and *there* they ought to find their food—the manure. All these statements of mine are as easily ascertainable and provable on a perch of ground, as on a thousand acres; therefore, I say, don't disbelieve, but try them.

I have often watched a corn and root crop, and so long as their roots only occupy the ploughed and manured surface, all goes on prosperously; but when, in stronger and later growth, they search the subsoil, then is the time to judge by their looks whether they are luxuriating in manure and aëration, or whether they have to contend against the too common evils of a stagnated and unaërated soil—unmanured, uncultivated, and undrained. The bilious and disappointed crop gives unmistakeable evidence of its condition, and ends in an unprofitable result.

The Cost of Improvement.—As a general estimate, you cannot effectually improve stiff land under £25 per acre, or, with buildings, £30 per acre; your drainage will cost you £6 per acre; fallowing, levelling, subsoiling, &c., £7; and a good heavy manuring, £7; lime or chalk and earth-burning, £5. Then comes the question—Are you not better off, having to pay 10 per cent., or £2 to £3 per acre extra, than if these improvements—buildings, drainage, fencing roads, &c.—were not made? I have no hesitation in saying that the difference is more often £6 per acre than £2. What a miserable miscalculation, then, not to make these amendments! Your sowings and harvesting become earlier and cheaper, your horse and manual labour less, and the *tout ensemble* one of prosperity in lieu of adversity.

Covered Yards are cheaper than the ordinary homesteads,

and can be effected completely for £5 to £7 per acre, a profitable investment at 5 per cent. for the tenant.

As this system of homesteads is rapidly growing, and as I know it to be the best and cheapest, I have asked Messrs. Beadel, Sons, and Chancellor, of Chelmsford, Essex, to send me a list of those which they have erected, and their cost.

Had the system existed when I commenced farming, I should have preferred it to my detached buildings.

Dr. Voelcker's valuable experiments show us that our manure does not suffer by exposure to air, but its washing by rains carries away its most valuable properties.*

Ever since I commenced farming, I have never lost any portion of my manure from such a cause: hence the improved fertility of my soil.

I annex Mr. Chancellor's letter:—

CHELMSFORD, *October* 8, 1858.

DEAR SIR,—I enclose you a Schedule of all the covered homesteads I have erected since about 1850. The amounts of the various "costs" are accurate, but I am not able to fill in all the acreages. In some instances, as in Park Hall, Ongar, the covered homestead is an addendum to the other farm buildings, and therefore could not be taken as a fair criterion of the proper cost of a homestead per acre; but I think you may very fairly assume that the cost on an average would be from £5 to £6 per acre. Of course, much depends upon locality, price of bricks, timber, slates, stone, &c. I have made numerous calculations upon this subject, as you may imagine, and I have invariably found that the covered homestead does not cost more than the usual mode of erecting farmeries; and, if you take into consideration the number of stock, the price of a covered yard is less *per head* than the open yards and bullock-houses in the old system.—I remain, yours faithfully,

FRED. CHANCELLOR.

I. J. MECHI, Esq., 4, Leadenhall-street, London.

---

* The following experiment (March, 1856) proves the possibility of perfect management of the manure accumulating under sheltered live stock, along with complete comfort and prosperous condition in the animals:—

I have removed 100 half-bred hoggets from an open boarded floor and placed them on straw in a walled and covered shed with paved bottom. The space allowed is 10 superficial feet per head, including in this space the necessary feeding troughs. Of course there is proper ventilation by openings in various directions, to carry away the impure corporeal exhalations. Each sheep receives daily 10 lbs. of mangold, three-quarters of a pound of rape-cake, and some finely-cut wheat-straw chaff. Their appetites and condition are in every way satisfactory. They have been now eight weeks in this shed without any removal of manure, and by an almost daily examination of the condition of the manure, I am enabled to arrive at definite conclusions. If straw was too abundantly supplied, the manure became warm—too warm; by stopping the supply it became cool. In fact, the degree of wetness of the manure regulated its temperature; when wet it was cool, when moist it heated. Finely-cut straw or short stuff absorbed moisture quickly, and had to be very sparingly supplied. A light covering of straw once a day keeps the manure in perfect order, solid and free from smell: but disturb it with a fork, and the odour is all-powerful. One pound and a half of straw per head per day for sheep is a sufficient foddering, and 9 to 12 lbs. for a bullock. We must not forget that 13-14ths of the manure is liquid. I was never before satisfied or confident as to feeding on straw bed, but now I see clearly that the failure or success depends upon the proper management of the manure. The late dry weather has caused the manure in many open farmyards in this neighbourhood to heat violently, and then "fire-fang."

Locality.	Acreage of Farm.	Owners.	Cost.	Remarks.
Fingrith Hall, Blackmore, Essex....	Abt. 500	Messrs. Smith, Payne & Smith.	£900	There are other buildings.
Broomfield Lodge, Chelmsford, Essex	25	Jas. Beadel, Esq.	250	
Frowicke Farm, St. Osyth, Essex ..	238	Thos. Alexander, Esq	350	This was built principally for fattening bullocks; there are other buildings besides.
Hormead Farm, near Buntingford, Herts.	..	J. W. Higgins, Esq...	1100	
Lobb Farm, Tetsworth, Oxon	..	Trustees of Sir Chas. Flower, Bart.	700	The cost is exclusive of some old buildings; there are other farm-buildings.
Stevens's Farm, Chignal St. James, Essex	360	Wm. Crush, Esq.	2000	
Gilston Park, Herts	Abt. 500	John Hodgson, Esq...	3000	There is a 10-horse power fixed steam engine, which works all the machinery.
Park Hall, Ongar, Essex	..	Capel Cure, Esq.	500	
Graffham, Hunts	..	Lady O. B. Sparrow..	1700	
Hall's Farm, Bury, Hunts	Between 400 & 500	Lady O. B. Sparrow..	1900	A portable steam-engine and fixed machinery.
Little Bardfield, Essex..............	Abt. 400	John Cutts, Esq. ...	1800	Fixed steam engine and machinery.
Berwick Hall, White Colne, Essex ..	Abt. 300	Rev. W. E. Hume...	900	
Elmington, near Oundle, Northamptonshire.	..	Corpus Christi College, Cambridge.	1150	Portable steam-engine and machinery.
Hinton Farm, near Twyford, Berks .	..	T. C. Garth, Esq.	1600	
Braffes House, nr. Shipton-on-Stour, Shropshire.	..	H. J. Sheldon, Esq. ..	About 1600	Portable steam-engine and machinery.
Haines Hill, near Twyford, Berks ..	Abt. 500	T. C. Garth, Esq.	3000	Fixed steam-engine with fixed machinery.
Rivenhall, Essex	Abt. 150	Mr. W. Porter	1200	
Edwards' Farm, Eye, near Peterboro, Northamptonshire	..	E. S. Knipe, Esq.	1220	Portable steam-engine and machinery; there are also other buildings.
Ham Farm, Nutfield, Surrey........	Abt. 400	H. E. Gurney, Esq. ..	2300	Portable steam-engine and machinery.
The Mill, Wakes Colne, Essex	About 10	H. Skingley, Esq.....	360	This is a small homestead for the accommodation of the mill horses, a few acres of land, &c.
The Rectory, Debden, Essex........	About 60	Rev. H. Hodgson	700	

CHELMSFORD, *Oct.* 8, 1858. FRED. CHANCELLOR, *Architect.*

Agricultural Education.—I have often alluded to the inconvenience, in a business point of view, of uneducated ignorance. I say uneducated, because the Almighty alone gives mind; man can only cultivate it: but many of my best workmen cannot read or write, and it is a drawback to their otherwise intelligent minds. It is true we have now a subscription school, but until the last two years there were little, if any, means of education for a parish of 5,000 acres, with a population of near 1,500 people.

It is a painful truth that a large number of farmers, uneducated themselves, are not sufficiently alive to the great advantages afforded by education. Rates to keep in repair the highways are readily granted, but the minds that are to direct the future farm operations of this kingdom remain unmended and uncared for, except by the unfair taxation of the benevolent.

Management of Estates.—The contrasts in the management of estates in this kingdom are as great as those in our farming. In some which I have had the privilege of inspecting (such as the Duke of Bedford's, the Duke of Richmond's, Lord Hatherton's, Lord Willoughby D'Eresby's, Earl Bathurst's, Earl Radnor's, Earl Fortescue's, &c., &c.), a judicious and continuous expenditure of a portion of the annual rental has tended greatly to augment that rental, besides producing food and employment for an increasing population. But beyond all this, the care for the physical and consequent moral condition of the labourer, by a system of proper and decent cottage accommodation and garden allotment, exhibits a sagacious recognition and appreciation of the bonds that tie so strongly together the various classes of our happy community.

But, as I said, in farming these are the exceptions, and not the rule, and I see too often, with sorrow and disgust, the opposite of all this. No annual appropriation for improvement or profit, but a dilapidatory and depressing influence extending banefully over every interest on the estate.

The power of an individual to influence and stimulate progression in his own immediate neighbourhood is often very effective and considerable, and, to a certain extent, it may be admitted that good tenants may be created or bred on the estate, having before them the example of a noble-minded and judicious proprietor who combines progress with profit.

Probably the Lincolnshire system of valuations ensures most permanently high farming as a system. It should never be forgotten that improvements create a new and extended market for our own agricultural produce.

Management of Stiff Clays.—In dealing with a stiff clay farm, deficient in buildings or shelter for stock, I should depend almost entirely on green crops that could be spring and summer fed—plenty of tares, clover, and rape. The mangold not to be commenced until March or April. Beans to be well manured, and thoroughly cleaned, and then consumed on the farm. As a general rule, I grow one-eighth beans, one-eighth clover, one-eighth tares, one-eighth mangold, the rest corn, thus making the rotation once in eight years.

As a golden rule, never omit ploughing or digging your land before the last frost. One night's frost will do more cultivation than all the harrows and rolls. Of course all your stubbles will be scarified during the hot month of September, when twenty-four hours' sunshine in our country will perish every weed.

Nothing is easier than working a drained heavy-land farm if you watch your opportunity, and avoid spring ploughing.

Crosskill's Roller.—If you do plough up deeply in the spring any of your stiff clay subsoil you will find that it dries hard and unmanageable. Crosskill's roller (with 5 cwt. added behind to balance the shafts), will crack the clods, which then again dry, and after another scarifying, another clod-crushing or two will so open and expose the hitherto hermetically sealed soil, that it is easily pulverized by the first shower, and if you have previously top-dressed it with lime it will become in a useful and sweet condition. Land, so Crosskilled, does not bind during summer—of course I speak of drained clays. Fine cultivation is the ruin of undrained clays,—I wish there were none left.

Profit in Agriculture.—Let him who enters on farming make up his mind to great vicissitudes in price, and in some degree in quantity and quality. It is the history of the past, and will be of the future. If the average is remunerative it is all we can expect. The historical ups and downs of agriculture are interesting and forewarning,—they may easily be obtained, if desired.

The Condition of my Soil.—Although my land for ten years was cropped every other year with wheat, and although it is in other respects "very hard worked," yet its fertility has every year increased.

My old bailiff complainingly exclaims "that guano does no good now—you cannot see where it goes," whilst fourteen years ago the smallest dusting of it showed a marked effect. He cannot be made to understand that the land was then undrained and full of poverty (like too much now in our neighbourhood), whereas now drainage, cultivation, and plenty of manure from stock have filled it with an enduring fertility, which renders the action of guano comparatively inoperative.

Three years ago I bought a field adjoining my own, and on putting down the fence my men could hardly believe that my own land could ever have been like that, so cold and benumbed, full of weak stubble and poverty-stricken weeds. The tread was entirely different. Although that field cost me £20 per acre in improvement, it is still visibly far in arrear of my earlier improved soil. These contrasts afford encouraging reflections for an agricultural improver.

The Average Yield of my Crops for several years has been—wheat, over 5 quarters; barley, 7 quarters; oats, 11 qrs.; and other things in proportion. My mangold wurzel are always good, varying from 25 to 40 tons per acre. In our dry climate, in Essex, these roots are more certain as a crop than swedes, which prefer a moister climate and a looser soil.

Farm Labourers will not be troublesome to manage, if they know that you or your bailiff know what a fair day's work is; without this knowledge you will be unfavourably placed. I prefer piece, or task work, with steady dependable men.

As my labour, including engineer, &c., costs me 45s. per acre, a mistake of 10 per cent. would add 4s. 6d. per acre to my rental.

Buying and Selling.—If you buy 5 per cent. too dear, and sell 5 per cent. too cheap, your farming profit is gone. Bear in mind that there are in every market men who are keen and thorough judges of the value of every article. If you are not so, you must find some good judge to act for you, otherwise you will soon fall a victim to superior power. The amount of fleecing from the inexperienced is something surprising. I have known an animal bought cheaply change hands several times in an hour, and afford a good profit at each change, excepting, perhaps, the last.

Light Lands.—Anybody with ordinary brains may farm light naturally-drained land, cover it with sheep eating rape-cake, oil-cake, or beans, or some of each. Let your corn crops get well rooted before the frost comes. Use Crosskill or the drill presser, and use plenty of artificials for your root crops. If you are troubled with wire-worm, never sow your corn crop without rape dust, 4 to 5 cwt. per acre: it will pay in the crop, especially if you use a little salt with it. Superphosphate of lime suits many light lands; on my clays it never shows the least result, proving, I suppose, that I have already in the land, or by my feeding, quite as much as the crops require. Claying or marling light soils pays well.

Reaping Machines.—A wise farmer will use a reaping machine. I have done so for several years; I never had any trouble with mine, because I *lent* it to my men, and they soon found it was to their advantage to keep it in perfect working order. The great economy is time, which it certainly saves in harvest.

Waggons on our farm would be considered by the men themselves as antiquated and obstructive inconveniences. They would increase the expenses, and delay the time of harvest materially. For fourteen years we have used Hannam's one-horse skeleton carts. (See Royal Agricultural Society's *Journal*, vol. ii., page 73.)

Comparative Merits of Corn and Cake.—A farmer, whom I knew, divided a field of rape: half was fed off with sheep eating barley, and half with sheep eating an equal value of oil-cake; the difference in the subsequent crop of barley was two quarters more after the cake than after the barley. This is consistent with chemical analysis, the cake containing nearly twice as much nitrogen and phosphate. Nobody will be ever ruined by using plenty of rape-cake, either for feeding or for manure; you may always see the results in the following crop. I have used 100 tons; it contains quite as much manurial element as oil-cake, and costs much less money.

I never saw a sheep that would not eat it. I have fattened some thousands on it. When sheep are on clover, giving them rape-cake and locusts will make them fatten most rapidly, and the mutton is peculiarly rich and palatable. They are wonderfully fond of the locusts, and will, if you permit them, eat a large quantity. When they know the locusts are in the troughs, they will race to the fold to be first; not so when there is only rape-cake. They are more fond of linseed-cake than rape-cake.

As a general rule, I think 7 lbs. of rape-cake, linseed-cake, or beans, will make 1 lb. of net mutton. If so, you get the manure for nothing, when 1 lb. of mutton is worth as much as 7 lbs. of either rape-cake, linseed-cake, or beans. This is cheaper manure than any you can buy at any price.

7 lbs. of barley will make 1 lb. of pork.

Farm Horses. — Inquire in your neighbourhood how many horses have died on a given number of acres during the last seven years, and you will be astonished at the gross total thus abstracted annually from the capital of agriculture;* much of this loss arises from mismanagement. Animals are allowed to gorge themselves with masses of indigestible green food, which ferments, generates gases, and produces swelling, inflammation, and death. Again, horses coming in heated are allowed to drink cold water *ad libitum*, producing gripes, surfeit, &c. It is notorious that brewers' horses drink when they please, but then their water is always *warm*, and no evil result takes place.

Another common cause of disease is want of ventilation in stables; hence a putrescent atmosphere, producing farcy and many other diseases. Our London horses, well housed, groomed, and fed on comminuted food, contrast strangely with the usual listless, pot-bellied farm horses, with undeveloped fore and hind quarters, and uncombed manes and tails. Is it not possible for agriculture not to be slovenly?

Great losses also occur amongst cattle, &c., for want of due attention to the commixing and dividing their food. Turning animals in to green food, when the hoar-frost is on it, causes abundant deaths.

I seldom give my horses any hay; they get two bushels per

* Comparing this with steam-power and its cost of replacement and reparation, the odds are sadly against the horses. My steam-engine, which is now perfectly good after ten years' use, would have worn out, in competition, £250 worth of horse-flesh. Thus leaving a large profit in favour of steam-power.

week of crushed oats, plenty of fine cut and sifted wheat-straw, or oat-straw, and 20 to 30 lbs.* of mangold wurzel per day; their condition is first-rate. The mangold is a perfect substitute for hay, and keeps the horses in excellent health. The mangold may be used immediately after being pulled, provided there is plenty of dry chaff with it. There is no reason why mangold should not fatten horses as well as bullocks and sheep. I know a very extensive farmer in Suffolk who uses mangold on a large scale for his horses, and finds it a great economy, as compared with hay.

The mangolds are cleaned from any soil, and thrown whole into the manger.

Pigs.—Few people have fattened more pigs than myself, or more successfully. Cooking meal for pigs in cold weather is desirable, but I have always depended on summer fattening as the most profitable, the carbon of the food going to make fat instead of heat. In winter, pigs, having no wool, are not so profitable to fatten; sheep do better then. Of course the price of corn and pork must be considered—when 1 lb. of pork is worth 7 lbs. weight of barley or peas, you may safely go largely into fattening.

I have had 300 to 400 pigs at one time for several years, and never had disease; but if you litter them on straw, and have many, they will get heaves, or lung-disease.

Mine have been on open sparred floors, so that air always circulated under and around them, and the atmosphere did not become putrescent, which is almost sure to take place on straw, especially if soft or barley-straw. Ten years of experience with the sparred floors, have more and more convinced me of their superiority for stock. The only difficulty is in getting the straw into manure.

Good strong reedy wheat-straw, frequently changed, is a good thing, because the air circulates under the animals amongst the straw, but there is nothing like boards. Beans alone, and lentils alone, will give pigs cramp when confined. If soaked twenty-four hours before giving them, I am told they will not do so.

I knew a farmer who manured his grass-land by sowing every day so much land with beans broadcast.

The pigs were turned in, and regularly picked up every bean, and manured the land so sown. By repeating this daily he regularly manured all his field. This is cheaper than the dung-cart. It is the filling, carting, turning over, re-filling, carting, and spreading, and wasting, that run away with the farmer's profit.

* I find, when hard worked they will eat 50 to 80 lbs. per diem. My horsemen keep them several hours in the stable, covered with straw, so that they attain the proper temperature; and thus do not gripe the horses. They seldom drink much water when eating mangold: 50 lbs. of mangold would contain about 44 lbs., or two pails, of water.

Nothing like the sheep-fold or pig-fold; washing the manure away by buildings' water is absolute ruin.

Iron as Manure.—A farmer once told me he manured his land with iron, and explained that it was the plough which furnished his manure. This is literally true, for so many ploughings, harrowings, scarifyings, Crosskillings, &c., in a summer will fill your heavy land with fertility, provided the inorganics are there. There is a love between the air and the soil, which ends in a fructifying attachment, if you will but expose them to each other's influence. This is thoroughly understood in the Rodings of Essex, where the crop and fallow system have existed for ages. A farmer is sure of his crop of barley after a long fallow, if the land is drained.

No such result would occur did we plough about so many billiard or bagatelle balls.

I knew a farmer who took a good farm wretchedly out of condition and full of weeds. He fallowed every acre of it, taking care to allow time between each ploughing for the vegetation of the seed weeds. The result was a crop of wheat, averaging 5½ quarters per acre, and other crops in proportion. He was a wise man.

In our eastern and southern counties weeds are far more easily destroyed than in Devonshire and other hilly and moist districts. Our burning and drying sunshine gives us cereal advantages, but we suffer in our turnips and grasses, except where we can get irrigation.

I believe that in our stiff clays we have a great store of mineral manures, in what Dr. Daubeney justly calls a passive condition. Drainage, aëration by cultivation, lime and clay burning, bring them into active disintegration and use. I am a great believer in Liebig's mineral theory, and, therefore, respect the alkalies of the stiff soils. The great secret is to keep such soils open and aërated. Of course, a root crop with ample space for cultivation is more profitable than a bare fallow, but where the capital is limited, the fallow comes in well.

Italian Rye-grass.—I sow this with the seed-barrow on the barley about May, when the barley is sufficiently grown to merely permit the germination of the seed. As soon as the barley is harvested the rye-grass begins to show itself. It then requires a good irrigation of liquefied manure. In the warm growing season you cannot give it too much moisture. Without this, after the first cutting there will be no crop. After its second year it is ploughed and followed by peas or beans, or turnips, never by a cereal crop.

Its value, as an early spring feed, is too well known to require comment. Land can never be too highly farmed for Italian rye-grass. I often cut it or feed it four or five times during the season.

Beans.—I am very fond of beans on heavy land. You cannot over-manure for them, and they are a capital preparation for wheat. We generally drill in February, harrow them when an inch high, horse-hoe them well, and hand-hoe them twice, and then the land, after harvesting, will be as clean as a garden. I grow an eighth of my heavy land in beans annually.

The Growth of Weeds costs Great Britain millions annually. From May 20th until the end of June all the mischief is done, for, if previously neglected, the rush of vegetation at that period in the South of England renders eradication hopeless. Of course in root crops there is no excuse for growing weeds.

As you cannot always get manual labour enough at the critical period, it is both cheaper and more effective to use Garrett's horse-hoe, which has been my mainstay in this respect for many years, all my drilled corn crops being cleaned by it between the rows.

As soon as the corn crops are removed the stubbles should be scarified, or the weeds will prosper.

Our yellow clays produce black grass, which vegetates in October and November. It is highly desirable to harrow this up ere you sow your wheat, or it will give you much trouble.

The Advantage of Deep Cultivation is particularly shown immediately over the drains, where the earth has been deeply disturbed; many people fancy that it is because it drains quicker, but the truth is that air has more ready access to the soil. Wherever a loaded cart-wheel consolidates the soil in wet weather, the ensuing crop does not prosper, especially barley and turnips, but wheat and beans have a greater power of penetrating strong soils.

Town and House Sewage.—Before the year 1957 the people of this country will have come to their senses on the value of this substance, which is literally their food; but there will be an immense extent of discussion, doubt, and disbelief, all which can alone be removed by time and *necessity*. Already the screw is put on—guano, or birds' dung, will soon be as dear as rappee, or perhaps, unobtainable, and then the British public will naturally inquire whether their own dung is not superior to that of birds. My own experience and opinions have been long since recorded (1843), and a few years' application of liquified manure to my farm has satisfied me how easy and profitable an operation it is to re-apply that which was taken from the land.

The Value of Green and Root Crops.—There is nothing that puzzles an inexperienced agriculturist more than this question. If you graze, and do not breed stock, you will have occasionally to pay very high prices for your lean animals. At this moment (March, 1857) you cannot buy lean sheep under 7*s*. per stone of 8 lbs. (net dead weight), whilst the price of fat sheep is only 6*s*. per stone; so that probably those who purchase lean stock now will have to give away their root and green crops without return, except the manure or at the end of sixteeen weeks sell the same sheep, fat, at no greater price than they now cost lean. In this instance the breeder has the advantage; at other times the reverse of this takes place.

On the whole, perhaps, there is no better average plan than breeding a portion of your stock, if the farm is suitable for it. Some years your root and green crops will realize, in meat, £7 to £8 per acre; at other times possibly not so much as a tithe of that sum. Turnips that cost £7 or £8 per acre are often let for feeding at £1 per acre, the owner of the sheep giving them ½ lb. of oil-cake per day. I have known that many acres of roots and green crops have been *given* for the purpose of sheep feeding, where farmers are deficient in capital. As a general rule, where much purchased food is used, a considerable loss or charge is incurred for the manure, but still it is the best and cheapest way of obtaining it.

If you are unfortunate in the health of your stock, then the loss is serious, indeed. A long experience has taught me that pigs lose less money than any other stock. Seeing that manure is so costly to produce, the waste of it is, indeed, an agricultural criminality.

Animals that are fed on hay, linseed-cake, and roots, seldom leave much price for the roots after paying for the hay and cake—leaving no margin for casualties, attendance, or shelter.

Cheap Manuring.—Mr. Lawes has shown beyond a doubt, in the Royal Agricultural Society's Journal, that there is no way of obtaining manure so cheaply as by feeding animals. Of course that system involves a larger capital per acre, inasmuch as we must keep more stock and employ more labour; but common calculation will enable a farmer who knows the chemical analysis of each feeding stuff and its market price to avail himself of opportunities.

For instance, beans are now about three farthings a pound, and mutton sevenpence half-penny. Now, if seven pounds of beans will make one pound of mutton, it is quite clear that you get your manure for nothing. Of course, I do not mean that sheep should have nothing but beans. Take pork, and, at the present falling prices of peas and beans, manure might be, through pigs, cheaply obtained.

One thousand five hundred sheep folded on an acre of land for twenty-four hours (or 100 sheep fifteen days) would manure that land sufficiently to carry it through a four years' rotation. Now, if each sheep had one pound of beans, or three-quarters per acre, it would tend greatly to fertility, and leave no immediate loss.

This system is the way to increase the fertility of your soil at the least possible expense, and it is the absence of this practice that I complain of as being so injurious to all classes, but particularly to the farmer himself. I may be asked—But where is the money to come from? I answer, that country bankers are but too happy to assist prudent, thriving farmers;

next to depositors, they are their best customers, because the improvements they make, being very profitable, enable them to pay a good interest for the money they borrow.

In order to make 14 score lbs. of meat per acre, it would be necessary to have 20 score lbs. of lean stock per acre. This and the feeding would involve a capital in live stock and food alone of some £10 to £15 per acre.

Artificial Manures.—I know a farmer with 600 acres, who says that if he spends £1 per acre in artificial manures, his farm pays; if not, it loses. I know some who spend double that sum. I have only placed 10*s*. per acre for artificial manure because I produce much manure by feeding animals, which, if there is capital, is the cheapest way of getting genuine manure.

Management.—This is a comprehensive term: it implies the right man in the right place, and the right thing done at the right time. In every undertaking, warlike or peaceful, it is alike essential, but particularly so in agriculture, where the fluctuations in weather render forethought and promptitude an essentiality for profit. For instance, take the question of Drilling,—you find a particular day or two when your heavy land is neither too wet nor too dry, but friable and lively: to lose such an opportunity would indeed be a loss.

Again, in wet weather a frost may form a thin crust, through which your drill will work pleasantly, and your harrows finish up; it is an occasion not to be passed over. Again, in October we have an average of twenty-one fine days—off with your mangold wurzel. In November, wet and fogs—woe be to your land, roads, and horses if you get caught. Begin your harvest a *little* too soon, you will find in a couple of days that all your corn has come on surprisingly. It is true reaping machines will make shorter and more certain work of our harvesting. In business matters it is desirable to make one's feelings subserve to one's interest. Good-natured people are apt to keep on incompetent persons for old acquaintance sake;—I have suffered somewhat myself occasionally from such a sentiment.

Stock-taking.—Book-keeping is as necessary on a farm as in a warehouse. How can we tell what each kind of live stock pays or loses, unless their value is taken once a year, and the quantity and value of food consumed, and of stock bought or sold, duly registered? If you buy and sell for cash, your cash-book will contain every item paid or received. From this you can post to every account. I use Swinborne's Farm Book, published at Colchester. It is by a rigid investigation of the cost and return of each particular crop that we detect the weak points in agriculture, and find out how to correct them.

Farm Expenditure.—In making out the expenses attached to each crop, I have found it necessary to distribute to each a charge of £1 2*s*. 6*d*. for a number of miscellaneous items as per list; and also to add the sum of £1 5*s*. on each acre for labour in yard, attending on live stock, for horse and manual labour of a miscellaneous and undefinable character, and for extra quantities of manure.

I have been minutely particular in estimating every item of expenditure, and which, diffused over the whole area, gives a charge of £7 17*s*. 2*d*. per acre. All beyond this realized by the crops will be interest or profit on capital invested.

For want of a remembrancer in detail of all charges, many are apt to take too favourable a view of farming, and thus lose their money, and become disgusted with the occupation.

My Course of Cropping for 1856-57 :—

	A.	R.	P.
Wheat	54	1	7
Barley	14	2	0
Oats	9	0	0
Grass	7	0	0
Mangold wurzel	12	2	0
Red clover	13	2	0
Beans	11	2	0
Italian rye grass	22	0	0
Tares and rye, to be followed by turnips	19	0	0
Fallow	1	0	0
	£164	1	7

My Prices for Field Operations.—As there is an erroneous supposition that I pay fancy prices for my work, I annex a list of what I pay, and imagine it will make some of my practical friends scratch their heads. The fact is, with a well-trained staff of regularly-employed agricultural labourers, who have been through the whole process of modern improvements, you may always do work on the easiest terms ; the men are so "handy," and there is scarcely one on my farm who could not work my steam-engine. Besides, with light carts, good roads, and easy access to every part of the farm, you may safely compete with the most pinching screw, who is surrounded by green muddy lanes, small fields, and badly placed buildings.

I am very fond of digging, or rather forking, a few acres every November—say about six to eight acres, for mangold. It pays well. When labour was cheap, I used to pay 2*d*. per rod, or 26*s*. 8*d*. per acre; but now I pay 3*d*. per rod, or £2 per acre. Some farmers seem quite astonished at my working my 170 acres of heavy land, all arable, with five horses, with an occasional additional horse; but steam is a great help.

HAND-HOEING.

Beans	4*s*. per acre.
Wheat	4*s*. do.
Turnips	4*s*. do.

WEEKLY WAGES (1856) .... 12*s*.

HARVEST WAGES.

	£.	s.	d.
Fagging or bagging wheat, and mowing oats and barley; then loading, carting, and stacking the same ready for thatching .... (with beer) per acre	0	11	6
Cutting and tying beans .... (ditto) do.	0	6	0

HAY-MAKING.

Cutting grass .... per acre, and beer	0	4	0
Cutting red clover .... do. do.	0	2	6
Filling manure into ¾ carts .... for 20 loads	0	2	0
Spreading ditto .... do. do.	0	1	3
Cutting drains in stiff tile-clays, 4 feet deep, at per rod or pole, including placing the pipes .... per rod	0	0	5½
Thatching per 100 square feet, and to keep them in order for a year	0	1	0
Shaving or trimming the stacks .... per stack, containing 25 qrs. of mowed wheat	0	1	0

COST OF TARE CROP AFTER WHEAT.

1 Ploughing	0	6	6
2 Harrowings	0	1	4
Drilling	0	1	6
2 bushels of seed	0	16	0
Rent, rates, tithes, &c.	2	5	6
Miscellaneous expenses	1	2	6
Labour in yards, attending on live stock, horse and manual labour of a miscellaneous character, some extra manure, &c.	1	5	0
	£5	18	4

Consumed by sheep, eating in addition beans and rape-cake, or locust and rape-cake.

Sometimes the tare crop is followed by white turnips, consumed on the land by sheep, eating also rape-cake or beans.

OATS AFTER TARES.

Ploughings	0	13	0
Harrowings	0	2	0
Drilling	0	1	6
Seed, 2 bushels	0	8	0
Harvesting, carting, and stacking	0	11	6
Thatching	0	1	0
Threshing 11 qrs., at 1s. 6d.	0	16	6
Rent, rates, and tithe	2	5	6
Miscellaneous charges	1	2	6
Labour in yards, attending on live stock, horse and manual labour of a miscellaneous character, some extra manure, &c.	1	5	0
	£7	6	6

Oats consumed on the farm by cart horses and carriage horses.

COST OF ITALIAN RYE-GRASS—TWO YEARS.

Seed, 2 bushels, sown in barley or wheat	0	15	0
Two years' rent, rate, and tithe	4	11	0
Two years' miscellaneous expenses	2	5	0
6 irrigations of 15,000 gallons each	3	0	0
Labour in yards, attending on live stock, horse and manual labour of a miscellaneous character, some extra manure, &c.	2	10	0
	£13	1	0

or £6 10*s*. 6*d*. per acre per annum.

On some very poor land I have kept 16½ sheep per acre during six summer months. Some portion is mowed off, but I generally consume much of it with sheep on the land eating rape-cake or beans. After two years' such treatment the land is in first-rate condition for beans or root crops, and after that for corn.

Much more manure may be put on, such as rape-cake, guano, &c. Of course that would have to be charged, and would be returned in the increased produce.

As a general rule, you cannot over-manure for Italian rye-grass, provided it is administered in a liquid state, or washed in by rain.

COST OF BEAN CROP AFTER WHEAT.

	£.	s.	d.
Scarifying	£0	2	2
Harrowing	0	0	8
Ploughing	0	6	6
Harrowing before and after drilling	0	1	4
Drilling	0	1	6
Seed—3 bushels, at 5*s.*	0	15	0
Two horse-hoeings	0	2	0
Two hand-hoeings	0	7	0
Harvesting (cutting)	0	6	0
Carting and stacking	0	3	0
Thrashing (1*s.* 3*d.* per quarter)	0	6	3
	2	11	5
No carting to market, as they are consumed on the farm.			
Rent, rates, and tithes	2	5	6
Miscellaneous expenses	1	2	6
Labour in yards, attending on live stock, horse and manual labour of a miscellaneous character, some extra manure, &c.	1	5	0
	7	4	5
Filling, carting, and spreading manure,—15 small carts	0	10	0
	£7	14	5

No charge for manure, as the crop is consumed on the farm.

COST OF MANGOLD WURZEL, OR SWEDES, AFTER WHEAT.

	£.	s.	d.
Scarifying	0	2	2
Harrowing	0	0	8
Filling, carting, and spreading manure	0	15	0
No charge for farm-yard manure, as it will be re-produced by consumption of the crop.			
Forking the land	2	0	0
2 cwt. guano	1	8	0
1 cwt. salt	0	2	0
5 cwt. rape-dust	1	8	0
Broad-sharing	0	2	2
Harrowing twice	0	1	4
Drilling	0	1	6
Seed—4 lbs.	0	2	0
2 horse-hoeings	0	2	0
3 hand-hoeings	0	12	0
Singling	0	1	0
Pulling, stacking, thatching, and earthing	0	11	0
Carried forward	£7	8	10

	£.	s.	d.
Brought forward	7	8	10
Carting (horse labour)	0	3	6
Rent, rates, and tithes	2	5	6
Miscellaneous expenses	1	2	6
Labour in yards, attending on live stock, horse, and manual labour of a miscellaneous character, some extra manure, &c.	1	5	0
	£12	5	4

RIVETT WHEAT AFTER RED WHEAT.

	£.	s.	d.
Scarifying	0	2	2
Ploughing	0	6	6
Three Harrowings	0	2	0
Drilling	0	1	6
Seed—5 pecks	0	8	0
Striking up furrows, &c.	0	0	11
Horse and hand-hoeing and weeding	0	5	0
Harvesting (excluding horse-labour)	0	11	6
Thatching and trimming stack	0	1	3
Thrashing and dressing, 2*s*. per quarter	0	10	0
Carting to market, 9*d*. per quarter	0	3	9
Two cwt. guano	1	4	0
Rent, rates, and tithes	2	5	6
Miscellaneous expenses	1	2	6
Labour in yards, attending on live stock, horse and manual labour of a miscellaneous character, some extra manure, &c.	1	5	0
	£8	9	7

COST OF A WHEAT CROP AFTER BEANS.

	£.	s.	d.
Scarifying per acre	0	2	2
Harrowing	0	0	8
Ploughing	0	6	6
Harrowing twice	0	1	4
Drilling	0	1	6
Harrowing once	0	0	8
Striking up furrows, with one horse and double tom	0	0	7
Water furrowing, &c. &c.	0	0	4
Seed, at 60*s*. per quarter	0	9	3
One horse-hoeing	0	1	0
One hand-hoeing	0	3	6
Weeding	0	0	6
Harvesting (excluding horse-labour)	0	11	6
Thatching	0	1	0
Trimming stack	0	0	3
Thrashing and dressing, 2*s*. per quarter	0	10	0
Carting to market, 8*d*. per quarter	0	3	4
Two cwt. guano	1	4	0
	£3	18	1
Rent, rates, tithes, &c.	2	5	0
Miscellaneous expenses	1	2	6
Labour in yards, attending on live stock, horse and manual labour of a miscellaneous character, some extra manure, &c.	1	5	0
	£8	10	7

COST OF WHEAT CROP AFTER CLOVER.

	£.	s.	d.
As above, deducting guano, &c.	6	0	0
Labour in yards, attending on live stock, horse and manual labour of a miscellaneous character, some extra manure, &c.	1	5	0
	£7	5	0

COST OF CLOVER AFTER BARLEY OR OATS.

	£.	s.	d.
Seed, 17½ lbs. .... average	0	10	0
Hoeing	0	1	0
Mowing	0	2	6
Making, carting, and stacking, including horse-labour	0	3	0
Thatching	0	1	6
Rent, rates, tithes, &c.	2	5	0
Miscellaneous expenses	1	2	6
Labour in yards, attending on live stock, horse and manual labour of a miscellaneous character, some extra manure, &c.	1	5	0
	£5	10	6

COST OF BARLEY AFTER MANGOLD DRAWN OFF.

	£.	s.	d.
Ploughing once	0	6	6
Scarifying, in spring	0	2	2
Harrowing	0	0	8
Drilling	0	1	6
Harrowing	0	0	8
Seed, 2 bushels, at average price, 35*s*.	0	8	9
Harvesting and stacking, including horse-labour	0	12	6
Thatching	0	2	0
Thrashing and dressing, 2*s*. per quarter	0	13	0
Carting to market, 7*d*. per quarter	0	3	9
Two cwt. guano	1	4	0
	£3	15	6
Rent, rates, and tithes	2	5	0
Miscellaneous expenses	1	2	6
Labour in yards, attending on live stock, horse and manual labour of a miscellaneous character, some extra manure, &c.	1	5	0
	£8	8	0

GROSS EXPENSES, PER ACRE, ON THE WHOLE FARM.

	£.	s.	d.
Rent	1	16	0
Tithes, great and small	0	5	0
Church rate	0	0	2
Road rate	0	0	3
Poor rate, including police and county rate	0	2	3
Manual labour, including engine-driver and bailiff	2	0	0
Horse labour	1	0	0
Seed	0	8	6
Depreciation, or wear and tear, of implements	0	2	0
Steam-power	0	8	0
Blacksmith, wheelwright, cooper, founder, saddler, basket-maker, bricklayer, carpenter, and veterinary	0	5	6
Thatcher	0	1	0
Depreciation of horses	0	2	0
Artificial manures, lime, chalk, and rape-cake	0	10	0
Wear, tear, and loss of sacks	0	0	3
Bean tiers	0	0	3
Loss of stock and casualties	0	1	0
Loss of land by roads, buildings, fences, and waste	0	2	0
Road-mending, ditch-cleaning, fence-trimming, &c.	0	1	0
Miscellaneous petty expenses	0	1	6
Irrigation, permanent charge per acre	0	6	0
Malt and hops used in brewing beer for men	0	2	0
	£7	14	2

Take my own case as an illustration of the principle which I am endeavouring to enforce. The original rental of my farm was a little over 20*s*. per acre. It is now more than double that sum, the excess being interest on improvements; now instead of £1 per acre difference in the crops as compared with what they used to be, fourteen years' experience has taught me that the difference is from £3 to £5 per acre, and in some crops £7 to £9 per acre. The average yield of the crops now and before the improvements may be represented as five to three at the very least. On comparing notes with an intelligent neighbour of mine, he admitted that my extra expenses of £2 per acre, as compared with his, were more than compensated in my increased crops.

In **Conclusion,** if I find a heavy-land farm properly drained, free from unnecessary fences, with good covered yards centrally placed, and proper and modern machinery; if I find it free from weeds, and, above all, if I know that on that arable farm at least 200 lbs. weight of meat is made per acre per annum, the result must be a certain profit. Nothing can prevent this but gross mismanagement or ignorance of the business. But how few such farms does merry England exhibit! Truth replies, how few!!!

All my life it has been my habit, in order to arrive at truth, to examine and compare various systems, with a view to form a judgment on the facts. I am quite satisfied that the mass of mankind do not adopt my practice, else it would be impossible that such miserable and unprofitable discrepancies could exist in agriculture. There are none so blind as those who will not see, and if self-interest will not prompt our landlords and tenants mutually to improve, nothing that I can say can have that desirable effect.

The food question is an important one. A month's holiday to the British stomach would settle all our manufactures, commerce, and philosophy. We must make the acres we have yield up a larger increase, as we cannot extend them.

It is true we are enabled to get corn from our neighbours by paying for it, but meat we cannot get, and unless much more meat is produced per acre than at present the prices will naturally rise much higher, and cramp consumption.

I can scarcely have patience when asked, "But where is the money to come from for all these improvements?" when I see daily the tendency to invest in every new speculation, British or Foreign, except "National Agricultural Improvement."

In conclusion, having proved my case, and exposed my farm for many years to public inspection, it is now my intention to sit down quietly and enjoy the privacy of agricultural peace and plenty.

PART II.

ON AGRICULTURAL IMPROVEMENT.

Letters written during 1844-45.

Tiptree Farm—Its drainage and details—General relations of agriculture—Farm valuations—Drainage of heavy land—Farm horses—Agriculture, manufactures, and commerce—Heavy-land drainage—Subsoiling after drainage—Thin sowing—Cattle-feeding—Leases—Cash—Inconsistencies—Thick and other sowing—Deep and shallow drains.

THIS series of letters, when collected and published in 1845, in pamphlet form, along with a number of papers from other pens, on kindred subjects, was prefaced by the following introduction:—

A nation is in peril when its willing labourers (the sinews of its strength) are looked upon and got rid of as incumbrances—when their cottages are considered nuisances, and placed as such in nooks and corners away from public view—when their gardens are curtailed and coveted by their wealthier neighbours. What would be said of a workman who, having to do a certain piece of work, casts away, despises, and is ashamed of the means by which he is to accomplish it? A nation having abundance of capital and labour, and sending abroad, or refusing to employ either, can only be compared to the able but idle workman, preferring poverty and danger to abundance and security.

A good workman will take a pride in his tools—see that they are bright and in perfect condition: his welfare depends on so doing. A nation is equally dependent on the employment, comfort, and education of its labouring classes; their wretchedness and ignorance are contaminous, and must infect the classes above them—poverty and demoralization are twin brothers.

Let a tenant's improvements be fairly valued at their worth to the incoming tenant, with corn, rents, and long leases, and we shall have millions invested in agricultural improvements. where now we have but thousands.

Improvements cause employment to the willing labourer, and through him to the merchant, manufacturer, and trader. It is the millions that support trade, manufactures, and commerce, not the wealthy few. Let us keep our men and our money at home. Would foreign countries be enabled, as they now are, to compete with us in manufactures and in agriculture, but for *British loans* and *British emigrants?* Certainly not; and yet loudly are we complaining of the very results, we, ourselves, have brought about: *that* money and *those emigrants were wanted at home in agricultural improvements.* It was a great mistake, the sending away our surplus capital to employ the labour of other countries, instead of using it in our own.

We have at home in agricultural improvement an inexhaustible fund of employment for labour and for capital, but it is a sealed book; we have no available means of bringing to bear on our superabundant labour and unimproved land, the surplus capital of trade, manufactures, and commerce. Nor shall we have, until there are agricultural improvement companies, with adequate capital and knowledge, eminent agriculturists and capitalists sitting side by side as a committee of directors. Let one such company show successful results (about which there cannot possibly be a doubt with common discretion and proper management), and you will have as many agricultural improvement companies as you have now railway companies.

The elements of and desire for agricultural improvement exist extensively in every district and in every city; but individual agricultural talent and science, of which there is an abundance, require to be called forth, marshalled, and applied by the force of ample concentrated capital.

The almost certainty of our population becoming doubled in a few years, leads us to some very serious reflections. The *acres* do not increase in size. How then is the population to be fed? Stern necessity will compel us to sweep from the land those pleasing green fences, trees, and pastures, whose agreeableness blinds us to their cruel unprofitableness. Like the Chinese (our superiors in agriculture), our land must be gardened to the very edge of our roads—artificial rivers must be made to carry from our towns and cities to our rural districts those precious streams of excrement, the means of reproducing our own food and employing our own labour, which are now conveyed through expensively arched conduits to be wasted (would nature allow it) in rivers and in seas—our moors and our wastes must feed men instead of game.

Let us, then, take time by the forelock, and do that willingly and profitably, which otherwise we must submit to grudgingly by stern compulsion.

1. TIPTREE-HALL FARM.

Allow me to mention an extreme case of agricultural improvement—the expenditure of £6,200 on a farm of mine, 130 acres (Tiptree-Hall, Kelvedon, Essex), that only cost £3,250. In due course, when the results are accurately ascertained, I shall deem it my duty to submit statistical details and drawings of the buildings to every agricultural society in the kingdom, in the hope that it may give confidence to those who, having the means to improve their property, are doubtful as to such improvements paying a remunerating profit to both landlord and tenant.

The Expenditure above mentioned has been applied to—

1st. The perfect and permanent drainage of the land with stones and pipes, 4 yards apart, and 32 inches deep—between 80 and 90 miles of drains.

2nd. The entire removal of all timber-trees, which cannot be profitably grown in corn-fields.

3rd. The removing of all old, crooked, and unnecessary banks, fences, and ditches.

4th. The cutting new parallel ditches and fences, so as to avoid short lands.

5th. The inclosure of waste, and conversion of useless bog into good soil.

6th. The economizing time and distance by new roads, arches, and more direct communications with the extremities of the farm.

7th. The erection of well-arranged farm-buildings, built of brick, iron, and slate, in a continuous range, excluding all cold winds and currents of air, but open to sunny warmth.

8th. The building a substantial and genteel residence, with all due requisites for domestic comfort and economy.

9th. The erection of an efficient thrashing-machine, and needful apparatus for shaking the straw, dressing the corn, cutting chaff, bruising oats, &c., so constructed as not to injure the straw; avoiding, by its perfect action, that immense waste of grain visible in almost every truss of straw we examine.

10th. The avoidance of thatching and risk of weather, by ample barn-room, with convenience for in-door horse labour at thrashing, &c., when not employable without, so as to have no idle days for man or beast.

11th. The saving of every pound and pint of manure by a tank (90 feet long, 6 feet deep, 8 feet wide, with slated roof facing the north, and with well and pump), into which is received the whole drainage from the farm-yard and stables.

12th. The conveyance by iron gutters and pipes of every drop of water from the roofs of each building, so as in no manner to dilute the manure in yards.

13th. The perfect drainage of the foundations of the barn, and every building on the farm.

14th. A cooking-house to prepare food for cattle.

TIPTREE HALL FARM.

I am thus particular in detail, because it is from each of the above branches of expenditure that some portion of remuneration is expected. But, during the progress of my undertaking, I have been warned, entreated, and dissuaded by my farming friends, who protested that a profitable return for such an enormous expenditure was impossible; my calculations, however, were made, and mere assertions without facts and figures weighed nothing with me. Although the operations were only commenced early in 1843, the results, so far as they go, are gratifying and convincing. As one instance of success, a field of oats, sown on the 16th of May, after drainage, was harvested and stacked before another (sown two months earlier, on better but undrained land) was ready to cut. Hereafter you shall have detailed statistics of every department in which saving is effected and increase produced.

In a Moral and Social point of view these improvements have acted beneficially. They have excited the energies of the tenant and his labourers, stimulating them to think, compare, and improve. They have awakened the attention and curiosity of the neighbouring farmers, who are watching the result, and already have they caused many undertakings in drainage, which otherwise would not have been thought of. Had I invested my money in the Funds, there would have been an end of the matter; but now I have the satisfaction of having fulfilled a public duty (without injury to myself) by calling into action temporarily and permanently, a considerable amount of labour. I conceive *that* the highest order of charity, which, by providing employment to the willing labourer, confers a favour unseen, and leaves uncompromised (his most valuable privilege) his self-dependence. If every one who has the means follows my example, where requisite, there will be little need to complain of the want of employment for our peasantry or our capital.

Whilst all this has been done for the farmer's profit and comfort, the cottagers have not been forgotten. A few gutters and pipes to their residences, and some drains in their gardens have rendered the former *dry* and *healthy*, and the latter *productive;* and this at the trifling cost of a few pounds.

I may be asked, "What can you, as a Londoner, know about farming?" I will answer: "I always loved the beauties of nature, the pure air of heaven, the sports of the field, and the hospitality of our honest yeomen. I have seen one farmer making a fortune, and his next neighbour losing one. I have seen one field all corn, and another nearly all weeds."

I asked, "How is this?"—inquired into the causes—noted the results—obtained from all the best farmers, and all the best agricultural books within my reach, every information bearing on agricultural pursuits—practised on my own little garden, on a small scale, a variety of experiments; and after carefully weighing the evidence, I came to the conclusion, that want of drainage, waste of manure, shallow ploughing, and short leases, are amongst the greatest curses to this country; and I, as far as my individual means will permit, am resolved on remedying them.—*March* 15, 1844.

---

2. THE DRAINAGE AT TIPTREE-HALL FARM.

The Land is of such various qualities, and so adapted thereby for the retention of both top and spring water, that the Essex people considered it never could be improved, even to become of tolerable goodness.

About two-thirds of it was a strong yellow loam subsoil, in a state between putty and bird-lime, according to the season, here and there mixed with a hodge-podge of stones, to which its attachment was so affectionate that there was no separating them, and it was only by the constant use of water that the land-drainers could get their spades into or rid of this adhesive substance; at intervals might be found veins of silt (the reverse of adhesive), and here and there the soil would assume a rusty appearance, indicating iron, with a bluish or slaty character; then a patch of gravel occasionally amongst the loam, in which would rise a small weak spring, sufficient, however, to ruin the crops in its immediate neighbourhood. Over this subsoil, and between it and the cultivated soil, was a hard, dry, and impervious pan, formed of the subsoil, but hardened and rendered solid by the heat of the sun and the constant action of the plough-sole. The soil itself partook in some considerable degree of the nature of the subsoil, being, however, ameliorated by mixture of manures, and by cultivation. Still, so great was the fear of the wretched subsoil that the pan was never disturbed; consequently, there being but nine or ten inches of cultivatable earth with an impervious basis, a dry summer burnt all up, and a wet one ruined the crop by rotting the roots. A showery season was the only suitable one for this description of land. Now, however, after draining, in the short space of a few months, we are subsoiling to the depth of fourteen or sixteen inches, and working it like a garden; the water having left it, and the frosty air following the water, it is as mellow and friable as could be desired. In fact, during the last month, whilst our neighbours were unable to move, we were harrowing in our wheat and beans like a rich garden; the earth crumbling down after the drill like sand—very much to the astonishment of the tenant and labourers; and this after so much carting and disturbance, and so much of the subsoil thrown up, that two months previously it was thought a whole summer would hardly suffice to condition the soil. The drains cross, at a very acute angle, the slope of the land; they are four yards apart, with a leader to every fourscore rods—the leader being rather deeper than the other drains, but not wider. Still, as it never runs full, it proves in practice my subsequent proposition, that "the filtration of water, in strong soils, is far inferior to the velocity of its passage through the drains." Each acre contains twelve score rods; and costs ten pounds,* requiring 3,200 pipes and 360 bushels of stones.

The Style of Drainage applied to this part of the farm is as follows:—

First, a double turn of the plough takes out nine inches; then a narrow spade (sufficiently wide to admit the drainer's foot) takes out ten inches; then comes a still narrower spade (fourteen inches long, three and one-eighth wide at top, and one and a half at bottom), which removes thirteen inches more —making the whole depth from the surface thirty-two inches. The drain being well cleared out, we first fill in the drains, to the depth of ten inches, with nice clean gravel-stones, and then place, *on the top* of these stones, a drain-pipe, thirteen inches long and three inches wide outside, having a two-inch bore. This fits so exactly into the space made by the last or narrow spade, that it not only rests on the stones, but binds against the sides of the drains, thereby preventing the stones being choked by the superincumbent earth, but also forming the earth above it into an arch; which in the stronger soil would, it is presumed, retain its form even if the pipe were broken or decayed. As this is a plan of my own, and contrary to the entertained opinions, that the tiles should be at the bottom, I will give my reasons for so doing; because,

1st. It is cheaper (wide drains take so large a quantity of stones).

2d. It is more durable, and less liable to choke.

3d. There is a larger *area* of *space* for the *escape* or *filtration* of the water; and this I consider of the utmost importance, and not sufficiently considered. It is quite evident, that the *filtration* of the water must be *according to the area of the pores presented to the air in the drains.*

It might be illustrated by saying, it is of little use having a large passage unless you have enough side-doors to admit a sufficient number of passengers to travel down it.

The other third of this farm was the reverse of the first two-thirds, and required an entirely different system of drainage. It is mostly black, sandy, and boggy soil, with numerous

* To those who have stones at hand, my drainage will appear dear, but I had to pay one penny per bushel for them, and cart them three miles. My pipes, 2-inch bore, and 13 inches long, cost, delivered, 20*s.* per thousand; but by Hatcher's Benenden tile machine, I presume they could now be made cheaper. There is also an admirable patent plan of socketing pipes into each other, which I should certainly have availed myself of, had it been then obtainable. Valuable information on draining is contained in Mr. Parkes's intelligent and scientific communication in the Royal Agricultural Society's *Journal.*—*March,* 1844.

springs rising at various points where obstructed by perpendicular walls or veins of dense clay or hard gravel.

The drainage here has been effected by a person named Pearson, from Warwickshire, a man of extensive knowledge and ability in this department of drainage, who, I understand, has essentially improved Lord Digby's estates by his judicious sub-draining of the springs. His plan is to take his fall from the lowest point, and gradually work up to where the spring shows itself, having previously ascertained the whereabouts by digging, and by those plants that invariably show themselves over a spring. As springs are generally attended by sandbeds, a single drain will often lay dry a large extent of ground. In one case, where there was a swamp of four acres, the drain was opened at two feet, and continued in a trench till it reached eleven feet in depth. The sand boiling up at intervals like water in a cauldron, of course it was necessary to shore up the sides, and when his level was accurately taken, he commenced laying his pipes on hay (two half-pipes, four-and-a-half inches diameter were put together, being internally nine inches by four-and-a-half), but so strong was the force of the water, it was necessary to have two strongly-made iron skeleton arches with wooden sides, about thirty inches high and the width of the drain. In these arches were laid the pipes, and firmly loaded to the top of the arch with soil to keep the pipes from being forced up by the boiling waters and sand; when loaded, the arches were removed by a lever, the mouths of the pipes being carefully stopped with hay, till the next length of pipes was laid in the next arch (two always being in use, one in front of the other).

The result is, that one such drain laid perfectly dry four acres of bog (having a smaller spring carried over or across it); the first drain runs *permanently* 30,000 *gallons every twenty-four hours*, and several others nearly as much. It has laid our neighbour's wells dry, a quarter of a mile off (being in a bed of sand, below their level). The land (which has been double spitted) is now always perfectly dry, although previously dangerous for cattle, and entirely worthless.—*March* 28, 1844.

---

3. DETAILS.

I am so constantly told, in tones varying from doubt and pity to ridicule and censure, "You will never see your money again,"—"You are a bold man," and so on—that I must endeavour to fill up the outline of my plan with details, and try to convince the prejudiced.

Most of my operations are approved of separately, but there is a dread of the sum total, as if what were individually right could be collectively wrong. Let me, then, attempt to show how the farm is to pay me, as landlord, an additional rent of

£240 per annum, with an increased benefit to the tenant as compared with his former holding.

In making the following estimates, I have adhered strictly to matters of fact, which I am prepared to discuss and substantiate. I have expressly undervalued the benefits, because I know how suspiciously and sceptically my statement will be scrutinized by those whose minds are pre-occupied by doubts and prejudices, rather than by calculation.

Statement of Gain or Saving:—

	£.	s.	d.
200 trees removed—estimated to damage by their roots and by their shade, 1*s*. each	10	0	0
950 linear rods (5½ yards each) of removed banks and fences (ditches filled up), averaging two yards wide—some were four yards wide, but the difference is set off against a few new ditches. It is estimated that each rod of these fences and banks damaged 6*d*. by their roots, their shades, and their encouragement of weeds and vermin	21	5	0
One-sixth saved in horse-labour and wear.—(This in the Prize Essay of the Royal Agricultural Society's Journal, vol. iv. part 2, p. 336, is estimated at one-fourth.)	21	0	0
One-eighth saved in manual labour	20	0	0
Seven acres gained in fences, banks, ditches, bog, and waste, which produced nothing, but cost the tenant rent, rates, tithes, &c., 36*s*. per acre	12	12	0
Profit in cultivation of the above seven acres, at 15*s*. per acre	5	5	0
105 quarters of wheat, thrashed by machine, gain in quantity one-twenty-eighth, or 2*s*. per quarter	10	10	0
150 quarters spring corn, at 1*s*.	7	10	0
Saving in thatching, removing stacks and straw, waste by birds, &c.	5	0	0
Liquid manure tank, calculated to contain 120,000 gallons, but we only reckon upon 20,000 gallons, at 50*s*. per thousand (each thousand gallons being equal to 4 cwt. of guano)	50	0	0
Improved quality of solid manure	10	0	0
Increased value of stock, by warmth, dryness, and diminished consumption of food	15	0	0
General increase on 90 acres of corn and clover crops, arising from *perfect* drainage, at £1 per acre	90	0	0
Saving in quantity of seed sown	20	0	0
Twenty acres that used to be long-fallowed, at an expense of £5 per acre, now calculated to pay their expenses, if not a profit, by bean or root crops	100	0	0
A first-rate house to live in, with every comfort and convenience: the lower rooms 11 feet high, the bed-rooms 10 feet high, and convenient rooms for the bailiff. (The tenant could not reside in the old dilapidated hovel, which was damp, unhealthy, and caused several deaths by fever)	30	0	0
	£428	2	0

To sum up, whereas the former gross annual return of the farm was under £5 per acre, we shall try to increase it to £10 per acre.

To this might be added several contingent advantages, of considerable value, but not so easily reduced to figures.

1st. The being able to fatten at least 100 to 150 sheep more than before, of a better quality, and earlier lambs. The tenant could breed, but never thoroughly fatten a lamb or sheep on the farm in its former cold, wet, and exposed state, with its homestead open to the cutting north-east winds, without gutters or drainage.

2nd. The facility of cooking and steaming food, and the economy of several acres that were required for horse food, by growing lucerne, tares, &c.

3rd. The very important benefit of early sowing and harvesting. We reckon we shall gain at least a fortnight in both, as proved last year, with superiority of sample, and avoidance of a catchy week in September.

4th. A perfect independence (by our efficient drainage) of a very wet season, which has often ruined the crops on this farm; witness 1842, when the oats yielded but three quarters two bushels per acre, and an inferior sample.

Lastly. The agreeable feeling of having a complete farm, with good roads, comfortable homestead, and good crops, instead of the former dilapidated, beggarly, and poverty-struck land and premises.

The saving of horse and manual labour is considerably underrated, when you consider the ready communication with each part of the farm, the abolition of all short-lands, the facility of ploughing or carting at almost any time with less power, the land being firm and mellow, instead of putty-and-paste-like;—no idle days in wet or cold weather, there being employment under cover for men and horses, grinding, chaff-cutting, or thrashing;—the facility, at harvest, of drawing the loaded carts into the bays of our large barn, and at once depositing the sheaves;—the ease with which they are transferred from both barns and stacks to the thrashing-machine, the straw being delivered by the machine into a gallery over the very sheds, yards, and stables where it is required;—no time lost or accidents in leading horses or cattle to water, there being tanks in every yard, and a yard to every stable—all the tanks filled simultaneously from a single pump.

There is another advantage of which no valuation is taken, I mean the farmer or bailiff's time; whilst writing up his accounts or arranging his plans, by stepping from one room to the other, he can at once *see* every man, boy, horse, or sheep, on *any* part of the farm, except about four acres. Any accident, mistake, neglect, maltreatment, or pilfering, is perceptible at a glance.

The General Application of the Expenditure is as follows:—

	£.	s.	d.
Draining, fencing, levelling, ditching, and roads......	2200	0	0
Barn, stabling, tanks, sheds, yards, &c..............	2000	0	0
House and offices	1000	0	0
Machinery, implements, cooking apparatus, &c.......	500	0	0
Manure, marl, &c....................................	500	0	0
	£6200	0	0

The item for house has been objected to; but I have yet to learn that a farmer is not entitled to be as well housed as a tradesman or manufacturer, and I am convinced brick and slate buildings are ultimately cheaper than board and thatch. I would caution gentlemen who may visit my farm this year, against raising their expectations too high, for although the land is all cropped and doing well, considering the dry season, I would have them remember that last year it was considered the poorest farm in Essex; that since January, 1843, we have cut eighty miles of drains, and spread their contents (nasty yellow stiff loam) on the surface; that we have removed 5,000 yards of banks and fences, filled up the ditches, cut new ditches (on the heavy land there should be one every seven or eight acres), made new roads, cut down and converted between 200 and 300 trees, carted across the land 60,000 bushels of stones, 300,000 drain-pipes, 400,000 bricks, 200 loads of timber, slates, iron, stone, sand, lime, and building materials; that we have removed all the old buildings, and erected new ones on a different site; that everything has been out of order and out of time, and that all this was done in sixteen months, *without long fallowing a single field*. It must be at least two or three years before the land is got into first-rate condition.—*June* 1, 1844.

---

4. GENERAL RELATIONS OF AGRICULTURE.

Superfluous Capital and Unemployed Population are in their co-existence a dangerous anomaly—threatening, in its continuance, ultimate destruction to our nation. Luxury for the wealthy few, and poverty for the unemployed many, must produce discontent, anarchy, and ruin. It is an alarming fact that much of our income is derived from the capital we lend to foreign countries; whilst, in our own, we dole out, grudgingly, in rates and in charities, a tithe of what ought to be the just and well-earned wages of the industrious, but not employed labourer.

Ask the majority of your independent friends whence they derive their income? The widow will tell you—"My money is making a road, cutting a canal, or building a town in America." The orphan will say, "Mine is supporting a civil war in Spain or South America, or growing corn in Russia for the London market." The capitalist will report his strong-box full of bonds —Chilian, Columbian, Peruvian, Mexican, French, Spanish, Dutch, Portuguese, Austrian, Prussian, and Neapolitan (some of which, by-the-by, do not pay interest or principal); but neither the widow, the orphan, nor the capitalist will tell you their money is profitably and delightfully engaged in growing food for themselves and their families—in providing employment and profit for their fellow-countrymen of every grade, from the labourer to the merchant. No; agriculture has had, as yet, no charms for the capitalist or speculator. We must reform, and quickly too, some of our errors, both as capitalists and farmers. The one lends his money to strengthen foreign competition in agriculture, commerce, and manufactures; the other sows uselessly and prejudicially more seed than the total annual amount of our wheat importation—the extra quantity sown actually diminishing the produce to a similar extent; yet all this takes place whilst we are complaining of superabundant capital and population, as if an industrious population could be too great. My opinion is, the more numerous we are the more prosperous we shall be, for we *live by one another*. The denser the population the greater our power and our trade, PROVIDED WE KEEP OUR CAPITAL AT HOME AND AT WORK AMONGST OURSELVES. To ship off our labourers and our money is nothing less than suicide. It is giving away, economically and politically, the sinews of our strength; and I call upon every man who has the welfare of his country at heart to put a stop to it.

This leads us to the question, "How is this to be done?" I answer, *easily;* and point to my operations at Tiptree Hall Farm, as a solution of the difficulty. If every capitalist were to expend, as I have done, forty-six pounds sterling money in improving each acre of poor and indifferent land, the sum total required would be *many hundred millions*. I need hardly point to the magical effect of this expenditure on our trade, commerce, and manufactures. Every individual in this country would feel it. It is too grand and delightful a prospect to hope to realize. There is too large a mass of miscalculation, ignorance, prejudice, pride, and long custom to be removed. Facts and results will scarcely do it; but reason and truth must prevail at last, and I look forward with hope that the wise, the patriotic, the intelligent, and the wealthy will exercise their influence, by example and precept, to procure so desirable a result. Agriculture is our sheet-anchor; to that we must look for employment and for profit; it is a vast field for enterprise; it is our vital strength as a nation; and our pride of country alone should stimulate us to be independent of foreigners for the supply of our daily bread—the staff of our lives.

Agricultural Improvements.—In considering how these improvements can be most readily effected, it is quite clear that individuals generally have seldom the means, the ability, or the inclination to carry out a *perfect* system of agricultural improvement; it must be done by companies of associated capitalists, the same as our railways and other great undertakings. I will venture to assert from experience, that there is not, in agricultural undertakings, *one-tithe* of the difficulty or uncertainty that attended railway operations.

Rival companies will be beneficial to the public by the protection of competition. General rules, however, on fundamental principles must be obtained by sanction of Act of Parliament;

and I apprehend an examination of competent authorities would lead to a table of laws adapted to the security and profit of the shareholders, the benefit of the landowner, and the welfare of the tenant.

Mortgagers might transfer their mortgages to the company, with full authority to carry out necessary improvements, on condition of receiving from the company all benefits over and above five per cent. interest for the company's capital. Should the landowner desire a sale, the company would have the opportunity of purchasing outright by public competition; or the landlord might have the power of redeeming his property, on paying the company principal and interest up to a period of sufficient notice.

In all cases where there is not an absolute sale, landlords should have the power of redeeming their property or transferring it to another company, under equitable arrangements to both parties. The variations in rents and prices of corn would be no greater, on an average, than the fluctuations in railway or other shares.

As to the fear of companies engrossing land, the same objection cannot apply to them as to charities. Shareholders invest for profit, and rivalry will necessarily prevent oppression. What tenant would not rather trust to fair competition under a company than to individual favour, cupidity, or caprice, to say nothing of the uncertainty of individual life?

Landlords would also benefit. Frequently now (I know several cases) a landlord, without agricultural knowledge, is prevailed upon by a designing or an incompetent tenant who shows an annual statement of heavy losses, to reduce his rent, till he receives but two per cent. for his money.

Farm Valuations.—I proceed to consider the defects in the present system of valuations.

Now a bad farmer is almost sure to get a new lease (for who is anxious to take it after him?), whilst a thoroughly good one is almost as certain to be turned out, or have his rent raised—the landlord being generally ready to avail himself of those improvements which a wise farmer is compelled to make for a profitable return. These improvements are *bonâ fide* his property, and ought to be legally as much so as the coat on his back; and it is a scandal and disgrace that they are not valued to the incoming tenant.

Let us see, in fact, how it acts on the landlord—I shall prove clearly he is a loser by it ultimately.

The outgoing tenant is obliged, in self-defence, to starve the land and injure his crops the last four years of his lease, whilst it takes the incoming tenant another four years to repair the damage done by his predecessor; so that between the two there is, during eight years, less labour and capital employed, less food grown, less profit made, and an increase in the poor's rate, without any corresponding benefit to the landlord. In nine cases out of ten an improving tenant resists being charged a large interest, in the shape of increased rent, on his own capital. He makes way for a miscalculating bad farmer, who ruins the land, ruins himself, and ultimately the landlord is obliged to put up with a small rent—not, however, till all parties have been put to considerable regret, inconvenience, and expense, arising from exchange of residence, to say nothing of expensive sales, valuations, and leases, a non-acquaintance with the peculiarities of a new farm, and the breaking-up of many friendly and relative ties, formed during a local residence.

Long Leases and a Corn-rent (that is, the value of so many bushels of wheat at the current price of the day) are essentially beneficial to both landlord and tenant, as well as to the country at large. Under this system landlord and tenant have but one common interest—they rise or fall together. The present custom of fixed money-rents acts alternately most injuriously on both. An unexpected war may find a tenant benefiting by an enormous price, whilst his landlord has only his four per cent.,—reduced, in fact, to two per cent. by all commodities having risen to war prices.

On the other hand, a tenant hires on a war lease—a sudden peace makes him bankrupt by the violent reaction; and still his landlord must let his farm at peace prices, whilst he was deprived of war benefits. The landlord is evidently the greatest sufferer, and should hasten to amend so unfair and so ruinous a system.

A Code of Rules for Agricultural Improvement is much wanted.

Our Royal Agricultural Society should have extensive model farms, with schools and libraries attached. *There* should be shown, after patient investigation, the most perfect and certain modes of drainage, irrigation, and warping; the most complete, durable, and economical arrangement of buildings; the most advantageous mode of tillage and course of crops; the greatest economy of manure and labour; the minimum of seed and maximum of distance in sowing; the most advantageous stage of ripeness; the effect of steeping seeds in manures; the most profitable mode of housing and feeding stock, and the advantages of removing all trees and fences. When all these national and important subjects are accurately ascertained by a competent but limited board of paid and responsible directors, deciding regardless of personal considerations, then let a code of unerring rules be promulgated and enforced with the full weight and sanction of the society, as a guide and beacon to the doubtful wanderer in search of agricultural knowledge, who, eager to avoid the shoals of error, is now distracted by multitudinous and conflicting opinions.

The whole question of foreign corn importation is, to my mind, trivial and insignificant, as compared with the importance of national agricultural improvement; and I hope to see the latter occupy the minds and speeches of our statesmen and orators, to the exclusion of the former. I consider our dependence on foreigners for food a glaring and national disgrace, unworthy of our wealthy and highly-civilized country.

Let us grow corn instead of timber, fences, and rubbish: we can do better without one than the other. I am told, "We must have timber! what should we do in case of war?" I answer, "How do we get our tea, coffee, wine, and every other foreign article in time of war?" So long as we have money to buy, and hearts of oak to defend and convoy our purchases, Old England can never feel a want, nor want a market to buy in.

Besides, what a gross folly it is to grow our own timber in corn fields, at a cost of four shillings a foot (I am sure it costs more) when we can import it at one-third the price.

A great error amongst farmers is the desire to grasp a large quantity of land, instead of concentrating their capital by improvement in a smaller compass. One of the important results of my suggestions as to valuing and making improvements would be, that instead of £6 to £8 per acre being (as it is now on an average) a sufficient tenant's capital, double that amount would be required, as on my farm. This alone would find employment for considerably more than one hundred millions of additional capital; so that, in fact, when we had disposed of all our foreign bonds and securities, I doubt if we should have near money enough to carry out entirely my practical scale of improvements, except slowly and gradually.

Agricultural Education.—Let agriculture form an honourable portion of our general education—why should it not? Let Tull and Tusser range side by side with Homer and Virgil. Then would our nobility and gentry be independent of incompetent or dishonest stewards and land-agents, and be able to appreciate those of a more worthy character. Agricultural education and apprenticeships for our young farmers are imperative.

How many a worthy person, retiring from the toils and turmoils of a busy city, to enjoy the tranquil peace of agriculture, regrets the want of agricultural knowledge!—often are his hopes and intentions frustrated and his property diminished by interested or erroneous advice, of which, till too late, he cannot judge. When I see landlords making returns in rent (in my opinion an injudicious operation), I think how much better it would be to present their tenants with an agricultural library. Farmers, from the very nature of their occupation, and their isolated position, are seldom able to travel from county to county in search of facts; but how readily is a multitude of agricultural experiments and experience brought to their fireside by a selection of good and practical books! Some may say, "Oh, farmers are too prejudiced to read." Experience has taught me the contrary. Bring them the book—

they may affect to despise it, but they will keenly, anxiously, and with sound sense, scrutinize all that concerns their pecuniary welfare. Reason tells us that the farmer, born, bred, and mixing with others of precisely the same way of acting and thinking as himself, cannot be expected to have so expanded a mind as a manufacturer or trader, who is daily in contact with strangers from every corner of the globe.

It is to be feared, too, that jealous landlords form too low an estimate of a farmer's character, and consider his success and elevation as degrading them—as if his gains were their loss. Let us hope this feeling will gradually give way to a better, and that a farmer who follows the hounds, and dresses and acts respectably, will be considered quite as likely to farm well and make as good a member of society as one who imitates in every respect one of his labourers.

---

5. THE DRAINAGE OF HEAVY LAND.

The conflicting opinions as to what is perfect drainage convince me that practice without theory is like a ship without a compass—dangerous, uncertain, and expensive. Having cut, during the past year, with good effect, sixty miles of drains, I will describe its action, and state what I consider to be the true theories of perfect drainage.

My operation being different to the usual custom, I beg to submit my theories and practice for discussion, approval, or disproof.

Theories of Drainage.*—1st. That in perfect drainage, twelve hours' rain should percolate and leave the land in less than twelve hours from the time the drains begin to act, the difference in time being equivalent to the proportion of water the earth chooses to retain for its use by capillary attraction.

2nd. That to effect this, the subterranean area of porosity should nearly equal the surface to be drained; so that if the space to be drained were one square yard, the sides and top of the drain should present an area for percolation equal to nine superficial feet, minus the allowance for pressure.

3rd. That the continuance of water in the soil longer than it would remain by capillary retention, is injurious, both chemically and mechanically, causing inequality, density, and sediment.

4th. That the earth and roots will abstract from the passing water those gases for which they have an affinity, and in which they may be deficient.

5th. That the form of drain should be deep and narrow, as affording the greatest area of porosity at the smallest cost,

* Some of these I have since seen reason to abandon.

increasing the quantity of porous earth available to roots—nothing, animal or vegetable, can exist in dense, undrained subsoils.

6th. That the material for filling the drains should comprise the greatest durability with the least power of capillary attraction.

7th. That where pipes are used their material should be durable, but porous; their form not round or square, but a very narrow and deep oblong, the object being to get a large area of porosity.

8th. That small, round, hard pebble-stones, with a pipe over them,* seem to present all the advantages desired, viz., the impossibility of choking by superincumbent earth, resistance of pressure from the sides, absence of capillary attraction; the round hard stones having but little mechanical affinity for the water, and offering but small resistance to its passage.

9th. That the passage of water in a pipe or drain is always quicker than its percolation through the earth or material of the pipe.

10th. That no drain should much exceed 100 yards in length (fifty or sixty would be better), without opening into a leading drain of greater dimensions. If the drain were in any part full, it would delay percolation.

11th. That neither bushes, straw, nor other perishable material should ever be used in a drain.

12th. That the deeper the drainage the better the crops; but in no case should any portion of the drain be nearer to the surface than 18 inches.

13th. There should be a leader to every 300 yards of drains, giving it ample capacity.

14th. That there should be an open ditch (but no fence) for every seven or eight acres drained. The absence of an occasional open ditch is what renders so much drainage useless. Long continuous narrow streets, without frequent outlets, get frequently obstructed; the same may be said of drains—a full drain with a slow egress sadly retards the filtration of water. Drains should be never more than half-full of water—the other half air. In this way the superior weight of water causes proper filtration by displacement of air and replacement of water by quick passage.

15th. That the rapidity of percolation depends on the subterranean area of porosity and the depth of drain combined. Shallow drains want a greater area of porosity than deeper ones; because (as water presses equally on all sides towards the vacant

* October 14th, 1844. Perhaps I may be wrong as to putting the pipe on the top; but in practice I find it answers admirably. One thing I am quite convinced of, that whilst the water at first enters the drain at both sides, its most rapid entrance is at the bottom of the drain, where the pressure is greatest.

space in the drain) the deeper the drain the greater the weight and column of water. Consequently, the greater the pressure the more rapid the filtration; filtration at two feet will be double that at one—at four feet four times as great, and so on in proportion to the superincumbent weight of water pressing equally on all sides towards the drain. It is on this principle that deep pipe drains act quicker and lay dry a greater extent of ground than shallow ones—consequently, the deeper your drainage the smaller may be your area of subterranean porosity. Pipes at the depth of five feet would hardly need stones; the pressure being about two-and-a-half pounds on every square inch at first, and as the water escapes and diminishes, so will the drains run slower and slower, in a ratio proportioned to the diminished pressure.

Still stones, with pipes, in my opinion, are the quickest conductors of water generally in heavy land.

Now, although my drainage is considered the most perfect in Essex, *I* only consider it one-fifth as perfect as it should be. My drains have one foot of subterranean porosity for every five feet of surface, instead of having five feet: still, as it is expensive, even so, I must be content with it; and I will assume it to be the *minimum* of perfect drainage.

During the recent nineteen hours' rain, after a very dry time, the stones and pipes poured out an immense volume of water, which, on the second, third, and fourth day, gradually decreased; proving my calculation correct, that if my drains had been perfect, it would have all run away in seventeen hours, instead of eighty.

Bush Drains.—On comparing notes with a farming friend of mine, who has *bush* drains from 200 to 300 yards long, in the same quality land, he said, "I know not what has become of the water, for none has appeared in the ditches;" and he seemed quite surprised at my drains running so much. What is the inference?—that bush and straw drains of great length are *perfectly worthless* as compared with pipes and stone drains of moderate length.

In fact, on one field I drained about three acres the same time, distance, depth, and soil, with scuds or bands of straw tightly fitted over the vacant space, and find it as compared with the tile and stone drained part, almost useless, so much so that we shall redrain it.

The consequence of my friend seeing no water is, that it stagnates and remains in the soil, keeping the roots cold, wet, and sour, resulting in late crops and densely working land. I hope, after this, we shall hear no more of scud or bush draining.

Permanent Grass, on very stiff clays, must be ploughed up before the drains can act. The impervious pan requires to be broken up. This may be a subject of regret, but ought *not* to be; for I quite agree with Mr. Morton, that no permanent grass can keep so much stock per acre as the turnip culture and green crops, fed, folded, or stall-fed, nor is it so profitable. Grass land is, therefore, a national loss, employing less labour and capital, and affording less profit, than it would do if cultivated with roots, green crops, and corn. I apprehend the affection for grass land arises, on the part of the landlord, from his being able to obtain a better rent for it than for arable, with fewer repairs; and on the part of the tenant, that he is aware it requires less skill and capital than arable land. In the mean time, the public welfare suffers much.

Spring Draining.—It must always be effected by drain-pipes (without stones) fitting into each other so as to form one continuous unbroken channel. Half-circular pipes, fitting on each other, are sometimes used; if properly loaded they answer, but are not so secure as the whole pipes.

I think we may lay down as a safe theory—

1st. That as the pressure of water is from *below*, spring-drainage should be *deep*, so that the superincumbent earth be equal to resisting the pressure on the pipes.

2nd. That the pipes should be always large enough to contain air as well as water.

3rd. That no stones, bushes, or straw should be used in spring-drains; it being evident the immense pressure I have mentioned would quickly choke them with earth. Pipes, for spring-draining, should alone be used.—*July 16th*, 1844.

---

6. TREATMENT OF FARM HORSES AND LIVE STOCK.

Ask a farmer if he prefers for himself a wet and rotten dung-heap to a clean, dry bed. Ask him if cleanliness in place and person, with proper ventilation, is not conducive to his health. Ask him if his food, nicely cooked and prepared, is not more agreeable to him than if raw and dirty. Ask him if he likes a cool residence in summer and a warm one in winter. He will say certainly, and laugh at you into the bargain; and yet he will not consider that what is good and profitable for himself, is quite as much so for his cattle. What would farmers say, if after a hard day's work, *they* were obliged to walk ten miles for a supper, and the same next morning for breakfast—losing six hours' rest, and adding 40 per cent. to their labour? And yet this is how they treat their horses daily. It seems too ridiculous to be tolerated. I object entirely to turning horses out, or to having pasture at all; in our midland and southern districts, the waste of food and manure is enormous.

If a horse is turned out twenty days on an acre, it is equal to twenty horses one day, or forty horses half a day. Imagine what they must destroy: their weight crushes and injures an amazing quantity of food. It may be said, "Oh, the blades rise again next morning." Yes, but with this constant treading do they grow as fast and as luxuriant as if allowed to remain undisturbed and erect—a foot-path or rabbit-run in a grass-field will convince you. Then, where the droppings are, the food is lost: supposing the droppings and urine to cover and taint four square yards per day, that is 130 square yards, or 3 per cent. of the whole surface per month. It is in fact thirty-six pounds lost in every hundred per annum. The only excuse for depasturing is the imperfect state of the farm-yard, which allows best part of the manure to be wasted.

Again, as to manure, there it lies, in hot sunshine and bleaching winds, till it almost becomes its original straw-colour, losing its ammonia and other gases; and what, perhaps, is of more consequence than all, deprived of the benefits of fermentation which it would receive in a well-arranged tank. Supposing a horse's liquid and solid manure to be one cwt. per day, or eighteen tons per annum, we lose one-third that quantity. In fact, it is not too much to say, that in the amount of labour the horse performs, his keep, and manure, we can, by manger-feeding on my principle save thirty or forty pounds out of every hundred.—This is enormous!!!

Well may our great manufacturers, who consider a difference of *one* per cent. a good profit, exclaim against the want of calculation and management in farmers. Sincere friend as I am to the agriculturists, I admit, with shame, they deserve the censure bestowed on them in this respect. I call upon them to make at once honourable amends by adopting my plan, and so save their money and their reputation. The idea of a man having forty horses, costing him £1,500 per annum, and refusing to save £400 or £500 per annum in their keep, manure, and labour, is absurd; it is paying preposterously for the maintenance of prejudice or obstinacy; and yet, I am afraid there are some who will do so rather than act on my suggestions. There are other inconveniences and dangers attending depasturing horses—frequent kicks and accidents, loss of time in catching them, broken knees in driving home, and injury to constitution by sudden atmospheric changes. Besides, no horses fed entirely on green food can undergo the labour of those manger-fed on mixed food. Green food does not afford sufficient material for muscle and bone. It is too washy.

I object *in toto* to permanent pasture, as a positive individual and national loss. Clovers are useful—but you cannot thoroughly hoe and clean the land when they are sown with a corn crop. Lucerne (and sainfoin) is my favourite, and you can grow it anywhere* if you keep it clean, supply it amply with lime and its constituent parts, drain very deep (not less than five or six feet), and protect it from frost in the winter by a strong coating of manure, with a dust of guano in summer.

* Some regard, however, must be had to climate; I apprehend our northern districts and hills are hardly mild enough for such productions.

Tares on heavy land and rye on light land are both profitable; and plenty of potatoes, swedes, carrots, &c., which can be grown *on any land*, however heavy, boggy, sandy, or gravelly, *if thoroughly drained, properly manured, and deeply cultivated.* By these means you may keep more than twice as much stock as by permanent grass.

Were we to treat our bullocks and our sheep as we do ourselves and our riding-horses, keep them clean, warm, dry, and well fed, we should increase strangely the quantity and quality of our animal food.

Let us imagine ourselves standing or lying day and night for months in the moisture and effluvia of our own accumulated excrements, uncleaned and ill-fed; it won't bear thinking of; and yet this is how most farmers treat their cattle: their food is presented to them in large unmanageable masses, with abundance of dirt (a corrector of acid it is called), uncooked and unprepared. We need not wonder at having to stab our bullocks to let out the accumulation of windy flatulence, or forcing strange-looking machines down their throats to remove solid lumps of unmasticated roots; we need not wonder at foot-rot, fevered feet, or other complaints. The idea of a man swallowing a quantity of frozen turnips on a frosty day—without a bit of bread, absorbent or stimulant of any kind!!! It is too ridiculous to think of.

I will lay it down as an indisputable fact, as proved by our greatest breeders of animals, that we must apply to them the same treatment as we would to ourselves—if we wish to render them profitable. It is high time we amended our absurdities in this respect, or we shall have Spain, Portugal, and other warm and genial climes stocking us with what we ought to produce ourselves.

Let us keep them warm in winter and cool in summer—free from tormenting flies. In fact, I shall never consider we are perfect till we can keep up a given warmth in winter—whilst we have in summer cool and shaded paved yards.

Food and Treatment.—I will proceed to detail the feeding of our horses, and the proposed treatment of our cattle and sheep:—They are never turned out, nor do they receive any grass-hay or clover-hay, except a small portion during the interval between green-crops and root-crops. In summer they are fed in mangers on wheat-straw chaff, cut one-eighth of an inch, and tares, lucerne, or green rye, cut also into chaff the same size, adding ground beans, oats, or meal, with linseed. In winter, our carrots, swedes, and mangold, will be well washed, passed through Gardner's turnip-cutter, and again passed through a toothed cutter machine, so us to become what I call root-chaff; it will then be mixed with very fine wheat, bean, or oat-straw chaff, and a little ground beans, barley, or oatmeal, soaked linseed, steamed potatoes, and a little salt, varying the food as much as possible, to stimulate their feeding.

In fact, to sum up, we shall present their food in the form occupying the smallest possible compass and requiring the least mastication. Every half-hour saved in feeding is so much added to their rest—a most important ingredient in fattening. The dry chaff will prevent laxity and flatulence, producing also a sufficient and healthy excitation of the stomach, whilst it will afford to the gastric juices a ready access to every part of the mass of food.

This mixture appears by its various constituents perfectly adapted to the formation of bone, muscle, fat, and flesh, all which are essential to the perfect development of a well-fatted animal.

Weekly Cost of keeping each Farm-horse in high condition and full working order:—

	s.	d.
Twenty-four bushels of wheat-straw chaff, cut one-eighth of an inch, at 2*d*.	4	0
Twelve bushels of green tares, cut into chaff, at 2*d*.	2	0
Four-and-a-half pecks of beans, ground into small pieces	5	0
Pollard	1	0
Cutting chaff	1	0
Straw for litter	2	0
	15	0

From this may be deducted 1*s*. 6*d*. per week, the value of one horse's solid and liquid manure.—*August* 8, 1844.

---

7. AGRICULTURAL IMPROVEMENT COMPANIES.

It is a fact, that there is in trade, manufactures, and commerce, a superabundance of capital, whilst in agriculture it is as sadly deficient. Ask any improving landlord or tenant why their various improvements are so scantily and temporarily effected: they will say, not that it is unprofitable to make them permanent, but because there is not a sufficient command of money to do so. It is painful to see talented and spirited agriculturists crippled and restrained by the want of that capital which in towns and cities so abounds as to scarcely command 3 per cent., and is in consequence forced into rash speculations, or invested in loans to foreign nations, with whom we may be to-morrow at war.

Labour is the very best of Capital WHEN EMPLOYED, but we will not employ it *with* money payments, nor allow it to employ itself *without* money payments *by means of allotments*. We grasp and grudge the industrious labourer's patch of ground, but inconsistently enough pay cheerfully heavy gaol, police, or pauper rates, to restrain or punish the crimes consequent on his non-employment, poverty, and demoralization. I mention these matters as strong evidence of the necessity of applying the surplus capital of towns to the improvement of agriculture. A man with his cow, pig, and an acre of ground, has a stake in the soil. If non-employment and poverty fill your gaols, it is a logical deduction that employment and comfort can alone empty them.

Self-interest should alone induce us to take up the question, but the higher moral sense of justice to the general welfare commands us so to do. Honour is due to those counties, Lincolnshire for one, where their cottagers can keep a pig or a cow without being suspected of robbing their masters. Those masters will be found to be, as a natural consequence, men of talent, capital, and education; and their workmen many degrees in advance of those without either cow, pig, or land (the comparative criminal records of these districts would be instructive), ragged, and half-starving, on seven or eight shillings per week. The condition of the cottager is too frequently a true index to the character and position of his employer.

Agricultural Capital.—Let us inquire why capital finds its way readily to every foreign loan or hazardous scheme,* that tends to give strength to foreign countries and to weaken our own. Why have we companies, British and Foreign, for *every* object, *except* agricultural improvement? Is it because the 3 per cents. pay only 3 per cent.? Certainly not! Is it because we do not feel confidence in our landed tenures? Is it that there is no *disposition* to improve the soil? I answer—decidedly none of these causes. It is *because we have no authorized and competent channel for the profitable investment of surplus capital in agricultural improvement.*

Ignorance and want of combination are at the root of the evil. Everything in this way is left to individual enterprize. As well might a single shareholder attempt constructing his portion of a railway, with all its complicated accompaniments! Imagine him attempting such an object, himself without experience, and unaided by all the various aggregation of talent necessary for the details of such an operation. The idea is absurd; and yet the scarcely less complicated operation of landed improvement is, up to this hour, left in the position I have described.

Ask a capitalist why he does not invest his money in land or agriculture? He will look sternly grave, and quote a hundred instances where individuals have ruined themselves by such a course. So now he rushes into some foreign loan or project, to the great injury of his own countrymen, fearful of the "law's delay" in conveyance, with all its multifarious objections *pro* and *con.*, most likely alarmed by the rumoured fate of some

* October 12th, 1844. The two following paragraphs appear in this day's *Spectator*, page 969:—

"A railway is proposed from Lisbon to Oporto, through Santarem and Coimbra, half the necessary capital *to be raised in England*, and half in Portugal."

"One hundred Thames Tunnel Shares, on which £5,000 have been paid, were sold the other day for *Thirty* pounds." Can Agricultural Improvement Companies turn out worse than this?—I. J. M.

friend who, having at last got his estate, knows nothing about the management of it, and after struggling with incompetent tenants or designing ones, new leases, valuations, tormenting applications for repairs to the old dilapidated buildings, appeals for returns of rent, and other vexations, finds his rental reduced to 2½ per cent., or less, sells at a loss, and retires from the contest in despair. His example is quoted, and his mishap magnified to many other capitalists, who, ever after, from father to son, shun the dangers of meddling with so disastrous an affair as a landed investment.

Now, all this might be easily obviated and prevented by a well-conducted company, having practical directors, with proper engineers and officers (such men as Mr. Parkes, for instance). Do away with the law of mortmain as regards such companies. Let them purchase waste or poor lands—drain, clear, trench, crop, and let them. Let there be rival companies and their shares quoted at the Stock Exchange, the same as railway companies. Their success would depend upon their abilities and results, and a man disposed to invest his money in agricultural improvement, could, without any personal trouble, buy or sell his shares or bequeath them without more anxiety or care than attends any other investment.

How much more grateful to see Mr. Cobden and Mr. Baker on the same committee, exercising their great abilities to stimulate the productive powers of our grateful, but neglected soil; throwing to the winds the question of foreign importation or protection! How pleasant to see in our shipping lists, that having abundance of corn, we are *exporters* of flax, oils, and other matters, which we are now obliged to purchase! Could we but produce food with as much skill as we do manufactures, we should indeed be a great nation; we have the *means* to do so had we but the *method*. Had such companies existed years ago, millions of our money, lent or wasted to strengthen other nations, would have been employed *at home* in adding to our happiness and welfare. My earnest wish is, that I might be spared to see my suggestions in practical operation; it will be amongst the happiest moments of my life! Our duty to our country and to ourselves claims our attention to this matter.—*October*, 1844.

P.S. There are already agricultural colleges and drainage companies, and no doubt there will be loan companies, improvement companies, and companies for the cultivation of flax, oils, &c., which are now purchased of foreigners.

---

8. ON DRAINING HEAVY LAND.

Let me say here that I perfectly agree with the editor of the *Agricultural Gazette*, that there is frequently too much width in drains, and too little depth; the mass of earth to be removed, or stones to fill it, adding greatly to the cost. I will also admit, that the small pipes alone (as mentioned by him, and as described by Mr. Parkes in his valuable communication to the Royal Agricultural Society) will after a time (a year or two) carry off one day's rain in three days. But this is only an imperfect mode of drainage, for several reasons: 1st. Because it is two or three years before it will act perfectly, instead of at once drying the soil and rendering it friable. 2nd. Because in dense soils—and to those my theories are applied—the retention of water forty-eight hours longer than is necessary must be very injurious, by depriving it for so considerable a period of the atmospheric action. It acts like drowning, or soaking earth in water for two days, and must unduly expand its particles, absorb heat, and retain in degree that sodden characteristic which drainage is intended to remedy. I consider it an axiom that the friability of the soil will be in proportion to the rapidity of percolation. Fltration may be too sudden, as is well enough shown by our hot sands and gravels; but I apprehend no one will ever fear rendering strong clays too porous and manageable. The object of drainage is to impart to such soils the mellowness and dark colour of self-drained rich and friable soil. That perfect drainage and cultivation will ultimately do this is a well-known fact. I know it in the case of my own garden. How it does so I am not chemist enough to explain in detail; but it is evident the effect is produced by the fibres of the growing crops intersecting every particle of the soil, which they never could do before draining; these, with their excretions, decompose on the removal of the crop, and are acted on by the alternating air and water, which also decompose and change in degree the inorganic substances of the soil. Thereby drained land, which was before impervious to air and water, and consequently unavailable to roots, to worms, or to vegetable or animal life, becomes, by drainage, populated by both, and is as great a chemical laboratory as our own atmosphere, subject to all the changes produced by animated nature. I apprehend that two days' stagnation of water would endanger either worms or roots. Mr. Parkes justly observed to me, that worms act as assistant drainers, occupying the soil which before never contained any living thing; and it is through the innumerable conduits they make, that water finds its way so readily to a small pipe at a considerable depth; but, I consider, and must maintain my theory, that he who carries the falling water through heavy land in the shortest period is the best drainer, and will the soonest render such land equal to the best. To do this, there must be in the drain a large area of porosity. The means of effecting it may vary as opinion varies; but the drain, to be economic, must have the largest porous area in the smallest possible space that will convey the water.

I consider that the falling water, descending uniformly through the whole surface, and mixing intimately with each grain or particle of earth, is far preferable, chemically and mechanically, to its forcing its way in streams towards the joints of the pipes, whilst the remainder is delayed, waiting a day or two to take its turn in the same worn channel. For this reason I object to waiting for gaping cracks to make drains act; because it is quite possible the water may rush down such cracks from the surface, and leave considerable masses of intermediate earth unmoistened. The principal utility in drains, is, in my opinion, to enable the earth to derive the full benefit of the various and all-important manures with which the falling water and renewed air are so amply charged. Another very considerable objection to the "wait a day or two" plan is, that the greater quantity of rain falls in the autumnal or winter months, when every day's ploughing lost is of consequence, economically, and as regards the welfare of the ensuing crops. This alone should stimulate us to get rid of the obstructive water in a trice; for our autumns are never deficient in moisture, but the reverse. A small pipe will readily carry water when it gets in, but the question as to how and when it enters are subjects worthy the attention and experiment of the numerous and valuable agricultural correspondents of the *Agricultural Gazette*.

Surface Drainage.—After all that has been said and written on this subject, I have arrived at the following conclusions:—

1st. That Mr. Parkes's statement is a convincing proof that one-inch pipes (*without* stones, straw, or bushes) placed four feet deep, at intervals of thirty feet, will effectually and permanently drain the heaviest soils of the utmost quantity of surface water that can possibly fall, at a cost of from £2 to £3 per acre. That in mixed soils, the one-inch pipes, four feet deep and fifty feet apart, will perfectly drain such soils at a cost of about 45*s*. per acre.

2nd. That although those drains do not, the first year after being made, act so effectually as stones with pipes on my plan, which carry off the water at once; still the immense difference in cost, and greater depth, render Mr. Parkes's plan by far most desirable.

3rd. That Mr. Hammond's experiment, as detailed by Mr. Parkes, proves that my theory of "the area of porosity in the drains," as explained in my fifth letter, is an incorrect theory. I therefore withdraw it as such, and at once admit I was so far in error—although it appears I am correct as to *depth* influencing the distance of the drains and quantity of their discharge. The "area of porosity," however, evidently expedites the time of action in the drains the first year.

There can be no doubt that it is the *depth* of the drain which regulates the escape of the surface-water in a given time; regard being had, as respects extreme distances, to the nature of the soil and a due capacity of the pipe. *The deeper the drain, even in the strongest soils, the quicker the water escapes.* This is an astounding but certain fact.

4th. That deep and distant drains, where a sufficient fall can be obtained, are by far the most profitable, by affording to the roots of plants a greater range for food.

5th. That had I to redrain my heavy land, I should do so at least four feet deep, with inch-pipes at intervals of thirty feet, carrying each pipe with the fall of the land direct to an open ditch of ample capacity. I should thus economize several open ditches on my farm, which are at present a waste of ground. Each drain would thus be its own leader.

I should place the pipes in the drains without stones, or other matter, merely covering them with the clay itself, leaving the drains open as long as possible, as practised by Mr. Hammond. I should thus save £7 per acre on the cost of my draining, and have a greater depth of soil. The loss would be the difference between a perfect and imperfect drainage the first two years.

In conclusion, I consider the balance of evidence, where stones and pipes are used, is in favour of the pipe being placed at the bottom.—*December* 21, 1844.

---

9. ON SUBSOILING AFTER DRAINAGE.

How frequently we hear of farmers who, having subsoiled poor thin-skinned land, find that their *first* crop is diminished thereby, particularly if a *corn* crop; and therefore subsoiling is at once condemned. Now this result might naturally have been expected. It is quite clear, if you disturb deeply a very shallow soil on a stiff clay subsoil, you ought to increase considerably your supply of manure the first two or three years, till the hungry substratum becomes full of roots and organic matter. You must bear in mind, this undrained subsoil has been like stiff Suffolk cheese, a dense mass of poverty, unoccupied by roots or worms, and unacted upon by the gases of the atmosphere.

Of course by disturbing and intermixing it with the cultivated surface, it naturally robs it of part of its goodness, and imparts to it a portion of its poverty. It often happens, on bringing up the subsoil, a crop of weeds grow up from long-buried seeds. I therefore strongly advise a Root Crop after subsoiling, because then the land is well manured, often hoed, and when the crop is removed, a vast quantity of strong roots remain in the subsoil, and afford food for the ensuing crop. (I have seen a calculation, that each acre of wheat plants leaves two tons of roots and fibres in the soil.) What must a crop of Swedes leave? All deep tap-rooted crops do well on newly-subsoiled land, such as beans, roots, and rape; but I prefer the land becoming more solidified for white crops, particularly

Yards and Sheds.—Another important comparative question is the superiority of yards and sheds over stalls. I think we may lay down as a general rule, that whatever conduces to the ease and comfort of the animal, tends to its early ripeness, and *vice versâ*. Now, when a bullock is tied up, its movements are confined, and in some degree cramped by its fixed position. We can judge by ourselves, sitting or standing long in one posture becomes irksome, and a change is agreeable. The muscles, for want of exercise, get relaxed, and in many cases are unable to support the animal, when he attains to a great weight. But we must avoid the other extreme of too much freedom, or we shall lose fat by increased action and respiration. The happy medium appears to be just sufficient room for the beast to turn round in and no more. It is on this principle I account for the superiority of the close-box feeding, as practised by Mr. Warnes and Mr. Warren. Another advantage is that the bullock can rub his hind quarters. This I compensate for in my stalls by brushing them thoroughly every day, especially those parts they cannot reach to lick. They like it much. Whether the friction acts beneficially by electricity, circulation, or warmth, or all of these, I cannot say. It is possible some of the benefits of the close-box system may arise from non-excitement inducing more repose, whilst the smaller abstraction of caloric, and absence of draughts, insure a higher and more uniform temperature. Less straw is required in stalls than in boxes, especially where (as at the duke of Bedford's, at Woburn) there is a fall of a few inches in the pavement immediately behind the animal's heels, which prevents their lying back in their dung, as they are too apt to do.

Temperature.—There can be no doubt that temperature has a very material influence on the fattening of cattle. I remember to have seen in the *Agricultural Gazette* an illustrative fact on this subject, in which it was clearly proved that cattle laid on a much larger quantity of fat, in proportion to their consumption of food, during April, May, and June, than in the colder and moister months. This is consistent with the well-known fact, that the rapid abstraction of caloric by a cold and *moist* atmosphere, renders necessary a larger quantity of food to keep up the supply of carbon. The food is therefore wasted, which, in a higher temperature, would be producing fat. We find the fact so in ourselves. Exposed to cold in open unsheltered situations during winter, our appetite increases strangely, whilst our weight remains unaltered. In a warm dry room no such effect is produced. Let us apply this knowledge.

But whilst there is warmth, there must be ventilation. I find, in practice, a few small iron air-bricks placed in the highest point of the stable, near the ceiling, in the back and front walls, answer admirably, allowing the heated foul air that passes from the animal's lungs to escape, whilst they admit a replacement of oxygen to compensate for that which is being consumed.

Our bullocks, approaching to *perfect ripeness*, do amazingly well at a temperature of 45° to 50° (January): at 55° to 60° we found they sweated profusely. A thermometer ought to be in every stable; it costs but 3*s*., and is a safe guide, whilst our personal sensations of temperature are not to be depended upon.

Mode of Feeding.—We have fourteen Galloway Scots, averaging each 110 stone of 8 lbs. each, butchers' or net dead weight, and they are putting on fat rapidly. They consume daily for each bullock,—

	s.	*d.*
Four bushels of Swedes, cut one quarter of an inch (weighing 56 lbs. per bushel, at 6*d*. per bushel)	2	0
Three oil-cakes, weighing 7 lbs.	0	6
Boiled linseed, 3 lbs., at 1½d. per lb.	0	4½
Barley meal	0	1½
	3	0

The roots are given uncooked; the linseed boiled and mixed with meal or barley, and 12 lbs. of wheat-straw chaff cut one-eighth of an inch, part of it steamed, part dry, with a sprinkling of clover chaff. No charge is made for cooking or fuel—their manure being considered an equivalent.

So that the quantity in weight they consume daily is from 246 to 250 lbs. This astonishes some folks; but the almost daily progression of the animals proves it is well employed. The chaff is given partly steamed and partly dry. They are never allowed to want food; still the moment they cease feeding and lie down (they are almost constantly down), the food they leave, if any, is immediately removed for the pigs or sheep. The minute subdivision of the food enables the stomach to contain at least 25 per cent. more in quantity than with loose straw and large angular pieces of dirty unwashed roots. I consider the *cleanliness*, comminution, and admixture of the food, so as to diminish its bulk without risk of fermentation, is greatly in favour of early ripeness, leaving more time for repose and rumination. Hay, finely comminuted and *un*mixed with straw-chaff, is dangerous for horses. They are apt to swallow it greedily unmasticated.

Our lambs and sheep eat steamed straw-chaff, with barley or other meal and linseed; of course, linseed must always be crushed first, and then simmered. I am convinced boiled linseed is cheaper and more profitable than oil-cake; and we shall, when our stock of oil-cake is reduced, feed principally with linseed. Still a little dry oil-cake, at intervals, makes a change, and stimulates their feeding; straw-chaff, in lieu of hay, admits of a larger consumption of linseed. Our pigs fatten rapidly on steamed roots, &c.

Importance of Condition and Breed.—I am quite con

vinced that it is more profitable to buy a half-fat or thriving animal than a very lean or half-starved one. The latter eats more, is longer getting ripe, and you have less weight to sell with a profit; but if you purchase a half-fat beast at *5d.* per lb., and get him out of hand quickly at *6d.* per lb., you get 20 per cent. *without cost* on what you bought, and in addition are paid at the rate of *6d.* per lb. for all the fat you put on. It requires no conjurer to prove that this is the most advantageous mode of proceeding, presuming you buy your half-fat beast at the same rate per lb. as a very poor one, which you will most likely do, for butchers do not like half-fat stock; which should warn us not to over-stock, but always get our animals well up to the mark.

I feel assured that the best-bred animals, although at a greater cost, pay better than those which are coarse, cross-bred, ill-shaped, large-headed, and big-boned; for make these as fat as you will, they only command a second-rate price. One reason why inferior stock is so frequently preferred is this:—An animal that has by good luck survived starvation and exposure on a common or bleak mountain, is less likely to be destroyed by the ordinary undrained land and miserable homesteads of many of our farmers. To bring a handsome, well-bred creature, whether bullock or sheep, from rich, dry ground and judicious treatment, to take the chance of much worse fare, has not been found to answer. Although no judge of stock myself, I know what pleases my eye. Plenty of length, breadth, and depth in fore and hind quarters, large above the knee and hook, and small below; a little head, with full, intelligent, and contented eye; a neat horn, a firm but yielding coat that fills the palm, and an outline level and pleasant to the eye,—in fact, a sort of rotund squareness.

Bullocks and Sheep.—I have been at some trouble to inquire and practically compare which are more profitable to keep, and I am quite convinced that beef should sell at least 20 per cent. higher than mutton to make them pay alike. I know several very respectable graziers who have not for years had a bullock on their premises, being practically convinced of their unprofitableness.

I have at this moment 100 lambs thriving well, at a cost of 1½*d.* to 1¾*d.* per day, valuing Swedes at *6d.* per bushel (the price I could sell them for), whilst my bullocks are consuming to the value of *3s.* per day each. Unfortunately I have not a weighing-machine to compare the relative proportion of fat laid on in proportion to their relative weight, but I am quite satisfied the sheep pay best in proportion.

To what are we to attribute this difference in fattening?—Why, in my opinion, it is clearly owing to the difference in their coats. The wool of the sheep affords them a greater protection against cold. There is less caloric given off, consequently a smaller supply of carbon or food is required.

The bullocks, having a thinner covering, lose more heat, and require more carbon or food, and consequently are less profitable. This is another proof how important it is to keep our cattle warm, and to calculate the *cost* in each department accurately.—*January* 8, 1845.

---

12. ON AGRICULTURAL LEASES.

The only way to treat the matter is, as we would any other transaction—each party looking to his own interest, so contracting that both shall have a coincident advantage in the progressive improvement of the soil. After all, a lease is a mere business transaction, a contract or bargain for a pecuniary result. If we let our farms at an exorbitant rent, we must expect a similar result to selling goods above their value to a needy or foolish person. In one case our land is ruined or deteriorated, in the other we get five or ten shillings in the pound in lieu of twenty.

Corn Rents.—I am decidedly of opinion a long lease and a corn rent (regulated by the rent-charge for tithe) and a valuation of tenants' improvements to the incoming tenant, are indispensable as a basis for leases.—Some say, "Oh, a landlord does not like a variable rent." Well, but are not all classes of income variable with circumstances? Where is your five per cent. government fund annuitant? Why, *nowhere* in that character; but we find him grumbling or contented with three and a quarter. Your shareholder in canals, with ten per cent. to-day, finds to-morrow the railways have reduced him to five. Where are your holders of road-trust bonds? Their capital annihilated and the traffic transferred to railways. It is the same in trade, commerce, and manufactures, one year thriving, another losing; and so with the farmer himself, his wheat £20 this season, and £10 the next. Then, pray, why is the landlord to be placed in a different position from all the world beside? Your landlords of houses find their property improved by a church or swept away by a railway, or their dearly-built old houses rendered tenantless by new ones, more fashionable, more commodious, and cheaper, being built when timber, iron, and labour happen to have fallen forty per cent., the manufacturers being depressed. There is nothing certain in this world—all is movement and change. Neither landlords nor tenants can escape the vicissitudes of circumstances any more than other classes of her Majesty's subjects.

With regard to the Tenants' Capital, the late Earl of Leicester (Mr. Coke), who was himself a great agriculturist, used to say, when applied to for a farm, "How much money have you?—and I will suit the acres to the money." Now, a landlord who desires his land to be well farmed must have a tenant who can command £10 per acre at least—£15 or £16 would be much better, but still £10 per acre might do; but then he must not tie down such a man to any particular system of farming; the most he should require would be that the whole of the land should be long fallowed within the last four years of the lease, if required, or considered necessary by the landlord: or the crops alternated, corn and root, during the last four years, the roots and straw consumed on the farm. This would prevent the land being distressed.

Terms of Lease.—Let us assume that the preliminaries of a lease are arranged (for I presume no man in his right senses would ever take a farm without a lease, if he could find one within a hundred miles with a lease); then come the terms or details:—

1st. *As to Time.*—Twenty-one years should be the *maximum*, seven the *minimum*, with a power on the part of the tenant to determine the lease at seven or fourteeen years, giving ample notice (say four years).

2nd. *As to Rent.*—Whatever rent is agreed upon in time of peace, it should be based upon the average price for the last seven years per quarter for wheat, rising or falling annually with the tithe-rent charge, in easy gradations.

3rd. *Draining.*—The landlord, if rich, should drain the land permanently with pipes or tiles, charging the tenant five or seven per cent. interest on the investment. If there be a needy landlord and a wealthy tenant, the latter should be bound to drain the land efficiently, and be allowed a reduction of rent equal to ten per cent. on the cost of drainage; say five per cent. interest of capital, and five per cent. for the capital sunk and lost to him in twenty years. If both are in good circumstances, the expense may be divided equally, or done by either, subject to the above conditions. It is a folly and a loss to attempt profitable cultivation on undrained shallow-ploughed land; progressive profit to both landlord and tenant attend thorough draining and deep cultivation.

4th. *Timber, Fences, and Squaring Fields.*—Above all things a tenant must bargain for the removal of all timber trees, pollards, and useless fences, with full permission (under a plan approved by the landlord) to remove useless banks, fill up ditches, open new ones, and lay the fields in straight or parallel lines, to avoid short lands. As this is an expensive operation, he should be allowed the cost out of the sale of the timber; and in all cases the tenant should be permitted to burn all old pollards into charcoal, to be applied to the soil, or used in burning the earth. Whenever the growing timber is a consideration (which it very seldom is, now foreign timber is so cheap), the tenant should covenant to give 1*s*. or 2*s*. per acre increase in rent for its removal.

5th. *Buildings.*—I speak guardedly, when I say the difference to the tenant between well-placed and ill-arranged buildings is in stock alone a profit or a loss of 10*s*. per acre. In every case the landlord should provide an efficient, capacious, roofed manure-tank; gutters to the eaves of buildings, to carry away the water without touching the manure, and the farmyard itself should always be under-drained into the manure-tank. The best way is to do with this as with the drainage. If the landlord has capital, pull down and rebuild the homestead, or allow the tenant to do so, where the latter is a wealthy man, diminishing the rent in an amount equivalent to ten per cent. on the cost of building; say, five per cent. annual interest, and five per cent. annual portion of the capital sunk on a twenty-one years' lease. Where neither feel inclined to do the thing as it ought to be done, patching and repairing must be considered. To secure this being properly attended to, a clause might be inserted in the lease allowing the tenant to expend out of his rent a certain sum annually (according to their extent) in improving the buildings. If a landlord has good and permanent buildings, let him strictly covenant for substantial, *not* tenantable repair, which latter means merely wind-and-water-tight.

Course of Cropping.—It appears to me, that the dictation by a landlord to a tenant of a particular course of cropping is a monstrous absurdity, intolerable in this age of civilization, and not answering its intended purpose; for, in the first place, the landlord may know nothing about farming; and, in the second, local custom may sanction a system so inferior, that a superior farmer from the Lothians, or the Lincolnshire Wolds, dare never compete for an occupancy under such restrictions.

What would be said of the owner of a mill, either cotton or corn, binding the occupier to make his flour one way, or his cotton-manufacture another. Or when you let a shop, or house, you may as well control the description of goods to be sold, the profit to be charged, or the style of furniture. The object of such restriction is, on the face of it, fair enough, but does it answer the desired purpose? Certainly not; for the continuous starvation of the soil by a bad farmer, or poor tenant, is far worse than an evasion of the terms by a good one. I know I would rather hire after two white crops on land previously *well farmed* than after fallowed land (full of weeds generally) on a half-starved farm. A good farmer knows that to injure the land is to punish himself.

A fair valuation of useful and necessary improvements to the incoming tenant would do away with these absurd anomalies, and allow the land to go into the possession of the succeeding tenant cleanly and highly cultivated.

---

13. BUT WHERE IS THE MONEY TO COME FROM?

"Landlords have it not, and tenants cannot afford it." This reply accompanies a tardy admission that agricultural perfection is desirable. As theory and practice are always best in combination, I will state *how* the means are to be found, and illustrate it by my own case, leaving it to the option of others to follow my example or not.

Having some spare capital I invested it in land, purchasing 260 acres. Subsequently I reflected on the imperfect condition of one of the farms, and considered I should be doing no more than a public and private duty by improving it. Well, having already invested, where was the cash to come from? Why, I resolved on selling the other farms, and invested the proceeds in improving the remaining one. This is a ready way of conferring a great national benefit, without injuring ourselves. It takes away the excuse (the last prop) of the non-improvers, and proves it is a true saying, that "where there is a will there is a way;" and where there is not a will, there is an excuse, good, bad, or indifferent. The struggles for tenures are surprising. A tenant will frequently purchase a farm at a high rate, and mortgage it forthwith for less than the purchase-money, in order to secure a holding, abstracting thereby a portion of his much-required means, and sometimes do so when his capital is barely adequate to his present tenure. If farmers, who plead as an excuse for not farming high, that *their means* are inadequate, would *diminish* their holdings *one-half*, they would lessen the competition for farms, and benefit themselves and the community. Their capital would thus be *doubled* in its relative proportion to their acres; and they would be at liberty to bestow deep and frequent tillage, with abundant stock and manure, where now the land, the landlord, the labourer, and themselves, are in an unsatisfactory and unprofitable condition. I maintain, and am prepared to prove, that there is no difficulty whatever in raising profitably and forthwith more food than we can require for our own consumption; but then we must try and grow beans seven feet high, instead of fences seven feet high: the one exhausts the soil quite as much as the other. Corn and cabbages must displace those ugly old pollards that mar the landscape, and are worth on an average 2*s*. each, to pay for a century's growth and cultivation (for their roots are regularly ploughed, harrowed, manured, and sown over). I will venture to assert as truth, that every villainous stump of this description has been a loss to the nation of 6*d*. annually; or, in the whole period of its growth, from 20*s*. to 50*s*. Multiply this by 40,000,000 and calculate the loss. As to hedge-row trees, the loss they occasion to the nation is certainly equivalent to £5,000,000 annually—assuming that there are but two on every acre, and that they cause an annual loss of 1*s*. each.

Possible Produce.—The question of what *may be* profitably produced from an acre of land, is a very important one. Professor Playfair (a first-rate authority) has, I believe, stated that £250 can be and has been produced from one acre of market-garden in one year; and we all know full well that in all gardens the produce is abundant compared with field culture. Why it is so needs no reply. "At blithesome morn and dewy eve," the crowds of men, women, and children issuing from market-gardens are living solutions of the problem, and stand in charming relief to the solitary farm-labourer, alone in a twenty-acre field, or scattered here and there over an extensive district, like plums in a school pudding.

The *average* annual return of the arable land of this country being about *five pounds ten shillings per acre*, stands in miserable comparison with Dr. Playfair's £250.

Valuation.—We all know that Lincolnshire is the best-cultivated county in the United Kingdom. The secret of this may be found in the fact that even leases are secondary to "a valuation of tenants' improvements," which *will* attract *capital* and *intelligence*.

I am perfectly convinced, from facts every day brought to my notice, that unless this system of valuation is made THE UNIFORM LAW OF THE UNITED KINGDOM, there is but little hope of improvements progressing as they should do. Improvements should be encouraged, but they are now discouraged; for I constantly meet with zealous and praiseworthy improvers, whose feelings are embittered, and operations cramped by the uncertainty of tenure OCCASIONED BY THEIR OWN IMPROVEMENTS. A non-improver, or bad farmer, has no such fears; *he is quite safe* in possession, for who is anxious to dispossess HIM?

Let us hope our legislators will see to this, for there is already too much indisposition to improve. In a recent instance, in Essex, a noble lord has abolished his tilery and sheds, established three years since, because his tenants *would not accept of the tiles "gratis,"* they finding the labour; and another landed proprietor in the same county is precisely in the same position. This is not creditable; but it is common in this and other counties, and shows the objection to amendment.—*June*, 1845.

---

14. AGRICULTURAL INCONSISTENCIES.

Prejudice and error generally go hand in hand: a man may be allowed to indulge in obstinacy for his own gratification, but when society is affected by it, the sooner a new light breaks in upon him the better.

Deep Drains.—Ask nineteen farmers out of twenty, who hold strong clay land, and they will tell you it is of no use placing deep four-foot drains in such soils, the water cannot get in; a horse's foot-hole (without an opening under it) will hold water like a basin; and so on. Well, five minutes after, you tell the same farmers you propose digging a cellar, well bricked, six or eight feet deep; what is their remark? "Oh! it's of no use your making an underground cellar in our soil, you *can't keep the water* OUT!" Was there ever such an illustration of prejudice as this? What is a drain-pipe but a small cellar full of air? Then, again, common sense tells us, you can't keep a light fluid under a heavy one. You might as well try to keep a cork under water as to keep air under water. "Oh! but then our soil isn't porous." If not, how can it hold water so readily? I am led to these observations by a strong controversy I am having with some Essex folks, who protest that I am mad or foolish for placing 1-inch pipes, at four feet depth, in strong clays. It is in vain I refer to the numerous proofs of my soundness brought forward by Mr. Parkes, engineer to the Royal Agricultural Society, and confirmed by Mr. Pusey. They still dispute it. It is in vain I tell them *I cannot keep the rain-water out* of socketed pipes, twelve feet deep, that convey a spring to my farm-yard. Let us try and convince this large class of doubters; for it is of *national* importance. Four feet of good porous clay would afford a far better meal to some strong bean or other tap-roots than the usual six inches; and a saving of £4 to £5 per acre in drainage is no trifle.

Tillage.—Another glaring inconsistency is the subject of tillage. I proposed subsoiling my heavy land for beans, so as to admit the action of frost and air abundantly. A demurrer was instantly raised by a farmer present, "Oh, we always plough shallow for beans." "Well, I know you do. Do you ever double-spit your gardens?" "Oh! certainly we do." "Do you ever grow beans in your garden?" "To be sure; capital ones." "What! and that on double-dug ground! impossible, surely." It would puzzle a conjurer to tell why a farmer always digs his garden twenty inches, and ploughs his land only five inches. Docks, thistles, couch, and other strong deep-rooted weeds are *not* to be found in *his garden*. What reason can a farmer give for drilling his beans at seven inches in his field and *twenty*-seven in his garden? Does the *former* mode give him a *larger* or *earlier* produce? Again, a farmer will caution you against sitting in a draught, or lying on a damp bed; of course he takes care not to do so himself: but while he practises this for himself, and recommends it to his friends, he pursues an entirely different plan with his cattle. They *must* be exposed to both; as if their sensations and physiology differed in that respect from our own! Let us keep our cattle warm, dry, and well-fed, and we shall seldom feel the *cramp* in our pockets.—*May* 1845.

---

15. ON THICK AND THIN SOWING.

The question of thin sowing is a most important one, involving the consideration whether we do not bury in the soil every year wastefully and prejudicially three million quarters of corn. I have endeavoured to bring my mind quite unprejudiced to the examination of this question, and present for the consideration of my brother agriculturists some facts and reasonings, with a view to stimulate unprejudiced experiments, which, I hope, will be fairly tried on a moderate scale, for an average of seasons, in every district.

Before proceeding to the general question, I would propound as theories, supported by facts on my own farm:—

1. That the tendency of *thin* sowing is to increase the size, vigour, and perfect development of the stem, ear, and kernel, prolonging its growth, and consequently *delaying* its maturity.
2. That, on the contrary, *thick* sowing hastens ripening, but renders the plant in every respect more diminutive and less productive.
3. That a large quantity of seed will not produce so large a crop in a short time as a small quantity of seed in a longer time, the supply of manure, soil, and climate being alike to both.
4. That dibbling delays the maturity of a corn crop, but promotes its tillering.
5. That drilling and broadcasting hasten its maturity, but diminish its tillering.
6. That the propriety of thick, moderate, or thin sowing must depend on the nature, quality, and condition of the soil; the comparative tempera-

ture and moisture of the climate, and the period at which it may be most convenient to the farmer to put in his seed.

7. That neither a large nor a small quantity of seed will produce a full crop if the soil contains *only food enough for half a crop.*
8. That a small quantity of seed sown at a proper early period, with deep and frequent cultivation between the widely-placed rows, will produce a much larger return than an abundantly-seeded close-sown crop in which the horse-hoe could not be worked.
9. That by varying the quantity of seed we sow in our different fields, we can cause an interval of succession in their ripening, and so prevent their all coming ready for the sickle at the same time.
10. That on land which has been subsoiled or trenched for the previous root crop, the wheat crop is delayed in its maturity at least one week.

Adverse Experience.—I have taken some pains to ascertain how results, adverse to the principle of thin sowing, have been obtained. The following are illustrations amongst others:—

Well, you sowed three pecks per acre: how did it answer?—We did not get quite so much as with eight pecks.

Did you give it more than the usual hoeings?—No, we gave it two hand-hoeings.

Were there not many weeds?—Oh yes, a great many more than usual.

It did not occur to you that the ground being so much less covered in the plant's early growth, that it was necessary to prevent entirely the growth of weeds by additional hoeing?—No, it did not.

And do you consider this a fair trial?—We do.

Frequent Tillage and comminution is our best and cheapest manure; and yet we obstinately decline following Jethro Tull's and Mr. Hewitt Davis's plan of a *fallow amongst the growing corn crops.* This is the great secret of Mr. Davis's *subsequent* good crops. The soil is *ready to receive them.* Were we to treat our turnip crop as we do our wheat crop, where would be the following crop? Imagine a crop of turnips on the ground *ten months* out of twelve, *not thinned*, and only a couple of scratchings, called hand-hoeings, bestowed on it. Oh! but a turnip swells so. Well, does not a wheat plant swell into a giant if you will but give it space and time, with deep and frequent cultivation and ample food?

I do not consider the system of thin sowing can be profitably carried out with the ordinary hand-hoe. My plan is to use Garrett's horse-hoe, which covers a whole stetch, 7 feet 2 inches wide, and will, with two horses, disturb deeply six acres per day, and remove all weeds from between the rows. I shall use it, weeds or no weeds, whenever the ground is dry, for the purpose of fallowing the land, and facilitating the escape of moisture and change of air by percolation and evaporation. Unless this is done, thin sowing must prove a failure. The horse-hoe should precede and succeed such little hand-hoeing as may be necessary between the plants. It is a singular corroborative fact, that our *dibbled* wheat (on the heavy, not the light land), which looked best all the winter, during the spring rains turned yellow, which I attribute entirely to our being unable to horse-hoe between the rows. The thin-sowed *drilled* wheat, which had been horse-hoed, looked beautifully green on the same description of soil. I am having Newberry's dibbling machine altered to cover the whole stetch, 7 feet 2, with a foot distance between the rows, so as to enable me to use Garrett's horse-hoe. I am not aware there was any other cause for the yellow appearance of the dibbled portion.

Induration of the Soil.—It is well known that on poor *light lands* wheats never tiller or branch so well as in heavier soils; there is a tendency to a more rapid or surface growth. In order to prevent this, they should, in such soils, be well rolled when sown, and *as soon as they are above ground;* and again shortly after, as well as in the spring. This checks their upward growth, and obliges the tap-root to descend into the subsoil, out of the way of frost and excessive drought; for there are two roots to wheat, a fibrous surface-root and a downward tap-root, which are connected by a neck between them (varying from one to six inches, according to the depth at which the seed is placed).

For want of this autumnal rolling, many thousand acres of light-land wheats have this severe winter been killed by the frost which destroyed the roots; especially on the north side of the stetches. A farmer, who lost fifty acres, told me to-day that where he rolled in autumn he saved his wheat, having previously observed that where cart-wheels had passed over the land, the plant was vigorous. No implement answers so well for this purpose as Crosskill's clod-roller. Of course in heavy land such rolling cannot be required in a *wet* autumn; in a very dry one it might be useful, although such land would seldom require pressure.

Supposing we are satisfied to receive as a crop five quarters, or 160 pecks of wheat per acre; what ratio of increase do we require from each kernel, assuming that we sow two pecks per acre? Why, eighty kernels or *one* full-sized *ear*. (I saw some ears last season containing 110 kernels.)

Now where is the man to deny that the average produce from each kernel *may* be, instead of eighty kernels, from 500 to 2000 or *more*, with *ample space, absence of weeds, wire-worm, and game?*

It is quite clear, that on the tillering or branching of wheat depends the whole question; that branching or tillering is indicative of vigour in the roots, both *tap* and *fibrous*. That vigour can alone be produced by deep drainage, early sowing, frequent, deep, and clean cultivation, a total absence of weeds, occasional top-dressings of manure, if the land is not of rich quality, or the plant be weak; and on light land, ample rollings. With the *present defective system of farming*, thin sowing must be a *failure*.

Early Sowing.—It has been stated, and correctly too, that thin-sown crops are later than thick-sown. This is correct, and consistent with the principle that the more vigorous and perfect the development of a plant, the longer must be its growth; although this may be remedied by early sowing, an improved condition of the soil by drainage, superior cultivation, and abundance of manure.

In a thick-sown crop, the growth of the plant is *premature*, as shown by the smallness of the ear and kernel, and the deficiency in the *number* and quality of grains. Time is thus economized at the cost of perfection.

I have proved practically on my farm this season that thin sowing in December and January makes the harvest a fortnight to three weeks later *in the same field* with thicker-sown, although both were put in on one day. The produce of the thin-sown is *estimated* to be smaller, but I am not prepared to admit this till the thin-sown has reached maturity, when it *may*, and very likely *will*, excel the thick-sown; but the bushel will settle that question. My *October thin-sown* and dibbled corn is admitted to be excellent.

The following will be about the quantities of wheat I shall sow, having regard to circumstances:—

In August	2 pecks	dibbled.
In September	3 pecks	dibbled.
In October	4 pecks	dibbled or drilled.
In November	5 pecks	dibbled or drilled.
In December	6 pecks	drilled.
In January	7 pecks	drilled.
In February	8 pecks	drilled.
In March	12 pecks	drilled or broadcast.

In northern and late districts, thick sowing presents the very great advantage of forwarding the harvest considerably. I should therefore always regulate the quantity of my seed by the period of its deposit, and the nature and condition of the soil and climate.

The Disadvantage of Thick Sowing in poor or moderate land is the want of sufficient support to mature each ear, thus causing death to many plants by starvation, whilst the survivors are crippled and debilitated by the contention they have had with their defunct companions—as clearly shown in Mr. Hewitt Davis's Essay. I would always, therefore, as I increased my quantity of seed, take care to supply a corresponding addition of manure, which is easily effected by occasional top-dressings of soot, guano, bone-dust, nitrate of soda, salt, or gypsum, in March and April, when vegetation becomes active and the roots move in search of food.

The quantity of corn to be produced depends not on the quantity of seed sown, but on the amount of food for plants the earth contains.

Thick-sown crops require more manure for their perfect

development than thin-sown. I know a farmer who grows from six to seven quarters of wheat per acre, by drilling three bushels of seed in October on strong land *very highly manured.* I recently examined the crops, which were very level, the ears numerous and evenly developed, the straw not very strong. Such crops suffer occasionally by lodging in a very wet season.

The Perfection of Wheat-growing is to produce a full crop of uniformly-ripened, large, well-developed ears, on strong upright stems.

The only way to accomplish this is by thin and early dibbling, frequent cultivation between the plants, and abundance of manure. The best crop I know of in Esse xis from five pecks of wheat per acre, dibbled in August by Newberry's dibbling machine: it promises to be seven quarters per acre. Not many miles from this is a crop from four, five, and six *bushels* of seed.

The six bushels promises to be better than the five and four, but not so good as the one I mentioned from five *pecks.* The saving here is five bushels of seed-wheat.

Manuring.—The maximum of size and number of ears combined, is the point we want to ascertain; much depends on the quality of the soil and character of the season, but still more on the supply of food we administer to the plant. I have no doubt in my own mind that by occasional top-dressings in a showery season, as much as thirteen quarters per acre could be grown by thin sowing, perhaps more. Of course this opinion will be ridiculed by those who *do not calculate.* Let such folks bear in mind that 240 kernels for one, supposing we sow two pecks per acre, would be FIFTEEN QUARTERS PER ACRE. But then we must apply to the soil *a sufficiency of food to mature such a crop.*

To attempt to grow fifteen quarters per acre with only food enough for five quarters, would be as absurd as trying to keep three horses in condition with only one horse's allowance. You can never ripen a large quantity of *large* ears unless you give a proportionate quantity of manure, and space for sufficient air or sunshine in which to mature them.

Starvation to either man, beast, or plants will reduce them to mere skeletons; abundance of suitable food, with cleanlin ss and warmth, will make them comparative giants. The concentration of manure and its consequences are plainly exemplified at our flower-shows, where enormous masses of flowers and foliage are produced by one solid foot of prepared earth. In a state of nature forty times the quantity of soil would fail to produce similar results. No doubt the frequent application of moisture, when requisite, assists in producing this effect; but a knowledge of this fact should stimulate us to study irrigation, and apply our liquid manure to the roots when the plant is in vigorous growth, instead of wasting it in our horse-ponds. I know and can appreciate practically the effects of such applications.—*July,* 1845.

16. DETAILS ON DRAINS.

[Some of the latter letters of this series were published subsequently to the other, in a pamphlet entitled "Mechi's Experience in Drainage," and were then prefaced by an introduction, from which the following extracts are taken]:—

The Question of Deep or Shallow Drainage which now so strongly agitates the public mind, is not a mere agricultural matter, but one deeply affecting every member of the community;—it is a question of producing one-fourth more food, at a less cost than at present,—it is a question of some millions annually, and it is, in fact, a matter of great national and political importance, involving the sanitary condition and physical strength of our whole population. If it be admitted that a diminution or a deficiency in our food is a great national calamity, it must also be allowed, as a converse of the proposition, that an abundance of the necessaries of life must be a great public blessing, influencing in its ramifications the welfare of every member of society, and our strength as a nation.

The shallow or non-drainers assume that tenacious subsoils are impervious or non-absorbent. This is entirely an erroneous assumption. If soils were impervious, how could they get wet?

I assert, and pledge my agricultural reputation for the fact, that there are no earths or clays in this kingdom, be they ever so tenacious, that will not readily receive, filter, and transmit rain-water to drains placed 5 or more feet deep.

A neighbour of mine drained 20 inches deep in strong clay; the ground cracked widely; the contraction destroyed the tiles, and the rains washed the surface-soil into the cracks and choked the drains. He has since abandoned shallow draining.

When I first began draining, I allowed myself to be overruled by my obstinate man, Pearson, who insisted that for top-water 2 feet was a sufficient depth in a veiny soil. I allowed him to try the experiment on two small fields: the result was, that nothing prospered; and I am redraining those fields at *one-half* the cost, 5 and 6 feet deep, at intervals of 70 and 80 feet.

I found iron-sand rocks, strong clay, silt, iron, &c., and an enormous quantity of water, all *below* the 2-feet drains. This accounted at once for the sudden check the crops always met with in May, when they wanted to send their roots down, but could not, without going into stagnant water.

On Digging a Drain.—Before I proceed to describe my mode of draining, I will remark that a very great mistake is made by most drainers in removing more earth than is necessary. My men for a 5-foot drain only open the surface 18 inches wide, and at 4 feet they can do it in 12 to 14 inches; at 6 feet deep they allow themselves 22 inches: this is when the land is tolerably dry; when very wet and adhesive, they sometimes allow themselves an inch or two more, to prevent the earth touching their clothes. As they are paid by the piece, they are very particular not to remove a bit more earth than is absolutely necessary. In stony or hard soils, requiring the frequent use of the pickaxe, the workmen require a rather wider opening; but, even so, at 6 feet deep, it is seldom necessary to open 2 feet wide. It must always be borne in mind that the pipes cannot be placed by hand in such narrow drains; the bottom not being 2 inches wide. The drainers have a stick with a piece of iron, like a long cockspur, on which they place the pipe, and standing astride on the top of the opening, place the pipes abutting against each other in a continuous line, giving them a tap or two to set them firm in their places. Great care is required to scoop out all crumbs, leaving the bottom of the drain smooth, with a sufficient fall. The bottom of the drain should not be wider if possible than the outside diameter of the pipe: it is thus kept firmly in its place. A common carpenter's level answers very well; but the workmen are generally sure to give fall enough to spare their labour in going too deep. We never plough out for the drainers. They stretch a garden-line, and so open their work straight and true. The ordinary spades are not at all calculated or proper for draining in tenacious soils. We use the patent grafting tools made by Mr. Lyndon, of Birmingham; they are thin, well plated with steel, and ring like a bell, and will go easily into hard clays, where the common spades could not be used at all. They may be had of Mr. Lyndon direct, or ordered through the ironmongers. The middle spits are removed by a narrow three-quarter spade, with a projecting iron for the foot; and the lowest spit is taken out by a long 14-inch dagger-like spade, with two cutting edges, a sharp point, and an iron rest for the foot: this is worked edgewise first, and then removes a considerable thin, but broad deep mass. The scoop follows for the crumbs. All these to 1s may be had of Mr. Lyndon.

Cost of Draining.—Now, in naming the prices I pay my men for draining, I must explain, first, that they earn as an average 12*s*. per week in short winter days; the usual weekly wages being 11*s*. in this neighbourhood. What we call 5-foot draining seldom averages more than 4 feet, because at the ditch the pipe is perhaps placed only 3 feet, and there are undulations and inequalities in most fields; but we get 5 feet deep in the rise as fast as we can. In stony soils, where there is much picking, it adds some extra cost to the labour. In strong *honest* clays or brick earths, without picking, we pay as follows:—

Six feet deep (*averaging* about 5 feet),	8*d*. per rod of 5½ yards.	
Five feet deep (averaging about 4 feet)	6*d*.	Ditto.
Four feet deep (averaging about 3½ feet),	5*d*.	Ditto.

This includes placing pipes and filling in. The drains are placed 40 feet apart, and, at least, 5 feet deep, where we can get quickly into the hill or rise. The pipes are 12 inches long, 1-inch bore, and cost 10*s.* to 15s. per 1,000, according to their weight. Each pipe weighs from 1 lb. to 1¾ lb., and is made of a superb whitish clay.

There must always be at least 20 per cent. difference in the price of pipes in different localities, because the clays are so various: in some cases they are to be had near the surface and quite free from stones, in others at a depth of twenty or thirty feet. Besides, coals may be in one place 10*s.* a ton, in another 20*s.* or 30*s.*; and some clays require more burning, and are obliged from their texture to be made into pipes of greater substance.

Also whether steam-power is used, and large quantities supplied, makes a great difference. At all events, 12-inch pipes, with a bore of 1 inch, are to be had at some kilns at 10*s.*, at others 12*s.*, but should never exceed 15*s.* per thousand.

Size of Pipes.—I seldom use any larger than 1-inch bore, except for large springs. I am practically convinced they are as large as are required. We make some sad mistakes as to water: a rope of water 1 inch thick, spread 8 inches wide, forms a *broad-looking* stream one-eighth of an inch thick. It is perfectly ludicrous to see immense 6, 9, and 12 inch bore pipes put in many cases to carry an insignificant stream that would fold up into a 1, 2, or 3 inch coil. We must bear in mind that a 2-inch pipe will carry as much as four 1-inch; a 3-inch pipe is equal to nine of 1-inch. It is desirable that a basin-shaped grating should guard the exit from the drain. to prevent rabbits or vermin entering. In ordinary leaders it is a good plan to have a long wooden box made with an iron grating, or have drain-pipes made pierced full of small holes at both ends, taking especial care that the openings between the gratings are equal to the discharge of the whole contents of the drain-pipe, or they would form an obstruction to the water.

Of course it is well understood that no tree or fence should be anywhere near a drain, or most certainly the roots will find out the drain and choke it.

On examining my 5-feet drains on the 24th December, I found the 1-inch pipes ran about one-fourth full, and discharged each one gallon per minute, or a hogshead per hour. The temperature of the water was 42°, whilst that of the air was 36°, the ground being deeply covered with snow. These 5-feet drains continued to run *three days* after the *thirty-two*-inch drains had *ceased.* On the 5th January some of the 1-inch pipe drains discharged four gallons per minute, or one ton per hour! It was after a melting snow. The air was 39°, the water 36°.

The deep drains always run, first and last, consequently render the land much drier than the shallow drains, by carrying away more water. I may be asked, "But what limit do you place to your deep drainage; surely you will not go *below* 5 feet?"

In strong tenacious clays, 4 to 5 feet is deep enough, with distances of 33 feet between each drain. In loose, friable, wet soils, deeper drains with wider intervals will be found the cheapest and most profitable where a fall can be got. I have drained from 6 to 8 feet deep in such soils.

Stoppages of Drains.—One great objection to *shallow* drains is, that the roots of weeds and of root crops will often fill and choke them.

I am quite sure that we know very little about the depth to which annual plants will send down their roots in search of food and moisture. I know of extraordinary instances, in deep friable soils, of Swede and white turnips running down several feet. In one case, where a pit had been cut through whilst cropped with parsnips, one root was traced *thirteen feet six inches*, and then broken off. This was in Mr. H. Dixon's brickfield, Witham, Essex.

There are cases where drains will not immediately act, where there is a hard crust or pan immediately under the plough-sole, which requires breaking up by the sub-soiler.

In parks or wet lands, full of coarse tussocky grass, the drains will not act until the surface is broken up and resown or relaid, so as to allow the surface to dry.

Philosophy of Draining.—I hazard the few following as my thoughts on this subject, without vouching for their correctness:—

I consider that drained earth is at various times in different degrees of moisture (some would say dryness; but there is always moisture in it, however dry it may appear). It is something like a great sponge—after much dry weather, it will absorb and retain a great quantity of rain-water; nor will it part with any of it to the drains until pores or molecules have received more than they have the power to hold in suspension by capillary attraction. Thus heavy rains may fall, and yet no water will pass out of the drains. If dry weather ensues, the moisture is drawn up to the surface by capillary attraction, caused by evaporation; the driest particles of earth, which are nearest the surfacce, depriving their lower neighbours of their moisture, and these again acting on a lower stratum. The deeper the drain, the higher will the water have to ascend, and the longer it will be in reaching the surface,—gravity, space, and friction acting as delaying forces; consequently, the slower will be the evaporation, and the warmer and drier will be the soil.

But why do deep drains discharge earlier than shallow ones in the same soil?

The capillary or suspensive power is more easily counteracted by the gravity, or weight of so large a body of water as can be held in a large sponge or deeply-drained soil. The pressure of falling water disturbs the capillary balance, and forces out the lower water until that balance is restored. There is a greater tendency to drip in a large sponge than in a small one.

I have observed in spring, wet friable soils, where drains have been cut from 42 to 48 inches, and left open for inspection, that no water flowed, although the land was obviously filled and black with water to within 12 inches of the surface; but when another foot of earth was removed, the water was given down, and continued ever after to flow in a rapid stream: *gravity had thus overcome the capillary or suspensive power.* In boggy or spongy soils it may be necessary even to go deeper than five feet to overcome the strong capillary or suspensive power.

PART III.

ESSAYS.

1. On burning clay.—2. On thin sowing.—3. Trip to North Devon.—4. Liquid manure and irrigation.—5. Sewage manure.

1. ON BURNING CLAY.*

I HAVE great pleasure in communicating what I know of the benefits of burned earth as a manure. I have used it for wheat and for root crops with decided advantage, although I have not, unfortunately, kept a statistical account of the difference; still so obvious were the results, that I have been induced to use a much larger quantity the present season, and my neighbours are following my example. It was used at the rate of 1,000 bushels per acre on a wheat-field sown with clover, leaving the middle of the field undone. The benefit was striking, not only in the wheat, but in the young clover. The whole of the field had been top-manured with guano, harrowed in with the seed. Where the burned earth was not used, the clover-plants and the wheat were inferior.

It may be proper to explain that it was not turfy earth full of vegetable matter, but a poor, cold, argillaceous, tenacious clay, such as is used for making bricks, yellow in colour, but becoming when burned a pale red or orange; the interior of some of the largest lumps being black or carbonaceous (I presume the small quantity of vegetable matter concentrates there). Occasionally this soil contains a fair proportion of round pebbles.

The mode of raising and burning is this—a strip of land is broken up in *very dry* weather with Ransome's Y. L. plough, drawn by three strong horses abreast, and a Scotch equilibrium whippletree. So great is the resistance, that it requires two men to hold the handles of the plough to counteract the leverage of the horses. The earth is thus broken, or I may say torn up, in immense rough masses or clods as much as a man can carry, which are admirably adapted to form walls and supports for the

* From the 7th volume of the *Journal* of the English Agricultural Society.

mass of fire. By this means heaps of nearly 200 solid yards may be readily burned. The earth being ploughed up, the fires are formed on the spot, the workmen placing a certain quantity of dried stumps or wood of sufficient solidity to maintain a body of heat, and enclosing the mass with large clods. These are carried by hand: subsequently, as they get more distant from the fire, a barrow is used, and beyond that a one-horse cart.

It is important to have the sides of the heap as upright as possible—not conical—because the heat always makes for the highest place. An important point in burning is to supply the fire sufficiently fast to prevent its burning through, and yet avoid overlaying it, which might exclude all air and put it out. Practice will indicate the medium. When the fire shows a tendency to break through, the outside of the burning mass is raked down, and more earth added.

If the ground is very dry, and no rain falls, the men are obliged to feed the fire almost continually night and day; but when there is moisture, it may be left for five or six hours, but seldom longer.

Something depends on the current of air. A strong wind would blow the fire *from* one side and out at the other. This is guarded against by placing hurdles interlaced with straw as a guard to windward.

The size of a heap is limited by the height to which a man can throw up the soil, and of course the diameter must be proportioned to the height, to prevent its slipping down. It is generally lighted so as to burn out by Saturday, and not require Sunday attendance.

This mode of burning may be essentially called summer burning, because we find practically that heavy rains put out the fires, or check their progress. Where fuel is abundant, or coal cheap, I have reason to believe fires may be kept up through the winter.

I have this autumn ploughed up, or rather broken up and burned, 4 acres of a poor rye-grass lea. This has produced 1,600 cubic yards, 1,000 of which I have carted on to the neighbouring fields, leaving 150 yards per acre on the field itself as a compensation. The cost per 100 cubic yards is as follows:—

	£	s.	d.
Labour and burning at 5*d*.	2	3	4
Fire-wood at 4*s*. 6*d*. per fathom	0	8	4
Ploughing and horse-labour	0	8	4

Carting and spreading according to distance.

When spread, as there are many large lumps, we roll the field with Crosskill's clod-crusher in a dry time. This pulverizes the burned earth, and we then bush-harrow, to distribute it equally. Our young clover so treated promises well.

As the portion of ground on which the fire is made is generally burned 6 inches below the surface, it is [illegible] out and spread it around, otherwise so rank will be the corn-crop there, that in spite of two or three flaggings, it is almost sure to go down and spoil. I find burned earth exceedingly useful for clamping potatoes, swedes, mangolds, &c.; but it is essential to allow roots to remain in a heap covered with straw three or four weeks previous to doing this, or they are apt to heat and rot, especially early-raised potatoes. The reasons why earth burned must be beneficial are sufficiently explained by Drs. Liebig and Playfair.

Of its cheapness as a manure there can be no question; for whilst it only costs 7*d.* a cubic yard on the spot, the mere cartage of London dung from our nearest port would be 2*s.* per cubic yard; nearly 4 times the cost of the earth itself.

It is much to be wished that tenants had permission to put down all old pollard trees, burning them on the spot with earth close at hand. Such pollards when carted home seldom clear 1*s.* each, after deducting expenses; whilst it is to be feared they damage the growing crops annually to that extent at least.

Tiptree Hall, Oct. 10*th*, 1846.

I should say that at 5*d.* per yard my men average (including occasional night-work) about 15*s.* or 16*s.* per week in dry weather.

To this may be added the following paragraph written by me seven years later, in the fourteenth volume of the same *Journal*:—

On the 10th of October, 1846, I made a communication to our society on the subject of burned clay (vol. vii. p. 299). I therein stated that I had burned 400 cubic yards per acre on a poor plastic yellow clay; that 250 loads or yards per acre had been removed to other fields, and that the remaining 150 yards per acre were spread where burned. The field is opposite my residence, and, years having elapsed, it may be interesting to deduce the results after so long a period. The field, before burning, was a poor 2-year ryegrass lea, and my neighbours seriously predicted that by removing 250 yards per acre of the top-soil I should ruin the field. Fortunately, anticipating such objection, and desirous to arrive at comparative results, I left about half an acre of the field undisturbed. It has been, since, all equally treated, viz. oats sown down with grass-seeds, and is still in grass. So far from the burning and removal of so much soil being injurious, in every crop, and to this very day, the worst portion of the field is that which was unburned and unpillaged. The fact is interesting and encouraging to earth-burners of strong clays. In every case in which I have used burned earth (I mean poor cold argillaceous subsoil clay, free from organic matter), I have during the last seven years had reason to be satisfied with its advantages, which are still obvious.

Tiptree Hall, Kelvedon, Essex, May 30, 1853.

2. ON THIN SOWING.*

Name of Field.	When sown.	How deposited.	Quantity of Seed per Acre.	Quantity of Land.		Produce per Acre.	Quality of Soil.	REMARKS.
	1845.		pks.	A.	R.	bush.		
Elm....	Oct. 29	Bentall's Dropper	4	3	0	40	Poor tile earth, very tenacious	2 to 3 kernels in each hole, 6 inches from row to row.
Elm....	Oct. 29	Newberry's Dibbler	4	3	0	38¾	do.	8 to 9 kernels in each hole, 11 inches from row to row.
Ash....	Nov. 1	Bentall's Dropper	4	1	0	35	do.	Most straw and corn from the smaller quantity of seed.
	Nov. 1	Drill	8	5	0	34½	do.	
Crooked Ridges	Nov. 24	Newberry's Dibbler	2½	0	1	30½	do.	The thin-sown a week later in ripening.†
		Drill and Dibbler	9	3	0	32	do.	
The Bog	Nov. 10 Nov. 20	Bentall's Dropper	4	1	0	48	Felty bog	The 4 and 5 pecks were unfortunately not kept separate. The smallest quantity of seed was estimated as the greater produce.
		Hand-dropped	5	1	0			

The quality of the wheat was good, weighing 63 and 64 lbs. per bushel; the straw strong and bright. The straw was larger and longer, and the ears largest, where thin-sown. My harvest commenced on the 14th July, and was completed on the 14th of August. I had only half an acre of wheat laid on 80 acres; about 20 acres more were dibbled on my light land with 4 and 5 pecks per acre.

No exact result is known, but they are estimated to produce from 40 to 44 bushels per acre, with abundance of straw. The land was very free from weeds; principally hoed by Garrett's horse-hoe.

Experiments in 1845.—1 peck of barley, dibbled 27th April, by Newberry's dibbler, on one-third of an acre of light soil, naturally poor, but fairly manured, produced 2 quarters, or at the rate of 6 quarters per acre.

* From the 7th volume of the *Journal* of the English Agricultural Society.

† I have invariably found the same result occur.—W. MILES.

Two fields of wheat were drilled, half with 1 bushel, 12 inches apart, half with 2 bushels, 6 inches apart.

In both cases the produce was as nearly as possible equal, although the thickest-sown *appeared* rather the best.

Thin sowing should be *early* sowing on heavy land. I consider I have been later in sowing than I ought to have been. It would be a dangerous experiment to sow thinly, unless the land were drained, subsoiled, and kept quite free from weeds by the horse-hoe. Some allowance should be made for game near preserves. On my light land and bog, my wheat plants would have been destroyed by wire-worm, had I not rolled them twice over in the spring with Crosskill's roller. On reclaimed bog, or deep rich vegetable soil, I find it imperative to sow thin, say 3 to 4 pecks per acre, or the crop would be mostly straw. Even with this quantity I had to flag my wheat three times on the bog, and then it was partially laid, especially so where 5 pecks per acre were used. Thin sowing somewhat delays the ripening of a crop, especially if sown on heavy land so late as November or December. In cold or elevated districts, thin sowing, to succeed, must be very early. In my experiments, anything beyond 1 bushel of seed per acre has not had the effect of increasing the yield, the extra seed being lost. It is a singular fact, that the 1 bushel per acre never changed yellow in the spring, but went on with a healthy green cast without a check. The 2 bushels turned yellow, and the 3 bushels yellower, and was decidedly the worst stetch in the field. I would venture to suggest that each farmer should satisfy his own mind, by trying part of an acre on each field.

We seldom hear complaints of the losses from *thick* sowing in rich soil. They are, however, serious in luxuriant summers.

Two friends of mine sowed 4 bushels per acre, and only got 4 quarters of grinding barley, which sold at 27*s*. 6*d*. They had an abundance of crowded weakly straw, which was laid early; mine dibbled, at 3 pecks per acre, in not near so good a soil, produced 6 quarters, which sold for 33*s*. 6*d*., with strong straws, and ears containing 17 to 19 kernels on each side. This was in 1845.

It is a fact worth observing, that where I sowed 1 bushel per acre of wheat, I have a plant of clover, but have no plant where I used 2 bushels, although in the same field. I drill the clover on the wheat in the spring.—*September* 26, 1846.

---

3. A TRIP TO NORTH DEVON.

At a time when we are all agreed that agriculture needs progress, it is well to watch and exhibit improvement wherever we find it. Having received a polite invitation from Earl Fortescue to inspect his agricultural operations, the Great Western Railway brought me to Tiverton, whence is a pleasant coach ride, of about twenty-five miles, to Castle Hill—quite a treat on a fine day in these railway times. The beautiful Devonshire hills form a strange and pleasant contrast to our level eastern counties. Imagine an endless vista of round hills, like so many inverted wash-basins of all heights and sizes, presenting at every turn delightful undulating perspectives. Towering high on your left, in sullen, misty grandeur, is Dartmoor, a wild waste of 250,000 acres, 800 feet high, frowning on you in the distance for several miles like some dark cloud. On your right rises Exmoor, another extensive waste, less stern and elevated than its opposite neighbour, exhibiting occasionally on its bald surface the powdering of lime and cultivation. In fact, for thirty miles, we see but hills and valleys;—such is the country between Tiverton and South Molton. The first three miles from Tiverton is on the red sandstone, and exhibits generally good soil and careful cultivation, the watered and well-drained hill-sides presenting an intense and pleasant verdure; but soon we pass to the cold and poverty-stricken clay-slate, showing too painfully and plainly poverty, and a low, neglected state of cultivation and buildings. It is true, occasionally the eye falls on a verdant patch, indicating combined irrigation and drainage, but this is the exception.

The most striking agricultural deformity is the miserably small dimension of the fields. From three-quarters of an acre to two and three acres is a common size. No doubt in a primitive pastoral country, without other shelter for stock, such enclosures were once found needful; but they must now give way to the introduction of a different system, or their occupiers will succumb, and the rental become depreciated. In fact one of the great wants of this district is accommodation for house-feeding, combined with drainage, irrigation, and turnip growing. The clay-slate—dirty white heavy unctuous clay, with tough and laminated layers cropping out on the sides of the numerous hills—keeps everything miserably wet. The climate, as may be supposed, from the physical character and conformation of the soil, must be mild and humid—the evaporation of the valleys and condensation of the hill-tops acting concurrently. In fact it is a grass country, so far as the climate goes; but the absence of calcareous matter in the soil produces a coarse hassocky herbage. Owing to the extreme moisture, it is very difficult to eradicate weeds, especially as the soil is undrained; so couch-grass reigns triumphant. Excess of moisture renders the growth of wheat precarious, and I was assured that twelve bushels per acre was a common average! Successive crops of oats are often grown, which I consider most injudicious, and in fact ruinous. Of course roots are seldom taken, as it would be impossible to feed or remove them without drainage. Some few attempts that met my eye looked abortive.

The beautiful North Devon cattle are seen to perfection, and deserve a better fate than eating turnips on an exposed and wet pasture.

But there is great hope for this part of Devonshire. It has an unfailing mine of gold when worked. I mean the constant means of irrigation. Every hill supplies its stream, and if the land were drained, would be available on the catch-meadow principle for the production of the finest grasses, which, immediately upon irrigation, supersede the coarse rushy herbage. Looking over an irrigated field, the intense green evidences unmistakably show the result, whilst any elevated portions that have not been covered, retain their rusty and worthless appearance. Our brother agriculturists who have never witnessed this operation, can easily appreciate the advantage of an abundant early feed of excellent grass, fed to the middle of April, and then in six weeks a crop of two tons of hay per acre. I have no doubt if sheep were folded after haytime, and fed with rape-cake, as is done by Mr. Pusey, summer irrigation might be available. The cost of the operation of catch-meadowing is seldom much more than 20*s*. per acre, with an annual charge of about 5*s*. Who would not covet such an advantage? and yet it is too seldom made use of, for want of drainage, which is an imperative preliminary, the soil being heavy.

I will now proceed to describe Earl Fortescue's improvements. His estate in that neighbourhood (South Molton) consists of about 12,000 acres, and partakes of the general character. There were seventy-two fields on 126 acres of one farm; now, only twelve enclosures. His lordship's own occupation consists of about 700 acres, which have been all drained under the drainage commissioners, superintended by Mr. Josiah Parkes. The pipes are placed 4 feet deep, at intervals of about 30 feet, and the drains answer admirably generally; but I am sure my friend Parkes will excuse me for saying there are several instances where the springs ought to have been tapped by deeper drains, so as to intercept their rising, and interfering with the surface water. The hills are full of springs, rising up through the patchy and party-coloured soil, which varies from a dirty drab to an occasional dark boggy, or silty, and sometimes yellow appearance. It is quite clear that these springs, rising up to the level of the drains, saturate the earth to a foot or two above them by capillary attraction, thus preventing the descent of the rain or surface water. This was clearly indicated by the almost impassable and wet state of many of the fields. The same remark does not apply to the clays of uniform character, having no springs.

Those springs should certainly be tapped at deeper levels. As a proof of this, the evil is not much felt in the spring or summer, when the springs are low. Another great mistake is the recommendation to lay such heavy land on the flat. I am aware that many of my Scotch friends, and my friend Parkes too, have condemned my practice of using furrows at intervals of every 7 feet; but experience has taught me its advantage, and that our county of Essex is right in this respect.

My own prejudices were originally strong against the system, but a trial of one acre on each field soon settled the question, and convinced me of my error. The fact is, however well drained heavy land may be, its physical and chemical character will not permit a percolation or permeation of the winter rains so fast as they sometimes fall. The open furrows here come in aid as auxiliaries, and prevent the bursting of the seed by stagnated saturation. This was forcibly evidenced by a gripped field at Earl Fortescue's, from which the water was rapidly passing away on the grips, the sub-drains also acting profusely. This field was infinitely drier than the adjoining ones. The cutting of these furrows does credit to Mr. Graburn's sound judgment in the matter.

His lordship has enlarged the fields by the removal of useless fences. The management of the farming operations, as well as the planning and erection of the buildings, machinery, &c., have been intrusted to Mr. Robert S. Graburn, of Butleigh, Glastonbury; and, in my opinion, are perfectly sound and business-like, in almost every respect. The most striking evidence of this was his first providing accommodation for house-feeding an immensely increased head of stock, and concurrently and cheaply providing an abundant supply of winter as well as summer food for them at a very moderate cost. The result of this will be a permanent increase of manure, cultivation, and production. The administration of the food, when grown, is equally judicious and economical. Greater results might have been produced by greater expenditure, but his lordship most judiciously determined to trust more to cultivation, and those economical means, the employment of manual labour within the immediate reach of small farmers, rather than to an extraordinary outlay for purchased manures.

I consider the raising of 120 acres of good swedes, turnips, mangold, &c., on a heavy land, that had never before produced them, quite a triumph; and this without much expensive cultivation on a previously exhausted and indeed partly deserted soil.

Let us see how this was done.

In some cases, where the surface, after drainage, was one mass of accumulated weeds, grass, rushes, &c., a spit was dug from the surface, and the grassy side placed on the surface of the undug ground next to it; thus raising a terrace, as it were, or an embankment, 27 inches wide, on which the turnips were to be grown. Another spit was then dug and turned over, not removed, so as to aërate the soil and facilitate the descent of the water through this adhesive clay.

The effect of this was the rotting of all the weeds and vegetable matter between the two layers under the turnips, whilst the intermediate dug soil became one mass of vegetable fibre. No one unacquainted with the moist Devonshire climate can imagine how soon a piece of raised earth becomes clothed with vegetation. The ridge is, after the removal of the turnips, split or turned over, nicely clean, on the dug furrow, ready for another crop of turnips, similarly treated, or for a corn crop, according to the state of the land.

The cost of the double-trenching above described is, I think, £3 per acre. But methinks I hear some of our friends, who plough six or eight times for turnips, inquire, Where is your fine seed-bed?

Now comes Mr. Graburn's strong point, borrowed from Mr. Huxtable, and improved upon. It is certainly a most admirable one, judging from the results. One man having a dibbler of the ordinary form, about the size of half a large pineapple, presses his foot on it, and leaves a hole large enough to contain one pound or pint of animal excrement (free from straw), a woman follows with a box of manure, and a half-circular trowel, which contains just a pint of manure, which she deposits in the hole made by the dibbler. Another woman, with a supply of superphosphate of lime, mixed with fine mould or ashes, uses a large extinguisher, with a handle, which she presses into the dung, and then empties its contents into the opening made. This extinguisher contains three drachms of superphosphate of lime mixed with fine earth and ashes. A child then follows and deposits a pinch of seed in the seed-bed of the extinguisher, pressing it gently in, and, if the adjoining earth is fine, pushing a little over it.

The combined operations, though tedious in description, are rapid and easy, as I can testify. The result is an unfailing plant of either mangold-wurzel or swedes, without regard to the condition of the surrounding soil or weather. The seed-bed derives moisture from the manure, and the plant having its food at immediate command, grows rapidly and luxuriantly. The cost of the operation is from 7*s.* 6*d.* to 10*s.* 6*d.* per acre. There will be about 17,000 plants to the acre; so 17,000 lbs. or pints of dung will be between 7 and 8 tons of dung per acre, and 3 cwt. of superphosphate of lime. I should say that a cross-piece on the dibbler serves to mark the distance for the next dibble-hole. The hand and horse-hoe may be at once employed, and I shall certainly practise it, especially after tares, in dry weather. If the land is in stetches, it would be desirable to mark the lines with the drill where no manure could be spared; the mould and superphosphate were alone used, at a cost of 20*s.* per acre.

A crop of turnips being now grown, how are they to be removed from heavy wet land in a wet climate? (Some idea may be formed of the wetness, when I state that they had scarcely a week's suitable condition for drilling since October, whilst in Essex our drains had not been called upon to act.)

By using 220 yards of Crosskill's movable railway (which cost, complete with trucks and turn-tables, £53) the whole 120 acres were removed by manual labour—advantage being taken of any incline in the ground. Mr. Graburn assured me that a man could move in the truck from 13 to 15 cwt. of roots. The cost of pulling, topping, tailing, and removing to the nearest headlands, is about 6*s.* to 7*s.* per acre. I was gratified to see a large supply in each field well thatched, in various clamps. I believe about 40 yards is the distance cleared, two each side of the rails. Of course, the railway itself is removed on a long light cart. Suitable occasions are made use of to cart home the roots in dry or frosty weather; or at other times by donkeys and panniers, each one bringing 112 lbs. A number of these useful animals are kept at a trifling expense.

Lord Fortescue's home farm consists of 373 acres arable, 339 grass (park, &c.). The live stock consists of 50 cows and heifers in calf, 2 bulls, 300 sheep, 50 pigs, 38 fat cattle, 16 working oxen, 11 three-year-old steers, 52 two-year-old steers, 118 calves. Total, 637. The breeding animals partially occupy the old farmery, but new, useful, and extensive buildings have been erected, at a cost of about £3,500. The arrangement is simple and economical, the whole being under one slated roof, having a wide span and considerable length. An open-sided barn, or hay and corn shed, is at one end, then comes the steam-engine, threshing machine, chaff-cutter, cooking-apparatus, with a ready access in direct lines to the feeding animals; at the other end is the dung-house and urine-tank. The roof is span, slated, and the timbers light, owing to the numerous supports it has on the uprights of the various departments.

The bullocks are mostly on boarded floors; no straw is used for litter; a few are in boxes, on Mr. Warnes's plan, but the boards are considered most convenient and economical, setting free the straw for feeding purposes. The floors between the bullocks being of slate, and perfectly smooth, offer a sort of railway facility in feeding, and in removing the solid excrement; the liquid flows in a gutter to its destination.

The whole arrangements of the feeding department appear to me regular and economical. The cut hay, straw, and turnips are all mixed; the meal and linseed, boiled by steam, is poured over and mixed with them, and given to the animals quite warm. The piggeries and external calves' places were not, in my opinion, warm enough, but in all other respects the general body of the building was well lighted, and perfectly ventilated. The steam-engine worked well, without smoke, having only cost 14*s.* for repairs in three years; the only defect being in a pair of vertical mill-stones. I noticed particularly that the draught and flues were well arranged for the economy of fuel and avoidance of smoke. The engine was by David Glasgow, of Birmingham; the chaff-cutter by Ransome; and the turnip-bruiser by Moody. The turnips were washed and elevated by machinery; the oats for food were thrashed daily; the straw was received from the shakers, and passed at once through the chaff-cutters, the chaff being carried up by elevators to its proper deposit. In fact, the interval between each meal was employed in thrashing and preparing corn, chaff, and roots for the succeeding one. The bullocks appeared to be doing well; their hind quarters would have been cleaner had the openings between the boards been wider. The most interesting objects were 60 fattening sheep, tied up to stakes in pairs, like bullocks. These occupied the vacant space in the roof, over the bullocks, their excrements following the same direction on an upper floor. I never saw any stock progress faster, being perfectly gentle and tranquil, except when disturbed by strangers. Those at Earl Bathursts's, at Cirencester, are treated much in the same way. Mr. Graburn told me it does not answer so well for lambs as for full-grown sheep. The undisturbed manner in which each animal gets its own share of food, and their perfect quiescence, almost lead me to prefer the tying up to the loose system. But it is still an open question in my mind.

The bullocks consume, daily, about 9 lbs. of hay, 9 lbs. of corn and linseed, 6 lbs. of straw, 50 lbs. of turnips, 2 oz. salt, 40 lbs. of water, given warm in three meals. The total of water, including that in the food, would be about 83 lbs. a day. —The sheep: 12 lbs. of turnips, 1½ lb. of oats, 1 lb. hay chaff. Not cooked; no water. The water in the food about 10 lbs. a day.—Calves eat about one-fifth as much as an ox. The working oxen eat about 30 per cent. more than the fattening oxen. A barren fattening cow eats in summer 100 lbs. of grass daily. A milking cow eats 150 lbs.—showing our milk to be a costly affair. There is a singular coincidence between the mode of fattening here, at Mr. M'Culloch's, at Auchness, and at Mr. Warnes's, in Norfolk.

One fact is interesting, viz., that the mixed bullock and other manure, free from straw litter, will neither ferment nor subside. This I have proved practically on my own farm. Mr. Graburn showed me a large accumulated mass, the produce of a twelvemonth, unaltered and undiminished. Its density excludes air, consequently it can neither ferment nor evaporate. It is on this principle that the bullock-pudding under my floors does not give off smell.

The use of straw, as food, is evidently and principally to give bulk and mechanical fitness to richer food, although we must not decide too hastily that it does not contain the carbonaceous elements of fat. On another part of the same farm an old store barn has been cheaply converted into a calf-house, where 80 calves, on boards, tied up to stakes and fed on cooked food, presented all the necessary evidence of progression, with comfort and economy both of food and manure.

To me the most interesting operation was the management of a small off-hand farm of 52 acres. It is an example worthy to be followed, where there are small holdings and limited means. It may be readily imagined that in its primitive state it produced neither much meat nor corn. The fields being enlarged and the land drained, I was most agreeably surprised to find twenty-seven bullocks fattening, tied up on boarded floors, in what had recently been a barn. There was the necessary accompaniment of a copper for cooking, a corn-bruiser, a turnip-cutter, a chaff-cutter, and a thrashing-machine! Do not be alarmed, gentle reader; a real thrashing-machine on a 52-acre poor farm. Well, there it was, a hand threshing-machine by Barret, Exall, and Co., but his lordship would not suffer such a barbarism as to make a beast or a steam-engine of mind and matter combined. No; a simple overshot water-wheel, supplied from the hill, gave power and velocity to all the machines I have described; and at what cost, think you!—about £63 for the whole. I buttoned up my coat and felt resolved that Old England could and should feed her own population; ay, and employ them too. But where is the food for twenty-seven bullocks? All provided, now and *in futuro*. Plenty of oats, of turnips, of tares on the wheat-stubble, of clover, and of straw, and 4 acres of nice watered meadow available at almost any period of summer. Plenty of manure in the manure-house to grow the next root crops. No guano bought—nothing but 2 cwt. of superphosphate of lime, and the home-made manure. Oh! it was a delightful sight, and a beautiful landscape. The abrupt and winding and shaded road, the primitive buildings, standing out in relief from the towering hill that sheltered them, the rushing water and simple wheel, the shaded vale beneath, all carried back the mind's eye to our choicest old landscapes.

But let us leave the enthusiastic for the practical. Here were the elements of compound fertility and reproduction. The produce of the farm is to be beef, pork, and wheat. Depend upon it if animals do not pay (which I do not admit) they leave us a legacy without which we cannot, as farmers, succeed.

Oh! but says some lynx-eyed critic, where are your horses, Mr. Mechi? Ay, where are the horses? Why, I am happy to say nowhere, on this 52 acre farm; but I saw a pair of young Devon bullocks (capital beef they will make some day) ploughing deep and well—an acre per day. These are the horses—they take their place and food beside the other bullocks. In fact, one of the most pleasing symptoms of my visit was not to find a horse (excepting three or four condemned ones) on his lordship's great farm.

The whole managment is simplicity itself. The father ploughs in the morning, the son in the afternoon. The intermediate periods are occupied in thrashing oats, crushing them, cutting turnips and chaff, and cooking, with the assistance of another man. By simply turning on the water, away goes all the machinery like mad—one fancies there must be a steam-engine.

Now, I do say that we must turn our barns into bullock-sheds—fill them with meat instead of corn. The question is settled in my mind. Some years ago Earl Ducie (I was told), writing to a friend, said,—"I agree with Mr. Mechi in nearly all his principles except his 'great barn.'" Hereafter I shall call it a bullock-house.

Altogether I do say this 52-acre farm of Lord Fortescue's is a most edifying and pleasurable fact, and stands in strange contrast and comparison with others of a similar size. I am hourly more convinced that the salvation of our heavy-land farms depends on boarded floors, more stock, and ample drainage.

Passing from this little farm, we examined the tilery on the estate (the first ever erected in Devonshire). The earth makes excellent pipes: the clay is prepared by Clayton's machine, and the pipes passed through Scragg's. His lordship finds wood-fluel (of which there is an abundance on the estate) and pays 8*s.* 6*d.* for the manufacturing, up to 4 inches in size.

The drying was going on by flues, but the sheds were not considered so advantageous for winter drying as those kilns now in connection with the heat of the burning kilns at Ainslie's tilery.

We now enter upon Lord Ebrington's farm of 126 acres, on which there were formerly 76 enclosures! now reduced to 12. Here are the same improvements as at his father's, Earl Fortescue's; drainage, root-growing, excellent new buildings, and abundance of stock, house fed—in fact, the same elements of increasing fertility: say, 62 fattening oxen on boards and in boxes; 8 working ditto ditto; 2 horses; 64 fattening sheep (tied up); 30 fattening hogs; 2 sows; manure-house, liquid-tank, &c. Some quiet practical agricultural friends of mine will open their eyes rather wide on comparing the stock with the acres.

The sheep were shorn early, as an experiment: they instantly consumed 2 to 3 lbs. more turnips per day each, showing that they required a warmer temperature. The pigs appeared to be doing well on turnips and meal, although I should strongly recommend boarded floors and more warmth for them also.

The Earl of Fortescue's rental is, I believe, about 16*s.* per acre for arable land, and 27*s.* for grass, tithe included. His lordship appears to me to be meeting the times with a just and liberal spirit. Although he pays 6½ per cent. to the drainage committee for drainage, he only charges his tenantry 5 per cent., and this does not commence till Lady-day twelve months after the completion of the work. He is willing to put up water-power and threshing-machines at 6 per cent. from the time of their completion; the tenants keeping them in repair, but being allowed rough timber for the purpose. He is also ready to consider favourably the case of any of his tenants who wish for more extensive and additional machinery.

With regard to grubbing up coppices and useless fences, making drains or water-meadows, or erecting additional buildings, he will give one-half of their reasonable cost, if done by the tenant with his lordship's approval, within the last seven years; or one quarter, if within the first seven, of the term of fourteen years. These allowances are made, not in money, but in guano or superphosphate of lime.

His lordship advances to any of his tenants guano for grain crops, or superphosphate for turnip crops, without requiring repayment till the Lady-day following, and then only at three-fourths of their cost. The same advantages extend to the purchase of lime.

In conclusion, I have been thus minute in the description of an improving entailed estate on public grounds, as an example to others. I consider the arrangements generally as insuring a greatly-improved condition of the land, the labourer, the tenant, and the proprietor; and, as a necessary consequence, of society at large, by diminishing crime and increasing the demand for manufactures. Let me impress respectfully but earnestly on our legislators the necessity and justice and advantage of extending the provisions of the Drainage Act to buildings and other necessary permanent improvements. If the individual instance before us is considered proper by the heir to the estate (whom I assume to have concurred in it), and if such provisions are found to work beneficially in a sister kingdom, let them no longer be delayed in England, so that our aristocracy may participate in the advantages of a general national progression.

The absence of railway communication is a sad drawback to this portion of North Devon. When larger quantities of food are produced by improved farming, it will become an indispensable requisite. I heard there was some good farming in the neighbourhood of Barnstaple, but had not time to visit there. Much farm produce is shipped from Barnstaple to the Welsh iron districts, but I heard great complaint of extravagant freights. A good deal of land had been formerly leased for lives, and exhibits the usual evil consequences. The want of root crops and suitable buildings for winter-housing compels the sale of much stock before winter sets in, although the winters are mild compared with those of our eastern counties.

Lord Fortescue has improved much land by catch and water-meadowing.—*January* 27, 1857.

4.—LIQUID MANURE AND IRRIGATION.

Preliminary Expectations.—I have already 100 acres completed, and shall finish 170 acres in about a fortnight. There will be about 1,100 iron 3-inch pipes, 3 yards long, making a total length of nearly 2 miles. Each pipe weighs 119 lbs., so that 55 tons of iron piping will be about the quantity.

The pair of pumps are of 20-inch stroke, and 5½ inches diameter, capable of raising and discharging, at their ordinary speed of 23 strokes per minute, about 80 gallons per minute. My great tank is about the size of a small chapel, 30 feet deep, and 30 feet diameter at the widest part. All the other tanks have a communication with it, and already it contains an imposing supply of XXX.

My bog spring, of 30,000 gallons per diem, will fall into the tank to the depth of 12 feet, which is a considerable advantage; in fact, without an abundant supply of water this operation cannot be carried out.

I shall expend £600 for the 170 acres, or about £3. 12*s*. per acre to cover the expense of tank, pumps, pipage, gutta-percha hose, and every expense except the steam-engine, which I have already. Possibly it would be safer to calculate generally on £4 to £4. 5*s*. per acre, but much depends on the neighbourhood of iron, price of labour, bricks, &c.

The pipes are jointed with tarred rope and boiling lead, like the common street water-pipes, and placed in the ground about 18 inches deep. There will be 1 hydrant or iron supply post for every 11 acres; 200 yards of gutta-percha pipe (half 2-inch, half 1½-inch) will reach any part of the farm. The pumps will be enabled, by means of various taps, to distribute either liquid manure or plain water, as may be found desirable.

A man and stout lad to assist him will, I expect, dispose of 600 hogsheads per diem, say enough for 10 acres. A branch pipe of 2 inches will intersect the farm-yard, from which a powerful jet will wash the solid manure from under the boards and cause it to flow into the great tank. This operation requires much water to render fluid the jelly-like manure of the ruminating animals; as the water will be propelled by a greater force than from an ordinary fire-engine, it is easy to imagine what a cleansing every corner will receive about twice a week. The flies in hot weather will be in considerable danger, and the heated roofs and buildings may be speedily cooled. The animals will, no doubt, get a shower-bath when deemed advisable. The whole affair is amazingly simple.

In our dry eastern counties we can grow wheat to perfection. That plant has already sent its roots nearly a foot deep, and before another month will have secured to itself sufficient moisture, by still deeper research and by shading the ground. But how stands the case with our early turnips, our second crops of grass and clover? The parched and heated ground awaits in vain the much-desired moisture. Well may the western and northern coasts boast of their humid atmosphere and luxuriant green and root crops.

By these subterranean pipes I expect to render more certain

and abundant all green, root, and leguminous crops. In fact, I expect to maintain a large number of live stock without much purchased food, and still grow wheat on half my land.

Assuming that 3-horse power of my engine will be required, the cost of a day's application on 10 acres will be—

	s.	*d.*
Interest on capital, at 7½ per cent	6	0
My engineer's pay for one day (a youth from the farm)	1	6
One man in the field	1	6
One youth in ditto	1	0
Coals for engine (this is, in fact, 1*s.* more than the cost, as we use screenings at 9*s.* per ton.)	3	0
	13	0

So, that in fact, 1*s.* 6*d.* per acre will more than cover the whole cost of applying 150 tons of manure, or water, on 10 acres of land; but even if it cost more, under less favourable circumstances than mine, the expense is ridiculously small in comparison with the ordinary cost and waste.—*April*, 1852.

Value of Liquid Manure.—*January* 12, 1853.—How frequently I am told by observant agriculturists that, although they have constructed tanks for the preservation of liquid manure, they could never perceive any good result from its application. To doubt the value of liquid excrements, would be to deny the utility of the sheepfold, and to disbelieve the science of agriculture. The great mistake is in using it insufficiently diluted on a growing crop, Its strength and pungency are injurious to the roots of growing plants. The urine of a cow or horse falling in dry hot weather on young clover, destroys it; no such result would take place during rain. On light dry soils the danger is greater than on tenacious clays, the latter having a fixing or neutralizing power. Plants having their rootlets near the surface suffer more than robust bulbs of an advanced growth whose tap roots deeply penetrate the soil.

Perhaps some of my readers may be surprised when I tell them that we irrigate all day long, and every day, wet or dry, Sundays and hard frosts only excepted. The quantity applied daily may average from 500 to 700 hogsheads. In dry weather it is no uncommon thing that we apply one inch per acre and cause the drains to discharge abundantly, as though it had been raining heavily for twenty-four hours. We feel that the poor hungry sub-soil is thus saturated and amended, and that a thousand affectionate or affinitive compliments are being interchanged and unions effected between the elements of air, water, and the infinitesimal soluble and insoluble granules of mother earth.

Solid manure might remain for ever inoperative but for Nature's drippings, which, in our dry eastern counties, with an annual rain-fall of 24 inches, are far too few for bulbous and leguminous plants. Hence the poverty of our grasses, the evaporations of summer demanding nearly all the rain-fall of that period; from April to September, 93 per cent. of the rain-fall is evaporated. When we are thoroughly convinced that water is manure, that it contains (see Liebig) all the organic elements of our bodies, we shall no longer wonder that proprietors in our lake and other districts, blessed with a triple rain-fall, should, if their land be drained naturally or artificially, consider that the breaking up of their pastures would be an act of insanity. Inorganic manure, where deficient, can always be cheaply supplied. I have no hesitation in saying, that by the new principle of irrigation our poor pastures, constituting so large an area of this kingdom, might be greatly increased in quality and fertility, assuming, of course, that the water of rivers or of springs were available. In Devonshire, irrigation is only made use of on the naturally drained soils; to put water on the heavy clays in their undrained state would be injurious. My process of irrigation may be described as giving an Irish or lake climate to my grass, root, and leguminous crops, whilst I retain the natural dryness and heat for my cereals; our natural rain-fall is about 24 inches; I increase it artificially to about 30 inches; 300 hogsheads per acre are equal to 75 tons.

With respect to the necessary dilution of our manure, in a dry summer you can hardly dilute it too much—say 1 hogshead of liquid to 50 of water. During winter, or on a fallow, it may be applied in considerable strength. Still, as a maxim, the greater amount of water we can pass through our soil, the greater will be its fertility, because the ammonia and carbonic acid, supplied by Nature without cost, will be proportionately increased.

The soluble form is the only true and profitable principle—searching, warming, and fructifying the barren subsoil by aëration, irrigation, and disintegration.

When we, as agriculturists, understand chemistry in its relation to agriculture, which shows us that there is no difference between a bullock and a shower of rain, except in *in*-organics; when we comprehend that three-fourths of the weight of our bodies are water—that nine-tenths of our turnips are water—then shall we believe that water is manure; then will the sewage of every town, village, and railway, be eagerly sought after and economized; then will covetous contentions arise about trickling brooks and gushing streams; then will the farmer's mind identify the carbonic acid and ammonia of wind and water with the fat and lean of his Christmas bullock; and then will the people of this great nation be better employed, and better and more cheaply fed.

It is easy to comprehend that if carbonic acid and ammonia are the two great fertilizing solvents and constituents, how important must be the maceration and reduction of *all* manure in abundance of water. The evolving gases are stored up in the water for fertility and profit, instead of escaping into the atmosphere and thus being lost to their owner.

Details of Irrigation.—*February* 10, 1853.—In depasturing grasses, which is always most advantageously done by cows or bullocks, it is well known that the portion covered by the solid manure is untouched for a year, causing ugly patches and wastes. Now, in irrigating, we turn the jet against these masses, which are immediately fluidized, dispersed, and sunk deeply into the soil; and, strange to say, that very spot, hitherto avoided by cattle, will almost immediately be more closely cropped than any other portion of the field.

Where sheep are folded or fed on clovers, &c., it is well known that they, in dry weather, need a change, the feed becoming foul. A heavy shower from the jet removes all offensive smell, freshens and sweetens the feed, manures the roots, encourages growth, and stimulates the appetite.

The Vicissitudes of Seasons have often a painful and unprofitable effect on agriculture. Peas and beans are considered a "gentleman's" crop; turnips mildew in a very dry summer; wireworm, slug, and grub, devour the crop. Now, all this is set right by the new system of irrigation, for no animalculæ can withstand the offensive ammoniacal shower; it either destroys them or drives them away.

The Seeds of Weeds are quickly destroyed by saturation in the liquid manure tank; as a proof of it, I soaked some oleaginous rape-seeds in liquid manure for twenty-four hours, as a preparation for sowing; and, to my great surprise, they had speared in that short period. The maceration of our manure will tend to prevent the increase of weeds.

Cost per Ton of applying Liquefied Manure.—Although 1*d.* per ton would pay 7½ per cent interest and all working charges, still, as there are occasional stoppages and hindrances arising from various causes, it is desirable to calculate on 1½*d.* or 2*d.* per ton. When it is considered that 100 tons per acre may be, as it were, filled into carts, carted from a half-mile to a mile, spread and ploughed in, or, what is better, deeply soaked into the soil, for from 12*s.* to 16*s.*, the charge is ridiculously low in comparison with the wear and tear and cost of men, horses, carts, roads, and gates. Open boarded floors are almost a necessary accessory to the irrigation. By directing a jet of water, as powerful as from a fire-engine, into the solid pudding, it flows from every shed in a lazy stream through a subterranean pipe to the great tank, whence, when still further diluted, it is propelled to the fields. It is hardly possible to appreciate the advantages of the irresistible and all-powerful jet; in five minutes it covers your buildings and yards with a torrent of rain. It is of a thousand scrubbing-brush power, cleansing every crack and cranny, washing away rats, mice, flies, and smells, and leaving at all times, but particularly in hot weather, a most refreshing sense of cleanliness. Excessively fat pigs and other animals in hot weather luxuriate in this shower-bath after recovering the first alarm. A hundred gallons of water per minute shot, as it were, out of a 32-bore muzzle, would hardly be faced with equanimity by courageous soldiers, especially in close quarters. It feels, close to the jet, like a solid substance, so great is the velocity under 4-horse pressure.

Iron Pipes.—My subterranean pipes are of 3 inches diameter, and it is most satisfactory to be able to state that in no instance have they choked. When it is considered that the pressure on every portion internally is 40 lbs. per inch, this may be easily conceived. The fluid is in fact a confined, rushing, irresistible stream, travelling about 120 feet per minute with an impelling force of 40 lbs. per square inch, which would of course compress or elongate any compressible substance. It is highly desirable that there should be no right angles in the pipes, all abrupt diversions proving great obstructions and causing waste of power. Easy curves are commendable, especially at the attachment of the hydrants. As a general rule, the larger the pipe the less the friction and resistance, the stream travelling more slowly. Bear in mind that it is impossible to force the contents of a large artery through a small vein without mischief. I work two jets attached to 1½-inch gutta-percha pipes. When we only worked one jet, there was much mischievous straining, and we were compelled to work at low speed.

The Tank.—Great mistakes are made in regard to tanks, which need by no means be expensive. For instance, my tank, which is 30 feet in diameter at the widest part, and 30 feet deep from the crown of the dome, is only 4½ inches thick, set in cement, the dome being of 9-inch brickwork, having a bearing or footing of 16-inch work. My tank, which holds from 70,000 to 80,000 gallons, cost only about £80 complete. All tanks should be circular, and worked from the surface downwards. For instance, a band or circle of brickwork, 5 feet deep, then another excavation of 5 feet, and another circle of brickwork, and so on to the bottom. By these means there is an avoidance of those dangerous slips which are caused by the pressure of the superincumbent mass, which pressure is received by the bricked circle. I speak of heavy clays. The dome is, of course, built upwards, and loaded or banked with earth as the work proceeds, to prevent its bulging outwards. No scaffolding is needed for the dome.

Summer's Sun and Winter's Frost must be guarded against, for on a hot day in July or August, gutta-percha pipes, when empty, will melt like wax; therefore a cork should be placed in the end, or, what is better still, there should be no stoppage, —one lad relieving the other at meal-times. In winter, your gutta-percha pipes would be full of ice in the morning; therefore, to avoid this, raise the suction above the liquid in the tank, and your pumps will draw and force air through the pipes and drive out all the fluid, leaving them empty. All the subterranean pipes may be thus emptied, if necessary, or the gutta-percha pipes may be emptied by the attendants on them. I may here mention that the gutta-percha pipes, when nipped or injured, are repaired by removing the damaged portion and bringing the two ends together like melted wax. It is worth while to see how it is done by the Gutta-Percha Company, as there will be frequent occasion for the operation.

Amongst several practical difficulties was that of preserving the fluid condition of heavy bullock manure, decomposing horseflesh, and other substances. If we stir up a pailful of such matter, the heavy particles soon subside, leaving the fluid on the surface. Now, with an abundance of manure, it became occasionally desirable to apply it to fallow land during winter in a dense semifluid condition. This we have successfully accomplished by agitating the contents of the tank in the vicinity of the suction-vessel, by air passing with great force and velocity through a gutta-percha jet, attached to a gutta-percha pipe. Of course it may be reduced by a larger supply of water. A ton of heavy bullock-pudding requires about 15 tons of water to make it comfortably available, although it may be proper in dry weather to use much more water. In the liquefaction of the solid pudding under the boards, the jet, as from a fire-engine, cuts and liquefies the mass until it flows in a stream like molten lead to the great tank through subterranean pipes.

Of course, the gruel may be either "thick and slab," or "thin and toast-and-water-like," according to the propriety of its application. Some idea may be formed of the liquefying power of the system I have described by my stating that at one time I had in my great tank about 20 or 30 dead horses and cows, besides some 250 loads of bullock-pudding, sheep and pig manure, &c., nearly all of which has flown through the jets in fertilizing showers. Of course, I need hardly say that an immense quantity of water has been used in the maceration, detachment, and liquefaction of so much solid matter, probably not less than from 30,000 to 40,000 gallons per diem.

Although the irrigation has only been in operation for eight months, it is telling very unmistakably on the profits of my farm.

For instance, a piece of red clover, of 8 acres, being an imperfect plant, was condemned to be ploughed up early; but on the application of the jet it produced enough to mantain 13 sheep per acre all the summer; thus setting free my other fields for hay. My young clovers were fed until late in November. Again, so greatly has it increased my produce of roots, both swedes and mangold-wurzel, that with 40 young bullocks and 100 sheep, besides cows and calves, they will, unless I largely increase my stock, carry me on into June.

I hope we shall never again be asked, "What has science done for agriculture?" It is impossible to see this mode of irrigation without feeling that we owe it all to science. Without mighty steam and imperishable gutta-percha, without cheap iron, vain would be any attempts at such an operation. Who can help loving and admiring science, which removes the veil of ignorance, and gives us some insight to those wondrous operations of nature, enlarging our minds, and filling them with awe and reverence?

The time is fast approaching when the farmer will receive back weekly, from our towns and cities, his supplies of food, altered in form, but scarcely in value. How reasonable and delightful to trace the bullock of to-day returning this day week, and passing through the jet to produce on the morrow the food for another bullock. The arterial supply and venous return will be the Harveian agricultural circulation.

We ought to be the richest agricultural country in the world. Not only do we consume all our own produce, but tax the world for necessaries and luxuries; not only may the farmer demand back his bullocks and sheep, his pigs and poultry, his bread, butter, cheese, eggs, and milk, but he may claim to have them flavoured with the spices of the east, the coffee of the west, and the tea of China; port, Madeira, sherry, brandy, and liquors; the luscious orange, and juicy grape, Turkey figs and Arab dates; and how thankful should he be that free trade will supply him with millions of quarters of American maize and Baltic wheat, hundreds of millions of French eggs, Dutch cheese, Holstein butter, and Ostend rabbits—all showering on his farm, in rich brown drops, to fill it with plenty and profit. No longer, then, should we hear of farmers feeding their animals on millions of oilcake and corn, at a certain loss of 33 per cent., for the sake of replacing that which has left their farm for ever to pass down sewers, to be food for the marine plants of the great ocean, or only to reach them again in the shape of Peruvian guano at £10 per ton. Let landlords and tenants believe that town sewage and bullocks and sheep, and guano and oilcake, are identical, and then this reckless folly will be redeemed. Like the great Jenner's vaccination, it will ultimately prevail, but "my hope is in the future," and another century may teach us all agricultural wisdom; some few have learned it already.

Details of the Steam Power Employed.—*March* 3, 1853.—I purpose to enter generally on a consideration of the agricultural steam-engine—its advantages as an economic agent, but more particularly the care, anxiety, vexation, trouble, and expense arising from the want of a proper knowledge of its management and requirements.

The very introduction of steam power is a monitor of intelligence and progression. It increases the farmer's care, attention, and responsibility; it stimulates and enlightens the labourer.

Unlike the two pieces of stick called a flail, with its one idea for the labourer and farmer, the steam-engine has almost a vitality; its 3,000 or 4,000 bolts, rivets, nuts, screws, brasses, straps, cogs, valves, slides, springs, flues, bars, water-gauge, steam-gauge, joints, packing, and a hundred other little matters, keep you always on the *qui vive*, and in a state of hopeful care and anxiety. You feel that you have under your care a monster or volcano ready to avenge your neglect, by sending you and your buildings flying into space, like a shower from Etna or Vesuvius. It throbs and pants in placid regularity; but neglect to lubricate its numerous bearings, and your ears will be assailed by screams of complaint and distress. Nothing perplexes and bewilders an ordinary farmer, from a backward district, so much as the apparent complication of bands and pulleys, and the various connections of the steam-engine. I honestly believe that the annual agricultural shows, with their now numerous machines in operation, are doing much to withdraw the agricultural mind from its obscurity. How much more quickly would this be done could agriculturists investigate the great economic applications of steam in our factories, workshops, mines, and steam-vessels? The railway locomotive is itself, perhaps, the greatest travelling monitor we have; and much was done by the machinery department of the great Exhibition. Let us hope that in the new Crystal Palace a more calm and less hurried opportunity may be likewise afforded and made use of by the million. As I see by recent accounts that the Marquis of Tweeddale has succeeded perfectly in working ploughs by steam power, we must all soon square our fields, knock down our fences, get rid of our prejudices about hedgerow timber, and learn our lesson about steam.

Our agricultural engine-makers will pardon me when I say, that *they* have had much to learn and improve upon during the last three or four years. When you first think of having an engine, your mind is racked with doubt whether it shall be vertical or horizontal, high pressure, low pressure, or expansive. But suppose this settled; then comes the number of horse-power—four, six, eight, or ten; then the size, form, and thickness of boiler—whether flue, ordinary, Cornish, or tubular. In fact, the use of a steam-engine is a sort of experimental school of improvement and alteration. It is a great chance but that, having decided upon your engine, you do not quite know whether you had better drive with cogs or bands; and whether the latter shall be of leather or of gutta-percha, or of both—the gutta-percha representing the slice of ham in a sandwich of two leathers, which is the latest and best improvement.

Now, as I have had to buy my experience, and undergo the sentiments of doubt, plague, and mystery which I have just expressed, I consider it a public duty to communicate the results of my lesson for the benefit of such of my brother agriculturists as have a desire to be informed.

The first and most general mistake is in having too small an engine, and particularly too small a boiler; always have an engine two-horse power larger than you think you shall require, as you are almost sure to impose some extra work upon it ultimately. It is a false economy to go to a cheap maker, or to screw down the estimate. A boiler should contain 25 cubic feet of space for each horse-power, which they seldom do, but which was a rule laid down by the memorable Watt and Tredgold; remember that the power is in the boiler, not in the engine, the quantity and pressure of steam being the measure of power. Mine is a flue boiler, three-eighths of an inch thick, which answers very well.

Now, with regard to flues or chimneys, or shafts, enormous mistakes are made, especially with flue boilers. Your engineer leaves you, as he did me, all trim and clean, with an assurance that steam-flues keep themselves clean, and free from soot, and require no cleansing. There never was a greater mistake than this. The consequence is, that you go off admirably the first two or three weeks, when you gradually require more coals, more stoking, and get less and less steam; your temper gets soured, and all goes wrong. This was precisely my case; so I broke open the brickwork at the back of the boiler, and found the bricked flues and the flue of the boiler almost choked with fine sand or inorganic matter, which, being the incombustible residuum of the coal, was carried along by the draught, and deposited gradually, like drifted snow or sand. The result of this obstruction was what we see almost daily—a black suffocating line of smoke spreading its nuisance far and wide, a sure indication of waste and mismanagement. I forthwith established iron trap doors at each end of every flue, and also wherever there was a bend or turn, so that once in a week or ten days every flue and corner may be cleansed of the sand, which often amounts to one or two sackfuls. By this and some other arrangements the smoke is converted into gas; we generate steam easily and abundantly, and little or no smoke issues from the chimney.

The importance of cleaning boilers inside and out is great, seeing that iron loses its conducting power when coated with inorganic earthy matter. Another very important matter is to have ample depth and space under the furnace-bars, so that an abundant supply of cold air may enter; otherwise your bars will be frequently melted and destroyed, and you will be tormented by an undue accumulation of vitreous masses or clinkers, which, adhering to the furnace-bars, obstruct the draught of air which ought to pass between them, and without which there cannot be perfect combustion. I have also a contrivance for admitting cold air at the end or back of the bridge or furnace-bars. We get smoke instead of gas, because we do not admit air in sufficient quantity. I am satisfied that air should be admitted at the two sides of the ash-pit, as well as in the front;

the colder the air the more oxygen it contains in a given space, and the more clear and brilliant will be the fire. A water-gauge and steam-gauge are both essential, the former of glass, like those on the railway engines, packed with vulcanized India-rubber rings, or you will always be breaking them. If we could always see the water playing or boiling in the gauge-glass, we should not hear of these melancholy explosions.

I have two steam-gauges—one a spring one, the other of quick-silver, like a barometer. This is a more correct and safe indicator than the former, the difference being very considerable, say 25 per cent., owing, no doubt, to the mode of fixing the spring. We work, at high pressure, say 40lbs. to the inch (sometimes 50 to 60), which is more economical in fuel than lower pressure; of course, every attention should be paid to the safety-valve. We keep our boiler about three-fourths full of water; the fire is banked up at night, so as to be ready for a start in the morning.

Before I proceed to the very important consideration of brasses and bearings, or supports, I would remark that our old tumble-down farmeries are by no means adapted for so mighty a power as steam, which would rack them to pieces. It is essential that the foundation for the engine, and the walls or supports for the axles or shafting, should be so strong as to allow of no movement, trembling, or vibration, which would cause a serious loss of power and increase of wear and tear. It is only those who have witnessed steam machinery that can properly appreciate the immensity of its force.

Having now your shaftings sufficiently strong with bearings at close intervals, take especial care to have the brasses long enough, which thus diminishes the ratio of pressure by increasing its area. Take care that, while your brasses are screwed sufficiently close to prevent play or oscillation, they do not press on the shafting. Most woful mistakes are made in this respect, as I know from annoying experience. Remember that if you screw the brasses tightly to the shafting, it acts like a skid on a wheel or a break on a railway-carriage—the lubricating oil is excluded; you get heated bearings, enormous friction, and most likely breakage or injury to your machinery by obstruction. Where we depend, as we must do, on agricultural labourers for our engine-drivers, it is highly essential to watch over and instruct them in these matters. It is no uncommon thing to see them pouring or wasting oil into the holes of the brasses without previously removing or picking out the dust or dirt, consequently the oil does not enter between the shaft and the brass, and they get hot and abraded.

In all rapid movements, such as the thrashing-machine drum, which in my case makes 1,200 revolutions per minute, a most vigilant attention to the brasses is indispensable. The brasses should be examined after each day's thrashing; and, if fluted or worn, should be cross-filed with a half-round smoothing file, so as to permit the lubricating oil to traverse. Good machine-makers have often sad reason to complain of the gross negligence and clumsiness of farm management of their engines, acting injuriously alike to all parties. As I look upon the highly-finished and smoothly-working engines at our great shows, attended by their vigilant makers and managers, hoping to receive the prize for economy in fuel and execution of work; when I subsequently examine the judges' reports, and read of 4 or 5 lbs. of coal per horse per hour, I ask myself, how will all this be altered when we find them on a farm, with foul flues and boilers, worn brasses, hot bearings, and careless management.

The cost of engines in the south of England may be taken at 25*l.* per horse-power, to which it will be safe to add 25*l.* more for thrashing, chaff-cutting machines, grinding-mill, turnip-cutter, shafting-bands, &c.; so that you get all paid in a six-horse power engine for about 350*l.* to 400*l.*, which will cover bricklayers' and carpenters' work in ordinary cases.

The annual cost of repairs to machinery, brasses, driving-bands, and occasional fractures, may be set down for the whole machinery at 5*l.* per horse power, or 30*l.* for a six-horse engine —assuming, of course, that it is worked all day long, and every day up to its full powers. The consumption of coals, with clean flues and good management, will be 6 to 7 cwt. per day, or 10 to 11 lbs. per horse per hour. As a matter of detail, you will require for your steam horses rape oil for bearings, Russian tallow for cylinder, white and red lead and soft hempen cord for packing, and leather thongs or rivets for your bands. Your engine-man should have a vice, anvil, forge, hammers, two half-round and two square files, pincers or blacksmith's tongs, spanners, screw hammers, &c. I prefer an intelligent agricultural labourer as my engine-driver, and give him 10*s.* a week, except at harvest, when he has double pay. I ought to say that all riggers or driving-wheels should be turned smooth, which causes the driving-band to cling to them by excluding air. If left rough from the casting, as mine were originally, the driving bands slip.

In conclusion, let me remark, if I have not been already too tedious, that horse power cannot be compared with steam-power. Horse-power is very variously estimated by engineers, according to the size and keep; but assuming it to be the power of raising 33,000 lbs. a foot high each minute, remember that four hours of such labour would constitute a day's horse work; whilst so long as you feed your steam-horse with coals and water, you may work it night and day. I have seen it stated that one-half the population of the whole globe would be required to turn out our manufacturing quota by manual labour. If we used horses, instead of steam, we had need sow every acre with oats and hay; we should want millions of grooms and whole cities of stables. If we should succeed in getting a few hundred thousand farriers and horse-doctors, where the hides would come from for harness I really can form no idea. Let our non-steaming agricultural friends imagine that one of our ocean steamers of 1600 horse power would require, working night and day, four relays of horses and two relays of men—that would be 6,400 horses; one man to every four horses would be 1,600 grooms and attendants, to say nothing of hay, straw, corn, water, for 14 days, with 6,400 sleeping stalls for the horses, with beds and provisions for the attendants. Noah's ark or Smithfield would be nothing to it. This is ridiculously though truthfully illustrative, but not more so than to oppose long custom and the flail to science and steam.

Let us not for a moment suppose that steam displaces manual labour. It has had the reverse effect in manufactures, and so it will in agriculture; for it brings with it general improvement, progression, abundance, and cheapness.

Pumps and Pumping.—*October*, 1853.—There is no action so simple as pumping, and yet which, in my case, occasioned us more vexation. Pumping water is easy enough, provided your valves fit closely on their seats, and provided you have no pin-hole above the water; for, however minute the aperture, your pump will draw air instead of water. Many have been plagued considerably by force-pumps attached to high-pressure steam-boilers; I was for a long time, and from a simple cause. When the supply of water was shut off from the force-pump, in its attempt to form a vacuum, it drew air through the packing, and forced it back again, and thus afterwards, when it should have drawn water, drew air. I have now in the pump-barrel a small tap, which we open before turning off the water, and through this the air enters and escapes without distressing the packing,—great has been its comfort.

The pump-valves should be accessible, for in pumping semi-fluid manure occasional obstructions will occur by pieces of turnips or mangolds, sticks, straws, or bones, getting under them, thus preventing their striking equally on the seats; the wear on them is considerable, seeing that they are struck down fifteen times a minute with a sledge-hammer blow, or at 60 lbs. per inch about 450 lbs. each blow. When these valves get fixed, or do not act, much time is lost in unscrewing the taps. It would be very desirable to have the power of flushing them with water by a pipe and tap from a cistern above, which would often remove the obstruction.

The valves and their stalks should, when not a ball, be of strong wrought iron, all in one piece. My original cast brass or iron stalks snapped off like glass, and were hurried away like straws. This reminds me that under the pump barrels should be a cast-iron roomy box, easily accessible, where pieces of iron, stones, &c., that are drawn in, may, when deposited, be occasionally removed, and thus prevent the ends of the barrels striking upon them to their injury. The threads of all the screw-bolts should be very deeply cut, and everything should be extra strong, otherwise with a pressure of 60 lbs. or 70 lbs. things will be all to pieces.

So dense has been the fluid of our manure, as compared with water, that the valves should have a sufficient weight to drop on their seat quickly, otherwise, as in my case, the semi-fluid manure will obstruct their descent and prevent their action. I find it perfectly unnecessary to have expensive brass valves; where the pumps are in frequent action the friction of the fluid keeps them free and smooth. My pump-barrels are of brass, 5-inch diameter and 20-inch stroke. Had I known what I do now, they should have been of iron, as a cheaper material and equally useful. They work through a packing of soft hempen cord, saturated with melted Russian tallow. This same tallow I use in a cup with tap, to lubricate my slide valve above the cylinder of my steam-engine.

The various taps in connection with the pumps and the subterranean pipes should be all repacked occasionally with well-greased rope, and if set fast by rust, in consequence of not being recently used, a little oil insinuating itself between the surfaces will render their detachment easy. In the first instance, for want of knowledge in these matters, I have seen three or four men straining with levers and destroying property where a boy could with ease have turned the taps or stop-cocks. Now, however, we scarcely know what it is to have an impediment.

I find it convenient that my engine will drive a pair of 4 feet 4 in. mill-stones, and also work one barrel of my pumps, throwing at 30 revolutions per minute 50 gallons per minute. I reckon four-horse power for the stones and two for the pump. If we work the two barrels, two jets should be open. The resistance of the jet or fountain costs some power; for when removed and the liquid merely flowing out of the 1½-inch or 2 inch pipe, the engine runs off as if it had but little work to do.

There is a great convenience in the fountain-like jet, especially amongst growing crops where a man must not move about, as he can thus command 50 or 60 feet on each side of him; but it is at some cost of power and waste of ammonia. If the pipe were pierced with holes like the eyes in a lamprey, the liquor would flow through easily, cheaply, and without the same loss of ammonia. There would be more labour in moving it.

When pumping manure up a steep incline, it is desirable to finish off by pumping water to cleanse the pipes; or at all events to turn off the tap, to prevent the return of the liquid, which would dribble away into the lower grounds from the solid matter, and leave it to incrust or choke the pipe. The only case in which we had a subterranean stoppage was from this cause; the tap was not turned off, and the other fields being lower, the liquor naturally flowed back each day of pumping. Not having occasion to return to that field for three months, some of the pipes were found choked with solid manure.

Retrospective.—My irrigation being now perfect, without check or hinderance of any kind, I consider it an agricultural duty to allude to the difficulties, and show how they have been overcome.

Smell from the Tank.—Although this tank is domed over, with trap doors, the effluvium was inconvenient at 100 yards distant: the introduction of a jet of waste steam cooks the smell as it rises. The steam must be introduced above the liquid, not into it. Steam is a wonderful purifier. A constant jet of air pumped through a gutta-percha tube into the liquid, causes a constant boiling up of the solid and liquid, so that they are both drawn into the suction. This air-tube is generally near to the suction-bulb, thus counteracting the tendency to solidification around the bulb which would otherwise take place. The suction-pipe and the air-pipe must all be of gutta-percha, so as to be easily pulled up, shaken, or examined. I began with iron pipes in the tank, but found them useless because they could not be lifted or examined. The bulb at the end of the suction-pipe should be at least 3 feet long and 2 feet diameter, with about 200 holes of 1 inch diameter, so as to admit a gradual, easy entrance for the manure. On the top of the tank you will have a winch or well-rope attached to the suction-bulb. An occasional shake or examination of the bulb will be useful. This may be done without stopping the pumps. If you have much solid matter in the tank, and only use it occasionally, the liquid will become sufficiently dense to float the whole mass several feet thick. In order to intermix and distribute this mass, a jet from the pumps will cut it to pieces and mix it with the fluid. A weighty collar should be placed round the nozzle of the air-pipe to keep it down in the liquid.

Pump Valves.—It is necessary to have spare valves, and have them turned true every now and then, otherwise you will draw air instead of liquid. Of course your plunger barrels must be carefully packed with greased rope. A very large air-vessel is indispensable, not less (for such pumps as mine) than the size of a 20-gallon cask. I have three in immediate connection with the pumps. If you are deficient in air-vessel you will break your machinery; and you must have in addition escape-valves close to the pumps, otherwise when there is a stoppage on the fields you will break your machinery by hydraulic pressure. If your pump-barrels are too large in proportion to your subterranean pipes, you will come to a dead lock, break machinery, or waste power. There is a proper proportion and velocity that cannot be violated with impunity. Again, long lengths of small gutta-percha tubing impede the transmission of fluids. I never use now smaller tubing than 2-inch, and this is inflexible unless you insert at intervals corrugated joints. The jet alone causes much resistance, and taking it off the engine at once increases its speed. Mr. Telfer uses no jet, and gets no fountain. This may answer well on his sandy soil, but on our hard and cracking clay such a system does not answer, for obvious reasons. Of course, in standing crops of roots, &c., a fountain or shower of at least 40 to 50 feet is imperative. Working a double set of 1½-inch hose with two jets greatly eases the engine.—1854.

---

4. SEWAGE MANURE.*

What is Sewage?—In it the chemist recognizes legs of mutton, rounds of beef, and basins of turtle; cargoes of sugar, coffee, and port wine, millions of 4lb. loaves, and thousands of tons of cheese and butter. Therein are not only all the alimentary productions of our own country, but also our enormous alimentary imports—altered in form, it is true, but scarcely in utility or value. It is truly a well-known but unworked mine of gold, equal in annual value to one-half the interest of our national debt. We might call it a stream of liquid guano. It exists in a form of peculiar availability, and almost self-portability; its fertilizing powers are enormous. We may estimate its value by the sums expended to compensate for its loss. We pay for our guano two millions annually? for unprofitable oil-cake and corn, to feed our manure-making animals, many millions; and vast sums are annually abstracted from the agricultural pocket for phosphates and other artificial manures.

Nationally this neglect of sewage is a great calamity, but one that, it is to be hoped, may receive a gradual and wholesome correction. If it is considered ruinous by the farmer to waste the excrementitious deposits of his animals, with still greater force does the objection apply to the waste of our sewage. Experience has taught the writer of this article, that there is no material practical difficulty to overcome in its economy and appliance to the soil as a fertilizing agent. It is not more difficult to convey than the water which intersects our streets, and finds its way into every house. It may, in fact, be considered the venous return of an arterial circulation; and the more abundant its liquefaction, the more valuable it becomes, seeing that water alone contains all the organic elements of our food. It is hardly possible to treat this subject except as a joint question of sewage and irrigation with drainage.

* From Morton's *Cyclopædia of Agriculture*. (Blackie.)

We said there was no practical difficulty in economizing this most valuable commodity, excepting the all-important one that public opinion has not yet appreciated its value. In vain would the iron arteries circulate their precious streams through British farmeries, unless the British farmer knew its value, and estimated the results of its application to his soil. The force of public opinion must be brought to bear on this great question. Teach him that it is liquid guano, brought to his door in its only available form; let him understand that the water of solution is independently a means of fructification; point out to him that every valued meadow whose rich crop of hay he covets, owes its powers of production principally to the abundant supply of moisture.

It is a question for the landlord and his tenant, for our legislators and for the country at large. When once convinced of its value, recorded registers of supply will be attached to each farm like our gasometers. Quarterly demands for its use will be cheerfully paid: our towns will be cleansed, and our country fertilized.

The evidence on this subject is too abundant and distinct to be doubted or denied. It is collated in a most authentic, comprehensive, and detailed form, in a document issued by the General Board of Health, Whitehall, London, entitled, "Minutes on Information, collected on the Practical Application of Sewage Water and Town Manures to Agricultural Production." The copious instances of cost and return there exemplified induced the writer of this to carry out the system on a farm of 170 acres; and an experience of nearly one year has sufficed to convince him of its easy practicability and great pecuniary advantages; he finds it, in fact, the key to profitable farming. The cost of the operation verifies the calculations quoted in the Board of Health paper:—

	£	s.	d.
Tank (to contain 80,000 gallons)	100	0	0
Engine (4-horse)	100	0	0
Pumps	60	0	0
Iron pipes, laying, and hydrants	350	0	0
Gutta-percha distributing pipes, &c.	50	0	0
Extra taps, air vessels, and sundry minor arrangements	60	0	0
	£720	0	0

or about £4. 5s. per imperial acre. The price of iron 3-inch pipes, delivered, was £5 per ton; at this moment (March, 1853) they are very considerably dearer, owing to the great rise in iron. The cheapest districts for iron pipes are probably Newcastle and Glasgow. The quantity used for 170 acres was 50 tons. Each nine-feet length of 3-inch pipe weighs about 118 lbs.; quantity of piping per acre about 15 yards, or

5½ cwt. to 6 cwt. per acre. The working cost per diem is as follows:—

	£	s.	d.
Coals, at 1s. per cwt.	0	6	0
Man at Engine	0	1	8
Three boys, } working two jets, and moving the pipes	0	1	6
One lad } working two jets, and moving the pipes	0	1	0
Wear and tear, and repairs	0	2	6
	0	12	8
7½ per cent. interest on first cost, £54 per annum, or for 300 days	0	3	7
	0	16	3

The quantity delivered daily would be, for ten working hours, 130 tons of *water;* but the specific gravity of liquid manure being so much greater, the cost of delivery may be fairly placed at from 1½*d.* to 2*d.* per ton. The writer has rather overrated all expenses, to prevent disappointment, and he has also allowed for many stoppages that will naturally occur.

In the manufacturing districts, both coals and machinery would be cheaper; labour dearer. On a very large scale, with economical expanding and condensing engines, and a rigid engineering supervision, the cost of application might be fairly reduced to 1*d.* per ton.

A primary essential to the application of sewage is a natural or artificial drainage. In Devonshire we find the springs profitably applied to irrigation wherever there is a natural drainage, whilst on the undrained clays they are not made use of.

A glance at the geology of the site of London and its surrounding country, will show to how great an extent it is available, even without drainage; for, although the immediate vicinity, being of London clay, would require drainage, the chalks, sands, and gravels, parched up by summer heats, almost pray for the fertilizing stream. It is not our province here to enter into minute statistical details of cost and remuneration, but taking the value of town sewage generally at £1 per head of inhabitants, and multiplying it by the resident urban population, the annual value can scarcely be less than ten to fifteen millions sterling. Unmistakable evidence of practical operations, as detailed in the minutes of information by the Board of Health, shows that the cost of the necessary means for appliance would be from £3 to £4 per acre, added, as it were, to the fee simple of the soil. The farmers, for many miles round our various towns and cities, would be largely benefited, after paying to public companies a liberal interest on outlay. In fact they would, by these means, receive back their agricultural products weekly, in the form of town sewage—enriched by the consumption of large foreign imports. A few years since, the Metropolitan Sewage Manure Company was established, and still exists; but, for the want of increased capital, and from other causes, has not yet proved remunerative. The supplies were abstracted from a suburban sewer, and led to some very rich market-gardens, already saturated with town manure, and on which the proprietors (who send large supplies of vegetables, and load back with manure, which they obtain at a mere nominal price) apply 100 tons of manure per acre per annum. Here the benefits derived from the sewage are considerable, particularly in summer, but the company lack the funds to convey it to the poor lands, more distant from the metropolis, beyond the economical reach of its solid manure, and which most need the sewage. No doubt it will ultimately be taken up and extended by capitalists having more means and experience. The present works are at Stanley Bridge, Fulham, near London. The evidences are all sufficiently clear, that the mere water irrigation of land on this principle of subterranean pipage, and at the cost named, is remunerative. How much more so, then, when saturated with the elements of our food. The question is a great one, and deserving the consideration of our landholders, statesmen, and of our corporate and parochial authorities.

The necessity for irrigation is becoming annually more apparent. The extensive removal of woods, fences, and the general clearing and improved cultivation of our country, added to the daily increasing drainage, render our soil and our climate warmer and drier, and consequently less favourable to succulent productions. By the proposed system of irrigation, we shall have a warm moisture for our roots and green crops, and dryness for our cereals; in fact, a desirable combination of food in abundance, for man and for beast.

The recent experiments of Mr. Way have shown indubitably, that we may apply our sewage to our clay soils at any period, and in any quantity, and that the valuable manurial solutions will remain in the soil, chemically arrested by an all-wise Providence for the use of plants, and for the ultimate food of man.

The facility of removing the London sewage by steam-power, is very obvious. The surplus water of the great Bedford Level, 280,000 acres, is disposed of by steam-power, of 1,200 to 1,500 horse. The area of the metropolis being so much less, half a dozen steam-pumps of (four-feet) moderate diameter would probably dispose of the whole. It is a most simple and easy operation, but it is only reasonable to anticipate that many years must elapse, and that a greatly increased knowledge of agricultural chemistry must be attained by our land-owners and farmers, ere their conviction of the advantages to be derived will induce them to avail themselves of town sewage, and of other similar local resources, too often now entirely neglected. The writer of this has applied the principle of liquid or sewage manuring to 170 acres of land. An experience of less than twelve months has proved to him that the operation is a very profitable one, and influences most favourably his future farming prospects. Numerous are the advantages which result from the system: suffice it to say, that his experience justifies and confirms the results obtained by others under similar circumstances. Hitherto, in farming, that portion of the farm which produces root crops has, as a general rule, failed to pay its own annual expenses, and has entailed a considerable charge on the cereal moiety. Sewage or liquefied manuring alters this, and renders the root and green crops self-supporting, by furnishing a great increase at a diminished per-centage of cost. It may be compared to growing the ordinary produce of 100 acres, on 50 acres, thus diminishing by 50 per cent. the rent, rates, tithes, taxes, horse and manual labour, and wear and tear of implements, roads, gates, &c. In many instances, as in those of poor grass lands, which probably constitute one-third the acreage of the United Kingdom, the writer has no hesitation in saying that the produce would be doubled, and greatly improved in feeding quality.

A neighbour of the writer has told him, that on a portion of land he had irrigated with plain water, he had increased the produce eightfold—say from a quarter of a ton per acre to two tons. Experience has taught the writer, that no amount of solid manuring, particularly on pastures, even at a great cost, will, in our dry climate, effect what may be done cheaply and quickly by irrigation with water alone, or with sewage. The facility and promptitude with which a barren soil may be fertilized, is surprising. A rank yellow clay subsoil, when thoroughly saturated with sewage, becomes at once capable of producing good crops. The chemical effects appear immediate; nor can this be a matter of surprise, seeing that the solution fills every interstice, and surrounds every granule of soil. In lands drained naturally or artificially, the writer has seen cabbages and roots luxuriate in a miserable plastic clay brought from the subsoil, immediately after its saturation with sewage or liquefied manure. Its effects are alike beneficial to every agricultural crop—cereal, bulbous, or leguminous; although, in the case of cereals, a due regard is required as to the necessity for its application, and a judicious regulation of the quantity of seed. With regard to the form of application, the writer's experience confirms the evidence collated by the General Board of Health, that the hose and jet present very great advantages in every respect.

As to the period of growth, or season for application, the writer has applied it at almost every stage of growth; in sunshine and wet weather, in winter and in summer: on fallows, in wet weather, very strong; in dry weather, more amply diluted. During the heats of summer, its frequent application to bulbous, leguminous, and green crops, is attended with the most profitable results, illustrating, in degree, the rapid vegetation produced by great heat and moisture in tropical climates. With an increasing population and limited acreage, the time is fast approaching when the concentration of capital on land for a greatly increased production will become a necessity. In no way can this be done more advantageously than by the application of town sewage, or liquefied manure. In lieu of two acres producing barely enough for one cow, six sheep, or one bullock, by these means from three to five cattle, or twenty sheep, may be maintained on one acre. In extreme cases, enormous results have been produced. The Meadows near Edinburgh, some of them once arid and worthless, have, by being flooded with the sewage of that city, risen to an enormous value, and are annually let by public auction, at prices varying from £15 to £32 per acre. It is estimated that the quantity of green food cut annually from each acre is from fifty to eighty tons. The supply of milk to our great cities would, by similar irrigations, become greatly improved in quantity, quality, and price.

It is singular that, as a closely-calculating people, we should nationally have neglected that which has been long economized by other nations. A friend of the writer, who visited Nankin, assured him, that at the corner of each street was a receptacle from which all excrement was carefully taken, a law of the Chinese forbidding its waste. It is the only manure applied to their corn-fields. It strikes one as a singular anomaly that there should be such a neglect and abhorrence of this ordure, whilst we import annually enormous supplies of birds'-dung from the Pacific. The extension of the sewage system in our southern and midland counties would necessitate the introduction of steam-power, and, as a natural consequence, enlarge and enlighten the minds of the tenants and labourers, who at present are by no means thoroughly convinced of the advantages of steam as an economic agent in agriculture.

It is interesting to see a boy quietly working his way down a field of mangolds or turnips as high as one's knees, distributing on each side of him, to the distance of fifty to eighty feet (and if the wind blows, much farther), heavy showers of liquefied manure. It is no uncommon thing to make the drains run at four feet depth in dry weather; thus affording ample food to the deeply buried roots, warming and fertilizing the too often wretched subsoil. The writer has applied the liquid manure to cereal crops as late as the end of May and beginning of June, with much advantage, on such portions of the field as required such assistance. One of the most important results is the destruction or driving away of injurious grubs or insects. Wire-worm, slug, and beetle either perish under the jet or quickly leave the field. Clovers do not fail, and roots are freed from knobs, and fingers and toes.

For a more detailed and comprehensive statement of the advantages resulting from liquid manuring, and from irrigation, the writer of this refers to some communications from him to the Editor of the *Agricultural Gazette*, recently published in that journal. The document issued by the General Board of Health, Whitehall, London, entitled, "Minutes of Information Collected on the Practical Application of Sewer Water and Town Manure to Agricultural Production," deserves the attentive perusal of every one interested in this question. No doubt, it may be obtained by those who can show that they are interested in its objects. Every local board of health in the United Kingdom possesses a copy of it.—*March* 1853.

PART IV.

SPEECHES.

Thorp-le-soken—Witham—East Essex—Wickham Market—Hadleigh—Drayton Manor—North Walsham—Saffron Walden—London—Hadleigh—Witham—Coggeshall—Hadleigh—Saffron Walden—Tiptree—Aberdeen—Witham—Tiptree—Braintree—London—Carlisle—London—Woodbridge—Manchester.

It is right to premise that in the following reports only a selection of the addresses given, and those very much curtailed, is attempted.

Thorp-le-soken, *June*, 1846.—Mr. Mechi said: It had all through life been his opinion that manufactures, commerce, and agriculture, were inseparably connected, and that it was impossible to make them antagonistic interests without injury to all. In his own case the greater part of his customers were manufacturers; while, on the other hand, he consumed corn and meat, some of it in all probability grown in the very neighbourhood where they were assembled: therefore, there was a beneficial intercourse between them. The manufacturers were still prepared to supply them with goods, but he hoped they should be none the worse customers of the farmers if they supplied other nations with what was not wanted for the home trade. He looked for the time when agriculturists would be in the same position—when they would be able to say to foreigners, "We have all the corn we want, and here is more to ship." He believed that would be their position, and that it would soon be brought about if they all farmed like his friend Mr. Hutley, of Witham. He had no hesitation in saying that whilst the agriculture of Essex was very far superior to that of other counties, it was very far inferior to what it ought to be. In the first place, as had been remarked by Mr. Nunn, it was impossible to grow corn without manure; and if so, why waste it? If the manufacturers had thrown money down the drains or into the ditches, they would not be in the position they now were of being able to supply not only the home consumer, but to go into foreign markets and offer their goods in competition with those dwelling on the spot, and living, as was thought in this country, much cheaper than themselves; and yet they could go 10,000 miles and say, "Here's a razor, or a piece of cotton, which we offer you for less than you can make it yourselves, although we live in a country in which bread is so dear." Could that be done without skill, science, and enterprise? It was the science and superior industry of the British manufacturers which enabled them to buy iron and other commodities of their opponents, and send them back in the shape of manufactured goods. There was another reason why manufacturers had progressed. When they wanted to build a factory they hired a piece of ground upon lease, and he believed that were it not for the power of getting a certain tenure for a definite period, the improvement which had been alluded to would never have taken place. He believed further, that the basis of agricultural improvement must be leases. He did not state this as being opposed to the landed interest of the country; he knew the land-owners to be men of noble sentiments, although of course with some prejudices; but he believed that the effect of leases would be to secure a superior class of tenantry—men of capital, and men whose land at the end of their leases would be more valuable than when they entered upon it. It was a painful thing to see men left to chance; a landlord might be taken away and all his best intentions be frustrated. A tenant ought to have security, that in improving his land he will have an opportunity of seeing part of his money back.

East Essex, *October*, 1846.—Mr. Mechi said: He was bound to condemn the general agriculture of this country, and this county also (though in a less degree), as being very far less perfect than it ought to be, or than it might be. Shallow cultivation was certainly a crime chargeable upon the agriculture of Essex; they heard very little of subsoiling, and with the great body of agriculturists he believed it was considered to have very little effect; but he was sure, from actual results, that in hard and tenacious subsoils, the effect of breaking them up and rendering them pervious to air and water improved the permanent fertility of the soil, and increased the return in the crops. It rid the land of an enormous quantity of jolly old thistles—and economized the expense of cultivation subsequently. It was a great misfortune for any individual, nation, or county to be self-satisfied, and to fancy themselves perfect in their avocation. He held it as a principle that the man who rose every morning with the conviction that he knew but little compared with what he might know, was much more likely to improve and to succeed than one who might think he had nothing to learn; and, therefore, he should be prepared hereafter to find his improving friend Barker admitting that he had learned a great deal, and hoped to learn a great deal more as an agriculturist. To a great extent he confirmed his (Mr. Mechi's) position, for he had expressed the belief that the rising generation required a better education, and that education would give them, as a body, greater power and more profit. He (Mr. Mechi) believed there was a great want of agricultural knowledge among the landlords as well as tenants. In his short drive that day it was impossible for him to avoid wondering how landlords could allow their tenants to be encumbered and robbed by ranks of trees, elbowing each other upon immense fences. No landlord could thus rob his tenant, without robbing himself at the same time, and therefore it was evident that they did not know their own interests. Look, for instance, at the miserable desire there was for old pastures; but what farmers were there who had had a quantity of it who were not aware that it was robbing them from day to day and from year to year. If it ever contained good wholesome grasses, which was very doubtful, they had long ago worn themselves out, and made way for twitch, weeds, and everything except that which could be profitable to the tenant. From his own observation he was quite sure that many an old pasture, which a landlord might consider it a crime to break up, would, if farmed upon the four-course shift, produce at least three times as much food both for man and beast, and employ three times as much labour as in its present form. Before he left the subject of education, he wished to recommend to their notice the agricultural college at Cirencester, of which noble institution he had the honour to be one of a committee of five. He could tell his friend Mr. Barker, that his principle of practice combined with science was there carried out; and farmers' sons were taught to top and tail turnips, and the elements of geology and agricultural chemistry at the same time. They had there a professor of agriculture; with teachers of geology, botany, and land surveying; an eminent practical chemist; and in fact everything calculated to remove from the rising generation of agriculturists those prejudices which had been the bane of their parents. It was not alone with the agriculture of this county that he had to find fault; he equally complained of one branch of its manufactures—that of draining-pipes. If the farmers were not sufficiently aware of their own interests, to prefer cheap steam-power to dear horse-power, the makers of pipes and tiles were not much further advanced. On his late visit to Sir Robert Peel, at Tamworth, he made inquiries for tile-works, and was delighted to find one with steam-power for hauling up the clay, rollers to press it, hot water to moisten it, steam-power to work it in the pug, and hot flues to dry the pipes when made, so that a good and sound article, such as the specimens he had shown them to-day, could be produced either in winter or summer, and be ready for the farmer in one week from the time of being dug from the clay-pit. With regard to quality, no person who had seen them could deny that they were worth 30 per cent. more than any of the same size made by hand, and charged at a much higher price; and therefore he hoped and believed, from conversations he had had with some of the intelligent pipe-makers of this county, that if landlords and tenants were disposed to drain their land as they ought, the manufacturers were prepared to go ahead with steam-power, and supply them as well as could be done in any other county. He saw at Sir R. Peel's 600 acres of land, drained with pipes put in 4 feet deep, where drains previously made 2 feet 8 inches had ceased to be of any use. Here was illustrated the principle that deep was far superior to shallow drainage. There was a particular character in that soil, a large quantity of ochreous and iron matter, which in shallow drains, with pipes and soles, choked them up. A slow stream caused a deposit, as they saw in their ditches, but a rapid stream cleared itself, and thus the much-sneered-at "pencil-cases," or 1-inch pipes, worked perfectly well when the old-fashioned pipe and sole choked up, showing that the latter were not only very expensive, but entirely useless. He lately saw a field of twenty acres perfectly drained by a single drain; it was not spring water, but a single drain took all the rain water that fell on the field. But how did he know that every part of that field was perfectly drained? He made holes in various parts of the field, and placed pipes in them, one on the other to the depth of 5 feet, and rammed earth round them; down this telescope of pipes he put a piece of stick, like a yard measure, but longer, and he thus found before he cut the drain that the level of the water was within 18 inches of the surface. Having cut a single drain through the field, he then found that the water in these trial-holes began to lower, more rapidly near the drain, and less rapidly farther from it, but ultimately there was no water nearer the surface than the depth of his drain, 4 feet 6 inches. The result was that the whole field was drained by one small and inexpensive drain, when others would probably have cut them every 20 or 30 feet, and multiplied the cost tenfold. Therefore a man, before he presumed to say what drains his land required, should cut his test-holes, and by examining his stick from time to time he would see what was drained and what was not. That was important, because he had himself thrown hundreds of pounds away by cutting drains too close, and he was sure others had thousands, and he wished to prevent this in future.

Wickham Market.—*November*, 1846.—Mr. Mechi said: Nature has favoured you in this district with a superior soil, and I am happy to say that you have shown proper discretion in cultivating it as it ought to be. But I do not consider that you are perfect farmers yet. So long as I see the liquid manure pouring—the strong tea running into the ponds, and so long as

I see you satisfied with keeping merely the tea-leaves, I consider that a great defect. Another great defect is the use of those lumbering, antiquated, barbarous affairs I would call them, waggons. Another point in which you are deficient, is deep cultivation by sub-soiling; and one more, which I am happy to see is being remedied, is deep drainage. I am quite aware that this county was the first that introduced drainage into this kingdom, or rather practised drainage in this kingdom; but that is no reason, having been tolerably well done, why it should not be perfectly done. We will come to this point, however, by-and-by. In the speech which your chairman has made, he has been kind enough to pronounce the meed of praise on myself, hoping that I may not lose my property. I am happy to inform you that I have already succeeded in doubling the returns on my farm, and I hope, now that the expenses are over —the expenses of improvements—I hope that I shall be able to derive a return for my capital; a small return as a landlord, a better return as a tenant. Gentlemen, we all know that agriculture is not a very profitable affair. The return is too slow for that. As a manufacturer and trader, if I vend an article I can very soon replace it by another; but if I, as a farmer, sell my crop of wheat, I have no prospect of another crop until one year has passed over my head. Therefore, farming must always remain a less profitable occupation than trade, commerce, and manufactures. There are, no doubt, many enjoyments which compensate for the loss of profit. There is a fine independence with plenty of open air, and a reference to one's farm-yard for a good dinner, if one requires it. But if farming is an operation slow and of small profit, how very essential is it that that business should be conducted in the most profitable manner. I am quite sure that a great deal more corn might be grown, and much more food produced, than there is at present. When I see those thousands and tens of thousands of ugly stumps called pollards, that meet me at every turn and corner, I consider their being allowed to remain, a disgrace to the landlords of this country. The value of these pollards, when cut down and carted home, is not on an average one shilling each. I believe I speak the truth in saying so, and I am quite prepared to prove that the damage they do annually to the land is more than their whole value. We see also a great many scrubby timbers, as they are called, worth two, three, and four shillings each, that annually do a damage to the tenant of two, three, and four shillings each. Multiply these losses by many millions, and I believe you will find the damage done equivalent to the whole of the malt-tax annually. That may be considered a bold assertion, but I believe by calculating the number of trees, the average number of trees on each acre of ground, you will find it a correct one, and that the damage is rather undervalued than otherwise. I believe that the desire on the part of the landlords for growing timber is very fast diminishing. I believe that it was not a desire to injure the tenants, but a mistaken notion that it was profitable to grow them, and that the rent was lower in consequence. But it never can be profitable to have in our corn-fields trees in competition with the unrented forests of America, and other parts of the world. And as to timber, there is no fear of our having timber for every purpose so long as we have money to buy it from other countries, and convoys to protect it home in times of war. I therefore hold it to be a prominent feature in the improvement of agriculture, that the landlord should cut down timber-trees, except those that are ornamental and pleasant to the eye; and I am sure the tenant would not object to pay on the average an increased rental of two shillings per acre, more or less, varying with the number of trees on the estate. No doubt the landlord would ultimately derive as great benefit as the tenant, because the tenant, deriving more profit, would become a man of better capital, and more able to pay his rent regularly, and the estate or farm when it changed hands would be decidedly at a premium.

Another great defect, as it appears to me, in your district, in common with many others, is the wretched form and state of the buildings. We have a queer-shaped barn here, and a cart-lodge there, and a granary in another place, and generally so arranged, that every wind that blows in winter can have a passage through the whole. The result is, that the cattle are much longer fattening, and of course much less profitable to the tenant. Temporary buildings in agriculture must no longer be the order of the day. I had the honour lately of an interview with his grace the duke of Bedford, who, as a great cultivator, and making a most profitable return from his estates, has found it answer his purpose better, when buildings require great repairs, to pull them down and rebuild them of bricks, slate, and iron.

The hedgerows of this county are certainly superior to ours in Essex, very much so; but still I think there is great room for improvement. I think it is a mistaken notion to grow our own timber for firing; it is much dearer than coals. It would cost but three-pence or four-pence an acre at the utmost to keep these fences neatly trimmed, as we see them in Norfolk and Cambridgeshire. We may as well take a lesson and do all that is desirable, because attention to fences is profitable; and also because, from being well kept up, they look exceedingly neat.

I do not think that the farmers of this country apply sufficient capital to the land; that is to say, I think they take too much land in proportion to their capital. The consequence is, the best use is not made of that capital. I do not believe that any man can farm to the utmost extent of profit in these days without purchasing artificial manures—*guano* for instance,—for his distant fields, thus avoiding cartage; and a larger quantity of yard manure for his near fields with deep cultivation, and better agricultural implements. Mr. Hutley, a great authority of our county, who farms 2,000 acres in a most profitable manner, said, at our Witham meeting, that he considered guano paid itself in the straw alone, besides the crop, and that he has now 100 acres of wheat dressed with 2 cwt. per acre of guano. And I can tell you further, he never feeds off a piece of clover, or a piece of fine rye-grass or tares, without giving his sheep one pound of oil-cake per day. It appears to be a great expense. But what is the result? Enormous crops both of roots and of wheat. And his system is profitable, because every two or three years he hires an additional farm.

The question of deep cultivation is very important. I know that the majority of agriculturists consider that sub-soiling is not either a profitable or a proper thing. Now that is one of the greatest mistakes that ever was made in agriculture. If you see a farmer ploughing his ground five inches, or six inches, you will find him digging his garden to fifteen or twenty inches' depth. If you ask him why, he says, "I can grow better crops in my garden by deep cultivation." How inconsistent then!—if the one operation be right, the other is wrong. Besides, if increased depth of cultivation be injurious, you must carry out the principle and say that two inches are better than three inches, and that one inch is better than two inches; and thus you must go backward, and in course of time there would be no cultivation at all. I say you must carry out the principle. What is there magical in the favourite depth of six inches, except in the power of a pair of horses to draw the plough and do an acre a day? Will any man say if his horses could take eighteen inches, he would not do it with a pair? I have sub-soiled and uniformly found it answer the desired purpose of increasing the crops. But woe betide the unfortunate wight who does this without deep drainage! If he sub-soil without drainage, he will make his land like the bottom of a pond, and ruin his crop. That is a distinction which should be particularly attended to, because many farmers have condemned sub-soiling when they ought to have condemned themselves for not having previously drained the land.

On draining I have had to combat with great difference of opinion, and a great deal of prejudice, amounting, in some instances, to a disbelief of facts. Which is the cheapest drainage? The deep drainage. It is cheaper than the shallow. I drained my clays actually 33 feet apart, 5 feet deep, with one-inch pipes. The cost of this was £3. 2*s*. 6*d*. per acre. I have reason to believe that the interest this will pay will amount to at least from 50 to 60 per cent. on the investment annually. Well then, I ask, should it not be done? I believe some of you saw the drainage last year, and I am happy to say that every drain runs freely, that the water all passes through the land, except in the particular case of a very heavy shower; for the pipes run like pumps. What is drainage to do? To carry off the water we see? That is a very small part of its operation. Water we have always considered our enemy; an abundance of water has always been considered our enemy on heavy land. Now I am prepared to prove that water is the very best friend we have; and that, if our land be thoroughly and deeply drained, we never can have too much of it, except at harvest. I am prepared to prove, and it is well known by chemists, that water is the richest manure we have. We know practically that irrigation is coveted by everybody for their meadows, and that it is exceedingly beneficial. What are the rains from heaven but the best kind of irrigation, providing we allow them to percolate the soil. They come down charged with ammonia, carbonic acid, and other gases, and, disintegrating the sub-soil, descend and form new chemical combinations. And there is another most particular use in the descent of water through the soil, and that is, that it is the only carrier of heat downwards. Nothing can you get to carry heat downwards, excepting water; therefore, it relieves the air and the top-soil of its heat, and warms the sub-soil. This is one of the most important operations of water. In summer, the surface of the ground is often 136 deg.; the sub-soil at the depth of 4 feet is about 46 deg. But the water falling on well-drained land, passes down to the drains, leaving behind it the heat it contained. That is a well-known scientific fact; and we all know the warmer our sub-soil is, the better our crops grow. Well then, what a sin and folly it is to make water-furrows, open furrows on the top to carry it away, instead of making drains below—furrows, which not only carry away the heavenly rains, but a great proportion of the soluble parts of the manure that lie near the top. I know perfectly well that, on undrained land, if you put a top-dressing of soot, and there happens to come in the course of the day a very heavy "shot" of rain, as it is called, you have the mortification to find the next morning that soot travelling down your ditches rather faster than you like to see it. Is not that a fact? But if the land be thoroughly drained and porous like a sponge, the particles of manure find their way down, the roots go in search of this manure, and up they bring it by capillary attraction.

The effect of agricultural improvement is not confined to the farmer's pocket. There are a great many classes dependent on the farmers. There are, first, the landlords. We know sometimes that good landlords do not get their rents. A kindly feeling towards tenants sometimes causes them to yield a portion of that which is really their right. I have known instances of it; but, at all events, the better the farmers are off, the better rents they can afford to pay. Then there are the tradesmen; the better the farmers are off, the better they are off. And last, but not least, there are the labourers. It is a delightful consideration, that as labour is applied to improvements, it is the happy means of affording the labourer future employment with cheaper bread, and there are certainly better wages. There is no doubt that the better the farmer does in the world, in the same proportion is he happy in expending the money freely as he gets it. I have a very high respect for the yeomen of this great country. I believe they form the basis on which society rests. There is nothing so large in amount as agricultural produce; there is no other occupation in which one quarter so much capital is invested. Bad will it be, then, for this country, when its agriculture ceases to be remunerative; because, I need not tell you, that the want of remuneration drives away capital; and, as the converse of the proposition, the more profit that is made, the more readily is capital attracted. The loss on heavy lands, by three or four wet seasons in succession, ruins many a farmer. And is not his also a national loss? Who are benefited by the money he has lost? None. In railway projects and in Stock Exchange speculations, the loss of one is the gain of another. But when a farmer on wet land in bad seasons has to fall back on the capital with which he started, and to part with the little he has at his command, why, every one connected with him, and everybody in the country, feels it alike. I have seen, with great pain, many an honest and industrious man struggling on cold and tenacious clays in wet seasons. I have witnessed changes in his temper, and the withdrawal of his domestic comforts, as year after year he has experienced his capital decreasing. I say this guardedly, because I knew in one of the hundreds of Essex, after several consecutive wet seasons, a farm that had been purchased for £18,000, being left unoccupied, could not be sold afterwards for more than £10,000. Well, then, if putting in a few inch-pipes, at an expense of £3. 2*s*. 6*d*. per acre—an expense that will not occur again—will render the agriculturist independent, as I am sure it will, of wet seasons, how important is it that such an expenditure should be undertaken!

I must allude to the protection the farmer ought to have when he invests his capital in improving the land of another. I am sure the effect of a well-regulated code of valuation, as regards incoming tenants, would be the means of calling forth a large amount of capital for agricultural improvements that is now held back. I believe I may say that with great truth. I believe that the landlords, by granting leases and such valuations, would ultimately improve their property very considerably. They would get a better class of men, for you may depend upon it that men of large capital and independent spirit will not run the risk of being turned out of their occupations. Why? Because they have laid out their money upon such occupations. His Grace the Duke of Bedford, who is a noble example to his country, and who is managing his land with great profit to himself, grants long leases at corn rents, determinable on the average value of wheat and barley; he drains all his tenants' lands, and charges them six per cent.

for it; and too happy are they to pay that rate of interest upon the capital so expended. He does not allow any obstinate man to say he will not do it, because he makes him do it by the terms of the lease. I am sure every farmer can afford to pay his landlord six per cent. for such improvements as are comprised in a good system of drainage. What is the result? His income is increasing annually. By doing away with the old trees and fences, you and I talk about, he is doing a service to his country, and everything is progressing in a satisfactory manner. The fields are straight, and the fences are straight, and there are no short lands. But there is also another part of the question. I must say that tenants very often neglect their farm-buildings. I would decidedly insert in the lease a clause, under heavy penalties, that when a tenant has got good and substantial buildings, he should be bound to keep them in good and substantial, not tenantable, repair. Fair play is a jewel. If landlords do all that is necessary to their tenants, the tenants are bound to do all that is right for the landlords.

Hadleigh.—*May*, 1847.—Mr. Mechi said, a long paper had been read about drainage, soils, rivers, and similar matters, but the writer (Mr. Hawkins) had not informed them that he had drained one acre of land in strong clay five feet deep and fifty feet apart; another acre five feet deep and forty feet apart; another five feet deep and thirty feet apart; and compared these drains with others done on the old-school principle. He (Mr. Mechi) was in hopes that he would have told them so, because a few experiments and facts saved a great deal of talking and discussion. He considered the question of deep drainage a settled one; as Abernethy said, if they had read his book on the subject, he thought they would have agreed with his practice, and with the practice of some of the most eminent men in the country, which was, Drain deep and drain wide, whether it was for springs or for top-water. In both cases they would lay their land most effectually dry; that he had proved beyond a doubt: and whether the clay happened to be ten feet below the surface, or the sand happened to be in a basin of clay, or on a hill of clay, if they would but cut their drains five feet deep, or from that to six feet, and put in an inch pipe, he would warrant that all the water would flow away, whether spring, surface, or rain water. He would make one remark upon the subject of spring-drainage, which was, that there was a great tendency in weeds to grow in strong-running springs. He recently had occasion to take up some pipes, for the purpose of making an alteration, through which ran a spring of twenty-five gallons per minute. He was surprised to find thistle-roots thirty feet long, catstail from twenty to thirty feet, all luxuriating in this subterranean drain, and in this rapid stream. He was not sure that ultimately they would not have choked the pipe altogether; and therefore he thought it was presumptuous to say that a spring-drain of constant running water would be a very durable one. There was another little fact about drainage that he would mention; that while an inch pipe, placed deeply in a strong clay, would effectually drain the land, chalk under clay, or even a coal-pit under clay of six feet or more in thickness, would not drain that clay. It was a singular fact, that a porous material under a bed of strong clay would not drain it; yet a pipe put into the clay itself would drain it. This was a fact that had come to his knowledge recently from several quarters. He would illustrate it by supposing a pail of water to be spilled in an upstairs room. They would find, as it came through, that instead of running immediately on to the floor, it had a tendency to run from end to end of the room; a few drops would fall in various parts, but the great bulk of the water would be absorbed by the ceiling. He believed that the same effect took place in chalk and various other formations under clay.

Now, they would consider the general question of agriculture. In his journey to-day he saw quite enough to convince him that they were but in its infancy. There appeared to him to be four principal causes for this unpleasant and unprofitable state of things. The first and most important was the want of what was called tenant-right. It was one of the greatest mistakes that was ever made, to suppose that the landlord and the tenant could have separate interests. He laid it down as a principle, and he thought it was undeniable, that the better the position of the tenant, the more respectable and intelligent he was, the better for the landlord.

In all matters of trade there was a security for the tenant's improvements. He had an instance in his own business in the city. He had the security of a lease, with permission to make such alterations as he thought proper, provided he did not deteriorate the property. He had the power of alienating that lease at any period of time he thought proper, deriving the full benefit of his alterations and improvements. He was quite sure if landlords generally were to grant security for the capital of their tenants, invested on their property, or rather, if the legislature once established the principle of a right to compensation for improvements, the able valuers of land in the different counties would very soon make up their minds as to what improvements really were. That would be one great benefit arising from the establishment of the principle. They would not then have Mr. Hawkins telling them that 2 feet 6 inches was the best mode of draining, and Mr. Mechi telling them that 5 feet was the best mode: it would be tried and proved, and not left to be a matter of fancy and discussion, but a matter of trial and fact. It would be the same with other questions. When a man was called upon to pay a certain sum to an outgoing tenant for an improvement, he would ask, Is this an improvement? Is it an improvement to put up a good sound building of brick or slate, or is it profitable to put it up of temporary board-and-thatch that is always requiring repair? These would be questions that would be decided by such a valuation for tenants' improvements as he had described. And he believed it would do more to produce a uniformity of practice throughout the kingdom than all the discussions that could happen at all the farmers' clubs throughout the country for the next one hundred years. It would then be a matter of pounds, shillings, and pence; and they knew practically, when they were touched in the pocket, they began to look at the question involving the outlay. He was sure that the effect of a valuation for tenants' improvements would be to turn out a large number of miserable farmers, men who were always ready to offer *5s.* an acre more for land that had been improved by some able, enterprising, and worthy tenant. He was sure it would attract, in the place of such men, a class of individuals with capital, who were ready now to invest in that agreeable occupation of agriculture, could they but see that their capital would be secured to themselves and families. But was it to be tolerated, if death struck a man in the midst of his improvements, that his family was to be sent adrift, and that the money expended in the soil was to pass into the hands of another who had not the slightest interest or share in the outlay either of time or money? He considered it a disgrace to the nineteenth century, and he was sure it reacted most unfavourably on the landlord.

Another great cause of non-improvement was the law of entail. Many a noble-minded man was desirous of improving his estates and encouraging his tenantry; but he had a large family. He knew that the eldest son of that family would have the whole of his estate at his death: and he knew if he expended money in improving that estate, that he was robbing the younger branches of the family. Therefore he did not make the improvement. He admired the aristocracy of this country. They were bright examples to the country at large; and so far the law of entail had been useful. But there was a great tendency to the increase of entails.* We had evidence that they were more than double; and the prospect and likelihood was that nearly the whole land in the country would, in the course of time, be entailed. Well, gentlemen, can we be all nobles? Can we be all men of extended property? No; we cannot become all aristocrats. If all the land were entailed, we should become, as they are in some foreign parts, *noble in name, ignoble in nature*. It might be said that the will of an

* We see new entails daily, by merchants, traders, and others, who have accumulated money and purchased lands. No doubt the pride of a name causes this interference with the liberties and rights of posterity. Why should not all other property be entailed, as well as landed property. It would be only fair play.

individual was to be respected as regarded his property. He apprehended, as a principle, the will of an individual could only be tolerated when it did not affect the welfare of the nation at large. He believed it was an established principle that the will of an individual must be made to succumb to the public welfare. Therefore, if entails were injurious to the nation, the sooner a ban was placed upon them the better.

Another cause of evil was, the *difficulty of transferring landed property*. If he had half a million of money in the three per cent. consols, he could go to town, walk into the Bank, and by paying *2s. 6d.* per cent. to a respectable broker, transfer the stock, and receive the money. The whole transfer would be settled in a few hours. But if he held a farm of 100 acres of land, and was desirous of selling it, there was a charge of $2\frac{1}{2}$ per cent. at a public auction; there were consultations and charges, and the production and signing of an enormous quantity of parchment, papers, and letters; and it was six months before he could hope to receive the money for his farm, and to have it properly transferred: and very possibly by his neglect, or the neglect of some party connected with him, he had lost or mislaid a musty old will, dated one hundred years back, of somebody who left the estate to somebody else; and he found when he had sold his property, that he could not make good the title-deed, but he was obliged to keep it whether he wished it or no, or mortgage it. He saw no reason why a piece of land should not change hands as a hat, or a coat, or a piece of calico. They were both articles of value, both articles of purchase and sale. And if they admitted the principle that the value of an article was increased by the facility of its transfer, they must take it as a converse of the proposition, that the more difficult it was to effect a transfer, the less was the value of the article. That was a subject, he thought, that must occupy the attention of the legislature; for, if landed property were as easily transferable as funded property, there was no doubt it would be increased in value, and that a great many improvements—as watercourses, roads, and fifty other things that were not now effected—would be done in employing capital and labour. Land was a thing easily identified: it could not run away. If the Government established a place similar to the Bank of England, in which all the land in the country could be properly mapped, measured, and divided, and the first title proved, there would be no more difficulty in identifying individuals in the case of a desire to purchase or sell, than there was in the transfer of three per cent. consols.

Another cause that interfered with improvement, was the want of a scientific education among agriculturists. He believed, if he had been born and bred a farmer, he should never have attempted any of his agricultural improvements. He should have done as most farmers did; he should have considered that his father had been doing what was right; that the custom of his country or village was right; and that anybody who attempted to say that it was not, knew much less about it than he did. That would have been his feeling. But when a trader, an apron-string farmer, commenced, he had no such prejudices. And he must say, that manufacturers, traders, and individuals who were trained to constant intercourse with large numbers of persons from various parts of the world, were more likely to have their ideas expanded, and to be less prejudiced than those who were confined by the particular nature of their occupation to a locality. It was in the course of nature that it should be so. He was quite sure, if science lent her aid more readily and more constantly to agriculture, they would see improvements progress more rapidly, as a matter of calculation. They would be thinking of the pounds, shillings, and pence, and of what was the most profitable way to do a thing; not how it had been done before, but how it could be done more effectually and more cheaply. He hoped the time would come when there should be an agricultural college in each county in England. He, however, did not believe they would get them until they had got the other causes removed that he had been commenting upon; but by-and-by he hoped they would have agricultural colleges like the one at Cirencester.

He would now revert a little to the practice of agriculture, for that was what they had to get their living by. He did think that what was wanted was a fixed number of agricultural principles, for the details could be worked out as each individual thought best. For instance, let them lay it down as a rule, when they had got valuation for tenants' improvements, that no farmer was a good farmer who had not got a high shaft above his premises, and a good steam-engine below. There was no doubt that as a principle, it was folly and waste of money to use man-power when they could get horse-power; and it was equally folly to use horse-power when they could get steam-power.* Because a man cost as much to keep as a horse that would do four times the amount of labour; and a real horse cost twice and sometimes three times as much as a steam-horse. If he was wrong, he should be happy to stand corrected. There were some gentlemen present who were using steam-power. He was about to use it himself, and he felt that he had acted with great want of calculation in not having used it before. Another principle was to use those implements that were necessary; never mind how many, provided a profit attached to the use of them. Never to hand-hoe when they could horse-hoe, was an important principle. It was folly to hand-hoe at 4*s.* 6*d.* per acre, when they could do the same thing better with a horse-hoe at 1*s.* 6*d.*: Mr. Garrett's

* Water-power is of course cheaper than steam, where it can be made available.

horse-hoe he meant. Another principle was, that brick, slate, or iron buildings, were cheaper to the tenant and the landlord, than board, and thatch, and poles. He could not agree with his friend Mr. Warren, who made his bullock-sheds for 30s., because he heard, in the course of a year or two, that the water came in everywhere, and the sheds were tumbling all to pieces. Was it not the same in the majority of their farm-buildings? Again, there should be no break or opening in the line of buildings. Place them as they liked as to the farm, but place them in such a way that the cold wind could not blow through them, and keep the cattle and yards cold. Another point was, never to omit to cultivate deeply. Every hour convinced him that deep cultivation was one of the farmer's greatest profits. He had been called, and he dare say, perhaps, by some gentlemen in that assembly he might be thought, an extravagant farmer:—"Oh, it was all very well for you to have these implements, and do this, and that, and the other." He was called an extravagant farmer; but the fact was, he could not afford to do as a great many people did here and in other parts of the country. He could not afford to waste his liquid manure. He could not afford to use waggons that were, when empty, a load for one horse, when he could take an ample load in a light cart, that cost half the money, with half the power. He could not afford to have hedgerows. He removed three miles and a half of hedgerows on his farm, and a nice little bit of ground they covered when collected together. He could not afford to have bad roads, getting a cart into a slough or a rut, and straining a good horse, which he had often seen done. There were many other points which at the moment did not occur to him, on which his money had been expended, and each of which had some object in view. For instance, the great principle of the quantity of seed was an important one. Last year, he believed, some individuals in that room saw his eighty acres of wheat. Nearly the whole of that was raised from one bushel of seed per acre, and a better crop for such poor land could scarcely be wished or expected. He had now some forty acres drilled with five pecks, and with one bushel, and he had every reason to believe that the crop would be a most satisfactory one at the harvest. This he had done to show them a fact—and facts were always better than mere opinions—he had one acre of barley dibbled with three and a half pecks; and one acre of oats with three and a half pecks; and every person who had yet seen them, admitted very candidly that there was a perfect plant, and enough. Now, it was a great national question, as there were something like 24,000,000 acres under corn crops annually, including beans and pease—it was of some national importance whether those 24,000,000 acres were to have 36,000,000 bushels less seed than they had at present. That was something like 4,000,000 quarters of corn. It might be more or less, but it was highly important, in these times of scarcity and starvation, that 3,000,000 or 4,000,000 quarters of corn should not be annually wasted in seed. His beans were put in at intervals of 2 feet 3 inches or 2 feet 4 inches; his peas the same. He acknowledged that during the spring he was very much pitied; his crops looked thinner than others. But, somehow or other, on the verge of harvest, there was a very different feeling; and if any of them came, he hoped to be able to see that they had also a different feeling. These questions must some day be settled. It was impossible that they could, with our increasing population and increasing intelligence, remain open questions. These were all matters of great consequence in the items of a farmer's expenditure. Then there was money wasted in another way in the washing, drying, and mangling of their dung-heaps. He did not put out his to be washed, dried, and mangled; but he took them from out of his tank or from under his animals, and carted them directly on to the land, and he ploughed them in, intermixing it all, in every possible way, with the various particles of the soil. He found practically that taking dung out of a yard after it had been well washed by the rains, and then making a heap of it, to be again well washed and dried, and then again to be moved and carted on to the land, was a great waste of time, and consequently of money. He did not chop any haulm; he could not afford it. He either mowed or bagged his wheats, and the moment they were safe in the barn or stack, the stubbles were scarified and harrowed, to prevent his having a stock of weeds that would employ a labourer in weeding for the next seven years. He thought it was very gross neglect to allow stubbles to remain through the winter: although he was a sportsman himself, and very fond of seeing a stubble for the partridge, still as a farmer he thought it was wrong. By burning the strong clay and useless subsoil on his heavy land (and he burned 1,600 loads last autumn), and applying them to his wheats and clover, he found it had been a very remunerative operation. He should follow it out this season; and while his money lasted, he should always be ready to lay out a pound to obtain 21*s*., and should endeavour to avoid laying out a pound to get 19*s*.

Agricultural Meeting at Drayton Manor.—On Thursday, the 23rd September, 1847, a party assembled at Drayton Manor, which included the following noblemen and gentlemen:—The Earl Talbot, Lord Forester, Lord Hatherton, Sir Francis Lawley, Bart., Capt. Dilke, of Maxtoke Castle; Mr. Edmund Peel, Sir Henry Delabeche, the Dean of Westminster (Dr. Buckland), Dr. Lindley, Dr. Lyon Playfair, Professor Wheatstone, Mr. George Stephenson, the Rev. Mr. Huxtable, Mr. F. Woodward, of Comberton; Mr. Josiah Parkes, and Mr. Mechi.

On the day following (Friday, September 24) Sir Robert Peel invited to dinner about sixty of the principal occupying tenants residing in the neighbourhood. Dinner was served at two o'clock, in the noble Gallery of Portraits recently completed at Drayton Manor, the whole party being assembled.

In the course of the evening, addresses on various agricultural topics were given by Mr. Woodward, Mr. Huxtable, Dr. Playfair, Dr. Buckland, and Mr. Mechi.

The following remarks were made by Mr. Mechi:—His practice in agriculture coincided so nearly with Mr. Woodward's, that it was only necessary to say that he grew alternately grain and root or leguminous crops, endeavouring as much as possible to grow wheat alternate years. He had originally drained his land 2 feet 8 inches deep, with pipes and stones, at a considerable expense; but since he had had the good fortune to meet with Mr. Parkes, he had amended his errors, and was draining more deeply and effectually with pipes alone, at one-third the cost. He rented some land adjoining his own; although he held but a seven years' lease, he drained it 5 feet deep with 1-inch pipes, at a cost of from 35*s*. to 50*s*. per acre. *He could not afford to deprive himself of the benefit of drainage.* He found it very unprofitable to farm such land undrained. The very first wheat crop remunerated him for the whole cost. The result of his improvements at Tiptree had been to double the produce of his farm and of his labour. A portion of it was formerly a swamp, not producing five shillings per acre. He had been entreated this year by a gardener in the neighbourhood to let those four acres to him, at an annual rental of £5 per acre. He had removed three and a half miles of unnecessary banks and fences. Taking the arable acreage of the United Kingdom, he thought they might safely dispense with 500,000 miles of unnecessary fencing, which, with its timber, displaced much food and labour. He considered the agriculture of this country in a very backward and unsatisfactory state compared with its manufactures. The agricultural mechanical appliances were rude, costly, and unprofitable. The farm-buildings generally were bad and uncentrally placed, causing a national loss of some millions; each ton of produce or manure costing an average carriage of sixpence per mile, renders the position of the building an important national consideration. Waggons were a most unphilosophical contrivance. It was quite clear, that a long, light, low cart of two wheels, having an area of capacity equal to a waggon, and only costing half as much, was a much more sensible and profitable mode of conveyance. The question was not now an open one, having been thoroughly discussed and decided upon at the London Farmers' Club; therefore the sooner the waggons were got rid of the better. With regard to the quantity of seed, his experiments (conducted now for three years and publicly recorded) had uniformly been in favour of thin sowing—say from four to five pecks of wheat, and six to seven pecks of barley and oats. Some of the best farmers in his neighbourhood adopted this system successfully. It was highly important in a national point of view, that this question should be settled; for if the quantities he had named were available, adieu at once to the necessity for foreign imports. It appeared to be admitted on all hands, that if a bushel of wheat vegetated, it was an ample seeding; and it was reasonable that it should be so, if each good kernel produced only one ear containing forty-eight kernels (and that was not a large one), because there was no allowance for increase by branching or tillering, which we know would take place to a considerable extent in well-farmed land containing an abundance of organic matter. Thin sowing delayed the ripening three or four days; consolidation by pressure prevented the development and action of wire-worm and slug. He had found salt tended to a similar result. He salted all his wheats at the rate of four to eight bushels per acre, *and was determined to use much more.* He knew a gentleman in Northamptonshire whose wheat crops could scarcely ever be kept from going down until he used salt, which had effectually kept it standing. He (Mr. M.) salted the manure in his yards. He found that it sweetened them (he supposed it fixed the ammonia). It was a singular fact that whilst salt tended to preserve animal substances, it, on the contrary, rapidly decomposed vegetable matter. It was a cheap alkali of native production, costing only about 20*s*. to 30*s*. per ton, whilst all other alkalies were nearly eight times as dear. He strongly recommended the abundant use of bones, with and without acid, for root and green crops. It was evident that the bones formed in our growing animals, and in our cows, from the produce of the farm, cost us 5*d*. per lb., or £45 per ton. Now if we could replace these, as we can do, by bone-dust, at £7 per ton, it was clearly good policy to use them. He considered the waste of the liquid portions of manure, in most farm-yards, a great national calamity. It was a great mistake ever to allow water to fall on manure. Water was a very heavy article. A thousand gallons weighed 10,000 lbs., and was expensive to cart. He had heard farmers say when rain was falling, that they should then litter their yards and make manure! *Straw and water in fact!* He found in practice that animals did well on their own excrements and straw under cover; that they consolidated the mass until it was four feet thick, when it would cut out like a good dung-heap, and be fit to carry on the land. But if rain-water were allowed to wash this mass, an injurious effect resulted both to the animal and to the manure. *He could not afford* to allow his manure to be well washed in the yards by drainage from the buildings, and afterwards to be washed, dried, and mangled, by pulling it out in heaps and turning over. It was a waste of time and of money. He found that his crops grew better with unwashed manure. *A farm-*

yard should be like a railway terminus, covered in, but amply ventilated. There was comfort and profit in keeping everything dry. It did away with the necessity for water-carts and tanks; the liquid portions of the excrements being just sufficient to moisten the straw and burnt earth, or other absorbent material. He admired, and practised to a certain extent, Mr. Huxtable's system of placing animals on boards. It would answer in a compact farm with good roads, and in cold climates, to feed sheep in the yards on roots. In mild climates, and dry, friable soils, it was most advantageous to consume the roots and green crops on the land, by folding with sheep. There was no expense of carting off and carting back manure. Farmers had found out that the whole of the excrements were thus applied to the land, whereas in open yards, with untroughed buildings, much was washed out and wasted. He hoped to see the time when tenants would consider it to be their interest (as in parts of Scotland) to pay 10*s*. per acre more rent for properly formed, permanent and convenient buildings and drainage, in lieu of the miserable and misplaced dilapidations of the present time. It was, no doubt, partly this difference that caused the Scotch rents to appear higher than our own. He was a decided subsoiler to the depth of at least 2 feet. It was a cheap and effective way of getting rid of strong-rooted weeds, their crowns being generally just below the ordinary depth of ploughing. He did this in dry weather, and, with the assistance of a heavy Crosskill roller and scarifier, made his fallows cheaply, quickly, and efficiently. He drilled his wheats at intervals of about 9 inches, so as to hoe them with Garret's horse-hoe. It cost about 1*s*. per acre. It was far more expeditious and efficacious than the hand-hoe, and only cost one-fourth the amount. He strongly advocated the abundant use of oil-cake and also of chalk on heavy clays deficient in calcareous matter. It had been proved that much more produce had resulted from oil-cake folding than where an equivalent amount was expended in corn. Good high farming was by far the most profitable; the starvation principle was a losing game. If we borrowed from the earth, we must repay, or we should soon find an empty exchequer.

North Walsham.—*April*, 1848.—Mr. Mechi said: When I reflect upon what has been done in Norfolk by that truly worthy member of society the late Lord Leicester, I am overwhelmed with the importance of the results produced by his extraordinary judgment and patriotism. I feel that to that noble landlord is due the great bulk of the improvement which I see has taken place in this county. I do hope and trust, and I feel, that his example is extending beyond the confines of this county. It was my good fortune to-day to travel with one of his late lordship's tenants. On asking him the former and present condition of his land, I was gratified to find that the rental had increased 300 per cent., that the land was worth four times as much now as it was twenty-five years ago. I was gratified also to find that that tenant had expended on a farm of 1,200 acres in the course of his holding, which extended over twenty-five years, the sum of £20,000 in artificial manures, and the sum of £40,000 in oil-cake; making together the sum of £60,000 in twenty-five years on a farm of 1,200 acres. Now, if that has been done with profit to the tenant, has it not been done with advantage to the landlord, and to the community at large? And is it not a most beautiful and impressive illustration of the advantage of landlords seeking for good and improving men as their tenantry, and encouraging such men when they have got them? I admire the landlords of this kingdom as a body, and I feel that many of them only require to know that it is their interest, and the interest of their successors, to have on their farms men of capital and intelligence, instead of poor, grovelling, and servile men. We know perfectly well that we are not all blessed with capital, nor all equally blessed with intelligence: but let those who are landlords and have an abundance of means at their disposal encourage such men, and seek for those who have capital. I will now proceed to the general question of agriculture, and touch upon my own practice.

I am but a young farmer, and as such I look around to those who are older and more practised than myself, to see if something cannot be learned. I think we are bound not to assume that we are perfect in our vocations, but to go on improving from day to day. I have been extremely gratified, on this my first visit to Norfolk, to see that in this district you have such good land, and that you have farmed it so excellently. It stands out in bold relief, compared with many parts of the kingdom that I have lately visited. Still, I think there are some weak points as well as strong ones. I think that your inclosures generally are far too small to be profitable, and that they are encumbered with a great deal too much timber, and timber that I think is not profitable to the landlord, certainly very unprofitable to the tenant. I think that the tenants, some of them, might trim their fences a little more neatly. The inclosures being so small, it would be very desirable that the fences which encompass them should be also exceedingly small; and when you consider that the cost of doing that is not more than threepence per acre per annum, I think that its being undone betrays a considerable amount of neglect. The waste of liquid manure, I perceive, is also rather common in this county, as it is in most others in the kingdom. I consider the waste of the liquid portion of the excrements a very great curse to this country generally; because science has told us that the liquid portion of the manure is essentially that part which will produce the kernel of our grain; the strawy and woody fibre of the solid parts of the excrements do not produce the kernel, except in a very slight degree, but the liquid portion of the manure is that which essentially forms the kernel of the grain: and as we already sell off from our farms quite enough grain which does not find its way back again, I think we ought especially to take care of that which will replace it. I am aware that it requires rather a different sort of building, and that troughing must be put up, and so on; and while I am aware that in every case it cannot be done, I am quite sure that, in a great many cases, it might be done with advantage to all parties.

The system of box-feeding is a very admirable one, and I believe that the country generally—certainly I for one—feel indebted to your neighbourhood for its introduction on my farm. I consider that all manure should be made under cover, free from water; for then the animals are sure to be maintained, and the manure will be in a more healthy condition, ready to go on to the soil uninjured, unwashed, and undried, whenever it is required. I have adopted the box system for my animals with great advantage, and I regret extremely that the whole of my farm-yards are not entirely covered up. If I had to rebuild them, not one drop of water should fall in any portion of them. I know of no model for a farm-yard so good as the large show-place in King-street. I saw there an enormous number of beautiful animals which seemed very comfortable, and I have no doubt that if the farm-yards of the kingdom were made on that principle, there would be considerably more beef produce and more corn grown. We should have less disease arising from those sudden changes of temperature which are so fatal to both man and beast. On the subject of feeding animals, I think it brings us to the consideration—a very important one—of the best and cheapest way of obtaining manure.

When I began farming, I had a notion that purchased manure —guano, nitrate of soda, and other things—was profitable; but experience has taught me that by far the most profitable way of obtaining manure—which is, in fact, obtaining additional produce—is to purchase a considerable quantity of grain, or of linseed, and to feed stock that is bred upon the farm. Mr. Lawes, in an admirable paper in the last number of the "Royal Agricultural Society's Journal," has clearly shown, that for every five pounds of flesh that is increased by the animal, twenty-five pounds is rejected or ejected in the manure. That has been proved beyond a doubt. Therefore, if we can purchase a large quantity of grain—I do not care of what sort or from what country—if we can purchase it, and sell that grain to our animals on the farm at the price we gave for it, it requires no conjurer to show that we are enormous gainers by getting our manure, of the best quality, for nothing. It was proved in the paper to which I have alluded, that where animals are purchased at a dear rate for grazing — where they are fed with hay, oil-cake, and grain, all purchased — that though by these animals we lose money, as we know we frequently do when the account is balanced, still the manure gained from them was not half the cost of guano; and of course it was far more advantageous in its bulk, which is, in my opinion, an important consideration. We know, practically, that where box manure is applied to the land—I see it clearly in my fields—that the land feels it at least a year or two longer than any artificial manure you can put on. I am not speaking of washed farm-yard manure, because I consider it is something like the tea-leaves that are left in the pot after the best of the tea has been poured away. But I am quite sure that I shall be glad to have my opinion confirmed by practical members present, that a farmer will never thrive so well as when he invests as much of his capital as he can possibly afford, in breeding stock, in fattening them with purchased food, and in fact, in selling to his stock that spring corn which is now frequently sold never to return to the farmer. He should send his spring corn to market on four legs, instead of through the merchant or miller. I consider *that* one of the most important points in agriculture; and, for my own part, I am now consuming and purchasing at the rate of 500 quarters of barleymeal annually, on a small farm of 170 acres; and I find that it answers my purpose so well, that next year I shall purchase 1000 quarters of corn. I do not tie myself to any particular sort, for it depends upon the price, but I shall purchase 1000 quarters of corn, and consume it on the farm with stock, in addition to the pease and beans that I now grow; of course in addition to all the roots and all the green crops. I am not at all satisfied that we do right in giving our animals a large quantity of roots or green food, unassisted by something of a more rich and solid character. I think that they ought to have the Swedes, the mangolds, the tares, and the rye as a sort of salad after dinner; but that their dinner should consist of oil-cake, of grain, or of Mr. Warnes's excellent compound; that the other part should form merely the small salad afterwards, and that they should not be kept, as is frequently the case, in a constant state of scouring or diarrnœa, by eating an unlimited quantity of this stuff. It may be said that the land would get too rich. There is not much fear of that; but if you think so, take a crop of wheat, or oats, or potatoes, which people will buy in London, and then take wheat again.

I hope your landlords will not tie you down when farming in this rich manner. I hope, when the farmer shows his landlord that he is not only consuming his own spring crops, but also that he is buying a good deal from other people—that he is buying beans from Egypt, Indian corn from America, or anywhere else; considering all this, I hope such a farmer will not be tied to any particular course of cropping—at all events during the greater part of his lease; because it is quite clear the effect of his making this purchase must be not only to make money for himself, but also to improve, to an incalculable degree, the permanent value of the soil.

At present, I say, we are only in the infancy of agriculture. When I go to London, I find a market-gardener, holding some hundreds of acres, who tells me that he puts on £45 worth of manure per acre for each crop. Now, when £45 per acre can be profitably invested in a market-garden in manure alone, I think we have a right to infer that we have the power of producing a very much larger amount of food, both for man and beast, than at present. I allude particularly to the green crops, such as tares and rye after wheat. Now I consider it a piece of bad farming, although it is customary, to attempt to grow those kinds of crops upon an exhausted wheat stubble. If we act on the principle that I have described, of producing a very much larger quantity of manure by purchasing food, we shall, if we are afraid of being overburdened with manure, put on forty or fifty loads per acre, for our tare or rye crop: depend upon it, it will grow all the better.

As to the mode of drainage, it ought to be up and down the hill. A very amusing instance of that occurred on my farm the other day. A piece of land on the slope had been drained across the hill, at only two feet deep. I had occasion to put in some posts for rails, on the incline below the drain, and I found that the holes were full of water, exactly level with the drain, which, although two feet deeper, being two feet higher in the rise, of course did not take the water from this post-hole. Now, if that drain, instead of being cut across the hill, had been cut down the hill, it would have met the water, and have been an equal distance from each portion of earth down the hill; or if cut four feet instead of two, the water would have found its way down to the drain: but by cutting shallow drains on a hill, and carrying them across a hill, it is clear that the water below the drain has no power to go into it, but has a long way to go to find the way into the next drain; whereas, if the drains were cut up and down the hill, every portion of soil, as it declined, would gradually find its way to the drain from both sides.

There is another point. I have been feeding on Mr. Huxtable's plan—what is called *board wages*. I find that it is a very successful practice, and I do not see that you have it in operation in this immediate neighbourhood. I have had eighty sheep on boards for several months, and they thrive admirably well; and when I tell you, that at one year old, several of them weigh twelve stone, which is twenty-four pounds a quarter for half-bred sheep, you will naturally agree with me that it is a profitable way of feeding them. I sold some of them the other day, at £3 apiece. I find, in practice, that no disease attacks sheep so situated. Occasionally, one or two, from being apoplectic and fat, were inclined to be giddy; and I was glad to see it, for they were immediately consigned to the butcher. There is no foot-rot, and they generally present a most healthy and comfortable appearance. On our cold and exposed land, they certainly thrive infinitely better than some I have tried on the old system of folding. They consume less food in proportion to the fat they put on. There is no expense for straw, and their manure falls through on some sawdust and burnt earth. By using about half a bushel of gypsum per day, and sweeping it down between the cracks, we have an excellent crop of manure to grow the turnips for next year. It is neither too wet nor too dry, but just in that state in which, on a hot summer's day, the turnip roots will find a very comfortable meal.

Saffron Walden.—*Dec.*, 1848.—Mr. Mechi spoke in the course of the evening, and said: I have a great affection for the agriculturists of this important county; they are an honest and kind-hearted race of men; but, almost as a natural consequence of that firmness and honesty, they are prejudiced; and while I esteem the former qualities, I shall never cease to war against the latter. My remarks will be esentially practical. Sir John Tyrrell says I am a good-natured man; but whether I am so or not, I am strictly a man of figures, and as you are so often referred to the balance-sheet, I devoted three whole days during the last wet week to examine into the proceedings of the last year, to see where they were satisfactory,—that is, profitable, and where they were unprofitable. I found that I had sold £500 worth of pork within the year; that, deducting the food purchased for them, they repaid me a small increase, and that I had all their manure for nothing. Those pigs were all bred on the farm; and so well does the operation suit my pocket, that next year, if I can breed enough, I hope, to sell £1,000 worth of them. My corn was satisfactory, but the labour was very high, and part of that labour was perhaps unduly charged, because the bailiff was occupied pretty well half his time in showing my visitors round the farm, instead of watching the operations of the labourers. On looking further, I found there was something wrong and unprofitable somewhere; and as I keep a minute account of every farthing paid and received, I was not long in finding out where the shoe pinched. I found that I had had 20 acres of very fine roots, which I could have sold for 10*s.* per ton, or £10 per acre, to draw off; but after I had taken the trouble to draw, cut, and hand them to the bullocks, I found, with what I paid for oilcake, linseed, and corn they consumed, that instead of those 20 acres bringing to me their worth of £200, I had absolutely lost the whole in exchange for the pleasure of feeding the beasts. I consider that when we can we ought to feed off every acre of roots with sheep upon the land, giving them oilcake too; since to grow root-crops to cart off for bullocks is a most unprofitable occupation. Why this is the case I will endeavour to explain: I find I can always sell my mutton at 1*s.* per stone, or 1½*d.* per lb. more than beef, while I find it costs me just as much, perhaps rather more, to make a pound of beef, than a pound of mutton; therefore, if I sell £500 worth of beef, instead of mutton, I have really lost one-fifth, or just £100; and, therefore, I say, let us feed off all we can upon the land with oilcake. And do not imagine that will make it too rich for corn. I hold that it could never be too rich for a corn crop if you put in the proper quantity of seed to suit the land. Where it is not practicable to feed, we must not grow mangold-wurzel; it must be a crop of tares or cabbages before the wet weather; and by that means we shall suffer less. I mention where I have lost, and that this has been the weakest part of my farming. Then comes the question, how is straw to be made into manure? There is a gentleman who does keep bullocks, but he gives them oilcake and not roots. I think we are bound to look at these matters purely in an £. *s*. *d*. point of view; and adopting that system, I think, will pay you good interest for your capital.

One point connected with drainage I had omitted to mention. There is an impression with some persons that stetch furrows are unnecessary. I have so often been asked by friends from the north, "Why do you dress your land with corduroy?" that I had to some extent imbibed the opinion that they were useless; but having on a late occasion tried a piece of land on the flat, I found that, whether in ploughing or any other operations, it was far more clung and less friable than when dressed in the usual way. That is an important fact; for, however well the drains may run, the furrows act as an additional drainage; and therefore I at once say, Do not do away with your stetches and furrows on heavy lands; and I am not quite sure that water-furrows in long lengths are not also advantages, because they prevent that running down of the land which will sometimes take place in very wet weather, even when the drains are running like pumps.

With regard to thin sowing, I have tried three experiments—one bushel per acre produced more corn than two; the increase being in one case two bushels and three pecks per acre, the other rather less than a bushel; and, in the third, the thick sowing had the advantage of about half a peck per acre. This is the third year I have tried thin sowing—one bushel against two, and, almost invariably, certainly the greatest balance of advantage, has been in favour of thin sowing. I am speaking now of moderately friable soils; and I must guard myself by saying that you ought to look to the condition of your land. Various things have a bearing upon it, and a wise man will not pass an opinion on what he sees, without the test of the bushel.

The next point to mention is my steam-engine, which I find by experience is very profitable. I use it very much for myself, and occasionally my neighbours avail themselves of it; so that it is often at work all night as well as all day. I find that the fuel, as I had previously estimated, costs 7*d*. per hour, and the attendance 3½*d*. per hour; and as it will grind 5 bushels of grain in that time, and do sundry other things, such as pump water, crush linseed, and cut chaff at the same time, I think it pays me a comfortable return of profit over and above the saving of horseflesh and taking horses from plough at particular times when they are wanted upon the land. Altogether it is a great advantage upon a farm, and I shall be happy to give any information respecting it which may be desired; but you must not calculate that a six-horse-power engine with grinding-stones, &c., complete, would cost less than £500, though I do not think that the same sum invested in three per cent. consols would yield you so much profit as you might derive from it upon your farms.

ON DEEP CULTIVATION.

London Farmers' Club: *April* 2, 1849.—Mr. Mechi said: We are all agreed that some degree of cultivation is necessary for our seed-bed; Nature herself has proved it by disintegrating the surface of our globe, using the chemical aids of air and water, and clothing it with vegetation, adapted by the Almighty Wisdom to the soil and to the climate, for the use of animated nature. In vain does man select the most imperishable material as a record of his skill; chemical affinity, by the ultimate action of heat and cold, of air and water, decomposes and crumbles to dust and to shapeless masses the architectural beauties of antiquity. It is a singular fact, that rarely do we meet with a farmer who could deny the benefit of a long summer fallow on tenacious soils — I mean a frequent ploughing of the surface-soil; and yet how few are prepared to admit the advantage of a similar operation to the subsoil! This seeming discrepancy is, however, not to be wondered at. The greater part of the heavy and hard-bottom land of this kingdom is undrained, or drained too shallow to admit of subsoiling. Experience has proved, that to subsoil without previous draining is most injurious. On undrained lands the open furrows act as drains to the disturbed soil; but, when the subsoil is broken up below those furrows, without any subterranean escape for water, it becomes after rains a puddled mass, into which the horses' feet force the upper soil or seed-bed, very much to its injury. In fact, it is a great impediment to cultivation, and hurtful to the crops; therefore drainage must precede subsoiling. There are many reasons why a disturbance of the subsoil may be profitable, where deep ploughing or digging would be ruinous. Let us beware of burying our seed-bed, which has so long been cultivated and manured; if we do this, and bring to the surface a bad, stagnated, undecomposed subsoil, we shall feel its ill effects for years. I speak practically in this matter; for wherever the yellow soapy subsoil of the new ditches has been spread on the surface, it makes a miserable seed-bed, and is most difficult to work. Let us keep the surface soil where it is; for in breaking up the subsoil quite enough of it will of necessity be mixed with the upper soil.

As the solutions of lime, manure, and atmospheric influence gradually ameliorate the under-soil, we can year by year gain one inch by deeper ploughing; remembering, however, that it will be one hundred tons of new earth per acre—a pretty strong dressing. In dealing with inferior subsoils we must be governed by our facilities for obtaining abundant supplies of lime, chalk, and manure, which would enable us to take a greater liberty with the under-soil.

I will now state what soils I consider require deep cultivation. Strong, heavy, tenacious clays of almost every description; these should be broken up in dry weather, because the treading of many horses is not then injurious; besides, the subsoil, being dry, is torn or broken up into fragments and irregular masses, which freely admit the summer heat and evening dews; whereas, if done when wet, the putty-like subsoil would collapse, and the surface become kneaded by the treading of horses. Sandy, silty, or gravelly soils, having a hard bottom of iron sandstone, or masses of pudding-stone (an admixture of pebbles with protoxide of iron, forming a sort of rusty rock-stone), these soils have generally contained much spring water, headed back by occasional veins of clay, and are much benefited by subsoiling. I find by breaking up these soils to the depth of 21 to 24 inches, instead of the common depth of 4 to 5 inches, that all crops succeed better, particularly roots, green crops, and clover. Their roots descend deeper, and are consequently less subject to injury by the vicissitudes of extreme cold or drought — of course, drainage secures them from stagnant water. I speak feelingly on this subject; for, before I drained and subsoiled my land, our winter crops were often injured, as well as our summer ones. I am convinced that it is the freezing of the roots in our shallow soils that often destroys our clover, our tares, and our wheats. I have traced the roots of wheat and tares from 9 to 18 inches below the surface, even so early as Christmas, where the soil has been sufficiently moved and pulverized; and we all know that clover roots descend very deeply into good friable subsoils. The pan or impervious mass that is often formed immediately below the plough, is a great impediment to the roots of plants: subsoiling remedies this evil. It often requires great force to break up this pan. The advantages of subsoiling on such soils as I have described are observable for several years. One result of deepening the staple is to cause a less rapid, but more perfect development of the plants. Their growth is prolonged, and forms a striking contrast to the hasty prematurity and inferior produce of shallow soils with a hard and unpulverized substratum. It is stated by Liebig, and other eminent chemists, that iron has the power of attracting ammonia from the atmosphere, which contains an unbounded supply.

If so, this at once accounts for the beneficial results of breaking up deeply, and exposing to atmospheric influences, our tenacious clays, which abound in iron: my heavy soils show by analysis near eight per cent. of peroxide of iron. Another advantage of subsoiling is the destruction of deep-rooted weeds. I know of instances where roots of thistles and other weeds, as thick as one's finger, have been disturbed by the fork and the subsoil-plough, but which were merely pruned by the ordinary plough. Dressings of chalk, marl, and heavy earths sink down in stratified layers, and in a few years are below the reach of ordinary ploughing.

Subsoiling and crossing the land by deep summer ploughings often restore to us the lost application. If we needed an argument against those immense mounds or lands so often met with in the midland counties, the impossibility of cross-ploughing them would be conclusive evidence; still, being so formed, it would be dangerous indeed to alter too suddenly the relative position of the seed-bed and subsoil. My own experience does not extend to calcareous soils; but we have evidence on Mr. Hewitt Davis's Surrey farms, that the gradual breaking up of the chalks is highly beneficial, especially in destroying or checking the growth of deep-rooted weeds. At the farm of the Royal Agricultural College, Cirencester, similar good results have been derived by deep cultivation, under the judicious management of Mr. Wilson. The soil there is mostly cornbrash or laminated limestone: the breaking up of this by deep-ploughing and subsoiling has a very noisy and rather ludicrous rattling effect.

I have generally a great respect for the practical experience of agriculturists; but I am bound to say, that on the chalks and limestones custom has assumed (without practical experience) that deep cultivation would be injurious. There are some soils in which subsoiling or deep cultivation is, perhaps, rarely requisite, except to remove deep-rooted weeds resulting from neglectful farming, or to recover a lost dressing of marl or chalk. These are loose, hot, dry sands and gravels; deep, loose, rich, friable, vegetable loams; and reclaimed felty bogs. In all these soils air and water have a very free passage. I have reason to know that in many instances some of them are most profitably managed by consolidation with sheep-folding, and by heavy rolling; the breast-plough and scarifier absolutely or nearly superseding the common plough. With regard to the mode and cost of deep-cultivation, my experience is, that where horse labour can be properly applied, it is always more profitable than manual labour; the relative weekly cost bearing no comparison with the relative power. In very strong clays during dry weather, manual labour is almost unavailable; so also in hard, concreted, rocky bottoms.

My mode of subsoiling is as follows: we open the ground 8 to 9 inches deep, with a strong, full-breasted iron plough, drawn by three horses abreast, having an equalizing Scotch-hinged iron whippletree. Smith of Deanston's subsoil-plough follows in the track of the first plough, drawn by six strong horses, breaking up 14 inches of the subsoil. The first plough turns a furrow-slice on this, and is again followed by the Deanston plough. The cost is as follows:—

Nine horses at 2*s*.	£0	18	0
Three men at 1*s*. 8*d*.	0	5	0
	£1	3	0

Quantity ploughed, 5-8ths to 6-8ths of an acre per day, seldom so much as the latter. Of course the chains and every part of the subsoil-plough are very strong: and it is severe work for six good horses in hard soils. I find a small wheel in front of the subsoil-plough a great advantage: it causes the plough to swim true, and prevents those violent jerks so injurious to the ploughman and his cattle. Compare a man using a pickaxe with the power of six strong horses applied to a point almost as small. The hard or stony subsoil, that doggedly resists the repeated hackings of the labourer, is broken up and shivered to atoms by the resistless plough, which groans and rattles as it wedges itself amongst the stubborn masses. The fork and the spade can only be advantageously employed during the winter months, in soils of a more workable character than some of mine, which are too clung and soapy in wet weather. In a more friable field I have forked, under the plough, 7 acres with advantage, at a cost of 42*s*. per acre, including ploughing. After subsoiling, the land is crossed and intermixed by a strong common drag-harrow, having teeth or spikes 18 inches long, and drawn by four horses abreast, the driver sitting on the frame. Although an old-fashioned tool, I can find none better suited to the purpose of deeply raking the ground, and bringing the unbroken lumps to the surface, to be crushed by Crosskill's roller, or to be pulverized by atmospheric influences. As to the recurrence of subsoiling, observation must guide us: there is a tendency in soils to settle down and become solid. We shall seldom err in trench-ploughing our land for root-crops once in four years. Trench-ploughing will be found easy where once the land has been subsoiled: this I sometimes do before winter, having three horses to each plough, so arranged as not to tread or solidify the work. The leading plough has a full bold breast; the second, that follows in the track of the first, has a smaller breast or mould-board. I have used Read's subsoil plough with advantage, and it is a very convenient tool for small farmers with a limited team; of course it does not go so deep as Smith of Deanston's powerful tool. In Scotland, it has (with some improvements by Mr. Slight, of Edinburgh) been considered to require less power than Smith's plough. It is the opinion of Mr. Smith, in which I entirely concur, that subsoiling greatly facilitates the passage of water to drains. I find that subsoiling materially assists the evaporative powers of tenacious soils, rendering them drier, and consequently much warmer; in fact, evaporation is a super-drainage of the soil after the ordinary drains have ceased running. When land is trench-ploughed a second time, it should be across, or at right angles with the first subsoiling. Although I advocate deep cultivation and a loose subsoil, I attach much importance to a fine, firm seed-bed; particularly for turnips, mangold, rape, and mustard: Crosskill's roller effects this comfortably in dry weather. We must all deeply regret the generally shallow tillage of this kingdom. In too many instances, the mouth of an ordinary wine-glass, or 2½ inches, is a common depth in some districts; whilst rarely can we find the furrow-slice cut deep enough from the solid land to cover the height of a wine-glass in a standing position, which is only 4½ inches. The result of this shallow cultivation is made apparent to all who travel by rail during summer; the question frequently being, which is the strongest crop, the weeds or the corn and roots?

ON THE USE OF AGRICULTURAL MACHINERY.

London Farmers' Club: *June* 4, 1849.—Mr. Thomas, of Lidlington, Woburn, had read a paper on this subject.

Mr. Mechi said: I do not think that the effect of using the steam-engine is to displace labour, for nearly its whole expense is expense of labour. If we consider the iron as taken from the mine, the coal employed in working the engine, and all the other processes which attend its completion, we cannot doubt that when a man has expended £500 in the erection of a steam-engine, and in providing its necessary accompaniments, the greater part of the amount has been expended in human labour. I am quite sure that the application of steam to agriculture is a profitable application, and I shall endeavour to give you a few facts in connection with the matter, which may be useful to those who, being possessed of steam-engines, are interested in their cost and management. But before I do so, allow me to say that I have but faint hopes in the use of steam extensively in agriculture, unless very great change be made in the system of letting farms in this kingdom. Our friend Mr. Thomas has alluded to Scotland. Why is it that steam-engines are found there almost invariably? Because the tenants have nineteen years' leases. It is quite impossible that any man can safely erect machinery involving a very large expenditure unless he has either a tenant-right enabling him to remove what he has constructed, or a long term of occupation on sure grounds, so as to be capable of remunerating himself for his outlay. If it be true that three-fourths, if not more, of the land of the United Kingdom, or of England in particular, is held by tenants at will, who are liable to removal through a change of temper, through accident, or through the death of other persons, I do say that under such circumstances there can be no difficulty in understanding why we are comparatively so backward in our agriculture. I feel strongly on this point. It comes home to the man who, while employing his capital on his own land, looks around him and feels that his neighbours cannot imitate his example with their present tenancies, without evincing an utter disregard for the welfare of themselves and their families. My steam-engine, which is of six-horse power, has cost me £150. There is then an expense of £40 for fixing; there are also required a pair of millstones, a linseed-crusher, pumps, a thrashing-machine, a dressing and winnowing-machine, chaff-cutters, and all the apparatus incidental to working. You cannot safely calculate the whole expense at less than £500. I have known instances—for example, there is the case of Mr. Bateson, of Hertfordshire—in which the cost has not exceeded £400; but from £400 to £600 is the average amount invested in the engine. Now, to come to the working or daily expenses. I find in practice that 5 cwt. of coals per day is the average consumption of ten hours' working; and that is confirmed by the statement of our friend Mr. Thomas. That gentleman says that 6 cwt. will do in his part of the country with the best sort of boiler and flue; 5 cwt. is amply sufficient for ordinary work: and with the price of coals in Essex at 20*s.* per ton, including cartage, that is 5*s.* a day for coals. Then you have to pay half a crown a day for a man. I have a boy at 6*d.* per day. I allow 1*s.* a day for wear and tear and deterioration. I also allow 1*s.* a day, and 4 per cent. as interest of money. The total expense of working the engine, for ten years, is 10*s.* per day. Now what will the engine do? She will grind, as the minimum quantity, her 10 sacks of corn per day: if I said 15 I should not be stating an impossibility. We pay, in our neighbourhood, 1*s.* 6*d.* a sack for grinding, or 3*s.* per quarter; she therefore earns 15*s.* a day in grinding. But in addition to this grinding she will cut up any quantity of chaff that I may require; she will drive a chaff-cutter, which required, under the old system, three horses; and at the same time pump water for the requirements of 200 head of stock in the yard—pigs and bullocks; crush the linseed, and work the sack tackling; and as I purchase 2,000 sacks of corn annually for the consumption of my stock, it is essential that the engine should be made to take that up to the second floor without any cost for labour. I have a strong opinion, that in addition to what she is now doing, I could render her exceedingly available for the irrigation of land. When I first had my steam-engine, I encountered what may be called the miseries of such an engine. We started remarkably well, but by-and-by we found that more coals were required, that more stoking was necessary to keep up the proper power. The coals, instead of being converted into gas, were converted into smoke. I opened the back of the breastwork, supposing that there was something wrong, where I found two barrowfuls of fine, very heavy material, like sand; it was, in fact, the mineral particles of the coal which had been carried along by the draught until they came to a corner, where they were deposited; and the consequence was, that they obstructed the free action of the chimney. I would recommend all who have engines to pay a bricklayer 2*s.* 6*d.* a month to have the bricks removed from the back of the furnace, and all foreign matters taken away, so that there may be a perfectly free draught. Mr. Thomas, in his able paper, has shown that steam-power is much more economical than horse-power. That is borne out by my own experience. I employed horse-power before I had formed any opinion as to the engine. I now find that the engine will do more work in ten hours, at a cost of 10*s.* than two relays of nine horses will accomplish during the same period. Eighteen horses can scarcely be kept at mill-work for half a crown a day each; and we now perform the whole operation for 10*s.* a day. But I must say I do not think that corn can be thrashed quite so cheaply as Mr. Thomas has stated it can.

Hadleigh: *November*, 1849.—Mr. Mechi said he was very glad to see the great changes that had come over the public mind in regard to some agricultural questions. Formerly the man who talked about tenant-right was considered an enemy to the landlords of the country; he was also generally looked on with disfavour, and it was thought that in asking for it he was asking something which was wrong for the landlord, and that he wanted to be taking something out of his pocket; but they had seen a committee of the House of Commons come to the unanimous decision that the question was a most vital one for the country, for the interests of the tenants as well as the landlord. They were aware that a bill was now progressing in the House of Commons which would certainly secure to every tenant his just rights; and no doubt the effect of that measure would be to draw out a vast amount of capital locked up and hitherto not employed in agriculture. It was impossible not to see that a great deal of money was accumulating in trade, manufactures, and commerce, and that there was a difficulty in employing it; they knew also, that practical agriculture was craving more capital. This bill, no doubt, would bring the superfluous capital of trade, commerce, and manufactures into agriculture. Though they cried out about distress, he believed it to be an admitted fact that the annual accumulated profits of this country were somewhere about fifty millions, and he should be happy to see a little of this accumulation employed in agriculture.

Witham Labourers'-Friend Society: *November,* 1849.—Mr. Mechi said they were all aware that for the last four years he had been trying comparisons between 1 bushel and 2 bushels an acre of seed; and having lately publicly reported, and having found invariably a considerable advantage in 1 bushel over 2, he had from all the circumstances given up trying the comparative results of 1 and 2 bushels; but this year he had tried the difference between a bushel and 5 pecks and a bushel and 6 pecks, changing the drill so as to deposit the desired quantity; and he found there was an advantage in favour of thick sowing this year, the 5 pecks giving an advantage over the bushel of 2 pecks an acre, and the 6 pecks of about 3 pecks an acre (that was as near as he could recollect, not having the figures with him); so that, deducting the difference of seed, the advantage was 1 to 2 pecks in favour of 5 and 6 pecks over the bushel. He thought the state and quality of the land had much to do with thick and thin sowing; for in another field, where he put in 6 pecks on the 21st of December, the land being strong with sheep's manure, they had too much straw, and had to flag it; there was a fair crop, but they all thought it would have gone down early in April, if not flagged. With regard to beans and pease he had also tried a similar experiment, and he found that the thick-sown had a considerable advantage in both cases over the thin. He drilled 4 bushels an acre of Mazagan beans as the thick-sown, and he drilled only three-sevenths of that quantity as the thin sowing—that was, he withdrew four of the coulters—and in one case the distance of the rows was about a foot apart, and in the thin sowing 2 feet 3 inches: they found the thick sowing produced very nearly 2 quarters an acre more than the thin sowing. In the one case he had 56 bushels, not a very bad crop, and in the other case only 48 bushels, showing a very great advantage of the thick-sown beans over the thin. But though that was the case with Mazagans, he did not assume it would be the case with the high-growing beans, because, once before he tried the experiment, and he found as much from three rows as he did from five; and he thought much depended on the nature of the bean. Now, as to pease, he put 3 bushels an acre as thick sowing, and three-sevenths of that quantity as thin sowing, being the white marrow pease, and he found an advantage of nearly 2 quarters an acre, the thick being 40 bushels produce, and the thin about 16 bushels less. He found that thick-sown beans were forwarder, and higher, and cleaner than the thin-sown; the thick-sown pease were the same; and there was a great deal more straw in both cases. With regard to wheat, he should certainly try the point again.

He would observe that, in regard to agriculture, it was a bad thing to assume they were too perfect. They could not go into any part of the kingdom without travelling down green lanes with great fences, 10 or 15 or 20 feet broad—they could not help seeing that the land was not half cultivated, the ditches blocked up, the buildings tumbling down, the manure washed away, &c.; and he did say that state of things must be and would be gradually remedied. Want of capital, want of skill, and want of security, were the causes of this in some cases; but he thought the force of these discussions and of public opinion would have a tendency to take away that fatal feeling in agriculture. They met with a man who was farming in the worst possible way, and if spoken to on the subject he would say, "I a bad farmer! My father farmed in the same way, and I shall keep on with it." Therefore he (Mr. M.) did say that the really go-ahead men, such as Mr. Hutley, Mr. Dixon, and others, who spent a great deal in artificial manures, and in improving their farms, did great injury when they patted on the back and encouraged the bad farmers. And now with regard to his own operations. He was perfectly satisfied with this year's crop; he never had so good a crop: he was sure it was remunerative, and that he was in the right road; and he looked to the pursuit of farming as a profitable one to himself. He was as close an accountant as any one in the room, and he knew where the money was spent, where it went, and where it came in. He did not say he had been perfect in all things, but he said the ground-work of all his operations was good drainage: part of the superstructure was good buildings; and though his 9-inch walls and slated roofs were called by the farmers of Essex extravagances, yet, if he went into details, and taking one building, stated what it cost, and then asked, will that pay? they said, "O yes! that will pay;" and so they went on. But if he said, "Would you like to pay 4 per cent. for them?" they replied, "Our rents are too high now." What he said was this, there was no part of his buildings, no part of his operations that he was not prepared to justify on the pounds, shillings, and pence argument. But when Mr. Hutley advised them to use guano and rape-cake, he said let them be careful how they dispensed with farm-yard manure, because Mr. Nesbit would tell them that rape-cake and guano did not contain all that farm-yard manure contained; for the best farm-yard manure contained everything that every plant could require; therefore, let them be careful how they parted with it. He admitted that the fatting of animals was very ruinous, and perhaps at times it would be advisable to avail themselves of these artificial manures instead; and as no farmer could make more manure than was sufficient for three-fourths of his farm, he ought to use artificial manures; but they ought not to neglect their farm-yard manure. It did not appear to him that he had anything else to say on these points; but he could not sit down without advocating the cause of agricultural improvement, which was attended with great benefit to all parties in the kingdom, in the progression of capital and the greater application of science and skill to the land. The agriculturists were not a reading class. He said they were a localized and nonreading class; but the next generation would be much improved. The son of his friend Mr. Hutley went to the agricultural college, or to Mr. Nesbit's, where he was instructed in science as applicable to farming, and therefore he would be less liable to prejudice than his father. (Laughter.) In conclusion, he would propose the health of Mr. Hutley, for he must say he admired his tendency to go ahead in everything. (Cheers.)

[The following discussion, which ensued on this speech, is very much condensed from the newspaper report:—

Mr. Hutley said he did not mean to spare Mr. Mechi an inch, for he intended to have a shot at him, and he would knock him down with sound argument, and proofs and facts. (Cheers.) They all knew, in the agricultural press, and in agriculture generally, that there were three great leviathans, who had been acting and talking, but had never shown their proofs—Mr. Mechi, Mr. Hewitt Davis, and Mr. Huxtable; and we had seen in the agricultural press within the last two or three weeks, a challenge from Mr. Hodgson, of Low Walton, near Whitehaven, to show his Swedes and his farm against theirs for so much money; and he (Mr. H.) meant, before he left Mr. Mechi, to make him a bet. Mr. Mechi had spent hundreds and thousands on his farm, which he (Mr. H.) never had to spend; and he thanked God that he had not, or he might have fooled it away as that gentleman had done; for, according to the last account, four years ago, he had expended £13,500 on 130 acres of his own and 40 acres of hired land. The offer he made Mr. Mechi was this—the farm he occupied was not the best land in the world, while Mr. Mechi had laid out £13,500 on his; but he would measure beans, wheat, and barley for £5 for the good of the society, to be laid out as the committee thought fit, and his produce shall exceed Mr. Mechi's by 8 bushels an acre. (Cheers.) He had no money laid out on his farm as Mr. Mechi had done; his was in the jog-trot way—he laid it out in the manner he thought convenient, and to employ the labourers and tradesmen; yet he would produce 8 bushels an acre more; and then came the straw, and he should say he had a load an acre more than Mr. Mechi. That was the effect of cultivation—not of talking about it, but doing it. (Cheers.) He considered Mr. Mechi as only a learner, though he set up as a teacher, and went about the country and said so and so must be done; but it was not done. Notwithstanding what Mr. Mechi had stated as to his heavy land, he would offer to thrash out his wheat and measure it against his; and then, as to the twitch, they all knew he was going to leave Abbott's Hall, and he should be a fool if he left much capital on it; yet he wou ldundertake to say it was in as good a condition as any farm in a hundred. There was a piece of Revet wheat there that was as good as any Mr. Mechi had got; and it should be recollected that Mr. Mechi was a tenant for life, while he (Mr. H.) was a tenant from year to year. Now he would stand by what he had said—he would produce 8 bushels an acre more than Mr. Mechi, and let them have it in black and white—let the result be fairly and strictly ascertained by impartial persons, for he would treat an honest man in deciding such a question as if he were a rogue. Mr. Mechi and the other great leviathans went talking about the country, and they had Mr. Caird, who had an extraordinary account of the Auchness Farm; and then it was turned to political purposes—the statements were handed to the Chancellor of the Exchequer. Mr. Mechi gave Sir Robert Peel a hint of what he was doing, and it was political altogether, for these men were subservient to their purposes.——Mr. Mechi: I deny it.——Mr. Hutley said here was Sir Robert Peel, who had done more hurt to the farmers than any other person, and he was supported by the way in which these free-trade farmers, who lived by mechanics, and not by farming, went talking about the country.——Mr. Blood said, some persons might begin to tire of these proceedings, which were generally of the same character. They began with an opening speech, and a fling at the landlords, to show how they could benefit their tenants; then came a gentleman, the best-tempered man in the world, who put himself up, like a buck, to be shot at, and was pretty well peppered (laughter); and whether he was right or wrong, he (Mr. B.) could not say. Then came a gentleman who gave them an account of some proceedings they did not know much about. But in the good old times of their meetings they had practical facts from practical men, who had tried them upon their own farms, and these he thought were more likely to benefit agriculture——Mr. Dixon would say he knew Mr. Mechi used his time, he used his tongue as every body knew, and he used his money; and he should like to know from that gentleman where he had failed and where he had succeeded; so that where he had failed they might avoid treading in his steps, and where he had succeeded they might follow him. It might tell against himself, but he knew Mr. Mechi had courage and fairness enough to tell them where he had failed and where he had succeeded, as that would relieve his personal friends of a great deal of anxiety (laughter); and it would do more. Mr. Mechi was quoted by the landlords in all parts of the kingdom, who said to the tenants, "Why don't you grow such crops as Mr. Mechi does? and you would succeed better than you do." Mr. Mechi was a great authority amongst the landlords; and if Mr. Mechi's influence was injurious to the tenant farmers, he knew no man who would be more willing to relieve them from it. He knew the landlords used Mr. Mechi's name against the tenants; that should only be done with justice, and he hoped they should have the matter clearly understood and stated, and no man, he was sure, would apply any remarks to Mr. Mechi for his failure. Let them have the books of the whole, and they should be content and satisfied.——Mr. Mechi said he was constantly twitted with the necessity of showing his accounts, and with the difficulty of his making a profit in agriculture. Now, would Mr. Hutley answer him the plain simple question he was going to put to him. He had held Abbott's Hall farm, of 680 acres, for twenty years, and had he not stated over and over again, that for years he never made a shilling out of that farm?——Mr. Hutley said he produced his books before the tithe commissioner, and by showing those books he was relieved from the compulsory agreement; for the first twelve years it was a dead loss to him.——Mr. Mechi: I feel relieved.——Mr. Hutley: It relieved me of something like £50 a year. (Laughter.)——Mr. Mechi said he was relieved by what Mr. Hutley had stated, as he had only farmed since 1844, and had to drain and do everything, and therefore he was placed in a more hopeful condition than Mr. Hutley, for the year before last he got 10 per cent. as a tenant, and 3½ per cent. as a landlord; last year, he confessed, he lost money; this year he had a brilliant prospect, and for the future a still more brilliant one. (Cheers.) He meant to bring out a book, "How to Farm Profitably," which he had in preparation, for he had no secrets on his farm; but it was rather unjust to him, after he had laid out money on things that had benefited the country, to twit him with the unprofitableness of farming, as if that did not extend to hundreds and thousands of the farmers in the kingdom. Let them look to the number of farms to be let, and no one they knew would leave a profitable farm. Therefore Mr. Mechi was not the only one who farmed unprofitably, if he did so. He challenged Mr. Hutley to discuss with him the whole management of the farm.——Mr. Hutley: I take you on the books—you have more words than I have.——Mr. Mechi: Mr. Hutley and I have a race in good farming, and when he backs a farm of twenty-one years of good cultivation against a bad farm of seven or eight years, I say it does not become Mr. Hutley. (Cheers.)——Mr. Dixon: Mr. Mechi began in 1844, and I will ask him for the return of 1847, 1848, and 1849, and will ask for no interest for capital, but for the common interest of the capital on the farm of that period, abandoning all his other expenditure, which I do not want to inquire about. I ask him this as a public man, as a teacher of agriculture, who blows everybody up—don't you? (Laughter.)——Mr. Mechi: If they deserve it.——Mr. Dixon: I ask him to give us the three last years of his farming.——Mr. Mechi: I have no objection.——Mr. Hutley said he had been in the West of England, where a person, after inquiring if he came from Essex, said to him, "My rent has been raised, and I am to farm as Mr. Mechi does, to pay that rent;" to which he replied, "If you farm as he does, you will pay no rent at all." (Laughter.) But they saw from this the injury it did. He looked at Mr. Mechi's farm with contempt. (Hear.) He (Mr. H.) stated here last year what he got from Mr. Mechi's man; then out came a one-sided letter from Mr. Mechi; and therefore he thought he would have him here this year. He repeated, the landlords took advantage of the statements made, and said to the tenant, "You must produce as much as Mr. Mechi does, or you must turn out." (Hear.)——Mr. Mechi said, in answer to that, he could state that at the Saffron Walden meeting last year, a farmer observed, he was tied hand and foot not to move tree or pollard; but six months after, his landlord came to him and said he might remove the trees, cut down the pollards, &c.; and when he asked, "What can have made such a change in your opinions?" he replied, "I have been reading Mr. Mechi's book, and I am perfectly convinced it is true." Therefore, if he (Mr. Mechi) had done evil, as Mr. Hutley wished them to believe, he had also done good. As to his crops, which Mr. Hutley looked on with such contempt, he would back against that the public approbation, and the opinion of the men who signed his book every day—men of as much intelligence, as much capital, and as much honour.]

STEAM-POWER IN AGRICULTURE.

Coggeshall.—*June*, 1850.—Mr. Mechi said: One thing is certain, that the general application of steam-power in cultivation will necessitate such a squaring and levelling and re-parcelling of the soil, as will thoroughly reform the hedge-and-ditch-row-ism and topography of this kingdom. It will equally compel a readjustment of the system of transfer or exchange of land, which should change hands as easily as the 3 per cents. A farm of 600 acres should represent a square mile, with a farmery in its centre, having half-mile diverging roads to its extremities; whereas now, under the system of old custom and unalterability, a farm of that size generally involves the intricate threadings of miles of almost impassable green and muddy lanes, with fields of every form except the right one. I am enabled to form a correct comparative estimate of the relative power of horses and steam, because, unfortunately, my first attempt was with six real horses; the remembrance of that great mistake awakens many unpleasant but profitable reflections. The mere working space required for the six horses is three times as great as that necessary for the engine and boilers, to say nothing of the stalls, attendance, and food. If a steam-horse costs only £25, it is quite clear that it is in its first cost, power, and maintenance, and durability, more advantageous than a real horse; besides, if you feed it well with coals and water, you may work it all night as well as all day.

	£	s.	d.
First cost and outlay of my own 6-horse-power engine, best wrought boiler	150	0	0
Fixing shaft, brickwork, &c.	70	0	0
Pair of millstones, gearing, and miller's tools	50	0	0
Carried forward	270	0	0

	£	s.	d.
Brought forward	270	0	0
Turner and Harwood's linseed crusher and gearing	15	0	0
Pump and gearing	15	0	0
Sack-tackle and gearing	10	0	0
Thrashing-machine and gearing, &c.	50	0	0
Dressing machine and gear	20	0	0
Chaff-cutter and gearing	20	0	0
Grindstone and gearing	10	0	0
	£410	0	0

Of course the cost must vary in some degree with the buildings. For a small additional cost I could, if necessary, drive an extra pair of stones.

DAILY CHARGE.

Coals	0	10	0
Wages of man as miller and engine-driver	0	3	4
Sperm oil, rags, candles, packing, &c.	0	0	6
Wear and repairs to engine, &c.	0	1	6
	0	15	4
Interest of capital, 400*l*. at 5 per cent.	0	1	4
	£0	16	8

DAILY WORK DONE.

(Charged at the price we should have to pay in the regular way, independent of cartage to mill, &c.)

Seven quarters of corn ground	1	1	0
130 bushels of chaff cut one-eighth of an inch long (less woman's time 7*d*.)	0	3	6
Miller's toll saved, 4 lbs. per sack, is 56 lbs.	0	3	6
Linseed crushed, water pumped, sacks raised, grindstone turned, water boiled, food steamed	gratis.		
	£1	8	0

Deducting expenses as above, this gives a daily profit of 11*s*. 4*d*., and the work done by the engine is more than ten horses could accomplish. But even if, instead of 11*s*. 4*d*. daily gain, we only conducted our business at the ordinary cost, still there would be an immense convenience in being able to do everything in our own way and at the right time, without cartage to mill, and the uncertainties of supply.

COST OF A DAY'S THRASHING.

Thirty quarters of long-mowed wheat (or 40 quarters of reaped ditto) thrashed, dressed, and sacked-up in eight hours. This would cost in addition to expense of the engine given above, viz.	0	16	8
Wages of seven men at 1*s*. 6*d*.	0	10	6
Three women and three boys at 8*d*. each	0	4	0
	£1	11	2

Or 1*s*. per quarter for the mowed and 9*d*. per quarter for the reaped wheat. The engine would do more, but these quantities

are as much as a good man can pass through his hands in the time. Having thus disposed of the statistical part of the question, I may observe that steam will have the effect of abolishing or diminishing the extent of land in grass. The facility of cutting straw into chaff, and grinding corn into meal by steam-power, will convince landlords, and tenants too, that the poor grass lands will be more advantageously converted into good corn-and-root-growing arable land. The Scotch system of two years grass for rest will naturally give way to the improved method of obtaining abundant manure, by purchased corn on boarded-floors or under sheds. My daily consumption of chaff is more than 130 bushels. If, by any mischance or repair, the engine is not at work for a few days, great is the outcry for its use. Everything seems out of joint without it. But on what-sized farms can steam be advantageously used? Here, I am sure, I shall differ most widely from the majority of landlords and of tenants of the present day. Before I answer the question, I should ask—What amount of live stock per acre do you mean to keep? If you determine to keep, as I do, £4 to £5 worth of live stock per acre, you will require a steam-engine on a farm of 130 to 200 acres varying in power from four to six-horse. Mine of six-horse power finds ample employment on a farm of 170 acres. In fact, as I extend my accommodation, I shall increase my quantity of live stock; being convinced that on this depends the increased fertility of our soil. It may be said, "If everybody did as you do, meat would be very cheap." I can honestly assure you there is no fear of everybody doing so: prejudice, or want of capital, both by landlords and tenants, will be an effectual bar to its general and immediate extension; but the sooner we begin the better, for it is quite clear that, even in this well-cultivated county, we are a desperately long way from perfection. It has been urged that the employment of steam-power displaces manual labour. However specious this objection may appear, it is not founded in fact, because the same principle of profit and economy that would induce an agriculturist to employ steam, would also cause him to drain and subsoil his land, open his ditches, square his fields, trim his fences, mend his roads, burn earth, cart chalk, keep his lands free from weeds, and do many things that tend to the increased employment of labour. Besides, the making of a steam-engine is nearly all labour, except the mere iron-ore obtained by labour. Thousands of labourers are rendered permanent and premature paupers by the slavery of agriculture—I mean, thrashing and chaff-cutting. These operations are generally paid for by the piece, or task work. The result is, over-exertion, a short cough, asthma, pain in the side, or some permanent disability. I see too many instances of this kind. Steam-power would prevent them. In conclusion, I recommend the use of steam-engines in agriculture:—1st, on the principle of humanity, as improving, by the cheapening and increase of food, the physical, moral, and social condition of the working classes: 2ndly, on the score of economy and profit, individual, parochial, and general: 3rdly, on the ground of providing food and employment for our mechanical engineers and miners, rather than for our horses: and last, though not least, as the basis for promoting the honour and safety of the nation, by increasing the number of hardy tars to navigate our coal-laden vessels, or, if need be, to man and defend "Old England's wooden walls."

Hadleigh.—*May*, 1850.—Mr. Mechi said: He had all his animals on boards, and was extending the operation; and he assured them they would succeed, as he had done, in making better manure, more manure, and more meat, by having their animals on boards, instead of putting them on straw and removing that straw after it had been worked into muck, and turning it over and recarting it after it had lost many of its valuable properties. Instead of that, let them take the pure excrement from the animals, carry it on the soil, and plough it in, and he was sure their crops so treated would exceed those grown with the primest guano. He should naturally be asked what he did with his straw. He replied, "Eat it;" that was, he let the cattle eat it, and he could keep four times as much stock. He could assure them, that if they increased their stock in proportion, taking care to add something better to the straw, they would get more manure, of a better quality, and grow more corn. He thought, also, that they did not manage their cattle well; that was, that they did not administer their food in the best mode. He was convinced that one-half the food administered in the usual way passed through the animal undigested. If they would do as he had done, and pour water on the excrements of various kinds of cattle and horses they fed, they would be astonished to find uncrushed beans, and even uncrushed oats and oilcake—it would be found almost in an entirely natural state, undigested. This would lead to the consideration whether it would pay the farmers to administer a smaller amount of food, but to render that food perfectly available to the stomach of the animal? He must think they were making a great mistake in giving so much food to their animals at so great waste. A bullock would not put on more than 2lbs. of meat per day, probably not more than one, and the average very likely would not be more than one and a half; a stone per week would be doing very well; 2 lbs. at *5d.* per lb. would be *10d.* a day. If they gave that animal half a crown's worth of food, which was often done (generally *2s.* worth), he could not pay for it. He might make muck in return for his food; but it was impossible that he could pay for more than a given quantity. He had said before, that his animals were all on boards. He assured the landlords of the country, whose duty he considered it to be to put up good buildings for good tenants, that brick and slated buildings of the best description, with boarded floors, could be put up, at an expense (if they wished or should choose to charge their tenants 5 per cent. for them), of only half a farthing per week for each pig or sheep, to keep that animal in the best way, and his manure in the best possible condition of dryness and availability; and for a bullock, ¾*d*. per week would give him an excellent lodging. He was particular on this point, because he was laying out £200 or £300 additional, and from a close calculation of the cost per score of slating, flooring, and every part connected with the buildings, he was charging himself 10 per cent., and a fat hog only paid ¼*d*. a week for his lodging. (A voice: "Is washing included with lodging?") He assured them that the animal neither required washing nor bedding, and it was one of the beauties of this principle that they might have 1,000 bullocks, hogs, or sheep on boards, and they would neither require sweeping, littering, or attending to in any way beyond the mere act of feeding them, yet they would be as clean as possible, and fit for a lady's drawing-room. He was often asked the question by those who came to look at his animals, both bullocks, pigs, and sheep—"How often do you sweep the floor?"—"Not at all; they sweep it themselves." He assured them, that by the addition of a little gypsum on the boards, the ammonia was perfectly fixed, there was no disagreeable smell at all, and the manure was taken away at intervals, just as it might be wanted. Nothing could be worse than the management of manure in this country generally. He had often asked farmers how they had grown their best turnips?—"Why, we take out the long manure, plough it in, and let it lie all the winter, and then we have far better turnips than when we put in the remainder of the muck-heap, 'washed, dried, and mangled,' by the road-side." The management of manure was a positive national and individual waste and loss; it was the very essence of losing money.

Saffron Walden.—*October* 1851.—Mr. Mechi, after alluding to the delightful bond of union that existed between Lord Braybrooke, his family, and the neighbourhood, said they had heard something of the difficult position of the agriculturists, which meant, he supposed, the position of the landlord, the tenant, and the labourer; and also, as was observed by Lord Hardwicke, of the tithe-owner and the government. There were five parties concerned, but they would allow him to invert the order, and begin with the labourer, because he thought industry was the parent of capital, and the labourer was the foundation of agricultural operations. Now, they were here to speak the truth; and he believed, from all the inquiry he had been able to make, that the condition of the agricultural labourer was most satisfactory. He was not alluding to the state of the poor-rates, because he knew the low price of produce had a tendency to diminish rates; but he said the labourer was in a prosperous condition. (Marks of dissent.) He should be happy to hear an objection, but he stated what he believed to be the truth, and why he believed it was this:—In Essex, the estimate of a labourer's week's wages was the value of a bushel of flour—that had been the general rule of action; and as the price of a bushel of flour now was *5s. 6d.*, and he heard they were giving *7s. 6d.* a week in this neighbourhood, and in his own neighbourhood they gave *8s.* and beer, it showed that the labourer was better off. (A person exclaimed, "The wages are not so high.") He knew there were some gave *6s. 6d.*, some *7s. 6d.*, some *8s.* and *9s.*; and probably the average would be about *8s.* or *7s. 6d.* Well, then, it must be quite clear that, wages being *7s. 6d.*, the labourer must be in a better state, and he was sure they were all delighted that it was so. (Hear.) Now, he went from the labourers to the tenants: he knew this was ticklish ground, and in the first place he must state that the low price of the farmer's produce—he meant of corn, for meat was dear enough—certainly entitled him to all the deductions in the cost of his productions that he could fairly claim. They knew the great items in that cost were rent, labour, tithe, and government taxation. Now, they could not complain particularly about labour; he did not think they did, and the labourer was well off; but he did think that rent should be reduced, if they were to have permanently a low price of corn, to something like a fair proportion to the price of their produce. He believed in many cases that had been done, and in many cases where it had not been done, it would be done, either from the good sense and calculations of the proprietors themselves, or from the stern force of compulsion and necessity. He came now to the tithe, and the clergy would find to their sorrow that they would sink or swim with the farmer. But the farmers must recollect that if they were paying the tithe rent-charge on a high price now, they had had that price, and were bound to pay on it. He did not say whether it was right or wrong to fix the charge on so high a scale, but he wished the tithes were higher on the farmers, because it proved that they had had more, and they should all be sorry to see it so low next year. Then they came to the landlord: and in reference to this point he felt they were in a comparatively happy district, for he was sure the landlords he saw there were too much men of business to expect their tenants to pay their rent out of capital; but if the tenants got a proportionate reduction, he did not think they would be so badly off. They heard a good deal about agricultural ruin. Now, in commerce, when they heard a man was ruined, when they looked for him he was gone, and his name was in the *Gazette*; but when he (Mr. M.) came here, he still saw the same happy faces. He did not say all, but he saw a great many that he had seen before, continuing in the same tenure. He could only say that he recognized those honoured names, the Claydons, and the Webbs, and the Jonases, as being still there, and long might they remain! But he would not hear of their being ruined, because he did not believe it to be the case. He believed, so far as foreign labour went, they had nothing to fear. Then, as to the manufactures, trade, and commerce of this country, let them look at the advantages the agriculturists possessed from these. He had said to these foreigners, "What do you do with your corn?" and they said, "We send it to England; we cannot afford to eat it ourselves, and we send it to you. It is with meat the same; it is half the price, because we have no one to sell it to;" and the agriculturists in this country would be in the same state if they had not a district which afforded a market to send their corn to; he sent his corn to the manufacturing districts, and, therefore, the greater the union between them the better for those two interests, and the happier for the country at large. Then, again, look to the difference in practice in agriculture in different parts of the country. There was as much as 2½ per cent. difference, and this, in any manufacture, would cause its entire removal from one part to another, and he did not know whether 1½ per cent. would not do it. Essex, for instance, ploughed with two horses, and stood pre-eminent for ploughing, while in some other counties they used six in a line; and having appealed to a surveyor in Herts on the subject, he sent him the allowances made there for the ploughing on heavy land, and he found the first ploughing 13*s.*, the second 11*s.*, the third 10*s.*, and the fourth 8*s.*; and he believed there were four ploughings for wheat. Then let them look at the extraordinary discrepancy as to the form and size of the fields, and the system of management. Look at Norfolk and Cambridge, and they sow large fields. He knew a farm in Norfolk of 1,000 acres in only four fields; he went into Devonshire, and he found there a farm that a gentleman told him the tenant had left, and he could not let it; and, on inquiring what it was, he said it was a farm of 67 acres, and there were 27 fields. Thus, he had 27 gates to open, had got 27 headlands, and 27 hedges full of trees, and then the tenant could not live. Was that a solitary instance? He appealed to a noble lord there, whether he did not know one whole parish in which there was an average of three-acre fields? Then, what conclusion could they draw but that agriculture was in a most backward state, as compared with manufactures and trade. He believed they would have to produce corn as the manufacturer did his cotton; for the manufacturer sold to them at one time for 3*s.* 6*d.* that which he now sold to them at 6*d.*, and got a better profit. How was that done? Not by the old clumsy system of weaving by hand; but let them look to what had been done in manufactures, to the capital invested in machines, not only to make the article, but to make the machinery, as shown in the Great Exhibition.

TIPTREE HALL.

Then he said to the agriculturists, compare your own clumsy contrivances with this; and I do say agriculture is far behind in its application of steam-power, in drainage, in fences, and timber; your buildings are badly placed, and before you can produce the article at a cheap price and in abundant quantity, you must remedy all these things. With respect to taxation, he thought it did not require any conjuror to show that they bought all their things at the cheapest rate. ("No, no.") Why, his lady bought two beautiful dresses the other day for 7*s*. 10*d*., and he bought an umbrella the day before yesterday for 18*d*. a very good one. He stated this to show that the expenses of the farmer were reduced in a great degree by the articles imported for his use.

Annual Gathering at Tiptree Hall.—*July*, 1852.—Mr. Mechi said: The number of our acres was unalterable, but the population was multiplying rapidly, and farmers' sons came of age every year, but acres had no sons; and therefore it was quite clear that, so long as we had order, peace, and good government, the rent of land could not be sensibly diminished. Well, then, if they were to continue to pay the same rent, and were to come in competition with those broad acres and those mighty rivers that Mr. Lawrence was so well acquainted with, it must be done by investing more capital, more skill, more intelligence, and he would say less prejudice on our own broad acres. Let them drain their lands; but before they could drain their lands they must drain their heads. When he met with a man full of prejudice and love for old customs, and he talked to him of draining or other improvements, that man did not tell him "The honest truth is, I am opposed to it from prejudice;" but he asked, "Where is the money to come from?" But he said, have a reform in the English brain; clear out prejudices, and the money would come whenever they like. Let them look at what was done about railways. At Colchester and at other places they would not have the railway come near the town—oh no, they drove it as far off as they could; but seven years after they had to make branch lines, in order to secure the benefits for the town, because they had prejudice, and opposed the plan in the first instance. Therefore, to effect improvements they must make an impression on the brain—they would then touch the pocket, and would find the money when it was wanted; only show it was profitable, and they removed prejudice, and the thing would be done. Therefore he had hopes that within 100 years, when his body was turned into a large cabbage or a great turnip, as it would be, for Nature would not let it be wasted—she would not let anything be wasted, but was carrying on a constant system of reproduction—then this matter would be understood, and the 5,000 oxen and all other things that were sent to London for the supply of the population, would speedily find their way back to those who sent them, to sustain their agriculture, and refresh and fertilize their fields, and reproduce the same articles to be sent up again.

Lord Ebrington had stated that they had eighty representatives of water companies in Parliament, and he believed in a century more they would have eighty representatives of manure companies. He said it was impossible for a man to travel through the country without seeing that there had not been capital enough, or education enough, or intelligence enough, employed to bring out the full capabilities of the soil. But they must alter that; and this brought him to the subject of education. He lived here in a parish of 5,000 acres—they were raising a subscription to build a school, for they had only a room 15 feet by 11 feet, and a female to superintend it; and how much did they think they had collected for education on this 5,000 acres, or a population of 1,200 persons? Why, among dissenters and all they raised £15 a year to build the house, pay a schoolmistress, and do all that was required for the education of that population. He hoped those whom he addressed had been to the Lewes show, and had seen the machines there, for they would have seen that they were of a nature that must involve the employment of a considerable degree of intelligence in those who were to superintend their operations; but where, he asked, were they to find the labourers to work them, with £15 a year for education. He was aware that various circumstances prevented the raising of a larger sum; but when the surveyor called on him for his rate, he found that they could raise 3*d*. an acre for the roads, but could not raise three farthings to develop the intelligence and the mind of the people about them; he did feel that it was a matter that wanted altering. His men felt it. His man had said to him, when he pointed out to him the principle and the nice action of a piece of machinery, "The Almighty has given to me the mind to understand, but man has not given me the power of developing it." And when, as Mr. Lawrence knew, they had annually devoted 200,000 dollars to the education of the people in the state of New York, they must feel we had been here asleep. It was his fate to belong to the Council of the Royal Agricultural College, to which he devoted twelve days in a year, and his friends pitied him, as they said they did not want science, they wanted practice; but the feeling on this was improving, and the Agricultural College at Cirencester was paying, though, he was sorry to say, they had not one farmer's son amongst the lot last year. He did not make this as a charge, but it was a misfortune. He said, give me science; it is the parent and guide of practice; and those who practise it would save millions in costly experiments, if they had science to guide them.

Royal Northern Agricultural.—*August*, 1853. —Mr. Mechi said: If farmers would only make an agreement with their friends in town, that all the beef, mutton, butter, and eggs which they sent in should be returned, after they had done with them, for the restoration and renovation of the land from which they came, they would be pursuing the plan which he adopted. They might think him a little visionary, or rather far-sighted, but he saw clearly that another half-century would not be permitted to elapse before the people would no longer pursue the thoughtless—not to call it by a worse name—plan of allowing the very best means of reproduction to run to waste into their rivers. There are 90,000 inhabitants in Aberdeen, and the refuse of this city, giving three persons to the acre, would fertilize no less than 30,000 acres of ground. Practical farmers know that a man with his 300 sheep upon 100 acres of ground, has no bad bargain in the way of manure. What, he might ask, became of the millions of quarters of corn which passed through the bodies of the citizens of London? He was satisfied that if the refuse of our food was turned to right account, this country might be the richest agricultural country in the world. The reason they had not attended to this hitherto was just because they had not thought of the thing. However, when a matter such as this was once brought before an Englishman's mind, it was not long before he tried it practically; and he believed that when agriculturists here once made up their mind to try this liquid manure, the thing would be done before they could say, "Jack Robinson."—He said: I have two miles of underground iron piping, and I can put on the liquefied manure, and pour it in three feet deep, and bring the cart home again for three farthings a ton, a sum so ridiculously small, compared with the usual expense, that I think I may strongly recommend the plan to your notice. You have heaps to make and turn, you have your carts to drive and bring back, you have roads to mend, and there is much expense in preparing manure for turnip crop; but in my case, supposing my bullocks deposit 100 loads of pudding upon the boards, I fire at it in the morning with this fire-engine, then it goes in a stream to the great tank, from this it is forced in a fluid form anywhere within two miles, sinks into the ground to the very roots of the crop, and is in action 24 hours after it is dropped. Suppose I wanted to put guano on my field: I put it into the tank, agitate it by an air-pump, and in a quarter of an hour you will see it pass out in a stream, going down into the subsoil to the roots of the plants. I believe I was the first who attempted to send out all the manure in this way. Last year I had 20 dead horses and some dead cows, besides the puddings, in my tank; I had 30 feet of solid stuff, and though I had air-pipes at the bottom I could not lift the mass. Luckily it dropped into my head to apply the air-pump—I pumped down the air, and the solid matter was set in motion till brought within the line of suction, and that took it away. All these dead horses, except the large bones, have gone through a hole the size of my finger. When a mass like that is brought into contact with water, you can have no idea of the chemical forces that act upon it. The gas of fermentation is taken care of by the water; it does not go into the air, but is laid up in store in the water, to go off in the fertilizing stream. Water itself is manure for grasses, as is well known by those who have moist meadows, and if it were mixed with the excrements of your animals the results would astonish you.

Witham.—*October*, 1853.—Mr. Mechi said: I assure you it affords me great pleasure once again to meet you at this table, in furtherance of the objects of the Witham Society. It is called the Labourer's Friend Society, and perhaps on that account I shall not be considered an intruder, as you are aware I have spent a good deal of money on my small piece of land at Tiptree, and, whether judiciously so or not, it is quite certain that it has conduced largely to the comfort and the morality of the neighbourhood. When I look at the million of bricks I have used, and the some 120 or 130 miles of drains I have made, nearly all of which was labour, I feel convinced it was a happy day for the neighbourhood that I was so inclined to spend my money, although it was a great source of satisfaction to me in other points of view. I do not admit I was wrong in so spending my money. I do not say I did everything as cheaply as it might be done; but I do think an investment in brick and slate is very much cheaper than board and thatch. I think it is a matter worthy the consideration of gentlemen, both landlords and tenants, that brick and slate are the things, after all, particularly for cottages and farm buildings; at the end of 10 or 12 years they are as good as the first day when they were put up, and are, therefore, the cheapest things we can use. The system of irrigation I have adopted certainly does wonderful things. It will change a bad pasture into a good one in the course a year. There is not a person in this meeting who will not be able to confirm what I say, that do what you will, and spend what you will, it is difficult to get good pasture on the hard yellow clay; but the irrigation appears to make the old plants die out, and brings you in a new stock of grasses and clover, that makes the animals look better, and enables you to keep more per acre. I have a strong opinion, which is confirmed more and more every day, that steam will shortly be the power to cultivate most of our soils, and for this simple reason, that horses soon get tired of hard work. We never allow them to plough more than an acre a day, when they are taken off and sent home, because you know it would be against your interest to make them do more. On the road, the power of a horse regularly worked is exhausted in an hour; he takes a coach 7 or 8 miles, that is one stage, and he is then taken off for the remainder of the day—he is worked

1 hour and he rests 23, and he cannot do more than 6 days out of the 7. But if you get a steam-horse, and feed him with coals and water, you may keep on to the end of time, or till it is worn out. I believe that steam-power is as important in the cultivation of the land as in any of the other operations in which it is employed. The great difficulty of the matter has been to get the great weight that was thought necessary to give the power on to the land, but, I think, by our machine (Romaine's) we shall get the power of 10 or 12 or 15 horses concentrated into the weight of 2 tons; and if we do get it in 2 tons, with the power of 15 horses we shall be able to move a great deal of soil at little cost. Whether the tilling of the soil, the preparing of it, and the seeding, can be be done all at one time remains to be seen. The inventor says that a rabbit, when it scratches up a piece of ground, covers it by what is scratched up from that which follows. This will be the principle of the machine. If it make a hole, it will fill it up in the same way; and if it succeed in that, and roll the land, it will be a great convenience to the farmers. But, I think, in seven years you will see forty different plans for cultivating land by steam. I can only say that so long as I commit any follies or do anything worth looking at, you will be quite welcome to come and look at it whenever you please.

Tiptree Gathering.—*July*, 1854.—Mr. Mechi said he thought this really a case of wind and water. He heard gentlemen on his right and left laugh, but he repeated it in all sincerity and gravity, that it was a case of wind and water: and when he told them that 75 per cent. of their bodies was water, that 20 per cent. was wind or gas, and 5 per cent. inorganic matter—or matter, he ought to say, that was soluble—he could only arrive at the conclusion that this was a very light meeting. Science would tell them—they had had Davy, and now Liebig and others, who would tell them—that if they had not wind and water they would be blocks of wood; for if there was not a fluid, where would be their circulation? When they came to have an agricultural education, such an education as would fit them for their calling—and this must come—the company would not laugh at such a statement as this; for, as his friend Caird said, he was beaten in grass because he had 1,000 tons less water than they had in the western parts of this kingdom. That water was what?—it was everything; and when he cleaned out his boiler after some time working it, and took cartloads of solid matter out of it, he at first wondered where it came from; but if it had not these things, which entered into the circulation of the plant, that plant would soon want strength and life. Plants searched for, and took up, and fed on these things. As an instance of it, if they put a vine within ten feet of a river, it would send a root out that would reach the water and take it up; thus showing that if the plant had not reason, it had instinct. But we did not understand this as we ought to do; and when they looked into the schools of the country, and asked, "Where are your books on agriculture?" they said, "Oh, we don't know anything about that." He told them that agriculture was not now what it would be 100 years hence. There were thousands of things in regard to it yet undeveloped, and our children would look back on their fathers and say, "What a stupid set of fellows they were; what a pity that science did not rise and enlighten their minds." But he would not quarrel with the farmers as to whether they should turn up the stiff clay, he would not go into matters of detail; but he took the broad principle of education, and he said, "You must teach these things to those who are to enter on the pursuit of agriculture; they must be pondered over, and studied, and understood, or you will not grow your quartern loaves as you ought to do." Let them look at the leading article of the *Times*, and see how it was that consols came to be at their present quotation. He said it was all a question of victuals. If they stopped the stomach, they stopped their commerce, their arts, their sciences, their manufactures; and as for their friend Dr. Lyon Playfair there, if he had no dinner for a fortnight, good-bye to all his science. He believed the time was coming when they should be awake, and not insane, as they were now; the dinner which they ate to-day, would reproduce itself to-morrow; that was, provided they did not send it down the Thames to pollute the water, instead of sending it to the land where it would fructify and reproduce itself again. Gentlemen had seen his children, and he would say that if those children fed on the milk of London, deprived of that nutritious quality which was lost by its being thrown away instead of being sent back to the pasture, they would find they would want bone, and muscle, and development, for that was the cause why all the children of London had crooked knees and bow legs; because the excrement that ought, by its use, to make the milk rich, thus bringing up the bone and muscle, and development of the child, was thrown into the Thames. So long as they threw that into the Thames, and went to Peru and purchased guano at a high price to replace it, he did say they were not acting as business-like and sensible men, and as they would act when the matter came to be understood. He would not measure this meeting, this great and important and scientific meeting, by details, but he took the principle, and he said, "If God does not give you ten inches of rain, you must go to a river, if you have one near you, and pour it on; you will thus double your stock, increase your corn, and thus you will increase the employment and the food of man. He would not detain the meeting, as he might do on the subject, he would write it out some day; but he did say it was a question that bore upon the moral, the social, and political welfare of this great country. He held it as a great principle, that that which was not profitable to agriculture was not a thing that it was proper to advocate; if it was not desirable on the ground of profit, it was worthless. Now, it would be said, "Where is the money to come from?" His reply was, he had now at that table the president of a body in London who would lend them the money for all these things if they could pay 6¼ per cent. for it, to be repaid in 21 years; and he did say, if they did not borrow it, they did not know their own interests. But he felt humbled when he saw those gentlemen from the city, and saw that they had companies in the first, second, and third floors for the improvement of the land in almost every country in the world; there was not a country they had not their money in, but they had not money in the improvement of English agriculture. He said it was a disgrace to them. Was there not ample scope in this country for that employment? When he travelled thousands of miles by railway through the country what did he see? Poverty, and a fixed rent, fixed tithe, fixed labour, fixed everything, and a limited production! It was like a gentleman having a large shop and nothing in it, and the rent of which was thus in effect doubled or trebled, because he had not sufficient stock in it to make a profit. These things must be altered; the change must come, and therefore in these meetings he called together the people of the towns and the people of the country, for he felt it was only by such a combination that they would get more agricultural knowledge; for if they went into agriculture and did not understand it, it was of no use. He said, therefore, have your college in every county, so that those who were to practise agriculture should thoroughly know their business. Depend on it a man must learn his business by acquiring information, by study, and by practical experiment; and what he wanted to see was for the towns to introduce schools for agriculturists, and see that they really did understand agriculture before they turned them into the country to employ their capital in the pursuit. For himself he followed his destiny in the course he took, feeling that he could not allow agriculture, for want of exertion on his part, to remain as it was in this great kingdom.

Braintree and Bocking.—*October*, 1854.—Mr. Mechi said that, somehow or other, however disagreeable his principles might be to some, he generally found that, personally, he was well received. The great question of the day was the question of manure. There was not a farmer who did not tell them that he could not produce a great deal more beef and mutton, and a great deal more corn, if he could obtain more manure. Let them therefore look to the sources from which it could be obtained. He had a letter from his friend Mr. Walker, of Rugby, who had taken all the good things from the people of that town, and, by the process by which it was carried on to the land, the sewage of the town was forming food for the people in the course of something like twenty-four hours. Now, they had 8,000 or 9,000 people in these two towns; and he asked them—Would not the manure of that number of sheep place any farmer in this neigbourhood in a much better position? He should like to ask Mr. Hobbs at what he valued the manure of one sheep per year? (Mr. Hobbs said he did not know.) Mr. Mechi: "Is it *5s.* a year?" (Several gentlemen replied "Yes," and some said more.) Mr. Mechi: "Then, if they had 8,000 people, it would be worth £400 at *1s.* per head; at *6s.*, £2,400; or at *5s.*, £2,000." Now, he was told he was a visionary man; but what he complained of was, that the farmers did not keep proper accounts. Mr. Walker had bought the manure of these 8,000 people of Rugby for £50 a year, under a lease of twenty-one years; and he (Mr. Mechi) hoped they had some calculating man amongst them here who would follow his example, and take the manure of Braintree, but not the manure only—the water also. At Rugby they had 150,000 gallons of water per day used, and Mr. Walker therefore not only got the sewage of Rugby, but 150,000 gallons of water a day to mix with it. Now, so important was this mixture, that Mr. Telfer, of Ayr, writing to him (Mr. Mechi) yesterday, said that he had put on guano in dry weather, and had watered one part, and left the other unwatered; and the difference was 75 per cent. against that which had not been washed in. Now, if this could be brought home to the farmers, he knew there was no class of men so keen as to the pounds and shillings as the farmers of England. If they were all agreed that a sheep's manure was worth *5s.* or *6s.* a year, that of a man must be much more valuable. So much for this subject, and it was a great one. They should, he hoped, no longer permit that the good things of this world should flow down their rivers while they were crying out for guano from Peru. Then it was asked—"Where is the money to come from?" A man of his acquaintance, who said so three years ago, had now found £300 to buy a steam-engine. Landlords had said they could not put up covered buildings; but when they came to learn that they were for the benefit of both landlord and tenant, they would put them up. The most difficult lands in this country to manage were those on which they could not keep sheep in the winter; but if gentlemen occupying such land had a covered yard and boarded floor, to which their animals could be brought home in wet or severe weather for a few days, eating straw and so on, there would be no hindrance to their keeping stock, because they had the opportunity of turning them out in the daytime, and bringing them home at night to warmth and cover. He contended that it would pay both the landlord and tenant to make the necessary outlay for putting up covered buildings. There was one other thing he should mention: it was exceedingly gratifying to him to see a large improvement in the housing of agricultural labourers. It was no use mincing the matter, but they were justified in getting out of their labourers all the work that they could in a proper manner; and if they had four miles to walk to and from their work every day, how materially must that lessen their capacity for work? Would any farmer think of sending his horses that distance, and was not the muscular power of the labourer of as much importance as that of the horse? He hoped that landlords, being no longer tempted by a particular law of settlement, would erect cottages on their estates, so that the men could have ready access to their work. Then their mechanics enjoyed the advantages of literary institutions, of reading-rooms, and museums; and why had not the agricultural labourer the same advantage? He would suggest that they establish reading-rooms in their several parishes, supplied with papers which they themselves had done with the day before; so that the labourer might read the spirit-stirring articles on the battle of the Alma, instead of retiring to his home, like his pigs, with his mind wholly unenlightened.

ON FARM BUILDINGS.

London Farmers' Club.—*November*, 1853.—A paper on this subject had been read by Mr. Bullock Webster.

Mr. Mechi agreed with Mr. Webster that it must be laid down as a rule that the cattle on the farm should be sheltered. One suggestion which he would venture to make was, that all farm buildings should have a steam-engine, fixed or movable, in connection with them. Then came the question whether the manure was to be removed daily, or to remain under the animals in covered yards, straw being added. He believed the latter practice to be sound, provided there was sufficient ventilation. He sold off his farm annually meat to the value of £2,500. His losses of late had been little more than nominal, and this he attributed to the circumstance that there was ample ventilation. As regarded the best method of securing ventilation, he thought it ought to be obtained from the bottom rather than the top of a building. He would tell them why he was of that opinion: in his sheds, the floors of which were boarded, he had on a level with the ground a number of 6-inch pipes, placed within 9 inches or a foot from the floor; and it was a singular fact that, while there were large openings above, the smell issued from the lower far more than the upper part of the building. The inference was unmistakable; and he considered it, therefore, highly important that in stables and cattle-sheds, especially such as were made of brick, and therefore impervious to the air, an opening should be made below as well as above, in order that the circulating air might be complete.

Another point for consideration was, the question of the construction of boarded floors as part of an improved system of farm buildings. He had always entertained a great dislike to boarded floors, as far as comfort and appearance were concerned; but after eight years' experience, he thought the balance was decidedly in favour of boarded floors. He could assure them from that experience that, if they divided a lot of bullocks, keeping one half on boards and the other half on straw, the butcher, when he came to make his selection, would go first to the bullocks on the boards. As regarded both sheep and pigs, he was convinced that boarded floors were best. When he put down his boarded floors, he certainly did not do so with reference to irrigation; but having commenced irrigating, he found he would have been obliged to adopt boarded floors if he had not done so previously, because the manure which fell to-day was, under the boarded system, washed out to-morrow and distributed over the land, so as to enter deeply into the growth of plants. He agreed with Mr. Webster, that barns should not be used for the future as they had been. In his opinion they should be used chiefly to keep a certain quantity of straw in a dry state, to be cut up as food for animals. He was glad to perceive that they were rapidly approaching a period when the system of cutting up food for animals was likely to be almost universally adopted; and if the great bulk of the straw were consumed, together with cake and roots, it would, he thought, be found a most valuable addition to the feeding powers of the farm. With regard to the amount per acre which it was necessary to invest in farm buildings, the evidence on the subject was to the effect that for the general purposes of farming, about £5 per acre would suffice. There might, indeed, be some advance on that, now that the cost of labour and materials was so greatly increased; but a great deal would of course depend on the circumstances of different localities.

Carlisle.—*July*, 1855.—Mr. Mechi said: I never enter an assemblage of agriculturists without feeling that they have looked upon me once, if they do not now, as a visionary enthusiast, only anxious to waste his money for the sake of obtaining notoriety, or gratifying some crotchet. I am constantly told, when I recommend certain improvements—"Oh! it is all very well for you, Mr. Mechi; you don't mind spending your money; and it is very kind of you to try experiments, and so on, but we have to *live* by *our* business." Now, gentlemen, we all agree that you can lay down no general rule as to course of cropping, period or quantity of sowing, or other details dependent on soil or climate, which vary almost in every district; but there are certain great principles quite independent of all such considerations, and also quite unconnected with Mr. Mechi's success or failure as a farmer. Drainage, on strong clays, wet bogs, or other soils—non-filtrative naturally—is a great general truth; so is the application of steam as a motive power instead of horses. Irrigation, when water of a proper quality is available, is another undeniable principle. So is the admixture of soils, the care and economy of manure, the erection of sufficient shelter in buildings—the convenient placement of buildings, good roads, the use of artificial manures for green and root crops. These operations all cost money—but they all pay—that is, if *any* farming will pay. I say again, the question of agricultural improvement is not dependent upon Mr. Mechi's success or failure. Tiptree farm might have been brought to the hammer, but deep drainage on strong clays would still have been a great truth. I know that many a hard battle has been fought over my agricultural suggestions or pretensions, but I only did in agriculture what I would do in any other business, prefer common-sense truths to old prejudices. I am happy to say I have succeeded, and am now well remunerated for my exertions. It is not the man who farms at the least expense who makes the most money,—on the contrary, the "bread-and-cheese" principle of non-improvement entails poverty and misery. The real question is, what does it cost per quarter to produce your corn? Nine times out of ten it will be found that those who spend the most money per acre get their produce at the lowest cost, and of course make the largest profit. I believe that if rents were doubled—(laughter)—don't be alarmed, gentlemen—(renewed laughter)—the farmers would be better off—(great laughter)—provided the increase represented the fair interest for drainage and other necessary improvements. It has been well stated by a well-known practical farmer (Mr. Hope, of Fenton Barns, East Lothian), that if he spends £1 per acre, or £600 a year, on artificial manures, he makes a profit; if he omits to do so, he farms at a loss—and I believe it. Some of the most successful and wealthy men I know of as farmers are those who have expended their improved means in large agricultural amendments. Indeed, I know one who, in the course of a long tenure of a large farm, has expended £50,000 on oil-cake and £25,000 in artificial manures—and I believe that is a point which particularly affects your county: there is no secret about it—the gentleman I refer to is Mr. Hudson, of Castleacre, one of the late Lord Leicester's best tenants. I can only say if you do as he has done you will make the best of it—buy estates for yourselves. The scythe is the farmer's great enemy. Cut off your green crops with sheep's teeth, and cram them well with linseed or rape cake. Thus you spare labour and two cartages, waste, and manure. He is a wise man who never makes a dungheap. The great want of agriculture is manure. You see evidences of this in almost every field. Every patch of luxuriance indicates by its contrast with the rest of the field the wonderful effect of a more abundant manuring. When travelling I always look out for oilcake-troughs in clover and turnip fields, and can pretty well judge, even at railway speed, by their presence or absence, how farming goes in that district. Don't tell me that land can ever be too rich for wheat. Give me a rich garden to grow wheat in, but then I would solidify it well before sowing, regulate my quantity of seed, and in the spring take care to hoe out the plants to a proper distance, according to the richness of the soil. A glance at your own well-farmed fields shows me that even your corn crops would be heavier if you used a little more cake or guano. It would enable you to break up your seeds after one year's crop, thus keeping your land clean. The streams of bread, meat, beer, milk, and vegetables, that constantly flow into London, so poison the Thames and the population, that folks are really thinking it will be prudent and profitable that the aforesaid necessary articles should be made to flow back to the lands from which they came, and that the farmer should no longer be compelled to restore what they have exhausted from the land by birds' dung from Peru, oilcake from every country in the world, and bones from all the yards and graveyards of Christendom. The recent investigations I have had occasion to make as juror at the French Exhibition have led me to the conclusion that our industrial superiority is mainly dependent upon the accessibility of raw material, and the vicinity of intercommunication by sea and land—but above all, by an abundant supply of cheap and good food. This can only be accomplished by an unflinching competition in production with other nations, by mighty steam, by economy of manual and animal labour, by larger productions in a given area, by increased cultivation and manure, by improved buildings, by drainage, by irrigation, and by a larger application of capital and intelligence. The necessity for a greater investment of capital in agriculture becomes every day more apparent; and yet, strange to say, the only two companies at present existing for the necessary advances are at the *West* end of the town. There is not one in our great city. On taking up the *Times* of Wednesday last, I found that Messrs. Rothschild and Barings are willing to become the medium for investing 750 millions of francs, or a considerable portion of it, as British capital in the new French Loan. How is it that agriculture does not ask for such a loan? There is plenty of money in Great Britain; but although the security on land is undeniable, the interest satisfactory, and the necessity great, there is an apathy in the matter to me perfectly incomprehensible. A hundred millions sterling might be forthwith invested with considerable advantage to borrower and lender. A much larger sum would be required for the full devolopment of our national agriculture; but the investment I speak of, in drainage and other immediate necessities, would increase our food supply in meat, corn, &c., to the extent of at least twelve millions annually. Such a result would, in all its ramifications, involve a great general addition to the national welfare and power.

TO WHAT EXTENT CAN TOWN SEWAGE BE PROFITABLY APPLIED TO THE PURPOSES OF AGRICULTURE?

London Farmers' Club: *February*, 1856.—Mr. Mechi said: One hundred years hence, which is not long in history, our successors will scarcely believe that a nation wanting annually many millions of quarters of grain to fill up its own inadequate production of food, should waste the only means by which such deficiency might be made good—I mean the productions of the land when they have fulfilled their office of nutrition to man and beast. Every one now at all conversant with modern agricultural chemistry must know that our agricultural produce loses little by such a process, and that the bulk of its elements are returned to us in the shape of excreta if we take the trouble to collect them.

If agriculturists studied attentively Professor Way's able paper on Town Sewage (see Royal Agricultural Society's *Journal*, vol. xv. part 1, page 135), it would teach them a great and profitable lesson. They would learn that of all the manure made by human beings (and I have no doubt by animals) 12 parts out of 13 in weight escape as urine, only 1-13th part being solid! Well may farmers love the sheep-fold, and well may they deplore yard feeding, where the rains from the untroughed roofs may, in too many instances, thus take away nearly all their manure. Mr. Way, with his usual care and exactness, has found that, taking the average of men, women, and children, each individual of the population will in the course of twenty-four hours contribute to the sewage of a town one quarter of a pound of solid and three pounds of liquid excrement. A knowledge of these facts shows us how trivial is the question of solid manure, for at a quarter of a pound each daily the total solid manure of 2,500,000 people in this metropolis will only weigh 279 tons.

According to Mr. Way, the excrement of each person is diluted with or distributed through 20 gallons, or 1,400 times its own weight, of water. It must appear singular to a disinterested observer, that whilst farmers seek eagerly after every new manure, and are subjected to much imposition in such purchases, they appear to be apathetic on the question of town sewage. I think much of this neglect must arise from the fact of its being in a fluid state.

Perhaps I may be here permitted to explain why I consider this mode of application far superior to the solid form. If you make a transverse cut or opening in the soil, you will find that the British agricultural pie-crust is only 5 to 8 inches thick. The slips and railway cuttings plainly reveal this humiliating fact. Below this thin crust we see a primitive soil, bearing most unmistakable evidence of antiquity and unalterability. The dark shades of the cultivated and manured surface have not been communicated to the pale subsoil; and we have evident proof that solid manure ploughed in, in the ordinary way, exercises little influence on the subsoil. Nor can this be wondered at, when the plough sole has been polishing and solidifying the floor at the same depth for the last few centuries. Now, when I apply liquefied manure (which means all the solid and liquid excrements of the farm animals mixed with water), it soaks deeply into the subsoil to the depth of the drains, which I have seen, on the very strongest clays, discharging the liquefied manure at a depth of 4 and 5 feet. I could show you 20 loads of rich oilcake bullock pudding, or manure; I would mix it with water, apply it in a shower, and you should search the surface in vain for any proof of its whereabout. It has gone down to do its work. What I want you to believe is, that town sewage is liquid guano, applicable to every soil and every crop, and worthy of your utmost attention. It is true that undrained land, requiring drainage, such as heavy clays and spring soil, must undergo that operation before they can derive the benefit of such an application; but there are extensive tracts of chalks, sands, and hot gravels, almost praying to be fertilized by the sewage of our towns.

One important reason for the superiority of liquefied over solid manures, is, that water is the great arrester and conveyer of ammonia, that invisible and truant spirit which is ever escaping unseen from reeking dung-heaps. It is this ammonia which dissolves the silica of the soil, and makes the kernel of our wheat, and the lean of our flesh; and it is for this ammonia that we so affectionately prize unwashed Peruvian guano, or birds' dung. When you have learned to apply fluid manure to the soil, you will find your crops yield as much as they do after the sheepfold, and you will get corn as well as straw, that is, if you do not sow too much seed.

Of course if the London sewage is used, I apprehend it would be pumped to elevated district reservoirs, whence it would flow from main pipes connected with smaller ones on the various farms, so that they would be always charged with a sufficient pressure to cause a jet; this would render unnecessary any steam-engine or tank on the farm.

As to the quantity required per acre, Mr. Telfer, of Canning Park, Ayr, tells me that he applies 500 tons of water per Scotch acre at five dressings, to his Italian rye-grass, with 5 cwt. of guano at each dressing, making a total annual application of 25 cwt. of guano per Scotch acre (one-fourth larger than the English acre). This is in a naturally moist climate, therefore we may estimate the water-absorbing power of the barren sandy wastes in the neighbourhood of the metropolis far more considerable. That those wastes would be rendered highly productive after the application of town sewage cannot be doubted.

Now, if you apply 500 tons per acre, you will only require

152,000 acres to absorb your 76 millions of tons. As 640 acres are a square mile, you would at that rate require 237 square miles, or a square area whose diameter would be about 15 miles. I have a strong conviction that a very much larger quantity of sewage, say 1,000 tons per acre at least, may be profitably applied to our sandy, gravelly, and chalky wastes. This would afford a great economy in distance and expense.

I apprehend no one will doubt the economy of transmission of fluids by tubes, seeing that by road carriage the charge of carting near the metropolis would be at least 8*d.* per ton, per mile. There is no fear of our being overwhelmed with cheap hay or superabundant milk by this process, for our metropolitan wants become annually more and more gigantic; but I do know, from extended and minute observation, that the infants and juveniles of this metropolis would present a very different muscular and general development if this scheme were carried out, for now the wretched wrecks of noble short-horned cows, observable on every green patch around the metropolis, speak volumes of the thin sky-blue which is vainly expected by fond parents to form the bone and flesh of their dear children. Their pallid faces and feeble limbs present infallible evidence of defective nutrition.

Tiptree Meeting: *July*, 1856.—Mr. Mechi said: I thought, when we called on the Hon. Mr. Cameron, he would have told you that while England has no agricultural statistics, they have in the young and comparatively new colony of Canada most correct statistics of every bushel of corn grown, and know what they are doing, for they have got over the old prejudice on this subject. And I believe the agricultural fear about the mischief of disclosing their affairs is a perfect phantom and delusion. Recollect this,—you cannot do away with the farmers of England—you cannot do without them—you cannot keep them in an humble position. Every day they are increasing in knowledge and intelligence—every day they are bringing the resources of science to bear with greater effect upon the cultivation of the soil, and better means of communication are being opened to them. Do not let us, then, be afraid of letting the world know that we are making a profit; for if we say we are all bankrupt, nobody will believe us. Now on looking round this large, intellectual, and influential meeting, I see that we have lots of doctors here, and I wish that amongst them I could get a physic that would cure prejudice. When I say this I do not intend to imply that prejudice is confined to agriculture. I hope my agricultural friends will not think that I look on them as singular in this respect, and as being the only class that entertain and cling to their prejudices. I recollect that it was said that steamboats would never do, and would never cross the Atlantic; that railways were impossible, and the electric telegraph was madness; and these are all evidences that prejudice is not solely an agricultural complaint.

Woodbridge: *November*, 1856.—Mr. Mechi asked himself what he had done to merit their good esteem and their kind favours? The conclusion he came to was that they had forgiven him for any agricultural follies he had committed, and that after ten or a dozen years' reflection they thought that he was not quite so wrong as they had conceived him to be. He believed that a great many of the farmers of England, at least many of the farmers of Suffolk thought, ten or fourteen years ago, as they had all thought in their time, that the farming of Suffolk was not so bad, and that the farming of England was not so bad after all, and that there was not so very much to learn as he had pointed out; but they must recollect this—that every year they were going on in their population by compound multiplication, which seemed to be such a favourite employment with Englishmen, and it was quite clear that that rapidly increasing population demanded a corresponding increase of production, which could not be carried out unless with improved means—unless they invested in the soil, on the part both of the landlord and tenant, a very much larger amount of capital and intelligence. Had it not been for their invitation to come to Suffolk, he should to-day have been at the Witham agricultural meeting, where he should have seen the steam-plough at work. Probably they were aware that there were two kinds of these ploughs now in use: one was by Mr. Fowler, which was worked with a wire rope, and which some of them might have seen in operation upon his farm; and he might mention that his neighbour Mr. Crump had also bought one and was now using it; but that gentleman's fields, it should be understood, were not limited to three or four acres: they were twenty, thirty, or forty acres in size, so that he had no difficulty in that respect, and with his common engine he was working the steam plough satisfactorily. Then there was Mr. Boydell's engine, as seen at the Royal Agricultural Show at Chelmsford, walking about like a Mammoth. It drew ploughs after it, and cultivated land at a great depth at a cost of only one-fifth of that incurred in ploughing-horses.

Manchester: *September*, 1858.—Mr. Alderman Mechi said: For sixteen years his experience and his outlay of money in agricultural improvement had taught him that there was nothing so certainly profitable as the judicious investment of capital in agricultural improvement. It had been the fashion to say, "Mr. Mechi carries out agricultural improvements as a hobby." But he only did that upon the farm which he would do in his business or house: if he found it out of order, he would put it in order, and that could not be done without an expenditure of capital and intelligence. If Manchester had been satisfied with the old hand-loom, would she have been able to clothe the world in calico, and to get large profits? No. But by a large intelligence, and a great availment of chemical, engineering, and manufacturing science, she was enabled to do this. Precisely the same thing must be done in agriculture, and by similar means. They must not remain satisfied with their present condition; but, feeling that they were only moving gradually on the way to perfection, they must make more haste than they had hitherto done. This was not a matter of easy accomplishment. Fortunately, however, there were railways now, and every facility for intercommunication. He did not charge it on agriculture that she was so backward. It was her misfortune, from the nature of distances and the impossibility of farmers meeting together as merchants and manufacturers did. Until agriculture had railways it was almost impossible for her to improve. A practical farmer seldom went out of his own county, and some seldom left their own parish. Every parish believed itself to be the most perfect parish in England, and that it had nothing to learn from any other. But all that was now done away with. The introduction of the locomotive had brought people to rub their heads together, and the result was a much greater amount of progress. There were now two great questions before the agricultural world. First, the introduction of steam to cultivation. He hoped that for all general purposes, as thrashing, grinding, and so forth, most farmers used the steam-engine. And his hearers might depend upon it that they would never develop the full powers of agriculture until they brought steam to bear on cultivation. Their five inches of cultivation would be exchanged for two feet or three feet; he said that very guardedly. They all knew how much was raised by market-gardeners; and that was done by depth of cultivation and great manuring. Perhaps gentlemen were not aware also that the horses now used in agriculture consumed one-fifth of the whole produce of the country. When they introduced steam their horses would eat coal instead of corn, and coals were much cheaper than the corn which would be eaten by the horses necessary to do the same amount of work. The next great question was, "What is to be done with the sewage of the towns?" They knew what it cost to feed the inhabitants of the country, and they could calculate what would be the value of the manure if it were re-applied to the soil. The Chinese were our superiors in this respect, for they husbanded the manure like gold, and not a particle was wasted. But he had no hope that that would be done just yet in this country. It would take a long time, and require a large unanimity of sentiment among the landowners and farmers, and the general public. When the public voice should be raised on the subject, and discussion upon it should be entered into in every society, they might hope that the time would come when we should have the gratification and profit of seeing the people better fed by means of that which was now considered positively injurious to them. He hoped they would believe him when he said that if they would employ a large capital in the soil in improvements, in drainage, in deeper and cleaner cultivation, in the use of a larger quantity of manure—if they would make their fields squarer, erect better shelter for their stock, and persuade the lawyers that it would be better to enable them to change their farms as they did their Consols, they would be able to compete with the most favoured countries in the world. He often met men from all parts of the world, and his inquiries from them had led him to conclude that English labour, judging by the amount of work done, was the cheapest in the world. He had found, upon examining some Polish and Russian freeholders, that their good crops were not much above half of what was grown on our best farms in this country. But then they said their cost was very little, they could buy the fee simple for £3 or £4 per acre. It would be a sorry thing for this country if the cost was so little, for it implied the absence of improvements, roads, and markets. He hoped to see the time when the rent would be about £3 per acre. It would be a happy thing for the farmers if the rent were doubled, supposing the increased rent represented a fair interest upon the improvements effected by the landlords. Non-improvement was unprofitable. If some one were to offer him a farm of a thousand acres of undrained land he would not have it as a gift to be compelled to farm it himself in its unimproved condition.

PART V.

LECTURES.

Four Lectures before the Society of Arts: November, 1850; December, 1851; December, 1853; December, 1854.—Lecture at Chelmsford: December, 1852.

1. READ BEFORE THE SOCIETY OF ARTS, *November* 27, 1850.—I purpose in this discourse to take a general review of our agriculture, adverting to certain practical points of interest, and remarking on my own agricultural position.

The physical and mental powers of a nation form its original capital. It is labour, directed by the mind, that feeds and clothes us, and procures, for our social adjustment, the metals which form the accepted standard of our currency. Therefore, the more numerous and concentrated the population, the more wealthy the nation, provided means are found for its employment. Can it be denied that we have yet, in this United Kingdom, a wide and untilled field for agricultural labour and investment? Look at our statistics of moor, bog, and waste. Oh, but I am asked, can these be profitably reclaimed? Request the poor peasant squatter to show you his cottage garden or allotment on such soils, and conviction will at once reach you. Carry your remembrance to the reclaimed rabbit-warrens, and quadrupled rentals of Norfolk and Lincolnshire; to the once sedgy, swampy wilds and wastes of the great Bedford Level, drained by mighty steam, which even now is doomed to be superseded by a costly and enormous but profitable estuary. See the warps of Yorkshire and Lincolnshire; the irrigations of the Edinburgh meadows, with their annual rental of from £15 to £20 the Scotch acre; the Portland Water meadows, and watered wastes of Teddesley. Take for evidence, the Woburn Sands, Chat Moss, Dartmoor, and endless other proofs; and then can you doubt that human labour, well directed, is profitable in agricultural progression?

But I am bound to give reasons for my dissatisfaction with

our present agriculture. Here they are:—The first and most direct evidence of the low scale of farming is the gross acreable produce of the United Kingdom. I have good reason to believe that the very largest estimate per acre, taking into account the poor grass and arable lands, and leaving out market and other gardens, does not reach £4 per acre. £3 15*s*. from one whole acre of land in the nineteenth century!

What each acre might produce by the application of more drainage, more manure, more labour, and deeper cultivation, more live stock, and better buildings, may be inferred by facts constantly obtruding themselves on our notice. As extreme cases, we may instance the production of eighty tons of mangold-wurzel per acre, sold at £1 per ton; of large productions of vegetables worth at least £100 to £150 per acre; of six to nine quarters of wheat per acre, worth, at only 40s. per quarter, from £14 to £18.

We see by Spackman's tables, that there are in—

	Acres.	Rental per acre.
England and Wales	36,995,000	21*s*. 8½*d*.
Scotland	18,944,000	5*s*. 1½*d*.
Ireland	20,177,446	13*s*. 5¼*d*.

(This estimate includes the rent of towns, and also all the bog and waste lands.)

Now it is quite clear that the mere increase of labour and production to the extent of only 10s. per acre, would afford us all food and employment, without recourse to foreign imports. Is this so fearful and difficult an object to attain?

It is a disgrace to agriculture that it produces no superabundance—nay, not even abundance, but leaves us to the mercy of large foreign importations.

I venture to predict that agriculture will never be rich until it produces superabundantly. This *can* be done, *will* be done, and *must* be done, for the concurrence of increased employment and food, with a multiplied population, can alone prevent anarchy and confusion. It is impossible to avoid seeing in every direction, the sluggishness, ignorance, and neglect of our national agriculture. Unlike our manufactures, it has availed itself of neither mighty steam nor general science. Enshrouded by prejudice, ignorance, and self-sufficiency, isolated localism has been her curse; but better times are coming.

Railway hedges are neatly trimmed and annually cultivated; they are thus rendered effective as well as neat. The farm hedges, diverging at right-angles from these, have never caught the pleasant infection. They still exhibit their huge, irregular, and ungainly proportions; shading and robbing the land, for the mere purpose of growing bushes to stop the gaps caused by their untrimmed and neglected condition.

Farmers dig their gardens two feet deep, but only plough

their land five inches. They take especial care of their nag-horse in a good warm stable, but expose their farm-horses and cattle to all weathers. They deny the utility of drainage in strong, tenacious clays, but dare not dig an underground cellar in such soils, because the water would get in. They waste their liquid manure, but buy guano from Peru—to repair the loss. I have known practical men seriously doubt the benefit of liquid manure, who are in ecstasies with the urine of the sheepfold.

The excreta of the vast importations which take place to this country of food and consumable luxuries, ought, if properly economized, to increase annually the fertility of these islands. But when I suggest new buildings, steam-engines, drainage, &c., I am asked, "Where is the capital to come from for all these improvements?" I reply, Where *does* the capital come from to make railways and docks; to build steam-vessels; to erect a whole town of new squares and streets, and to carry out every other useful and profitable undertaking? I believe the surplus profits of the nation are estimated at fifty millions annually. Every ten years, this accumulated wealth has found vent in rash or dangerous speculations. Fortunately, foreign loans have been superseded by British railways; and I can perceive clearly, that the surplus gains of the present times are destined to pass into agricultural improvement. I see in mental review, a long list of bankers, merchants, shipowners, manufacturers, traders, and professionals, who have become owners or cultivators of our soil. These, not having the agricultural precedents or prejudices of their predecessors, are devoting their powerful means and energetic common-sense principles, to the amendment of our agritulture, and the increase of employment and of food.

But there is one sad and most unjustifiable obstruction to landed investment and amendment. I mean the antiquated and semi-barbarous difficulty of transfer. In all other properties, possession is *primâ facie* evidence of ownership. It does appear to me a monstrous and intolerable nuisance, that the same principles of possession and transfer are not applied to land as to the Funds, or any other article of value. A public registry-office, with district maps, would at once obviate the difficulty. Land would then change hands twenty times for once now, and be subjected to a proportionably increased chance of improvements.

With regard to the practice of agriculture, there are certain things on which, from experience, I am competent to pass a decided opinion, and recommend as economical and profitable.

The Moral and Physical Condition of our Labourers has, in my opinion, a most important influence on our successful cultivation of the soil. They should be the apt and polished tools with which we carry on our work. To me, one of the most delightful results of agricultural improvement, has been its good effects in the immediate neighbourhood. I speak practically on this matter, and can testify that the expenditure of my money on a wild tract of bleak and barren heath has diminished crime, and conduced greatly to the security of property, and to the moral condition of the hitherto irregular and insufficient employed peasantry. The want of a better education is severely felt by the men themselves, especially when I have had occasion to send them as drainers to distant counties.

I find it advantageous to myself and to my labourers, to let every job as task or piece work. The work is more quickly and cheaply done; the men earn more money, are consequently in a better physical and social condition, and larger consumers of the farmer's and manufacturer's produce.

Every man who values the working condition of his horses will naturally extend the same consideration to his labourers. It is impossible too strongly to condemn the miserable policy of allowing itinerant speculators to monopolize the housing of our labourers. The social and physical pestilences resulting from these wretched hovels should make us wiser in this respect. Honour be to his Grace the Duke of Bedford, and to others, who have set a brilliant example, by providing ample and convenient residences for the peasantry on their estates.

Farm Horses should be clipped early, and gradually, piece by piece. If you doubt this, try on your plough, one clipped, and the other unclipped, and you will soon come to a conclusion.

I assume that you will never turn out your horses, but treat them exactly as you do your nag-horses, taking especial care that there should be ventilation at the highest point in the stable; this is well effected by iron air-bricks worked in with the brickwork. All their hay and straw should be cut up into chaff, the corn ground into meal, and mixed with it. Two-thirds hay chaff, and one-third straw chaff, is the right proportion; but cut hay alone does not answer, being apt to ball in the stomach. If their water were always warm, as at the London breweries, they might drink at any time; otherwise it would be as injurious to them as to ourselves to drink cold water when overheated by violent exertion.

Animals never do well under slated roofs, unless you interpose a lining of boards or woollen thick felt, such as is used in shipping. Slates conduct heat *to* the animal in summer and *from* it in winter. Thatching under slate is useful, though apt to encourage vermin.

Old horses do admirably well on cut food, and in warm and well-ventilated stables.

We never need lose a horse by gripes, provided we administer, when first attacked, one ounce each of spirits of nitre and paregoric, in a quart of warm water. I always keep a few doses ready.

Deep Cultivation after Drainage is essential to profitable farming on heavy lands. I effect this by removing the breast from a plough, and letting it follow, drawn by a pair of horses, in the tract of the first plough. We thus gain a greater depth. In summer, I use a very large plough with four horses, to open the work, and follow with another plough and four horses in the same track. This brings up immense clods and blocks of the nasty undisturbed soil. When dried by the sun, the Crosskill roller, with five cwt. added, cracks them; the scarifier operates, and again the Croskill renews the attack, all in dry hot weather, until you have a perfect garden —yellow-looking, it is true, but aërated, and deprived of many noxious properties, and ready for mixing with abundant manure and calcareous matter. You thus bid adieu to root-weeds that have tormented you for years; you facilitate the percolation of water, air, manure, and roots. Your crops do not dry up in summer, or freeze in winter; for it is the drying or freezing of the *roots* that destroys the plant.

I apprehend that, if a pair of horses could plough two feet deep instead of five inches, *that* would have been our general depth of cultivation.

This dry summer, all the manure for our root crops, being within five or six inches of the surface, got dried, and the root crop failed. Not so where it was buried deeper, like garden cultivation, below the solar influences. Our root crops send down their roots many feet in summer, provided the manure is there, as I have proved by examination.

The Potato Question.—I suppose if I grow potatoes I shall be told that I am not a farmer, but a market-gardener. I shall be proud of the appellation: it implies superior cultivation. Surely it will not be objected that potatoes are not food for man, as much so as bread and beef, and that a man may not grow what pays him best! The fact is, bad farmers, who do not keep much stock, or buy much manure, *dare not* grow potatoes with the ordinary mode of farming. I have heard them say a potato crop exhausts their land for years. For my own part, I like a heavy exhausting crop. It implies a heavy return, with means for restoring the deficiency occasioned by it. Miserable crops, occasioned by the save-all and cheese-paring principle, cause us to feel severely the pressure of our rent, tithes, and rates. They re-act on the landlord, labourer, tenant, and community at large.

Farm Buildings.—Had I to re-erect my farmery, I could materially improve the economy of its arrangement. Supposing, of course, that a steam-engine would be used, the waste steam, after passing under and boiling the necessary number of iron tubs or cooking coppers, should, passing through iron pipes, warm all the feeding-houses, keeping their temperature at a profitable heat for cheap fattening.

In the passages, which should be rectangular, with a turntable in the centre, I would place a light cheap iron tramway, on which the feeding-carriage would work with facility, having on it the baskets of turnips or other food. This would economize much labour, and the feeder would no longer be in the position of the man who had to pick up a hundred eggs at intervals of a yard, having each time to return and multiply his labour.

Feeding on Open Boarded Floors.—Experience has taught me, and will teach others, that in order to succeed in farming, we must produce a much larger quantity of meat on our farms than at present, and at less cost. In order to do this advantageously, it becomes necessary to consume a large portion of the straw of the farm, cut into chaff, and cook it with meal or ground oil-cake. We are thus deprived of the usual cattle-bedding, and must find a substitute.

Having practised the system rather extensively, I will communicate to you the details; observing, that although attended, as every system must be, with certain disadvantages, the balance of benefit is sufficiently considerable to induce me to continue and extend it.

The quantity of stock I now have on boards is—

Lambs	100	Bullocks	30
Sheep	50	Cows	10
Calves	60	Pigs	200

We are indebted to the worthy and Rev. A. Huxtable for the idea; but I found his space of three-quarters of an inch between the planks insufficient. I therefore measured the hoofs of the various animals, and arranged my openings accordingly. Thus:—

	Inches thick.	Inches wide.	Inches space.
For bullocks	3	4	1⅞
For sheep	1½	3	1¼
For pigs	1½	3	1⅜
For small pigs and lambs	1½	3	1
For calves..............	2	3	1⅝

For large Cotswold or Kent sheep, 1⅜ opening would not be too large. 1¼ openings do well for Hampshire Down lambs, but are rather too large for small Sussex Downs.

One cannot too highly appreciate the system on heavy lands, where animals cannot be profitably folded during winter. The area allowed for each animal and its feeding apparatus, is thus:

	Superficial feet.
Small sheep	8
Large ditto..................................	10
Small bullocks	30 to 40
Large ditto..................................	50 to 60
Small pigs	6 to 8
Large ditto..................................	9 to 11

Very much depends on the season and weather. In cold weather, pigs and bullocks can scarcely be packed too close, so long as there is room for them to lie down comfortably. Sheep require a little more room, or ventilation. In fact, it requires a nice observation to adjust the ventilation and temperature. This is best done by a thermometer, because our own feelings are not always a sufficient criterion. Every cattle-shed should feel as comfortably warm as a drawing-room. The opening for ventilation should be at the highest point.

Fine-bred pigs, having little hair, must have a much warmer temperature than sheep. When pigs huddle together, it is a sure sign that they are not warm enough. Cold, stopping the circulation in the skin, drives the blood to the internal organs, and causes inflammation.

I have often been struck on seeing how soon my groom will get a horse into condition, by warmth, cleanliness, and food. The same remark applies to a lady's lap-dog. My bullocks are all groomed daily by a boy, whose sole occupation it is. The cost is about one farthing per head per week, and I am sure it pays. Before I leave the open boards, I should say that the bars or planks may be either of straight yellow deals, or of straight-grained hard woods. The latter are to be preferred for heavy animals, as they wear off the edges of the deals. The depth of the pits may be from two to four feet. It is necessary, once in a way, to level the manure to prevent its touching the boards; it would soften them, and cause them to break.

I should say that we never sweep the floor; but the animals are perfectly clean. Of course the manure is taken at once from under the boards to the field, without the interventional expense of a double carting, shooting, or turning over of a dung-heap. The effect on the crops is unmistakable.

In order to pay you 10 per cent. on your investment for the whole building and floor, complete, with troughing, &c., you would charge your bullocks 1½*d*. per week; sheep and pigs, ¼*d*. per week. The cost of erecting covered homestalls, complete with boarded floors, will not exceed 1*s*. to 1*s*. 3*d*. per superficial foot.

One man on my farm feeds, and entirely attends to 250 pigs. It would require two men on the old straw-bed system. Our pigs are never cramped now. Formerly, they used to be, owing to the manure heating under them, and the cold giving those parts rheumatism.

One stout lad, at 3*s*. 6*d*. per week, will feed and attend to 30 bullocks; another attends to 60 growing calves.

I smile occasionally at the current belief that Mr. Mechi is a reckless, extravagant fellow—not at all pinching or farmer-like. An inspection of my future published accounts will possibly show, that whilst my workmen are well paid, my work is cheaply done by the task; and that certain folks have been under a considerable delusion. Before I leave the boarded floors, I must confess that I never like the look of my animals so well on them as I do on a little mountain of clean straw, or a nice green pasture; but this is not a question of fancy, but profit, and I am quite sure that the system is very advantageous. It is true we like a soft bed, and so do the animals; but our medical advisers recommend a hard one.

There is a very powerful development of the muscles on boards—so much so, that with fattening pigs, not bred on the boards, I have known some of them get capped hocks. It is surprising how quickly you may fatten *young* pigs on these floors. They find it inconvenient to run about, so divide their time between eating and sleeping—a most agreeable operation for the account-book.

There can be no doubt the animals are perfectly healthy on these boards. Considering the confinement and heat, this rather surprises me, especially with the pigs fed entirely on meal; for the ammonia or effluvia from under them certainly is powerful enough to discolour the paint.

Another question connected with the boarded system is the fly question. Where you have plenty of food, warmth, and stock, you will have abundance of flies. My bullocks could never lie down in the daytime, owing to their attacks; and of course, the continued lifting of their feet prevented fattening. By darkening the feeding-houses, I entirely removed this nuisance, and had the gratification of putting my animals in a most profitable state of repose; for if you have ten millions of flies, not one will bite in the dark.

To those who consider me "too fast," and are not prepared to go with me in boarded floors, I would say—By all means, then, have covered homesteads, such as may be seen at the Rev. Mr. Cooke's, of Semer, near Hadleigh, Suffolk; and at Mr. James Beadel's, Broomfield Lodge, near Chelmsford, Essex.

Whilst searching for facts to guide me to the most profitable mode, I met with the accounts of two farms, variously managed, which confirm by comparison, my own impression, that on the quantity and management of our live stock depends much of our success in farming.

For your information, I annex a comparison of Mr. M'Culloch's Auchness farming, with a similar one in Suffolk.

ACCOUNT OF AVERAGE MIXED SOIL FARM IN SUFFOLK.

INCOME.

	£.	s.	d.
47 acres wheat, 32 bushels per acre, 1504 at 5s	376	0	0
7 acres barley, 36 bushels per acre, 1692 at 3s. 6d. ..	296	2	0
23½ acres pease and beans, 32 bush. per acre, 752 at 3s. 6d.	131	12	0
*23½ acres clover, &c., cut once for hay.			
*10 acres pasture, ditto.			
*34 acres pasture marshes fed.			
*47 acres mangold-wurzels and turnips.			
232			
18 acres waste, fences, roads, &c.			
250			
* These 114½ acres kept ten cart-horses and one nag-horse; and, in addition, produced in feeding:—			
20 bullocks, at £7. 10s. £150 0 0			
120 sheep, at 15s. 90 0 0			
6 cows, at £9. 10s. 57 0 0			
10 young stock 25 0 0			
Swine..................... 25 0 0			
Fowls..................... 5 0 0			
	352	0	0
	£1155	14	0

N

EXPENDITURE.

	£.	s.	d.
Rent, 28s.; tithe, 7s.; rates, 3s. 6d.	481	5	0
Taxes	9	0	0
Wages	319	14	0
Bills, &c.	68	2	0
Seed, &c.	82	3	3
Miscellaneous	15	10	0
Interest on capital, £2250 at 5 per cent.	112	10	0
Losses of stock	25	0	0
Depreciation of horse-stock and implements	28	0	0
Loss to balance	14	10	0
	£1155	14	3

ACCOUNT OF AUCHNESS FARM.—1849.

EXTENT—260 Imperial Acres.

INCOME.

		£. s. d.
22 acres oats, 50 bushels per acre, 1100 bushels, consumed by the horses.		
55 acres wheat, 38 bushels per acre.. 2090 bush.		
Off seed........................ 168 do.		
Disposable............1922 do. at 5s.,		480 10 0
92 acres potatoes, 400 tons, sound roots, worth £3 per ton		1200 0 0
91 { 1 acre Italian rye-grass (seed)		5 0 0
50 acres turnips.		
15 acres grass, cut green.		
25 acres pasture.		
For feeding the following stock, viz.:—		
44 cattle, which were bought in June, and have been already sold at an advance of £5. 5s. per head on price paid for them	231 0 0	
86 cattle in course of feeding, at £5. 5s. per head in advance	451 10 0	
208 wethers, at 9s. per head advance	93 12 0	
52 hoggets, at 7s. per head advance	18 4 0	
6 cows, produce	60 0 0	
4 young horses, £5 each	20 0 0	
6 ewes	10 0 0	
Produce of 91 acres, besides manure		884 6 0
		£2569 16 0

EXPENDITURE.

		£. s. d.
1. Rent		262 0 0
2. Purchased manures:—		
Guano	192 0 0	
Bones	138 0 0	
		330 0 0
3. Purchased food, &c.		
For cattle and sheep (including £37. 10s. for summering 23 cattle)	284 0 0	
Oats, &c., for servants and horses	105 0 0	
		389 0 0
4. Bills and wages		510 0 0
5. Seeds purchased		25 0 0
6. Sundries, &c.		86 0 0
7. Taxes		24 10 0
8. Interest on sunk capital, £1000 at 10 per cent.	100 0 0	
Interest on floating capital, £2500 at 5 per cent.	125 0 0	
		225 0 0
Sum chargeable against the farm		1851 10 0
Tenant's remuneration		718 6 0
		£2569 16 0

The Suffolk Farm, of a superior quality, employing an equal capital, but less labour than the Auchness Farm, shows a considerable loss, whilst the latter produces an ample profit. In the Suffolk Farm there is no purchased manure or imported food; on the Auchness Farm we have £719 so expended. On the Auchness Farm the amount of meat made is £884—being the produce of ninety-one acres, and the purchased food; on the Suffolk Farm only £352 was received for meat, although 111 acres were used for that purpose.

On the Auchness Farm, £1,680 worth of corn and potatoes were sold for the consumption of man; on the Suffolk Farm, only £793 was the value of the grain crops.

Here we have a clear explanation of the cause of success in one case, and failure in the other. In one we see the animals housed, warmed, ventilated, groomed, their food cooked, and the utmost made of it, chemically and physiologically; in the other, the usual mode of turning out, and consequent waste and misapplication of food. Here we have a dependence on the *natural* production of the soil, unaided by imported food or manure, and consequently a minimum production with almost a maximum expense; there, a constant addition to the productive powers of the soil, with a maximum produce, and consequent diminished per-centage of expense. I need hardly say that I shall in my own practice follow the farmer who makes money, and not him who loses it.

Our success as farmers evidently depends greatly on our making the most of our root and green crops. The great question of the value of a ton of turnips in its meat-making powers can only be solved by the variety of modes in which it is applied to nutrition. The estimate of value by different persons is from 2*s.* 6*d.* to 12*s.* per ton.

In Norfolk, where house-feeding with oil-cake is extensively practised, its estimate is about 7*s.*, varying, of course, in some degree, according to the price paid for lean stock. In my neighbourhood, they are frequently purchased for house-feeding at 10*s.* to 12*s.* per ton; whilst for open or field-feeding they only command from 1*s.* to 3*s.* 6*d.*, and the manure left.

I know frequent instances where large flocks of sheep have consumed whole fields of turnips, coming from them absolutely leaner than before. Cold, wet, and comfortless, the frozen turnips acted as a purgative, being unaided and uncorrected by dry hay, oil-cake, or warmth or shelter. The value of the turnip crop was here absolutely nothing, and an enormous loss attended its production.

Review of my own Agricultural Position.—The publication of my agricultural proceedings has naturally exposed me to public criticism. All sorts of motives, good, bad, and indifferent, have been imputed to me. Of this I do not at all complain. I considered my farm in its original state, neither creditable nor profitable. I expended my capital in its improvement. The result of that expenditure was a decided benefit to my fellow-creatures. My agricultural opponents say the money was thrown away, the property not improved, and that I am losing much money by farming. In order to test the correctness of these opinions, I have, under the advice and suggestion of my friends, submitted to a valuation by three eminent surveyors, whose character and capabilities are beyond cavil. I am informed (though I have not yet received the official document) that they have fixed my rent at 36*s.* per acre, adding another 7*s.* per acre for the use of my machinery, &c. Now, as plenty of land such as mine was in its unimproved state can be hired for 12*s.* per acre, it follows clearly that the fee-simple of my estate is more than trebled in value, leaving out of view altogether the extra expenditure for my own personal convenience.

Whether I shall be able, with present prices, to pay a rental of 43*s.* per acre, besides tithes and all other charges, as well as a profit on my tenant-capital invested, remains to be proved. My incoming valuation as a new tenant was effected on the 30th of October, by the same gentlemen who set my rent. On the 30th of next October, and at all similar periods, so long as I continue to farm, my outgoing valuation will also take place. The much-desired balance-sheet will appear in the public prints, either for good or for evil, as the case may be. It will either be an example to follow, or a beacon to avoid. It will be done in honesty and good faith; but it would be premature now to prejudge its results.

---

2. Read before the Society of Arts, *December* 11, 1851.—We are met here this evening to talk about "Mr. Mechi's Farming Balance-sheet."

Portentous words! Methinks I see on the one hand melancholy Protectionists desirous to prove by it the utter ruin of British agriculture; and, on the other, zealous and too sanguine Free-traders, anticipating a large development of farming profits.

I am fully aware that the question, as regards myself individually, is totally unworthy of public consideration; but I know that your excellent society is desirous of testing how far our national agriculture may be promoted and encouraged by an accession of capital from trade, commerce, and manufactures; and also whether its practice cannot be stimulated and amended by the introduction of minds unfettered by long custom and prejudice.

Let us first consider the labourer.—I have no hesitation in affirming that his position is one of unusual prosperity. As overseer in my own parish of some 8,000 acres, I beg to state that the poor-rates for the last twelve months are lower than they have been for many years; and from a comparison with my books in former years, I am satisfied that the poor-rates rise and fall with the price of corn, in the same way and ratio as our tithe commutation. In this part of the country it has always been the custon to estimate a week's wages by a bushel of best wheaten flour, independent of extra harvest wages. Now our able-bodied labourers are receiving 8*s*. per week, whilst the bushel of flour can be had for 6*s*., leaving a comfortable margin for clothes, firing, and shop goods, their annual rent being paid by their extra earnings during the harvest month.

As landlords can live now so much cheaper than they used to do, I hope the question of a fair reduction of cottage rents will be duly entertained.

Foreign Competition.—Our agricultural friends having been bewailing the ruin likely to come upon them by a compe-tition with foreign agricultural labour, I have taken some pains to satisfy my mind on this point. Our glorious Industrial Exhibition has given me a fine opportunity to do so; for my farm has been almost daily visited by crowds of inquiring foreign agriculturists from every country, both as proprietors and tenants.

We compared notes as to the price per acre paid in labour for almost every operation on the farm, and they have frankly ad-mitted, with some surprise, that British labour, in relation to the quantity and quality of work done, is quite as cheap as their own.

I honestly believe and expect that we shall win the race of agriculture, and leave behind us those nations which are in any way deficient by comparison in capital, intelligence, or opportunity. And why should we not do so?

Have we not here every facility—good markets, plenty of con-sumers, and ready access and intercommunication by road, canal, or railway? Is not every implement of agriculture enormously reduced in cost? Good ploughs at 45*s*. each; plough-shares at 7*s*. per dozen; iron for blacksmith's work at less than one-third its former price; labour at two-thirds its former value; timber at 6*d*. to 1*s*. 6*d*. per foot; bricks at 20*s*. per thousand; to say nothing of steam and other thrashing-machines, scarifiers, drags, and all sorts of improved imple-ments, pipes for drainage, &c. &c. I cannot, for the life of me, see what equivalent advantage is possessed by foreigners. The only possible counterbalance can be an apparently cheaper rent, but not really so, when other circumstances are taken into con-sideration. I do not, therefore, fear the supposed unlimited powers of multiplying production in foreign parts. I have good reason to know that the restrictive and prohibitive principles of foreign nations tend to cripple and abridge their agricultural opportunities. But remember, the advantages I have named are useless until used. Have they been used? I say, Decidedly not.

Prejudices and inert self-sufficiency, fostered by a conviction that Agriculture must be sustained, whether she exerted herself or not, has kept her in the rear of our general advancement. I say this firmly and guardedly.

Go where you will, you may find abundant evidences of unused opportunities. Tumble-down and misplaced buildings, full ditches, great and ugly fences, queer, small, and misshapen fields, stagnant water for want of drainage, and well-washed animals and manure; cumbrous and antiquated conveyances, an enormous waste of manual and animal labour, most extraordinary discrepancies in agricultural practice and valuations in various counties, under the same circumstances of soil and climate. In one place a pair of horses abreast will plough one acre per day; in another, four, five, and six horses *in a line* will only plough three-quarters of an acre. In one county they will sow six bushels of oats and three or four of wheat per acre, in another half the quantity. In Essex we plough once for wheat; in some other counties, three or four times (in some places nine ploughings for turnips; in another, only two). Here we allow 7*s.* per acre for ploughing, whilst elsewhere 13*s.* is a common price. In one county an improving tenant is allowed by valuers for many things, in another nothing. The price of agricultural labour is similarly various:—

In Suffolk, parts of Essex, and other counties, 6*s.* 6*d.* to 7*s.* 6*d.* per week is a common price; whilst in parts of Yorkshire, Lancashire, Kent, Surrey, and elsewhere, 11*s.* to 13*s.* is no uncommon rate, particularly in the manufacturing districts.

But there is no end to agricultural discrepancy. In Norfolk I can find a farm of 1,000 acres, with only four fields, of 250 acres each; the fences neatly trimmed, free from hedgerow timber, and the whole a pattern of good farming. I turn to Devonshire and many other counties, and there I see sixty and seventy-acre farms, with twenty-five fields, on an average of about two and a half acres each. Who can wonder at the complaints of agricultural distress? Imagine on such a farm, twenty-five gates to open, shut, and keep in repair; twenty-five squares of hedgerows and timber trees, eating up the poor farmer's crops; twenty-five squares of headland to turn upon and destroy; and yet all these nuisances are measured to the tenant as *land*, and he has to pay rent, rates, tithes, and taxes upon them.

Again, in parts of Norfolk, Lincolnshire, and Scotland, steam-engines are almost as plentiful as blackberries, whilst in most other counties, they have few or none. In my own, with one million of acres, we have less than half a dozen.

In fact, from beginning to end there is such a total discrepant custom and practice that we cannot hope for some time for that uniform system which distinguishes so pre-eminently our manufactures, where a difference of one or two per cent. would make or ruin a trade. But the change is fast coming, and agriculture can no longer escape that science which ministers so extensively to the elegancies, utilities, and necessities of our every-day condition. I do not concur in any anticipation of agricultural ruin, nor do I fear that land will go out of cultivation. With the three per cents. at 96, land, however poor, will always have a value as an investment; and, no doubt, it is very properly passing from the hands of those who cannot or will not improve it, into the possession of more calculating and spirited proprietors.

Legal Difficulties.—Agriculture has not advanced with the other material interests of this great country, nor can she do so whilst under the trammels of antiquated feudalism. So long as landed property continues involved in mystical legalities, copyholds, live and dead heriots, &c., and withdrawn from the common-sense principles of possession and ready transfer, so long will agriculture be in the rear.

Until you treat your purchase and sale of lands as you do your three per cent. consols, by an authorized registry and immediate transfer, there are no hopes for the perfect development of our agricultural powers. 'Tis true that such a system would test *bonâ fide* possession, and affect the mortgage system; but this would confer a great national benefit, by passing land into the hands of *bonâ fide* capitalists, able and willing to improve it, and responsible for its duties, as well as entitled to its rights. We have evidence of this in the Irish Encumbered Estates Bill.

The Balance-Sheet. —Begging pardon for this long digression I now proceed to lay this before you; and I hope to be able to prove to you, that although there appears a large deficiency, the results of my operations, on the whole, are profitable. I have no hesitation in admitting that, in the hands of a practical farmer, more favourable results might be shown.

The numerous public and private duties devolving on me, will not permit that close attendance at markets, and rigidly vigilant observance of fractionalities and details, so necessary to agricultural success.

A desire not to remove old faces has caused me to retain on the farm the old original bailiff, who was not versed in the purchase and sale of stock: his time is much occupied in exhibiting the farm to numerous visitors. I permit this on public grounds, but it by no means conduces to my pecuniary advantage.

What is called "a gentleman farmer," in a poor neighbourhood, had need look rather sharply into matters; for he is considered "fair prey," by jobbers, dealers, butchers, and others with whom he deals. I have also more implements than are absolutely necessary; many having been presented to me, and others purchased experimentally.

I do not hold up my farm as an example for the ordinary class of landlords and farmers, for it is quite clear that their general capital is totally inadequate to similar proceedings; but, remember, that with our large national annual accumulation of profits, estimated at fifty millions, something must be done to absorb it, and thinking minds will reflect with pleasure on the multitudinous national advantages resulting from such operations as mine.

TIPTREE HALL FARM.

Dr.

	£.	s.	d.	£.	s.	d.
To valuation,* 30th October, 1850:						
Horses, eight	80	0	0			
Sheep	169	0	0			
Bullocks, cows, and calves	473	0	0			
Pigs	296	19	6			
Implements, including 12 iron stack-frames, iron hurdles, &c.	394	17	6			
Tillages, hay and manure (including cost of unconsumed root crops)	557	5	7			
				1971	2	7
To labour (ordinary farm)	264	5	6			
Ditto (treble-trenching 15 acres of land)	90	0	0			
Ditto, in connection with the live stock in yards, &c.	150	0	0			
				504	5	6
To rent on 125 acres, at 36s. per acre; Ditto, on 45 acres I rent, at 20s. per acre, with 5s. which I add for my improvements on it				281	5	0
Tithes, rates, taxes				58	18	5½
Tradesmen's bills, including purchase of a Bentall's broadshare				104	4	10½
Coals for steam-engine				55	15	0
Repairs to engine				20	0	0
Miscellaneous payments				6	4	4
Man's wages, acting as engineer, miller, and stoker to engine				39	8	11
Seed-corn, &c.				48	8	0
Live stock bought				710	12	0
Oil-cake and corn bought as food for stock				1558	17	6
Guano, superphosphate of lime, and chalk, bought as manure				135	7	8
Interest on farm capital, £2,700, at 3½ per cent.				94	10	0
				£5588	19	10

Cr.

	£.	s.	d.	£.	s.	d.
By Valuation, 30th October, 1851:						
Horses, five	55	0	0			
Sheep	167	8	0			
Bullocks, cows, and calves	479	0	0			
Pigs	278	3	0			
Implements	367	5	0			
Tillages and manure	499	8	3			
				1846	4	3
By wheat crop, 72 acres: average (including one field injured by blight) 36 bushels of marketable wheat per acre, is 2,592 bushels, at 5s. per bushel				648	0	0
27½ acres of potatoes, only half a crop, having been injured by drought, quality of potatoes good, selling at an average of 1s. to 1s. 2d. per bushel; 4,000 bushels in all, the small ones for seed and consumption by stock				150	0	0
Meat and live stock sold				2181	0	4
Wool sold				30	17	2
Butter, &c., produce of eight cows				60	10	0
Miscellaneous receipts				17	9	9
				4934	1	6
By apparent deficiency to balance, arising entirely from the large quantity of food purchased for feeding stock, as per account annexed, and £90 labour in treble-trenching and removing rocks—a permanent improvement. This apparent deficiency is amply compensated by the additional manure obtained				654	18	4
				£5588	19	10

* In both cases the valuation is by Messrs. Alfred May, James Beadel, and Robert Clutton.

MEMORANDUM.

The wear and tear of implements, depreciation on horses, &c., are all considered in the valuation.

No seed potatoes are charged for, or taken credit for.

The farm would be fairly entitled to a considerable sum for food consumed by visitors' horses, and occasionally by my own private horses, dogs, &c.; but no credit has been taken for this.

The credit price for wheat is taken at 40*s*. per quarter, because already above 100 quarters of this year's crop have been sold to average as near that price as possible.

No account is taken of the straw on either side; the custom of valuation in this county being to allow it to the incoming tenant gratis, as a set-off against thrashing and marketing the crop.

The root-crops are all valued at their actual cost, both at incoming and outgoing.

The charge for labour includes the bailiff's salary.

In addition to the 72 acres of wheat, and 27½ of potatoes, I have 20 acres of mangold-wurzel, 30 tons per acre; 6 ditto of Swedes, 18 tons per acre; 13½ acres of red clover, consumed; 12 acres of green-top turnips, after tares.

Although, by landlord's measure, I have 170 acres of land, the actual available land is only 155 acres, and 2 acres of lawn, garden, &c.; buildings, stack-yard, &c., occupying the rest: so that, although I did away with 4½ miles of useless fencing, there is still a considerable degree of waste.

It is necessary to remark, with reference to my statement of last year, that on receipt of the valuation for rent I found it to be 36*s*. per acre, *including* the 5*s*. for machinery.

A summary of my accounts will show that there was £10 worth of meat made, and £5 worth of corn produced, *for every acre on the farm*. Compare this with the Down farming, as described in Mr. Farncombe's prize essay "On the Farming of Sussex" (Society's Journ. vol. XI. p. 75), where the *gross annual return* is only from 12*s*. to 17*s*. per acre! Consider the effects on the country at large. The land is certainly as good and improvable as my own. At all events, the Yorkshire and Lincolnshire wolds and Norfolk heaths, with their bountiful productions, should shame the proprietors of our southern and other downs, into a more improved system than mere natural production. On downs similar to these, the Rev. A. Huxtable (to his lasting honour be it said) is paying £3 per acre in labour alone, and making abundant returns of meat and corn.

Whilst witnessing those splendid results, I sorrowed that his example had been so little followed by the neighbouring proprietors.

The time will come, when landed proprietors will be esteemed for the *condition* of their acres, rather than for their *extent* of territory.

Acting on the principles defined by Mr. Lawes, in his able paper (Royal Agricultural Society's Journal, vol. VIII. p. 256), I availed myself of the low price of cattle-food and fed a disproportionately large number of live stock, with a view to the permanent fertility of my soil.* This has been done at a very considerable cost, as shown by the stock balance-sheet; but I apprehend there will be but few practical farmers who will deny that this investment must be ultimately remunerative. The Lincolnshire or Norfolk farmer, who gives his fattening bullocks from ten to twenty pounds of linseed-cake per day (and there are plenty who do this), knows full well that a great immediate loss attends this system; but so thoroughly is this principle admitted, understood, and acted upon in the best-farmed district of Lincolnshire, that an outgoing tenant would receive from his successor, by custom, one-third the cost of purchased food consumed, in addition to the ordinary value of the farmyard manure. On this principle I should be allowed between £500 and £600 on account of my purchased food, besides a proportion of the bones, chalk, &c., used this year, and also a portion of the permanent improvement by treble-trenching.

This would have converted my apparent deficiency into a real profit. Unfortunately for the *appearance* of my balance-sheet, no such allowances are made in Essex, where a man may expend a fortune as tenant-farmer in drainage, chalking, marling, boning, &c., without receiving a shilling allowance —a pretty premium this to bad or low farming!

Of course the high state of fertility of my once miserable soil will render unnecessary for the future so extensive a purchase of food or manures, and I have now only to take out, by severe cropping, the fruits of my investment.

In order to illustrate the exact position of the feeding question, I annex my balance-sheet, freed from the charges of purchased food and stock; and in its ordinary condition it is evidently profitable, after paying me the high rent fixed on my former improvements by the valuers last year.

* The relative profitableness of thus enriching home-made manure, and of buying guano or other fertilizers, may be thus illustrated.—

100 quarters of feeding barley at 30*s*. would leave a loss in pig-feeding of at most 4*s*. per quarter, or £20 in all, and would be equal to the consumption of nearly seven quarters per acre on fifteen acres. £20 worth of guano would manure fifteen acres.

I should prefer the barley manuring, believing it will produce the greater result. But with the same value fed out in rape-cake, I feel sure that the profit would be still greater, if the sheep were well bought in and fairly sold.

Guano pays best on distant fields, by economizing cartage.

Dr. FARM ACCOUNT (IRRESPECTIVE OF LIVE STOCK AND PURCHASED FOOD). *Cr.*

	£.	s.	d.		£.	s.	d.
To labour, including bailiff's wages	264	5	6	By 72 acres of wheat—36 bushels per acre, at 4*s.* 9*d.* per bushel	615	12	0
Rent	241	5	0	27½ acres of potatoes—4,000 bushels	150	0	0
Rates, tithes, &c.	58	15	5	20 acres of mangold-wurzels—30 tons per acre, at *consuming* price, 6*s.* per ton	180	0	0
Seed	48	8	0	6 acres of swedes—18 tons per acre at 5*s.* 6*d.* per ton, *consuming* price	29	14	0
Tradesmen's bills	60	0	0	6 acres of pasture, *consuming* price	18	0	0
Horse labour—six horses at £25 per annum	150	0	0	13½ acres red clover, *consuming* price	54	0	0
Portion of engine-work for thrashing	30	0	0	13 acres tares, at £4; 12 acres white turnips after tares, at £3	88	0	0
Purchased manures	135	0	0				
Interest on capital, £1500, at 3½	52	10	0				
Wear and tear of implements and miscellaneous expenses—casualties	25	0	0				
	1065	3	11				
To profit beyond interest of capital	70	2	1				
	£1135	6	0		£1135	6	0

I have valued the wheat crop at only 38*s.* per quarter, although the 100 quarters already sold average over that price. I apprehend the most critical cannot object to this account. All the green and root crops (and part of the potatoes) are consumed on the farm, besides the 100 tons of wheat straw and the wheat chaff. In addition to all this, £135 is paid for guano, superphosphate, &c.; so that the farm will actually increase in fertility under this system.

It is my custom to take wheat alternately on half my farm, the soil not being adapted for barley, and the climate is too dry for oats. A very heavy rent is charged, to cover former improvements, and there has been no sparing of hand-labour. My land is annually improving in fertility.

Many will no doubt say that I have undervalued my root crops. I have certainly not overvalued them, for I could sell the mangold-wurzels here, without cartage, in any quantity, at 9*s.* 6*d.* per ton; but then I should lose the manure made from their consumption.

LIVE STOCK, TIPTREE HALL FARM.

Dr.

				£.	s.	d.
To valuation of live stock, 30th October, 1850				1018	19	6
Stock since bought				710	12	0
Corn, linseed, and rape-cake bought				1558	0	0
To produce of root and green crop, hay, &c., grown on farm*				350	0	0
				3637	11	6
To expenses—Man occupied as miller, stoker, and engineer	39	8	11			
Coals and repairs	75	15	0			
	115	3	11			
Less charged to farm	30	0	0			
				85	3	11
Labour—three men feeding stock, two boys, and extra labour cutting chaff, carting extra manure, &c.†				150	0	0
Interest on capital in live stock, £1,000 at 3½				35	0	0
Rent on extra buildings, and machinery required by stock				40	0	0
				£3947	15	5

Cr.

	£.	s.	d.
By valuation of live stock, 30th October, 1851	979	0	0
Meat and live stock sold	2181	0	0
Wool	31	0	0
Produce of eight cows	60	0	0
	3251	0	0
Consumed by horses, as charged in the farm account	120	0	0
	3371	0	0
Loss on live stock, chargeable against manure	576	15	5
	£3947	15	5

Now the allowance of one-third value of the purchased food, which I should receive by the most recent custom in the best-farmed district in Lincolnshire, would about equal the balance of loss shown; and it is a remarkable evidence of the importance attached by those eminent farmers to imported food, that even when I should have cropped all the land in 1852, still they would allow me *one-sixth* of the food consumed in 1851, assuming, of course, that I had not received any valuation in 1851.

* The roots (crop of 1850) are charged at 9*s.* per ton; the hay and other food in proportion.
† This includes every charge, even to carting and spreading the extra manure.

In summing up the results of my year's proceedings, I have clearly shown that the transaction is, under all circumstances, profitable. The farm-account shows an actual profit, beyond the interest on capital invested.

The sum of £90 for permanent improvement by treble-trenching would have to be spread over many years at an annual charge.

The stock-account shows an apparent heavy loss, but this is compensated for by the value of the manure.

When I first began farming, I depended principally on artificial manures; but experience very soon taught me, that they were far more costly than the manure produced by feeding stock. It is true the artificials act immediately, but they are also expended quickly, having little durability.

Mr. Lawes's admirable researches have now quite settled this question in favour of unwashed animal manure.

Permit me to say that both practical and scientific men can sufficiently appreciate the effects of my bringing on to a farm of 170 acres in one year nearly 300 tons of cake and corn in addition to the consumption of 50 acres of root and green crops, 35 tons of hay, and 120 tons of strong wheat straw, besides guano, bones, chalk, &c. I might, by proceeding more slowly and gradually, have followed the ordinary mode of sinking money the first few years to recover it afterwards; but I preferred availing myself of my capital and position as owner of the soil to do all at once, and thus get an earlier return.

The Durability of Manures in Heavy Soils.—This is a subject worthy the attention of agriculturists, especially those farming their own land, or on long leases, because it gives confidence in the free expenditure of money for cattle food, as a means of producing manure.

Walking, before harvest, with a friend in his wheat-field, I was struck with the marked superiority of one corner, and asked for an explanation. "Oh!" he said, "this portion was once a cottage garden."—"How long ago?"—"Why," said he, "I have known the field fifty years, and it was ten years before that time."

I felt there was hope for agriculturists who improved their own properties by drainage, deep cultivation, and ample manuring.

Mr. Robert Baker, in his prize Essay on the Farming of Essex (Royal Agricultural Society's Journal, vol. V. page 1), says, in speaking of the heavy calcareous clays, "The application of manure, whether from the farmyard or otherwise, increases not only bulk in straw, but quantity and quality also in grain; and from the retentive nature of the soil, manure continues to benefit for several years after the application."

On undrained heavy land the results would hardly be shown, because, if the manures were applied during winter, the land, being then saturated with water, would not absorb the manure.

Some idea of the permanently improved condition of the

clayey portion of my land may be formed when I tell you that the yellow subsoil would formerly be found in a four-inch ploughing, but now a good digging in the furrows will fail to reveal it; and even at lower depths the pale birdlime-like appearance is changed to a mellow and darker-coloured friability. So much for drainage, cultivation, and manure!

The Labourer's Balance-Sheet.—As we are talking of balance-sheets, permit me to lay before you the Labourer's Balance-sheet. As there are many in our towns and cities, with tolerably good wages, who don't know how to live—it may be useful.

LABOURER'S BALANCE-SHEET.

Analysis of Labourer's expenditure, average of family—man, wife, and three children :—	£	s.	d.
9 4-lb. loaves, at 5d.		3	9
1½ lb. of the fat of pork, at 6d.		0	9
1 lb. of cheese		0	7
½ lb. of butter		0	6
2 oz. of tea		0	6
1 lb. of soft sugar		0	4
¼ lb. of soap		0	3
¼ lb. of candles		0	2¾
Coals and firing		0	8
Boots for the man		0	4½
Boots and shoes for his family		0	4½
Clothing for man		0	7
Clothing for woman and family		0	9
Pins, needles, thread, worsted, &c.		0	1
Confinements (doctor's fee, &c.)		0	4
General medical attendance, by 5s. annual club payments		0	1
		10	1¾
52 weeks at 10s. 1¾d.	£26	7	7
Rent	3	10	0
	£29	17	7

Income	£	s.	d.
48 weeks' labour, at 8s.	19	4	0
4 weeks' harvest, at 21s. 6d.	4	6	0
Extra wages, earned occasionally by hoeing, dibbling, &c.	1	0	0
Wife's earnings at gleaning, weeding, &c.	2	10	0
4 bushels of wheat in the garden, at 5s.	1	0	0
	£28	0	0

From the above statement, which I believe to be strictly accurate, it is quite clear that unless the wife earns more than the sum I have stated, they cannot have the comforts I have described.

But how often do we find the labourer many weeks unemployed, and occasionally suffering from illness? Then again, with large families of five or six small children, they are compelled to be satisfied with bread only, and the vegetables they grow in their gardens. If the potatoes fail, from disease, it is difficult to estimate the amount of privation many families undergo. How cruel it is to pull down cottages and curtail gardens!—driving the labourer into lodgings, or miserable tenements with mere scraps of garden, erected by itinerant speculators in the neighbourhood, who know the increasing population must inhabit them. Every estate should afford comfortable cottages, well drained and well troughed, for the workmen employed upon it, and at least one-eighth of an acre of garden-ground, or as much as the man can cultivate during his leisure hours.

It is grateful to my feelings that by "task-work" my men are enabled to earn more per week by extra exertions, without loss to me. It almost astonishes me, as director of a provident association, that in my poor neighbourhood, we should muster some fifty members paying their 2½*d.* to 4½*d.* per week. Sometimes, when out of work, there is a sore struggle to raise this money; but how delightful, in cases of sickness or accident, to see them independent of parochial removal or relief.

We often complain of the slowness of country boys; but do we allow for their low physical condition? I asked a boy once,—"What do you have for breakfast?" "Bread!"—"For dinner?" "Bread!"—"For supper?" "Oh! some hot cabbage." Now, the latter was a *treat*, but I know this to be a fact. It is astonishing how much bread a labourer will eat. A hearty hard-working man will consume 1½ lb. to 2 lbs. for his dinner, and eat upon an average 3 lb. to 3½ lbs. of bread per day, some 4 lbs. The reason they only buy the salted fat pork, without lean or bone (which comes to London as bald pork) is, that there is no waste. It is fried in thin slices, and every drop of fat or grease used as a "relish!"

Few farmers sell their milk; consequently *skimmed* milk is a rarity, and only obtainable by a walk of one to three miles, at a halfpenny per quart.

In closing my remarks and reflections on the labourer's position, it is quite clear that a low price of bread is of the utmost importance to him, it being almost his only food; already he feels the reduction in sugar, and it is to be hoped that tea will be more within his reach; for so long as beer is inaccessible to the family, tea is the only stimulant. I have seen it on the labourer's table three times a day: coffee is not so much a favourite.

The poor labourer buys all his shop goods at the dearest possible market. The little village shop which supplies his tiny and fractional demands, derives its supply through the medium of a neighbouring town, laden with railway carriage and intermediate profits. The oft-repeated turn of the scale, and numerous wrappers, all tell against him.

Concluding Reflections.—It has been too much the habit of mere agriculturists to look with some degree of jealousy, if not of dislike, on those who invest in agriculture the proceeds of their successful operations in other occupations. But I conceive such transactions should be hailed with rejoicing, more especially by landed proprietors, who so frequently regret the absence of that capital which can alone assist to develop agricultural perfection.

In tracing the relations and results of a manufacturing surplusage, as applied to agricultural amendment, my heart warms with pleasing and cheering reflections, when I see the grim poverty, squalor, ignorance, and crime of a notorious and barren nighbourhood superseded by unmistakable evidences of an altered and improved condition.

A new post-office, an extra general shop, a couple of additional butchers, and many new cottages, all indicate an increase of business, of means, and of comfort; a new dissenting school, in connection with a humble chapel, spreads its benefits around, and only awaits the wholesome rivalry of an established church and school, long prayed for and long needed. I hope I may here be permitted to say, that it is to be regretted, that whilst increasing population and capital have gradually extended, encroached upon, and given greater value to this once wild and waste country, the ancient parish-church should still stand seven long miles from this neglected extremity, unavailable by time and by distance to myself or my poorer neighbours, and unaided by any auxiliary provisions.

Mr. Mechi's Reflections upon the Objections to his Farming Balance-Sheet.—What a storm has burst upon my poor devoted head! and how various its ingredients! Political rancour, personal insult, friendly pity, serious censure, malicious imputation! Surely, I may say with Yorick, "No crown of fame can ever fit it!"

I do confess that I am an agricultural sinner—that I have deviated from the beaten track—that I pulled down rotten buildings and substituted 9-inch walls and slated roofs—that I have made tanks and erected steam-power—that I have well drained and subsoiled—that I have removed trees and fences—that I have made good roads—that I have employed much labour—made much, but wasted little, manure—that I have made no long fallows—that I have cropped half my land every year with wheat—and that I have greatly and permanently increased its fertility!

All this is bad enough, but it was infinitely worse to let the world know it; and, above all (wretch that I am!), to express an opinion that such operations might possibly ultimately prove remunerative. I am clearly paying the penalty of my indiscretion, and can never again hope to recover from my disgrace, and look practical agriculture full in the face! Even *Punch* says, I am "Dun-up;" so I must hide myself carefully in the deepest recesses of agricultural consolation.

Amid the general gloom, an occasional ray from philosophical intelligence (thanks to Mr. Hill's penny postage) lights my dreary path, and supports my faltering steps. How delightful is this consolation from uncommon minds! It compensates for whole volumes of vulgar abuse.

Well, let us veil the disagreeables, and proceed to business; for, after all, is it a simple matter of fact and figures, quite independent of politics, passion, or prejudice? I am not at all disappointed that even my showing an apparent loss has not pleased everybody, although I am quite sure that, had circumstances permitted (which they will some day), a very large profit—much greater would have been the discontent and disbelief. There is really a mania for agricultural ruin just now.

Before I proceed to the question at issue, permit me to correct a few of the erroneous assumptions and statements that sometimes beset me. First, then, my land is all perfectly drained, and has not been redrained; secondly, my buildings have not been pulled down and rebuilt, although I have added to them; thirdly (and I say it without vanity), I am not a bad manager of stock, for it is the opinion of my immediate practical neighbours and labourers that I do make as much meat out of a given quantity of food as most people. I readily admit that our Essex stock is generally hardly so well bred as in more favoured districts, excepting always our pigs, which formed a material feature of my stock. In my balance-sheet there was an apparent loss of about £600 upon £1,600 of purchased food, which I said is compensated for by the extra manure. "Oh," says one, "but you didn't value the manure from food purchased in 1850, which of course was as much as in 1851." I reply—Of course it was only during the last four years that I saw the advantage of feeding with purchased food, and I remember, when first I commenced farming, being considerably abused and laughed at about my "solitary pig," which was all the live stock the critic then happened to see in the yards. There is one important fact that some of my objectors, and even my friends, appear to have most unaccountably overlooked, and it is that the revaluation of the land for a new rental was made on the 30th October, 1850, and instead of being fixed at 12*s*., the then value of similar unimproved lands in the neighbourhood, it was raised to 36*s*. per acre; thus, in fact, tripling the fee-simple. Why was it so raised? Not because it was poorer, but because by buildings, drainage, and improvements, and by the greatly increased fertility and improved condition of the soil itself, it was more prolific, although it had been cropped alternate years with wheat. The benefits of former manures were partially the causes of that increased valuation, and you will see that I have charged this greatly increased rent in my accounts. "Oh," but says another critic, "because you have expended £1,600 in 1851 in purchased food, of course you will continue to do so, and thus lose £600 annually."

Now, a reasonable person would infer that, having bought so unusual a quantity, and thus brought my land into such a state of fertility, I should not require to buy any more artificial food or manures; and, in fact, it is my present impression that my outlay in food and manures will seldom exceed £150 per annum, or 20*s*. per acre; and still I shall be able to keep plenty of stock from the produce of half my farm, it being now in a thriving condition, well filled with manure.

It has been assumed that £600 is too great a loss on the consumption of £1,600 purchased food, and that one-third of the cost is too great a sum for the value of the manure. Now, as this is the great question of agriculture, with every deference, I beg to state that no animal will pay for feeding on purchased food if you leave out of view the value of the manure.

It matters not whether it be hay, turnips, corn, straw, or oil-cake; and, further, if you deduct attendance, labour, &c., in connection with the extra manure made, also allow for casualties to stock, one-third loss on the purchased food will be a fair and safe calculation.

You cannot buy turnips or mangold wurzel, for removal, under 12*s*. to 15*s*. per ton, and certainly the stock will not pay more than 6*s*. for them. If you pay 30s. a ton for straw, or £3 for hay, the animals will not return above half the cost. I do not agree with the able and intelligent editor of an excellent agricultural publication, that I have over-valued my mangold wurzel at 6*s*., and my swedes at 5*s*. 6*d*. per ton, consuming price.

	s.	*d*.
If it takes 160 lbs. of turnips to make 1 lb., net weight, of meat, a ton would make 14 lbs. at 5*d*.	5	10
560 lbs. of fine straw-chaff, consumed with the ton of turnips (90 lbs. of straw to make 1 lb. of meat), = 6 lbs. at 5*d*.	2	6
	8	4

This I consider the value of the ton of roots with the [illegible] (minus attendance, &c.). Of course, if you used as an auxiliary purchased food, the loss on the purchased food would absorb much of the value of your turnips. It is well to have a proper understanding on this important question, both as to the loss on the purchase of food, and the benefit derived in the manure, which are about equivalent. The principle is the same whether it be £1 or £1,000. I, therefore, insist on this truth, that all purchased food (rape-cake, perhaps, excepted) must leave a loss or charge for the manure resulting from it. Still it is clearly shown to be a cheaper way of restoring fertility than purchased manure. A wise farmer, therefore, having his land in a state of fertility, will endeavour to maintain it by deep and ample cultivation, and by the consumption of one-half its produce with the straw of the other half. I predict the time to be coming when the boarded-floor system will be generally adopted for animals, and straw will be deemed far too precious to be trampled under foot—it will be used as food.

Before I conclude these remarks, let me entreat those who have capital to consider the poor unemployed labourer, at this dull season of the year. I have forty extra men now employed digging the land ten inches deep, and throwing it up in ridges at 2*d*. per rod of 5½ yards square, or £1 6*s*. 8*d*. per acre. It is a labour test, combining, in my opinion, charity with profit. It is true they can earn but about 1*s*. per day, but I offer it to all the odd men and strong youths who can get nothing else to do, and who must otherwise starve, go into the detested Union, or involve themselves in debt. This operation is cheaper and infinitely better than ploughing, and the eagerness with which it is accepted, impresses me with a very high sentiment of respect for the industry of our rural population, and their distaste for idleness. Of course, I supply them with steel spades and forks, made in Birmingham, which are far superior in ease, effect, and price, to the ordinary bungling utensils of most agricultural localities. A great reform is required in this matter of tools.

In conclusion, I repeat, that my transaction has been on the whole, profitable; and we may easily imagine what would be the effect of tripling (by the application of skill and capital) the rentals and fee-simples of the poor lands of this kingdom. It has been done in my case, and may in others, under the same circumstances. No doubt many will be horrified at the idea of an overwhelming supply of bread and beef; but if their principle is worth anything, the less we produce the happier we shall be. I do not envy such people their logic or their feelings. I shall go on unflinchingly, so long as it pleases God to spare me, in what I believe to be the path of agricultural profit and truth.—*January* 1, 1852.

---

3. Read before the Society of Arts: *December* 14, 1853.—When last I addressed you, agriculture presented an aspect of doubt and melancholy; forsaken by legislation and politics, she was abandoned to her own resources, that unknown mine from which she is now beginning to draw important and untold treasures.

On the occasion to which I allude, my celebrated balance-sheet was held up with political triumph, or mourned over by sincere doubt and mistrust; but those times are past, never to return: so we can now breathe freely, and discourse about the strength or weakness of agriculture, unbiassed by political asperities.

I shall have to-night to present to you another balance-sheet, and I purpose very particularly to call your attention to the new method of irrigation as practised successfully by me, involving in its consideration our water supply, sanitary condition, and physical support; the application of steam to cultivation will also deserve our notice. However gloomy our last meeting, individually, I never despaired, and you will remember that I said, "I apprehend nobody expects that corn will long continue at the present low prices; such an expectation would be contrary to all our historic evidences of fluctuations." And I also said, "No doubt, whatever the price of food may be, the land of this kingdom will continue to be cultivated; no one can seriously suppose for a moment that the large and active population of this kingdom is to be unemployed or unfed." These were bold assertions with wheat at 40*s*., but wheat now at near 80*s*., proves me to have been a true prophet.

Steam-power.—I am concerned to see that still so little steam is used in our own agriculture. Every farmer with 200 to 300 acres, who has not an engine, has a great lesson to learn, and I would have him to understand, that a strong four-horse power steam-engine, worked at 70 lbs. to 90 lbs. to the inch, will tire any sixteen real horses he can find, the comparative cost being £150 against £600, besides eating nothing when not at work, occupying less space, and economizing an immense outlay in casualties by disease, cost of attendance, and daily food—six to seven hundredweight of coal *versus* 32s. horse feed.

I little thought, seven years ago, that I should outlive the storm of ridicule and censure poured upon me by my practical friends. But it is gratifying to me, on personal and public grounds, to find the Mechian medicine gradually taking effect. I have often to "congratulate" my neighbours, with sly gravity, on their steam-engines, Garrett's horse-hoes, covered yards, boarded floors, and drainage of tenacious clays; waggons and board and thatched buildings are still clung to with considerable affection, but with a somewhat doubtful and half-calculating glance, at my *new-looking* brick and slated buildings, although erected ten years since.

If I meet the strong tea half a mile in advance of the farmery, after a heavy rain, and make some inquiries as to the condition of the tea-leaves in the yards, glancing at the untroughed eaves, I am told "My landlord ought to do this;" and sometimes I say, "I suppose you would repay him interest for it?" In fact, however unpalatable and unpopular it may be to uncover and expose agricultural errors or shortcomings, time convinces me that it is attended with the happiest ultimate results, and I can never afford to feel angry at former censures, when I see that many a sturdy old pollard has bowed to my influence, and that many a crooked hedge and way have been made straight by my example.

Balance-sheet.—I now proceed to produce my balance-sheet, and I am sure most of you will rejoice with me, that it shows a most favourable and encouraging result, the benefit I derive for this year being, in rent, profit, and interest, nearly £600. I will say nothing of a further sum I ought to claim, for improved condition of soil, owing to my having purchased, for consumption by my live stock, £700 worth of corn, oil-cake, &c. I shall have the benefit of this in next year's crop.

Dr.

	£	s.	d.	£	s.	d.
To Valuation, 31 October, 1852:—						
Horses	86	0	0			
Pigs	117	2	6			
Sheep	203	6	0			
Cattle and cows	347	0	0			
Implements	390	12	0			
Tillages, hay, &c.	526	10	0			
				1670	10	6
Rent of chapel land				45	0	0
Tithes, rates				68	0	0
Labour, including engineer, bailiff, &c.				407	0	0
Guano, bones, and superphosphate lime				98	0	0
Seed-corn and seeds				45	0	0
Live stock bought				1280	0	0
Corn and cake bought, for feeding purposes, horses' keep, &c.				648	0	0
Coals for engine, tradesmen's bills, &c.				130	0	0
				4391	10	6
My improved rent, 36*s*. per acre	240	0	0			
Profit	343	16	3			
				583	16	3
				£4975	6	9

Cr.

	£	s.	d.	£	s.	d.
By Valuation, 31 October, 1853:—						
Horses	74	0	0			
Pigs, &c.	255	6	0			
Sheep	448	0	0			
Cattle and cows	239	10	0			
Implements	390	12	0			
Tillages, hay, &c.	471	18	9			
				1879	6	9
Wheat, 3½ quarters per acre—50 acres				630	0	0
Barley, 5 ,, ,, —11				114	0	0
Beans, 5 ,, ,, —13				145	0	0
Oats				10	0	0
Produce of cows and poultry				50	0	0
Hay sold				55	0	0
Horse work, labour, hay, manure, &c., for private establishment				60	0	0
Live stock and wool sold				2002	0	0
Three stacks of old straw				30	0	0
				£4975	6	9

Cattle Feeding.—I recently incurred a brisk agricultural censure, for stating that "live stock is a necessary evil." We cannot do without it, because it produces manure, which enables us to sell grain; but, leaving out of view its manurial gain, it certainly "does not pay." Those who have a fancy for keeping pigs and other animals, will find, that after paying market prices for their food, adding shelter, attendance, and casualties, there will be a considerable loss, or charge, against the manure. If you have a fine crop of turnips, which in rent, manure, labour, &c., has cost you £10 per acre, and offer it on the market to be folded off for sheep, it is a great chance if you are bid £5 per acre; and if the parties give their sheep oil-cake whilst so feeding them, they would probably give nothing for the turnips.

These questions puzzle amateur farmers, but are well understood by the knowing old practical hands. Therefore, bear in mind that every pound you spend in purchased food diminishes the value of your root, or green crop.

My stock balance-sheet results very satisfactorily, compared with my last, owing to irrigation; but, had I not consumed so much purchased food, it would have been now far more favourable, although I should have been minus much manure, which may compensate me hereafter.

A Lancashire farmer told me a few days since, that a fine crop of turnips which cost him £10 per acre, he once sold for 10*s*. per acre, to be fed off with sheep. This was owing to the general abundance of turnips, and the necessity for feeding them off in time for barley. The £9 10*s*. per acre loss would evidently become a heavy drag, or charge, on the barley, clover, and wheat of the rotation.

Another large grazier told me, "If I buy a thousand pounds worth of oil-cake, I charge half to the bullocks and half to the manure."

Mr. Lawes's experiments on the comparative fattening qualities of sheep, in the Royal Agriculture Society's *Journal*, furnish correct data on this subject, and show that after paying for purchased food, *nothing* was left for the turnips, although we know they cost 10*s*. per ton, or more.

Breeding-stock of first-rate quality, if you have judgment and suitable land, is perhaps, remunerative, although there are many expenses and anxieties attending it.

Amateur farmers will do well to consider that 10 per cent. on capital, or £1 per acre, is, on an average of years, considered a fair remuneration by farmers. It is true there is house-rent free, besides some other advantages; but we see a great many ruined by farming, either from want of judgment, or by unpropitious seasons. In farming, as in all trades, a want of judgment is soon found out, and availed of by knowing hands who will buy of yout oo cheap and sell to you too dear. Your labourers, likewise, will take an exact measure of your capabilities.

LIVE STOCK ACCOUNT.

Cr.	£	s.	d.	Dr.	£	s.	d.
To valuation, 1852	753	8	6	By valuation, 1853	1016	16	0
Feeding-stuffs bought	648	0	0	Live stock and wool sold	2002	0	0
Live stock bought ..	1280	0	0				
	2681	8	6				
Profit, or rather price paid for produce of farm, in roots, green crops, and straw, consumed	337	7	6				
	£3018	16	0		£3018	16	0

The quantity of green and root food consumed by the stock, is estimated as follows (this includes the keep of farm horses):—

20 Acres of mangold wurzel, about 600 tons.
6 Acres of Italian rye-grass, well irrigated, and five times cut or fed (a very heavy crop).
A good second growth of clover, irrigated, about sixteen acres.
13 Acres of very heavy tares and winter oats.
50 Tons of swedes.
30 Tons of cabbage.
The wheat-straw of the farm.

Irrigation.—Now this balance-sheet opens up a vast question for reflection, both in town and country. Why is it so different from my former one?—Principally because I have the power of irrigation.

It is true that prices are higher now than then, but crops are less productive, and expenses are higher. Nearly the whole difference between this balance-sheet and the former one arises in the live-stock account. By irrigation I am enabled to double, if not triple, my green and root crops, and thus render them profitable instead of unprofitable. It is quite clear that if I can double my stock, I also double the quantity of my manure, and thus affect importantly the cereal crops. If I double my green and root crops I diminish their cost one-half. This is actually the fact, and therein is my present and most agreeable position. Every practical farmer knows that the losing part of his farm is the root crop (I mean in the Midland, Southern, and Eastern Counties, where we have hot summers and little rain). That root crop costs him more than the animals repay, and leaves a heavy charge on the ensuing grain crops. Irrigation changes all this, and permits each crop to be responsible for its own annual charge, thus rendering them all remunerative.

I am forcibly and frequently reminded of the truth of this statement by a five-acre pasture opposite my residence. Vainly did I try, by solid manures, to render this vile plastic clay into a useful pasture. It was like birdlime in winter, and cast iron in summer—poor, indigenous, and drab-coloured grasses choked and eradicated the finer kinds I had sown—and the animals wandered about, hollow and dissatisfied. In the space of eighteen months irrigation has changed all this: new fine and fattening grasses have clothed the field with perpetual verdure; it keeps three times as many animals, and the close and shaven pasture indicates their affection for it; butter, milk, and cream, alike testify, by their richness, to the fertility of irrigation; whilst the animals are improved in their condition.

Professor Way, in his recent valuable analysis of grasses, in the Royal Agricultural Society's *Journal*, has revealed the astounding truth, that irrigated grasses contain twenty-five per cent. more meat-making matter than those not irrigated.

We all know that grasses are voracious drinkers—they cannot stand drowning on undrained land in stagnant water, from which their roots soon extract all the oxygen; but see how prim and green they look beside any trickling rivulet. I venture, therefore, to predict, that the people of this country will soon connect ample water-supply, cleanliness, and health, with the idea of ample and cheap physical supplies—they will identify the well-washed contents of their closets with rounds of beef, saddles of mutton, big loaves, and rich milk. The ladies, whom I am too happy to see here to-night, knowing their great and proper influence, will recognize in every slop that leaves the house a richer, cheaper, and more abundant supply of that element, milk, which is to develope in their offspring, by bone and muscle, beauty and power, mental and physical.

In these times of advancement and common sense, let us call things by their proper names. The light of science has dispelled the darkness of our ignorance on these subjects. We know by our great chemists, that our sewers contain the elements of our food—of, in fact, our very selves,—and that to waste them, as we now do, is a cruel robbery on the welfare and happiness of our people.

Practical experience has taught me that this sewage is all the better for ample dilution; that the more you flood your cities with limpid streams, washing from every tainted and poverty-stricken court and alley the elements of pestilence and suffering, the grateful earth will absorb them in her bosom, and return them to you as treasures of health and strength.

The difficulties are insignificant; they exist in the *brain*, not in the fact. It is of no use to send a stream of sewage to a farmer who allows his own manure to run down the ditches, and sends to Peru to bring it back again in the shape of birds' dung at £10 per ton. No! landlords, and tenants too, must be taught or brought to believe that food and liquefied manure are one and the same thing, merely altered in form. Then you may make a small well by the side of each present sewer, and with your steam force-pump take *all* that comes down that source, and distribute it through subterranean arterial pipes on the whole country; not a drop need run past your pump to taint your streams. There is no more difficulty in it than in the water supply; but you must work a change in the minds of the agriculturists, or they will hardly take it as a gift, much less pay you for it.

When I speak of liquefied manure, I must be understood as meaning all excrementitious matter, solid or liquid, rendered fluid or semi-fluid by the addition of water, or by decomposition in water. In dealing with large quantities of such decomposing matter, a disagreeable and unhealthy effluvium will arise, however small the trap or cover of the tank; but experience has at length taught me that a jet of waste steam admitted into the tank above the agitated mass of putrefaction, effectually prevents any noisome odour. Vain are all other fixers or antidotes compared with this cheap and simple remedy.

The effects of liquefied manure are so striking, in improving our crops, that the cause is worth tracing. We know that there is nothing of which a farmer is so much afraid as the subsoil six or seven inches below the surface: if he brings this at once to the surface, he will grow nothing for some time. This proves clearly that that dreaded subsoil has never received, or been improved by, the solid manure ploughed into the surface soil; but by applying the solid manure in a liquefied form, it sinks deeply into the subsoil, saturating every granule, and by a thousand affectionate affinities improves its chemical condition, rendering its particles available and agreeable to the fibres of plants. Change of air and change of water are as necessary to roots of plants as to living animals: all this is effected by drainage and irrigation. It is no uncommon thing for us to saturate the soil to the depth of five feet, in the very strongest clays, making the drains run with the precious fluid, diminished, of course, in strength and value.

Experience has taught our farmers that the ammoniacal portion of our manures is the most costly, and yet the most difficult to retain; owing to its extreme volatility, admixture with water is the only profitable way to prevent its escape into the atmosphere: therefore the washing away of the fresh-made manure into a copious tank for irrigation, is in every way a great economy and advantage. Science has taught us that the earth is as necessary a composition of plants as air, water, and manure. It has also recently been shown by Mr. Way's experiments, as recorded in the Royal Agricultural Society's *Journal*, that nothing will dissolve the silica, or hardest part of our earth, so readily as ammonia. Hence the necessity for its economy, if we are to grow grain-crops more frequently and abundantly than we used to do; for, as you are no doubt aware, the glass coating on the straw of our cereals is a solution of silica, which is necessary, not only as a mechanical support, but as a protection to the vitality and circulation of the juices of the plant. I really believe that many of our spongy laid cereal crops may be traced to a want of soluble silica; the ammonia that should have dissolved it having escaped during the wasteful process of dung-heaps, or washed away by the rain from the untroughed farm buildings.

As this is a general discourse, I will not overlay it with tedious statistics of costs, but will state generally that to irrigate a farm of 200 acres, you would require—

Four-horse steam-power, worked at 60 lbs. to 70 lbs. per inch.

Fifteen yards per acre of 3-inch pipe.

A circular tank, about 30 feet in diameter and 20 feet deep.

Two hundred yards of 2-inch gutta-percha hose, with corrugated joints to render it flexible.

Gutta-percha jet.

A pair of force-pumps, capable of discharging 100 gallons per minute. (Mine are of 5-inch diameter, and 20-inch stroke, making 30 strokes per minute; but I would recommend larger barrels, and a slower action, to prevent wear and tear.)

At present prices, all this can be accomplished for about £6 per acre, so that the tenant paying 9*s*. per acre to his landlord for such an improvement would be a great gainer.

The question of economizing the sewage of our towns and cities will soon force itself upon our landowners and agriculturists. Admiral Moresby's recent announcement—that the guano supply will be exhausted in 10 years, will bring the matter to a crisis; our annual supply of 200,000 tons may be said to produce two million quarters of corn, or its equivalent in meat, &c. With an increased population, such a deprivation will compel us to look after our own guano.

Steam Cultivation.—I place before you the model of a steam-cultivator,* which I think is about to introduce a new economy in British agriculture. I have become, as it were, a parent to it, against my inclination. Mr. Romaine, the intelligent inventor, was consigned to me by the Agricultural Department of the Canadian Government, who had a high opinion of it. After trying in vain to interest some of our implement makers in this invention, I found that it would be lost to agriculture, unless I advanced the necessary funds for its manufacture, and for the securing of the various patents. On public grounds, I did this, and happy I am to say that its

* Mr. Mechi here pointed to the drawings and diagrams of Mr. Romaine's and Mr. Usher's steam cultivators, and being asked how they were to be got over the land, he explained that they were much lighter, in proportion to their power, than horses; for a horse weighed fifteen cwt., or more, and dynamometers showed that he could only exert a force of two cwt. in drawing the plough or other instrument, the remainder of his power being absorbed in moving his own body. A horse carrying on his back a man of sixteen stone weight for eight hours would find it to be a day's work.

success promises all that the inventor anticipated. If, with the assistance of a pair of horses and 5s. worth of coke, we can effectually comminute and cultivate ten acres per day, we may bid farewell to the whole tribe of tormentors, scarifiers, grubbers, harrows, broad-shares, and clod-crushers, that consume, through our horses, so much of the food of this country. If it does not supersede the plough, it will limit its operations. When once the steam-cultivator is shown to answer, no doubt many others will appear, and I venture to predict that, within seven years, steam will become the grand motive cultivating power. I also exhibit drawings of Mr. Usher's steam-plough: great credit is due to that gentleman, and I trust and believe it will answer his expectation, and be a great agricultural economy, on level land.

You will perceive by the models and drawings, that each of these implements may be compared to a steam-vessel on land instead of water. The internal steam-power causes the paddles or wheel-cultivators to revolve against the earth, and the resistance offered by the latter to the power exerted, causes the machine to be propelled.

You will also see, that Mr. Romaine's machine will, if required, deposit the seed and roll the land at one and the same time. These may be called dry-weather implements.

Every heavy-land farmer will easily appreciate the advantage of being able to complete his cultivation during the long and bright days, when the land works and admixes well. Steam, which never tires, will enable him to do this; and he will no longer be pained by seeing his exhausted horses brought home at two or three o'clock in the day, deferring his cultivation until the rains and fogs of November convert his aluminous clays into putty or birdlime.

If these machines answer, I see no reason why they should not be made sufficiently powerful to do 30 or 40 acres, or even 100 acres per day. I have no doubt that we shall see on our land what we now see on the wide ocean—monstrous moving volcanoes, rendered by science useful and subservient to man, each representing the powers of some thousands of horses, which we shall feed with coals instead of corn. Adieu, then, to small fields and narrow lanes.

Transfer of Land.—But before all the improvements, necessitated by our altered condition can take place, there must be a thorough reform of our present absurd, clumsy, dilatory, and costly mode of transferring land. I really believe it would benefit gentlemen of the law, for now (and I speak practically in this matter) a man of business avoids land, except as a permanent investment, or if he does purchase, takes especial care to avoid a separation from it as long as possible. I purchased the other day three acres of land that intersected my fields, and was highly amused at the production of as many parchments and documents as, when spread out, would cover the great charity dining-table at the London Tavern. After travelling back seventy-five years to trace the enclosure or kidnapping of this piece from a heath, it traced the deaths of the parties, their wills, their successors' wills, three or four mortgages several times transferred, and a mass of writing out of which any clever lawyer could, I should think, extract fifty objections. Apply the same principle to our funded, and every other description of property, and we should come to a dead fix like the Irish encumbered estates. Like those, the very absurdity of the evil will, I fancy, some day work its cure. It certainly keeps down the price of land, by greatly diminishing the competition for it.

---

4. Read before the Society of Arts, *December*, 1854.—This is the fourth time I have had the honour to appear before your Society; but I offer no apology, because I believe that there is no question at the present moment so important to the national welfare, as the attempt to increase our supply of food by improved British agriculture.

There is something of stern admonition in our present food position. With an abundant harvest, for which we have just returned grateful thanks, the prices of corn are enormous. An abundant home harvest is not now enough for the increased population; and, therefore, because some of our foreign supplies are cut off by accidental circumstances, Consols are depressed, confidence is withdrawn, circulation contracted, trade, commerce, and manufactures are paralyzed, with a prospect of much individual suffering and privation.

I venture to assert, from my own experience, that we could grow more than all the food that is required by the British people; but it must be done by investment and improvement.

The mere drainage of all the land that requires it would add millions of quarters of corn, and much additional meat to our present supply.

If I were asked "Why so little town capital finds its way to agricultural improvement?" I should say—"You have hitherto not held out to it the hand of invitation."

Great landed proprietors, with poor, unimproved, and entailed estates, either from want of knowing that means for their improvement exist, or from a false delicacy as to borrowing the money, or from a disbelief or doubt of the improvements resulting profitably to themselves and their tenantry, have not generally availed themselves, to any extent, of the two or three existing companies which have the means and legal powers to effect every necessary amendment, even on strictly entailed estates.

I know a great many small landholders whose property and tenantry would be equally benefited by such investments.

In a national point of view, it would be highly desirable that some hundred millions of our surplus capital should be engaged in producing British food on British soil by British means and labour—rather than that the cash-boxes of our capitalists should be crammed with bonds and responsibilities from every foreign nation and foreign undertaking—to the very casting of Russian cannon, to be used against our own troops. I could readily point out how one hundred millions could be at once *profitably* employed in agricultural amendment. But ere this can be done there is an immense amount of prejudice to be removed and self-satisfaction to be disturbed.

I venture to predict that, in a comparatively short period, we shall see every farmery covered in with sufficient shelter for its stock, lighted with gas, its fixed steam-engine economizing the costly labour of horses, and warming by its waste steam the various sheds. The food which the farm produces having done its office in the town will run back to restore the fertility which it had exhausted—our land will be drained and irrigated—the residences will be worthy of a more intelligent and more capitalled tenantry, rejoicing in pianos and libraries. The waste and loss occasioned by misplaced buildings, bad roads, and queer-shaped fields will be corrected by the facile sale or transfer and interchange caused by an easy legal registration.

If we have capital in this country — and who can deny that we have it in superabundance?—let it avail to give to agriculture a higher and more dignified, more intelligent, and consequently a more profitable position. The clumsy appliances and prejudiced neglects of antiquated agricultural customs are *not* profitable. The men who now suffer most in agriculture are precisely those whose ill-farmed, wooded, small, and undrained fields, and unimproved buildings are slowly but surely absorbing the tenant's capital, binding him in poverty and discontent. It will be a happy day for the tenantry of this country when their rents are doubled, provided that increase represents a proper interest for necessary improvements. This takes place in our towns and cities—why not in our agriculture?

Town Sewage. — I do attach much importance to the application of our town sewage to agricultural fructification.

Our excrement is literally our food, disagreeable and disgusting in form and smell, but unaltered in elementary value.

Injurious to man, it is vitality to plants; and many of the luxuriant vegetables that grace our tables, are a mere re-embodiment of our *excretæ*.

The time is gone by for false delicacy in these matters — we must entertain this great privy question. The Chinese would be starved, did they follow our example; but that wise people economize with rigid care that which they alone depend upon for the reproduction of their food.

I am informed they do not, as we do, fatten cattle at a loss, with purchased food, to produce manure for the growth of corn.

In order to form some idea of the extent to which our food might be increased by the application of town sewage, let us consider that 300 sheep on a farm of 100 acres, would keep it in a high state of fertility, and that, therefore, reckoning 450 men, women, and children as equivalent to 300 sheep, our population would fertilize 500,000 additional acres.

I say nothing of dogs, cats, parrots, canary birds, and horses: they consume largely, each horse consuming the food of eight men. Then you have enormous supplies of waste blood and offal, and a thousand other things that should add millions of quarters to your food.

The mere disintegration of your alkaline granites by the abrasion and triturition of traffic—the carbon or smuts from your roofs, which is but too perceptible after a shower, are all sources of fertility.

Farming Capital.—I may, perhaps, be permitted to say, generally, that to farm 400 acres of land you should have at least £5,000, or £12 per acre: but if you are to carry out subterranean irrigation, and all the modern improvements, you will want £6,000 to £7,000, irrespective of landlord's improvements, for building, drainage, &c.

You will then be in a condition to avail yourself of opportunities—to buy when you see anything cheap, and to sell when things are dear. I assume that you have judgment and a thorough knowledge of your business in all its details; for, unless by yourself or others acting for you, the most is made of everything, you must expect to lose your capital.

Look at my own live-stock account: if five per cent. mistake were made in buying and selling, it would derange my balance-sheet to the extent of £250.

Farm Profits.—As a general rule, 10 per cent. on the capital invested is considered a very good profit in farming. There are thousands who do not realize half of it; here and there a man of extraordinary powers and great personal economy accumulates a large fortune—but it is the exception, not the rule.

A return of four rents per acre is generally considered satisfactory—the average of the kingdom is, I think, less. In cases of improved farms, it is sometimes five rents, or more.

The necessity for diminishing the fixed expense by an increased produce is illustrated by the statement of a first-rate north-country farmer, who says that, if he spends £1 per acre, or £600 per year, for artificial manures, he makes a profit—if he omits it he makes a loss.

If stock is too dear, or you are short of capital, plough in green and root crops—particularly on heavy land.

Disposal of Capital.—As a general rule, your capital will be absorbed as follows:—

	£ s. d.		£ s. d.
Valuation	2 10 0		
Live stock	2 0 0	to	6 0 0
Implements*	1 0 0		
Labour	1 15 0	to	2 5 0
Seed	0 10 0		
Tradesmen's bills	0 5 0		
Rent	1 10 0		
Poor-rates, tithes, &c.	0 10 0		
Artificial manure	1 0 0		
Farm horses	1 0 0		
Personal expenditure			
	£12 0 0		

Farmers have generally the advantage of house-rent free, although too many of our farmeries are entirely unfit for a tenant of capital and intelligence, who will seldom enter upon such occupations.

Supposing we take a farm of 400 acres, on the four-course or mixed husbandry system, we shall find that one-half the farm produces nothing in the way of profit, but, on the contrary, leaves a considerable charge against, or upon the remaining half, which is in corn. For instance, the horses consume one quarter of the farm, the sheep and cattle consume the other quarter; and you will find, if you give your live stock much oil-cake or corn, that the whole of the expenses of one half the farm have to be paid by the other half, which is in corn—and whether that corn is at 40*s*. or 80*s*. per quarter makes a very serious difference to the occupier:—

400 acres (minus fences, buildings, roads, and waste, for which the tenant always pays rent), really 380 acres (more likely 370) will contain:—

	Acres.
In clover	50
In beans	30
In pasture	20
In tares, rye-grass, &c.	40
In roots	50
In wheat	100
In barley and oats	90
	380

It follows, then, that your 190 acres of corn have to pay—

Two rents,	Two manual labours,
Two tithes,	Two seedings,
Two rates,	Two tradesmen's bills;

and merely make a polite bow to the other half of the farm for the manure left, by the consumption of its crops.

Now, it seems very ungracious that when you have grown

* If with steam machinery, more than double that sum.

a splendid crop of turnips, at an expense of £7 to £10 the acre, the sheep are to consume it, leaving you nothing but the price of the hay and cake you gave them with it; but it is a system that can't be avoided, until you find some cheaper sources of manure.

In pastoral and dairy and cheese districts, where a suitable soil and climate combine to produce a natural fertility, live stock may be reared, or sustained with advantage on the natural produce; and I believe in parts of Scotland the turnip is produced more cheaply and nutritively than elsewhere, owing to the climate, but my remarks will apply to a great portion of this kingdom, especially where the rain-fall is under 26 inches, and the climate dry and suitable for the cereals—as on the eastern and south-eastern coast. In such districts the retention of poor, worthless pastures is a great mistake, and they should give way to a mixed husbandry.

On the subject of live stock I once asked a Lincolnshire farmer, who consumed £500 worth of cake annually, how he charged it.—"Oh!" said he, "I charge half to the bullocks and half to the manure."

As a general rule, when we are buying sheep for fattening, we pay 1*d*. per pound more for them than we could realize for the same weight when fat.

This is the penalty we have to pay to the breeder, who has to provide the bone and offal in the animal.

Breeding is not all profit, for it robs the corn side of the farm, unless much purchased food and manure is used to restore the balance: but to return to my 400-acre farm.

Now, I have no doubt this statement will startle many a practical farmer, and will raise a storm of indignation amongst stock-feeders and stock-breeders; but the naked truth is best told, which is, "that live-stock are necessary evils, mere manufacturers of manure, and unattended with any direct profit."

And if you give them cake and hay whilst feeding off your turnips and green crops, the return for these green and root crops will be *nil*, and their cost must be charged to the corn crops against the manure.

Agricultural Vicissitudes.—Three years ago, when I had the honour of addressing you, wheat was at 38*s*. per quarter, and agriculture gloomy and desponding. Now wheat is 78*s*. per quarter, with an abundant harvest, and agriculturists happy. Those who will refer to my predictions at that period will admit that I was a true prophet.

On a farm of 400 acres of highly-farmed arable land, the discrepancy in price between the two periods would be enormous. Take the 200 acres in grain, the difference would be something like £1,500.

If I were to advise you, I would say never take a farm that is not thoroughly drained, more particularly if of heavy clay:

the alternative is one of profit or ruin. I know so many estates where I see the tenant's capital wasting away under the evil influence of undrained clay, that it is quite a painful consideration. I am prepared to prove, that if a tenant will pay his landlord 5*s*. per acre extra, or 5 per cent. on £5 per acre drainage, the gain will; in various ways, far exceed the charge.

I will illustrate this :—A tenant of mine at the expiration of his lease, appealed for a reduction of rent. I declined acceding to it: I said, "If I reduce your rent 5*s*. per acre, that will be the whole amount of your gain; but if I drain your strong clay four feet deep, at an expense of £5 per acre, it will, particularly in wet untoward seasons, increase your crop from eight to twelve bushels per acre, or in money from 20*s*. to £4 per acre." I saw, by a certain expression of countenance, that he doubted the benefits of deep drainage in strong soils; but he said, "Suppose we try one field." Well, we did try one field, the drains poured forth their volumes of water after rain, the surface was dry and easy to work, and the crop succeeded where it had always before failed; this led to the drainage of other fields, and then came a covered yard or shed, on the same terms. The result appears already—a property more valuable and more marketable to the landlord, more remunerative to the tenant, and certainly more useful to the country at large. The neighbouring farmers watched the operation, which, I believe, was not without its influence on their proceedings and sentiments.

There is something very distressing in seeing men full of hope taking unimproved farms, and plunging into destruction; they are "booked" by the knowing ones on their first entrance with, "Ah, poor fellow, a very few years on that nasty soil will settle him!"

I may be asked why I attach so much importance to drainage. Why, you might as well ask me why I attach importance to circulation, vital or monetary. Stagnated water, or stagnated air, are as ruinous to the plants as they would be to our own vitality. Fix a cork in the drainage-hole of your flower-pot, and you will soon have a practical illustration of my meaning.

The sallow and billious plants,—like many turnip crops I know of on undrained land,—will show by their expression what is denied to them in speech.

This is not the occasion to enter into a subterranean examination of gravity, capillarity, aëration, or filtration, much less of all those affectionate or repulsive interchanges that turn air, water, and earth into food for man or beast; but, be assured, circulation is vitality—stagnation death and ruin.

Agricultural Power.—I lay down as a great axiom in agriculture, in the mere question of physical labour or power, independent of skill, that steam is cheaper than horse, and horse cheaper than man. A steam-horse costs 1*s*. 6*d*. per day, and will do as much work as two real horses. A real horse costs 2*s*. per day (including harness, shoeing, &c.), and a farm labourer nearly the same. But as a good horse weighs 1,600 lbs. and a man only 160 lbs., the power being as from eight or ten to one in favour of the horse, it follows that horse-power is considerably the cheaper, probably (including the necessity for manual superintendence) as four to one.

This brings me to the fearful question—What portion of the acreage of this kingdom do farm horses consume? I answer, nearly one-fourth of all the arable land in the kingdom. In ordinary arable culture, where there is little permanent grass, it requires four farm horses to 100 acres. Each of these horses will consume on the average from five to six acres (landlord's measure, which includes hedges, roads, waste, farm buildings, &c.)

Forty-two weeks { 84 bushels oats,
157 trusses hay, or 78½ cwt.
Ten summer weeks (no corn) will clear 2½ acres of clover.

This will be found to amount to 10*s*. per week, or £26 per annum, and will be the produce of about six acres at £4. 10*s*., or four rents per acre. I speak, of course, of average land, rented at 20*s*. to 22*s*. 6*d*. per acre, ordinary farming. Many farmers give oats all the year round.

On very poor farming, like some I know of, ten acres would hardly keep a horse, whilst on very high farming (especially on the irrigation system), one or two acres would suffice.* This brings us to consider the imperious necessity and advantage of forcing from the land its utmost possible development. If one acre will keep a horse, there is only one rent, one tithe, one rate, one seeding, and so on; but all these are multiplied from five to ten times, by middling and bad farming.

Those who have watched the discrepant productions of three tons to fifty tons of green food per acre, can at once apply my observations.

But a great economy may be effected in horse-keep, by crushing the oats, cutting the green food, and mixing with it a proper proportion of straw, &c., instead of turning the horses out to trample down and defile their food.

On the whole, I think we may congratulate ourselves on a considerable advance; facility of intercourse, and ventilation of the question by public meetings, remove, both on the part of landlord and tenant, many erroneous and antiquated prejudices.

In conclusion, permit me to state that there is ample scope for a noble future in our agriculture. The same principles apply to it as to all other branches of national industry. Self-satisfaction and immovability are ruin, but a rapid availment of science, capital, and amendment, is wealth and profit.

* Mine consume 2 to 2½ acres per horse. Some of my neighbours' horses consume 5 acres, some more.

Dr.

	£	s.	d.	£	s.	d.
To Valuation, 31 October 1853—						
Horses	74	0	0			
Pigs	255	6	0			
Sheep	448	0	0			
Cattle and cows	239	10	0			
Implements	390	12	0			
Tillages, hay, &c.	471	18	9			
				1879	6	9
Rent of chapel land				45	0	0
Tithes, rates				75	0	0
Labour, including engineer, bailiff, &c.				450	0	0
Guano, bones, superphosphate of lime				100	0	0
Seed-corn and seeds				50	0	0
Live stock bought				1619	0	6
Corn & cake for feeding purposes, horses' keep, &c.				1021	10	9
Coals for engine, tradesmen's bills, &c.				160	0	0
Interest on irrigation-pipes, 7½ per cent.				55	0	0
				5454	18	0
My improved rent, 36*s.* per acre	240	0	0			
Profit	517	15	0			
				757	15	0
				£6212	13	0

Cr.

	Acres.	£	s.	d.	£	s.	d.
By Valuation, 31 October 1854—							
Horses		140	0	0			
Pigs, &c.		131	14	0			
Sheep		555	2	0			
Cattle and cows		189	10	0			
Implements		390	12	0			
Tillages, hay, &c.		542	6	7			
					1949	4	7
Wheat, 4 qrs. 6 bush. per acre, 70*s.*	50				831	5	0
Barley, 7 ,, ,, 35*s.*	16				196	0	0
Beans, 5 ,, ,,	13				100	16	0
Oats, 13 ,, ,, 28*s.*	12				218	8	0
Produce of cows and poultry					50	0	0
Hay sold					—		
Horse work, labour, hay, manure, &c. for private establishment					90	0	0
Live stock and wool sold					2576	19	5
200 tons of mangold-wurzel, to be sold to London cowkeepers, at 20*s.*					200	0	0
					£6212	13	0

LIVE STOCK ACCOUNT.

Dr.	£.	s.	d.	Cr.	£.	s.	d.
To valuation, 1853	1016	16	0	By valuation, 1854	1016	6	0
Feeding stuffs bought	1021	10	9	Live stock and wool sold................	2576	19	5
Live stock bought (including two horses)	1619	0	6	Loss, independent of the root and green crops consumed....	64	11	10
	£3657	7	3		£3657	7	3

The quantity of green and root food consumed by the stock is estimated as follows (this includes the keep of six farm horses):—

12 acres of mangold-wurzels.
6 acres of Italian rye-grass, well irrigated, and five times cut or fed (a very heavy crop).
A good second growth of clover, irrigated, about nine acres. A first growth on eight acres.
20 acres of tares and winter oats.
16 acres of good white turnips and swedes.
The straw of the farm.
5 acres of pasture.

Grinding meal, attendance, interest for shelter, &c., may be considered as a set off against the horse-keep.

---

5. READ BEFORE THE CHELMSFORD LITERARY INSTITUTE: *Dec.* 1852.—**Agriculture, as compared with other Industrial Occupations.**—Seeing that this county, with its million of acres, is almost purely agricultural, and that this the county town, like others, is almost entirely dependent on the welfare of agriculture, I trust the subject I have chosen may be deemed neither tedious nor inopportune.

My object is to show that our great manufacturing prosperity has arisen from a diminution of price, and an enormously increased production and consumption; and I shall consider that I have a right to censure our national agriculture, if it has not availed itself of similar advantages to produce equal results. We must lay down as a sound axiom, that the greatest possible supply of comforts and necessaries is consistent with the utmost happiness and welfare of a people. To doubt this, were to approve the converse of the proposition.

This is taking place in our manufactures, but not in our food; for although a recent legislative enactment has enabled us to tax the world for supplies, a dependence on our own agricultural resources would be attended with want and extreme privation. And why is this? Has the land yielded its maximum of fertility? Has science and mechanism done its utmost? Most certainly not. Who will deny that the production, or I may almost say the manufacture, of our food is the primary necessity of our well-being and well-doing?

Has agriculture been treated as a business? Certainly not; our landed proprietors have yet to learn the fullest development of the trade of agriculture.

It astonishes me, that whilst our merchants combine for every useful purpose their capital and their energies, agricultural proprietors are disunited and inert. One would suppose that if in one case gigantic docks and warehouses, immense steam-navies, and twenty other useful associations, are in active operation, that at least Agriculture would exert herself to obtain from our towns and cities that golden stream of liquid guano that now pollutes our rivers. I will not drag you through the details of our enormous manufacturing progress; suffice it to say that by the mighty steam and all its concurrent developments, our pig-iron produce was:—

	TONS.	PRICE.
In 1800	180,000	£9 per ton.
In 1851	2,500,000	£3 „

and even now it is rapidly increasing; for our iron masters, like our agriculturists, have much to learn, and have, in some districts, not banished all their local prejudices, although they have greatly improved since they lost the protecting duty of £6. 10*s*. per ton.

By the bye, everything on a farm should be of iron; —an iron barrow of 30*s*. has worn out all the wooden ones on my farm, and it is now in capital order.

Let us take cotton, another great staple manufacture. Last year the consumption of cotton-wool was 760 millions of pounds weight, for which we paid eighteen millions of sovereigns. After making it up into every conceivable form and pattern, and supplying all our own people, we sent as much abroad as brought us home thirty millions of sovereigns. Our use or consumption of cotton last year was seven hundred times greater than it was one hundred and fifty years ago, and fourteen times greater than in 1800.

You all know that the price has decreased enormously, and that it is now within the reach of the million. The same remarks apply to the silk, woollen, earthenware, and other every-day commodities. Then how has all this abundance and cheapness been produced? Not by an overweening and inflexible attachment to the waggon and flail—not by a rejection of steam. No! manufacture discarded its pack-horses for canals, and its canals for railways. The spinning-jenny, the mule, and the power loom, impelled by mighty steam, perfected by the results of innumerable and costly experiments, have blessed the inhabitants of this happy kingdom with employment and comfort.

Instead of displacing labour, it has enormously increased it, for the actual workers in all departments of the cotton manufacture are now upwards of a million and a quarter, but, including their families, there are not fewer than three millions and a half, or one-eighth of the population of the United Kingdom dependent upon this manufacture. And what a pleasant thing it must be for us, in this purely agricultural county, to reflect upon, that they are all consumers of agricultural produce. Surely, if they, by improved means, supply us cheaply and abundantly, have they not a moral right to demand of agriculture similar advantages?

Our "Manchester School," as it has been called,—and I, for one, consider it an excellent school,—has always been ready to seize upon every new useful improvement; — I wish I could say as much of agriculture. On the very first invention of gas, it was applied as an economy in lighting our cotton factories; prejudice subserved to calculation and profit. Imagine to yourself one of these new cotton factories, 410 feet long, 76 feet wide, six storeys high, with a steam power of 150 horses, which will drive 150,000 spindles.

These manufacturers don't pull down their labourers' cottages o save rates, and make them walk two or three miles to their work, but actually spare them the trouble of walking up stairs, for they are raised from floor to floor by steam; and it is even calculated that if they were compelled to walk up so many stairs, the loss of time would absorb much of the profit. Large returns and small profits is the creed of the Manchester school, and, judging by results, it has not been an unsound maxim: I commend it to agriculture.

But has agriculture progressed with manufactures? Let us test it by price. Unfortunately there is an absence of agricultural statistics, which I hope to see some day remedied. It might easily be done, if we had a government board of agriculture, as well as of trade; for it is quite as important. But a reference to Mr. Caird's admirable book, published last year, shows that, since 1770, the price of butter has increased 100 per cent., meat about 70 to 80 per cent., and wool more than 100 per cent.; bread remains about the same price as in 1770; but it is evident, by our importations, that not near enough is produced.

Perhaps the most astounding fact in agriculture just now is this, that we imported last year 200,000 tons of Peruvian birds' dung, for which we paid nearly *two millions sterling*, and that a much larger sum is expected to be paid hereafter. The sewage of London, on the most moderate computation of eminent men, is worth two millions sterling annually, or the exact amount we paid the past year to Peru for birds' dung.

Now if a comprehensive scheme of subterranean pipage, like that of the gas or water of London, and like that on my arm, were carried out to irrigate the country surrounding

London, and even supposing the cost of it to be thirty-three millions sterling, the two millions we now pay to Peru would be six per cent. upon the investment; but, in reality, the affair could be done for infinitely less money, and with much greater results. In my case, iron pipage cost £250 per mile; but even if it cost £1,500 per mile, your thirty-three millions might enable you to lay down some 20,000 miles of pipage. Of course all these matters are easily reducible to correct calculations in detail. My only object now is to draw attention to this all-important question.

My own experience of irrigation this year has satisfied me that, in the production of root and green crops, I can, on my miserable soil, surpass all efforts on the very richest valley lands. If it can be done in my case, it can in others where the land is naturally or artificially drained.

How delightful to combine a system of sanitary cleanliness with a vast increase of the means of subsistence for man and animals. The facile and abundant production of milk of first-rate quality around each great city or town would arrest the rapid deterioration of race taking place in our crowded towns by "sky-blue," the produce of wash-fed and closely-packed cows.

The irrigation, irrespective of manure, by the water used in our towns and cities would be most valuable. Surely all classes of thinking men will not much longer neglect this gigantic and important subject.

The land is like a purse: you cannot keep taking out without replenishing, or you bring certain ruin. It seems nationally ridiculous to go to Peru for what we are wasting at home.

There is not half the difficulty in the economizing and application of our sewage as in the making of railways. Only create the will, and the way will quickly follow.

Those who would interpose the rights or prejudices of individuals, must remember that, for the public good, our iron railways have pushed themselves rudely through the very vitals of prejudice, and individual interest and feeling. An Englishman's house, valued beyond price from various associations, is no longer his castle; enormous vested interests have been destroyed, and others created, and all, it is to be hoped, for the public good.

The Labourer, and the Law of Settlement.—Economy in the means of production is indicative of success. How stands the case with the great agricultural tool, the labourer?

Our great manufacturers are compelled by law to take care of the education and morals of their juvenile operatives; but, independent of this, their own sagacity and humanity have dictated in a great many a watchful regard for the moral and social condition of their work-people. The manufacturer finds it to his interest to congregate around him the elements of his success. How is it with the agriculturist? I mean the landholder, under the temptation offered by the miserable law of allocation or settlement. Cottages are pulled down, and the labourers removed to other districts or towns, as encumbrances or nuisances. This suicidal policy reacts fearfully on the farmer.

The physical condition of a man is the measure of his bodily power. His labour is sufficient without the addition of a three-mile walk morning and evening. It is a perpetuating of ignorance and vice. The time thus wasted might be employed in acquiring learning and intelligence, if there were schools or opportunities for doing so, *which there are not.*

One is struck with the fact, that our towns and cities are now abounding with food for mind and cleanliness for body, by literary societies, mechanics' institutes, and baths and wash-houses, whilst the majority of our agricultural labourers are unsoaped and untaught. Every medical man knows, too well, that our wretched agricultural hovels, untroughed and undrained, foster crime and breed disease. I could point out numerous cases in my own neighbourhood, where the aged, the adult, and the youthful of both sexes, are huddled together, in indecent propinquity, in a single sleeping-room not much better than a pig-sty. So long as summer lasts, with open doors and casements, and short nights, matters are endurable; but when chilly autumn, scanty clothing, and deficient fuel, compel a shutting up for warmth, then come typhus and scarlet fever, and all the malignant consequences of a polluted and putrescent atmosphere. Thence ensue long sufferings, heavy parish charges for burials and other relief, a deteriorated peasantry, and a national loss. It is a bitter but truthful sarcasm on agriculture, that while the agricultural labourer may live anywhere, and come any distance, the cart or plough horse is carefully provided for in the immediate neighbourhood of his intended labour.

I think I see the time is coming, when the condition and sufficiency of cottages on an estate, and the general appearance of its farmeries, will be taken as a measure of the intelligence and humanity of its owner. The sooner our legislature extends the law of settlement, and removes the premium for destroying cottages, the better for the country at large.

There is an inherent sense of decency amongst the labourers themselves, which often finds vent in truthful but severe comments on these evils. The enormous rents produced by this system of allowing the population to outgrow their tenements, are surprising. I know scores of cottages that are not actually worth a £20 note, rented at £3 to £4 per annum. Their crazy and tottering forms indicate their age and frailty, and occasionally they lean on some common outward prop, to prevent their falling. Thus is the housing of our best agricultural tools, our peasantry, left to the itinerant speculator, who knows the labourer's sense of decency and comfort must succumb to the necessity for shelter. Our law of settlement perpetuates prejudices, and prevents the knowledge and introduction of different or improved modes of culture. Each isolated district thus plumes itself on the perfection of its practice, in happy ignorance of what is going on elsewhere.

If early travel enlarges the mind and improves the taste of our aristocracy, does not the principle hold good for our democracy? Many of our labourers, and farmers too, never went beyond the precincts of their parish, or adjoining markets, and have most vague and odd ideas of what is going on in the world; but railways and newspapers are working a change, and our Great Exhibition of last year did wonders in drawing our rural population from their seclusion.

It is impossible to avoid being struck, whilst scanning the maps and plans of various farms, with the monstrous arrangement of the estates. A farm of 640 acres (or a square mile) should be reachable at half a mile every way from the centre. On the four-course shift, an intersection of four tramroads, railroads, or common roads, would render the removal of crops and transmission of manure cheap and facile; but the whole system now is abominable and unbusiness-like, and so it will remain, until our landed proprietors urge upon our legislature the necessity of applying the ordinary business principles of register and immediate transfer. Queer-shaped fields of every ungainly form, green and muddy lanes, bad roads, high fences, and deep ditches, absorb the farmer's profit in twenty different ways. I declare, that this very September I have scrambled over huge banks embroiled with immense "lawyers," as the natives call them, although they are really sharp and entangling briars and brambles. Having surmounted this *chevaux de frise* I sink in up to my chin into a ditch. This is no exaggeration, but an ordinary real matter of fact. I cannot help exclaiming on such occasions, "What on earth can these be wanted for, when a direct pipe would convey all the water from so small an area!" It is the same in agriculture as in our great cities; there has been no calculation of rain-fall and velocity of transit; a well glazed pipe of a foot diameter would convey more water than a five-foot crooked ditch, the latter encumbered with all sorts of obstructions, washing into holes, bends, and eddies. The minutes of evidence collected by our excellent Board of Health in London have exposed equally gross mismanagement in our sewers, which, ineffective at five feet diameter, become efficient at five inches, velocity of current preventing that sedimentary deposit which will accumulate from a slow dribbling stream.

I remember full well, and so must every other landowner, that when it became necessary to commute the tithe into a rent-charge, the whole kingdom was at once surveyed, measured, and mapped; and the landowners were compelled to disburse as much as 4s. per acre for the expense. Well then, here is a precedent with a vengeance; I can't, for the life of me, see why I should not be able to exchange my land, or sell it, as readily as I could any other property I possess. Remember that the interposition of a difficulty of exchange, or transfer, diminishes seriously the value of landed property; if immediately salable and transferable, it would be preferred as a security to exchequer bills or consols, and money might be raised upon it at least one per cent. cheaper than at present. I cannot conceive why the same dependence on personal responsibility should not exist in land as in consols, provided a proper public office for the registration of sales or interchanges were established. I believe this is done in Scotland.

Steam.—It must be quite clear to the most superficial observer, that the main instrument of our rapid manufacturing and commercial progression is steam. The mere thought of its influences, in a moral, social, and economic point of view, is overwhelming. It facilitates intercourse, economizes time, multiplies labour, and cheapens production. Volumes might be written of its wonders, past, present, and to come; and well have manufacturers and commerce availed themselves of it.

But is it really credible that prejudiced and stolid agriculture has alone rejected its advances and disdained its aids? If I were a perfect stranger to this country, and to its history and circumstances, and were told that the steam-power of this mighty interest was less than 10,000 horse, I should at once condemn its fatal ignorance, or prejudice. Why, there is scarcely any article of luxury or necessity used by the farmer and his landlord that they do not owe to steam. From the button of his coat to the shoe of his horse—for every colour in his apparel—for the very newspaper he reads, and the impress of its characters, he is indebted to steam. His very loaf is now no longer dependent on wind or water, but is secured by steam. And yet we hear the miserable flail tapping the barn-door, and see the exhausted and haggard thrasher evidencing alike the misery and miscalculation of making man a mere automaton.

Don't tell me of the want of capital in agriculture, when land can always be transferred (barring the law's delay) into cash at £25 to £50 the acre. Good tenants are to be got in agriculture; but then the landlords must make it worth their while—they must be tempted, encouraged, and secured: capital is independent and fertilizing, and wants inviting; want of capital is humble and exhaustive, and wastes itself.

Such men as the late Mr. Coke, of Norfolk, who combined business principles with hereditary nobility, knew well how to improve his tenantry, increase his rental, and benefit his country; there are others like him, but far too few.

We are slow to give up our *predilection for land as an honourable qualification*. A man may be a millionaire in mills, machinery, consols, or shipping—his mind may be gigantic in learning, or science; but unless wedded to a certain acreage of cold clay or hard gravel, vain must be his aspirations to a legislatorial seat in St. Stephen's. This is absurd and inconsistent with our great commercial and manufacturing dignity. When ours was a merely pastoral and agricultural nation, such a system was proper and natural.

So long as you make land the sole basis of legislative qualification, so long you will perpetuate non-improvement. Having only this object in view, an immense number of proprietors, holding deeply embarrassed estates, have no means or desire to improve the condition of their wretchedly-managed properties. I find fault with our legislature for permitting such a temptation to neglect, resulting as it does in a great public injury.

Agricultural Statistics are much to be desired. I wish some member would move for returns of the amount of steam-power used in agriculture—the amount of money per acre collected for education in the various agricultural districts—the number of hedgerow trees per acre in various counties—and the miles of fences. The comparison of various districts would show such frightful discrepancies that we should no longer wonder at the wealth of some and poverty of others.

On the one hand, we have men like the late Mr. Coke and like many I could now name, looking around for tenants of large intelligence and sufficient capital, likely to improve permanently the value and rental of the estate, and impart by their example a high and improved state of cultivation. Such men are only to be obtained by suitable residences and farm-buildings adapted to the shelter of a large number of cattle, by liberal covenants and leases, by drainage, by the removal of injurious trees and fences, and by an exemption from an excess of game.

On the other hand, we have numerous districts permitted to remain in a miserable state of primitive neglect, and unparticipating in the general progression of landed value.

I see too many of this class in my mind's eye. The land cold, wet, and shaded by numerous small enclosures, studded with stunted trees, which can never be profitable to the landlord, and are certainly most injurious to the occupier. The humble tenant, though parsimoniously economical, sees his limited capital swallowed up, bit by bit, by poverty and weeds; his temper sours in the struggle, as, year by year, the quality of his productions deteriorates, and sinks lower in the unremunerative scale of marketable value. At last he leaves his farm a ruined man, doomed to seek some menial office, or to compete with the ordinary labourer. The landlord of such a property gets what is called a bad name, is pitied or censured, and must put up with an indifferent tenantry and a depreciated rental. The tradesmen and labourers of the neighbourhood participate in the depressive influence; and it extends through them, in a degree, to the country at large.

I know one unimproved farm which has had three tenants in

three years. A single year sufficed to ruin one tenant; the other two each lost about £700 in the year—the farm being about 300 to 400 acres in extent. This is only one instance out of a great many I could name.

The only parties who benefit by these changes are the agents who make the valuation from one tenant to another, and the auctioneers.

The want of means to improve entailed or other estates can no longer be pleaded as an excuse for non-improvement; for we have now associated companies, authorized by Acts of Parliament, to erect buildings, drain, make roads, or effect any necessary improvement, chargeable as against the estate. The competition between high-farmed and low-farmed estates, is becoming daily more obvious and severe; it requires no conjuror to predict which will be the first to succumb.

Let us see how stands our acreage, and whether there is not abundant opportunity for an enormous agricultural increase at even lower prices. Now surely something might be done to increase the produce only 10*s.* per acre; and that would at once add fifteen or twenty millions sterling to our food, or much more than the whole of our foreign imports.

I will take, for instance, one great source of economy—I mean the removal of unnecessary banks and fences, and the better management of those which remain, which should be assimilated to our effective railway fences. Recent statistics show that the mere ground occupied by fences in some counties amounts to ten per cent. of the acreage, to say nothing of the damage by their roots and shading, insects, &c., and also by an enormous number of unprofitable trees. Taking the kingdom through, I believe all valuers will allow that from five to seven and a half per cent. is not too large an allowance for fences and waste on a farm. Here, then, is at once an enormous opportunity of adding millions to our acreage. I am afraid even to estimate the damage done by trees, it is so enormous. I know some districts where there are twenty to fifty to the acre, and their roots may be traced from 30 to 100 feet. If we only removed two from each acre, we should have 100 millions less, and I think we might spare 500,000 miles of fences. I know plenty of tenants who would rather go to a timber-yard and buy foreign deals, than be at the expense of removing and cutting up the worthless timber offered by their landlords. We cannot compete with the natural forests of Canada.

The non-economy of Manure is also a serious consideration, especially deserving the landlord's attention. The loss resulting from a month's continued rain must be to the farmer enormous. The ammonia of his yard and of his heaps, with other valuable solutions, are lost to him for ever. When landlords and farmers understand agricultural chemistry, they will naturally combine to establish covered yards, and other protective means to economize that costly production. I say costly, for I know from my own experience that you cannot feed cattle with food at market prices without a loss, or charge for manure, of from twenty to thirty per cent., and often much more.

I am glad that covered farm-yards are extending in this neighbourhood. The owners and occupiers will soon follow them up by an erection of steam-engines.

If we take the literature of agriculture as an evidence of its educational and mental condition, one is struck with the feebleness and paucity of county journals in certain districts of England. In lieu of great commercial, agricultural, social, and scientific questions, the limited sheet is occupied by petty and local occurrences of every-day life. I know full well, that in many cases the talented editors are compelled to write down to the level of the ignorance and prejudice of their readers. I trust and believe that the establishment of so many societies like yours, in the heart of agricultural districts, may lead to enlightenment.

It is to be regretted that the peculiar occupations and distant locations of our agricultural population lead considerably to prevent their enjoying, to the full extent, similar advantages. Still, much might be done by local book-clubs, and other arrangements.

In these times we have clubs and societies of most sorts, but not a land-valuer's society—which I should very much like to see established.

Here is a large body of active, educated, and influential men, forming the connecting link between landlords and tenants, but hitherto not amalgamating their aggregated and practical agricultural knowledge for the improvement of agriculture. It is highly desirable, that the extremely opposite and anomalous practices of valuation, in particular localities, should undergo a thorough reformation. I am aware how large an amount of influence is exercised by this class of individuals, and how much they are looked up to by both landlords and tenants. Taking them as a body, I am sure that a periodical conference and interchange of sentiments would greatly tend to assimilate, gradually and prudently, the most incongruous of local valuations and farm practice.

I do not know a greater evil in this country than the over-trading in land. Now in business we do not measure a man by the size of his shop and warehouse; but by the judicious sufficiency of his stock, and compactness of his arrangements.

In agriculture, the desire appears to be for quantity, rather than for quality, too often as regards both landlord and tenant; and hence the cry, when improvement is suggested, "Where is the money to come from?" When I wished to expend money in this way, I sold one farm, and applied the money to the improvement of another; this must be done more generally, if we are to go a-head, and compete with foreigners and with the well-farmed districts of this kingdom.

Improvement is costly, although profitable; for instance—

	£. s. d.		£. s. d.
Pipe drainage, per acre, costs	4 0 0	to	6 0 0
Brick and slated buildings, with steam-power, &c.	6 0 0	to	8 0 0
Irrigation by subterranean iron pipes, with hose and jet	5 0 0		

So here is a sum of £15 to £20 per acre, irrespective of chalking, marling, claying, clay-burning, the removal of trees, fences, &c., the making good roads, and the subsoiling and levelling. The tenants' residence would probably cost £5 per acre.

Now, it is by such means as those above mentioned, that our most valuable estates have attained their increased rentals, and withstood these heavy claims for abatement which have thrown into the landlords' hands many unimproved farms.

Whilst treating of the great question of our national agriculture, I would fain have avoided an allusion to my own agricultural proceedings; but living as I do amongst you, who have witnessed my battles and my struggles, I cannot help feeling that it is no longer now in this county considered extravagant or ridiculous to drain heavy clays, to erect steam-engines and substantial buildings, to aërate the subsoil, to substitute carts for waggons, or even to lay down subterranean iron pipes for the economical application of that essential liquid which too frequently embrowns our horseponds and ditches.

Being now disentrammelled from the leading-strings of an imaginative protection, let the noble art of Agriculture strive to rival her sister Manufacture in the science, abundance, and cheapness of production. To have enough and to spare will be as great and as necessary triumph for our agriculture as for our manufactures.

Signs of the Times.—Our social position in regard to the proprietorship of land is undergoing rapid changes. When this country was pastoral and agricultural only, seigneurial dignity assumed a dominant and almost patriarchal character. But now, the overflowing and accumulating wealth of commerce, manufactures, and trade finds vent in the purchase of unsettled estates, and is partially superseding the ancient aristocracy.

Great good will result from this to the nation at large. The new comers will bring with them common-sense habits of business and active progression, which they will impart to their more astute neighbours; whilst, in return, they will by degrees imbibe the higher education, refined manners, and dignity of position which characterize so pre-eminently our high aristocracy.

I have often been amused by a distant and disinterested survey of my own agricultural position. I unwittingly, and very naturally, in my desire to apply common-sense principles of improvement to agriculture, stumbled against the old antiquated castle of prejudice. Instantaneously there descended from its turrets on my poor devoted head such a storm of missiles—indignation, imputation, ridicule, censure, disbelief—that had I not been clothed with the strong armour of truth, I must have succumbed.

Years have elapsed, and asperities have softened down; but even now certain honest portly yeomen look at me askance with gravity, and honestly believe that I have done a great agricultural mischief—that I have opened landlords' eyes, and made them believe that farming was profitable. I hope my balance-sheet of last year has somewhat diminished the prejudice on this score. Careful non-improving landlords have, too, been rather shy of me, and (for I can tell at a glance by their looks) eye me as a rash and speculative innovator. But time alters many things. I see an improving feeling towards me.

One hears now of deep draining here, a cleared country there, a range of substantial buildings, a few boarded floors, and some are actually so rash as to *talk* of having steam-engines.

One in this county, whose old premises were destroyed by fire, has reluctantly consented to covered yards, but will not hear of steam, although he always rides to town behind it. His successors will be free from this prejudice.

Farmers are getting gradually apologetic for their old waggons and exposed dung-heaps, and are making the "*amende honorable*" to our friend the Rev. G. Wilkins, by sowing less seed.

My last new "scheme" of subterranean irrigation is far too strong a dose to be swallowed at present, so my agricultural friends are only looking on to watch how it agrees with me. I feel remarkably comfortable under it at present, and am glad to find that an offer for the sewage of your town has been already made for agricultural purposes.

Joking apart, I can afford to hold out the hand of forgiveness to my bitterest opponents. The conscious triumph of having successfully stimulated the progression and development of agriculture, gives me firmness and good humour. I have all along had the moral support of thinking and intelligent minds—great has been its comfort! I feel, like the good old Duke, that my battles have been fought and won; and I still hope to live to see our national agriculture rank side by side with our manufactures, for the good of our people and for the national honour.

Our lamented departed hero knew full well the importance of abundant supplies for his brave armies. Let us then remember, that the indomitable courage and endurance of Englishmen well deserve the encouragement of ample physical support. It is, therefore, our duty to elevate the character of British agriculture, not only on the low ground of profit, but on the nobler consideration of national dignity and policy.

In Conclusion.—I see, in perspective, a railway activity pervading agriculture. The time is coming when farms will be squared, trees removed, and game moderated—when tramways will intersect estates, and one horse will draw to market the load of four—when the sewage of our towns will ebb back to its original source—when the waters of our rivers and drains will be applied to the irrigation of our fields—when our millers will use steam instead of water—when our farmers and their children will be better educated, and rank higher in the social scale—when our labourers will be better housed, taught, and fed. Then will the blundering rudeness and clumsiness of ignorance be exchanged for the watchfulness and thought of an enlightened intelligence—then will the fractional calculations of profit outweigh the fears of cost—then will antiquated territorial legalities be superseded by personal responsibility, identity, and possession. I see all this in the distance: it is a mere question of time. I see mighty engines on railwayed open fields, tearing up furrows a yard deep, making the land look like a sea—I see these hungry earthy masses saturated and immediately fertilized with the sewage of our towns—I see ample evaporation and facile percolation. Tottering and dilapidated farmeries will give way to permanent and convenient homesteads—the pinching economy of a penurious and pernicious system will be exchanged for liberal views and large operations—capital will develop its giant strength, unfettered by seigneurial restrictions—agriculture, commerce, and manufactures will unite by the ties of a great common interest and common intelligence, for the good of our people and for the honour of this great nation.

PART VI.

OCCASIONAL CORRESPONDENCE.

Addressed to the Agricultural Journals during the years 1842-58.

Drainage—Personal—Instruction—Roads—Demoralization—Carts—Feeding—Thin-seeding—Steam-engines—Forking—Hedgerows—Irrigation—Iron per acre—Reapers—Thin-sowing—Small Farms—Burned Clay—Feeding Straw—The Miseries of a Public Improver.

The Importance of Draining Land.—In illustration, I cultivated two pieces of stiff brick-earth, both richly manured—the one drained, the other not; both, however, having a considerable fall. In the drained land everything luxuriated and was early; in the other the very reverse—all stunted and late. So wonderful a contrast convinced me that there were powerful chemical agencies at work. Well may vegetation improve after a shower, where the rain can percolate through the well-drained land, bringing down with it, to the roots, the much-desired ammonia; and equally clear must it be that undrained land, already saturated with stale water, can derive no such benefit, for the rain cannot filtrate, but runs off the surface. Again, without drainage, the only escape for moisture is by evaporation, which, it is well known, causes excessive coldness; besides, wet land, not being porous, is deprived of the rays of light, of heat, and of the atmosphere, which would naturally occupy the pores vacated by the water in its downward course. It is lamentable to see the immense sums wasted in this country on undrained lands—in manure, extra manual and animal labour,—with an unprofitable return of capital. Was there ever a farmer who drained, but would tell you it paid itself, principal and interest, in the very first or second crop? There is little doubt that the perfect drainage of all the heavy and spongy land in the United Kingdom would increase the produce at least one-fourth, at a diminished expense, and render us no longer dependent on foreign supplies. I have heard many persons say that "their land was so stiff, that it was of no use draining it"—illustrating their remark by saying that "water will remain in a horse's foot-hole till it evaporates." Do try and convince them that it cannot go down unless they *make a way for it*.—1842.

A Personal Discussion.—Mr. Cunnington should consider that Tiptree Heath has never boasted of prize ploughmen or prize cattle. My feelings will not allow me to send adrift old servants; they are willing to learn and improve, and the greater will be my merit should I succeed in carrying out my views with the resident labourers, rather than introducing fresh faces from more highly cultivated districts. Tiptree has charms for me, and happy shall I be to see the whole of that neighbourhood take a foremost rank in agriculture. A critic should be *just* if he means to be *respected*, but Mr. Cunnington is like Sterne's critic, "all find-fault," no redeeming merit "to save my reputation in his jaundiced eye." All vile, wrong, and ridiculous—"profit" attracts him like a talisman, excluding all philanthropic or patriotic views. Now, really this Mr. Cunnington is not a very "cunning" man, or he would hesitate as to *alarming* "metropolitan gentlemen, who know nothing about land," but who "come to spend their money foolishly in Essex." The money does good, if even the owner loses it. Mr. Cunnington *might* have said, "Mr. Mechi, you are a great fool for spending your money so lavishly; but, at all events, *we in the neighbourhood* have derived considerable benefit therefrom. It has given employment to many a poor man who sadly wanted it. You have stimulated others to follow your example in drainage and the removal of timber," &c. But no! in Mr. Cunnington's eye it is a crime to erect good buildings, to drain the land, to save the manure, to give warmth, dryness, and employment to human beings, and to shelter your cattle from the cutting blast; with him the rotten thatch and dripping eaves are the very *beau idéal* of rustic landscape. Oh, how he will miss the brown and trickling stream of liquid dung! no idle labourers now to watch the pitiless storm as it rushes past the shivering steer.

With sighs he deplores the loss of eastern cutting winds. To him the sunny south brings cares and pangs and discontent. Sternly he says, "Give me a cold and northern aspect; away with your soft, voluptuous gales."

Pity he had not visited the farm in its original condition. He might then have felt keenly for the misfortunes of the honest and worthy steward, who still remains with me; he who in the old wretched house lost by fever in one short month his affectionate wife and two daughters. He might have seen in those rooms peas in a corner, growing, from moisture. He would have walked across the land in a wet September day up to his knees in bog (serve him right too), or be struggling in the stiffer soil with solid encrustments of birdlime-like clay.

Some insinuation is made as to the operation being connected with my trade. I scorn the imputation. It is *worthy the narrow minds of those who make it;* they cannot see it possible for a man to have his heart in the "right place;" that he may feel he is "but a steward in trust of his own wealth;" that it is his duty to look around, and benefit, so far as lies in his power, his fellow-creatures.

I will not believe, till I hear it from their own lips, that either Mr. Hutley, Mr. Baker, Mr. Hobbs, or Mr. Surridge, entertain any such feelings; they are too great advocates for improvement. I say now, and will maintain the position by proof, that the homesteads of Essex are, in too many instances, not creditable to so wealthy a county; and that disgrace is more pungent when contrasted with the extensive, durable, and well-arranged receptacles for its unemployed paupers.—1845.

When our Soil is poorly, let us consult the Chemist.—I hope the time is fast approaching when we shall, for complaints of the soil, get advice from proper analytical chemists as readily as we would for ourselves, so that they may investigate the disease, and prescribe a proper remedy, depending on the patient's constitution and the nature of the ailment, whether chronic or transient, whether arising from plethora, starvation, or dropsy—too much water without the means of escape, a very usual complaint in earthy patients.

Farmers make frequent mistakes when they trust to their own notions of doctoring: they readily perceive, by the external symptoms, that their patient is in an unsatisfactory state, but make sad havoc with their nostrums. How frequently do we see a dressing of dung forced on an already satiated patient, who cries out for an alterative of chalk or cold clay. Another administers a strong stimulant of lime, where the sufferer is already exhausted by previous excitement, and requires a tranquillizing tonic of good old mellow manure. A third gives alkalies, where acids and phosphates can alone avail. They do not consider that, if troubled with stone, gravel, or density of the substratum, a gentle operation with the subsoiler might give ease by causing a loosening of the parts; or that in cases of scurviness and poverty, light, air, cleanliness, exercise, and good feeding might prove a restorative.—1845.

Cutting Chaff answers admirably for manure. It instantly absorbs the liquid manure, and mixes intimately with the solid, where trod, making a dense compact mass, requiring much less room and carriage, for a load of this is certainly equivalent to two of long loose strawy stuff. It is astonishing how small a space a truss of straw occupies when cut half-inch; of course there is just as much of it when cut as before, although some folks seem alarmed at the diminution in bulk. We cut with two-horse power and Wilkes' (of Sheffield) cutter. We can cut 32 trusses per hour, but do cut from 22 to 26 at a common pace. I consider the cost of cutting is amply repaid by other saving. Of course decomposition proceeds more effectually; there is less shaking, turning, &c., and far less waste by escape of ammonia than in large loose masses. In bedding our horses and cattle we always put long straw over it to prevent their getting dirty by lying on the moist and filthy mass; but for pigs this is unnecessary, as they will not dung near the bed.—*May* 7, 1846.

National Agricultural Instruction.—"The National Assembly adopted on Tuesday the project of decree on agricultural instruction by a majority of 579 to 100."—*Times, Oct.* 5, 1848.

A perusal of the foregoing paragraph suggests many serious and painful considerations. Where are our institutions for national agricultural instruction? Where the senatorial or ministerial orations in favour of so worthy an object? Where the grant of public money for its establishment? Is the condition of our agriculture perfection? Is food produced in such superabundance that we need no improved scientific practice? Does no convulsive struggle of nervous susceptibility agitate our monetary system, our ministry, and our exchanges on the eve of a doubtful harvest? Are rents so punctually paid that the prosperity of our agriculturists is unquestionable? Is there no superabundance of willing but unemployed labour, no consequent misery, crime, and discontent? Are there no uncultivated or half-cultivated acres almost imploring the application of skill, labour, and capital? Is it possible that, amidst the crash and turmoil of fierce political elements, our Gallic neighbours should deem this a question of paramount necessity, which we in tranquil security so utterly neglect? Alas! it is too true that the science and practice of agriculture do not occupy their proper position socially or politically. Everything is left to chance, or to individual exertion and experiment—no order, no system, no uniformity; nothing but agricultural discrepancy. We have colleges and schools in connection with the arts and sciences, the army, the navy, the clergy, and the bar; but the production of our daily bread, our very existence, is too commonplace and contemptible an object to be fashionable.

If this is doubted, look at the position of the only public institution of this kind, the Royal Agricultural College at Cirencester. Perfect in its instructional and practical arrangements, well supplied with students, yet a considerable portion of its shares are not yet taken up. This noble and national undertaking is unaided by our Government or by the Royal Agricultural Society of England, who have both been solicited, but in vain. The frigid indifference of our landed proprietors to this institution is of itself sufficient and painful evidence of the little value attached to agricultural instruction. If knowledge is power, ignorance must be weakness, agriculturally as in other matters. The time is approaching when the surplus capital of trade, commerce, and manufactures must find its way to agriculture and to agricultural improvement. Already have railways and foreign loans absorbed their share. To employ capital in agriculture without practical and scientific knowledge would be ruin. It behoves, then, capitalists of all classes to take an interest in national agricultural instruction.

The necessity for employing and feeding our daily increasing population is an obvious and fearful proposition. The acres do not multiply; capital and skill must therefore unite to employ more labour and raise more food from our present limited area. I call therefore on our legislature, and on the patriotic and wealthy, to lend a willing aid in so good a cause. Our manufacturers and traders have as deep an interest in this question as our landed aristocracy. Our government can only expect order and good feeling when the able and willing are employed and fed. I entreat you, sir, to exercise your powerful pen in aid and to the attainment of "National Agricultural Education."—*Oct.* 24, 1848.

Parish Roads.—At a time when able-bodied labourers are compelled to seek refuge in our union-houses, for want of employment, it is our duty to look round and see whether there is not an opportunity of availing ourselves of their labour with advantage. Look at the condition of our parish roads generally; instead of being nicely rounded, so as to shoot the water, the middles are worn into holes, in which the water stands in pools, the high shoulders on each side preventing its escape. As surveyor in this district, I have improved a piece of road very cheaply, by removing the turf from the sides, picking and sifting the earth on each side, and throwing the gravel into the middle and into the holes, so as to form a gentle elliptic, sufficiently rounded to keep itself dry. This employs labour, and saves much cartage and expense of stones or gravel; for, owing to the inefficient manner in which many of these roads were originally made, it is found that a large mass of the gravel has worked to the sides, where it is not wanted, and where it is generally overgrown with grass or turf. It is melancholy to see many good roads ruined because the ditches and archways are filled up with vegetable matter, and are consequently unable to carry the water, so that it runs over and scours the middle of the road, causing deep furrows, the gravel being washed into the ditches. Neglect in roads, as in all other things, is costly and unprofitable—a stitch in time saves nine. In every respect, morally and economically, a little more attention to these matters would be advantageous. I find that breaking the largest stones is very convenient and profitable.—*Dec.*, 1848.

Agricultural Demoralization.—By residing three years in this neighbourhood, almost surrounded by barren heath, far from any church or school, and without any resident gentry, I am enabled to state a few facts on this matter. It is a great mistake to assume, under any circumstances, that human beings are naturally ill-disposed or ungrateful. On the contrary, I have great dependence on the general kind feeling existing in society; good being the rule, evil the exception. This is proved by the ready submission to law and order in our densely populated island, frequently, too, under the severe trials of great misery and want.

Tiptree Heath has always been notorious in Essex for its poverty in land and person, poaching, pilfering, and a generally low state of morals. Is it to be wondered at? Situated on the verge of several extensive parishes, without religious or moral example or instruction, uncared for, unsought after, this barren spot became occupied by squatters, or persons of poor and irregular habits; scores of mud huts (called cottages), grotesque in appearance, and scarcely fit for dog-kennels, have at various periods sprung up, as it were, from the heath, until we have a numerous though scattered population. Willing stewards of manors readily assented to any applicant who would build (?), and enclose a patch of the heath, satisfied that death and transfer must soon add something to the manorial advantages and legal charges. No system, no architectural design, no drainage! all left to accident or chance! poor Tiptree Heath was not worthy of such consideration.

The facilities for keeping a half-starved pony or donkey on the heath encouraged every third man to be a higgler, jobber, itinerant butcher, or beershop-keeper, or all of these; and, no doubt, in former times there was a very great facility for the transfer of property, legally or otherwise: at all events, our well-enclosed and wealthier neighbours in the valley had a very poor opinion of us. It was no uncommon thing to see knots of able but ragged and unemployed men lounging before the public-house or beer-shop. But mark the result of agricultural improvements: the erection of new buildings, draining the land, and levelling the fences, acted as if by magic, and our cases of crime diminished, as I am informed, seven-eighths. Am I not justified, then, in asserting that the first and principal cause of crime is non-employment, resulting first in poverty, and ultimately in robbery. It may be said, "Oh! there is the Union." Ay, but strong, able, and willing men, in the full vigour of life, will rarely submit to the privations, semi-imprisonment, and restraints of a Union, in which they are looked upon as incumbrances. I have reason to know that such men feel irritated and excited, when, observing (acutely enough) the half-cultivated soil almost imploring their labour, they go to be browbeaten before a board of economic guardians. The more bold the spirit, the more pungent the disgrace. It has been my lot to employ men known as poachers, and having a bad reputation as to temper and regularity, but hard workers when employed; I have reasoned with them, and they candidly admitted that so long as they could find employment it was all they required, but they would catch every hare in the parish rather than go to the Union. I have found that employing such men, and reasoning with them in a kindly but firm remonstrance, is far more repressive of crime than severity or neglect.

In the course of three years, with my property much exposed, my whole losses have been three ducks and a sheep. The parties who were assumed to have taken the latter were subjected to the usual legal process (we should always strictly endeavour to punish offenders), but the evidence was inconclusive. Having failed in punishing, my next step was to employ, and thus give them an opportunity of redeeming their character and of avoiding a repetition of offence. My motives have been appreciated, and the desired result has been accomplished. Do not suppose for a moment that I would pass by a man of known good character; such men must and do always command a preference; but I am quite sure that a discreet regard to the well-being and well-doing of our poorer neighbours, a trifling solace in sickness or affliction, a little aid where we know it is required and deserved, wins for us their respect and affection, and stimulates them to act up to our advice or remonstrance;—moreover, it is our duty. Indiscriminate charity is a great evil; there are most powerful objections to pecuniary relief, except under particular circumstances; employment is the great boon.

If our poorer neighbours are uneducated, they are not unobservant; the motives and actions of their superiors are keenly and faithfully discussed, and their example for good or for evil must ever have a considerable and important local influence. We are situated six miles from the parish church, and no other Church-of-England establishment exists within a radius of four to five miles. Although a member of the church, I have considered it my duty to aid the only place of worship and education in this neighbourhood—a small dissenting chapel and school, feeling that without that we should be heathens indeed, and hoping that the time may come when the numerous, increasing, and neglected population of this neighbourhood may be provided with a state church and school, to which end I would most willingly contribute. Let us also hope and expect that our heathy waste may be enclosed, and afford food and employment to its inhabitants. The time I hope may soon come when the local position of our churches will receive legislative consideration and correction. At present I could point out numerous instances where the old dilapidated churches are at the extremity of a parish, and without congregations, the congregations being at another part of the parishes, without churches. This is the case in our neighbourhood.—*January* 9, 1849.

On Land Drainage.—It is now and then well to talk a little on this matter, to interchange our facts and ideas, and to admit and correct our errors. It is a subject one cannot easily forget, as an agriculturist, with so smart a remembrancer as the storm of February 28th. Since I published my pamphlet on draining, I have been watching for facts to prove where I am right and where wrong in my views. First, as to whether we should have furrows and water-furrows. North-countrymen often say to me, "Why dress your land in corduroy?" whilst our Essex farmers would consider it an act of insanity to lay the land flat during winter. I confess, after draining the land, my inclinations sided with the flat-landers, but, to satisfy my mind, and avoid an extensive failure, I laid on the flat one acre in three fields; I am glad that I did so, for it convinced me that the practice of stetch and furrow on strong lands is correct, and that my predilections were wrong. I am not alluding to those absurd mounds which are to be seen in some of our midland counties, but to the stetches about 7 feet wide and perfectly flat on the surface, the furrow being narrow and just the depth to which the land is ploughed. This furrow is neatly struck up or cleared out with a double-breasted plough, affording a free passage to the water when more falls in a given time than can filter to the drains.

I will give my reasons for changing my opinion, and wish it to be clearly understood that my remarks apply to very strong adhesive clays during the winter season, for that is the period of danger in such soils. It is important in heavy soils to have a friable seed-bed. I found that where I laid the land flat, the surface soil was much more difficult to work in the spring, and not nearly so friable as the rest of the field. The difference was strikingly obvious, both in ploughing, drilling, harrowing, and hoeing. It was even observable two years afterwards, in plowing a clover lea, the furrow-slice turning up whole and shining in the flat acre, whilst on each side it crumbled and broke. In hoeing the mangold wurzel the same difference was perceptible, and the crop was not so good on the flat, either of corn or roots.

In very long lengths, with a considerable fall, the utility of water-furrows intersecting the stetch furrows is obvious; they prevent that accumulation of water and accelerated velocity which would wash into the ditches enormous quantities of soil. I presume the serpentine form of the enormous mounds in our midland counties was given to delay and break the force of the current after very sudden and heavy rains.

Theoretically, one would say that in well-drained land the water should descend to the drains; but practically, it is found that dense tenacious soils have not the power to transmit water so quickly as it often falls from the clouds, especially where the fall is considerable, and the surface smooth, fine, or caked. In fact, in dry weather, when the surface was cracked and the incline great, I have seen a hasty thunder-storm rush over the cracks, the momentum of the water overcoming its gravity. In heavy clays there is a great tendency to contraction when dry, and expansion when wet. It is worth our while to consider whether the open furrows, by allowing room for expansion, do not facilitate that extra friability which is wanting on the flat, where the lateral expansion forces the particles of soil into close, dense masses.

But to return to the various modes of draining: it will be remembered that my first 60 or 70 miles of drains were cut 32 inches deep, filled 10 inches with stones, and then a circular pipe placed on the top of the stones, to prevent any earth falling amongst them. These drains were only 12 feet apart, cut obliquely to the fall, having a leader to a certain number of drains. It is now six years since these drains were cut; every one of them runs perfectly after rains, with every prospect of continuing to do so for the next century. Still I considered that mode of draining too expensive, and hardly deep enough; but I wish it to be distinctly understood — for there has been some misapprehension on the subject — that I never altered or changed those original drains. My next mode was with 1-inch pipes, at intervals of 30 feet, 40 feet, and 50 feet, the depth averaging about 4 feet, being, in fact, 5 feet in the hill, and 3 to 4 feet as the ground declined; each drain being its own leader to the open ditch. Three years' observation of these drains convinces me that in our very heavy tenacious clays 40 and 50 feet are rather too far apart, but the ground is very perfectly drained at 30 feet apart. We shall always err on the safe side by draining close. I think there is but little danger as to pipes becoming displaced in heavy soils, if properly done. I had occasion to cut a cross-drain, intersecting the inch-pipe drains that were laid three years ago, and was gratified to find them all as perfect a line of pipe as when first put in, not one of them having moved its position in the slightest degree. In fact, although we cut above and below them, they maintained their places, and were not disturbed; they looked like a continuous pipe, tightly wedged and abutted against each other by the clay. Collars in this soil appeared quite unnecessary: of course the careful placement of the pipe is assumed.

Some six years ago a field of mine was drained two feet deep with pipes, but when I found the crops unsatisfactory, I re-drained it six feet deep at wide intervals—100 feet apart or more, to take away the springs which I knew must be there, and which I found did not enter the shallow drains. Of course the deep drains took the top water as well as the spring-water; but when rains were continuous and abundant, the top and bottom drains both acted and discharged abundantly. I mention this to prevent the removal of shallow drains.

I compare land during heavy rains to a cask kept constantly filled with water; if there were four taps in the cask, one above the other, they would all run when there was enough to fill the cask, but when the supply diminished, the upper tap or drain would cease running first, and so on gradually till the lowest tap also ceased running. If water was only poured in as fast as the lowest tap would carry it, the three upper ones would not run at all; this is exactly what takes place on land. In winter, with much rain, two or three courses of drains one above the other would empty the land quicker than only one line of drain. This, however, is a question of cost and not of necessity, because although one drain may not take the water so quickly as two, still it does enough if it takes it away sufficiently quick to prevent stagnation and preserve the friability of the seed-bed. The power of soil to transmit water to drains within given times must vary with their porosity or permeability.—*March* 13, 1849.

The Value of a Ton of Turnips.—The price paid in the neighbourhood of Colchester for good crops of white turnips and of swedes, to be fed off on the land, without oil-cake or any other food, is as follows:—white turnips, 30*s*. to 40*s*. per acre; swedes, 40*s*. to 60*s*. per acre. This will give an average of about 3*s*. 6*d*. per ton for swedes, and 2*s*. 6*d*. per ton for white turnips. A large sheep-dealer in this neighbourhood tells me he has from 800 to 1,000 sheep consuming turnips at the price per acre which I have named. What the turnips cost to grow is another affair; but the price singularly confirms Mr. Lawes's experiment, that 1 ton of turnips (without any other food) only produced 5 lbs. net dead weight of mutton.—*November* 28, 1849.

The Cart Controversy.—My carts are long, low, and light—not exceeding 7 cwt.,—12 feet long, 7 feet wide; in fact, they are Mr. Hannam's harvest-cart, but we use them for carting coals (2 tons), corn (wheat 80 bushels, barley 100 bushels), lime 80 to 100 bushels, hay 35 cwt., straw *ad libitum*, also for planks and bricks, when we require them. My man brought home 70 trusses of hay to-day—56 lbs. to the truss,—with a pony and old horse that cost together, years since, £18. They never turned a hair, although they came three miles. My waggon-neighbours so often wanted to borrow the said carts that I now charge 1*s*. per day in self-defence. I do not find the Scotch cart so useful; it is not large or low enough. Our light Essex three-quarter carts do well for dung only, but Hannam's are always wanted, and at harvest we never use more than one horse in them, and a boy to drive. With four horses, four carts, and two boys to drive, we harvested quickly 80 acres of mowed wheat, and 20 acres of beans and peas. For carting home green crops they are most valuable. They are made for £10 each; I used to pay £14 or £15. My labourer shrewdly observed to-day that there were 60 trusses of hay on the cart, before it attained the level of the floor of the ordinary Essex waggon. The use of the latter, except from necessity, I consider an act of agricultural insanity. I presume everyone has read Mr. Hannam's admirable paper, with diagrams, at page 73, vol. ii. of the Royal Agricultural Society's *Journal*. It exhausts the subject and settles the question. I, for one, am grateful to him for his valuable facts.—*February* 7, 1850.

MR. MECHI'S LIVE STOCK ACCOUNT FOR 1849.

Dr.	£.	s.	d.	*Cr.*	£	s.	d.
To Grazing stock in hand 1st of October, 1848, valued at the then market prices	621	0	0	By Grazing stock in hand 1st October, 1849, valued at the then market prices	569	18	0
Grazing stock purchased, from 1st October, 1848, to 1st October, 1849	306	17	0	Cash received for live stock sold and slaughtered,	1067	16	3
Corn, hay, straw, linseed, &c., bought	1037	4	6	Cash for wool	24	1	6
Coals, miller's wages, repairs to engine, &c.	128	2	9	Butter, poultry, eggs, milk, and cream	25	0	0
Labour, feeding and attending stock	50	0	0	Cash received for barley-meal sold	84	4	11
				Hay, corn, &c., consumed by two nag-horses, visitors' horses, &c.	75	0	0
				Keep of eight farm horses out of purchased corn and hay	210	0	0
					£2056	0	8
				Charge against manure kept	87	3	7
	£2143	4	3		£2143	4	3

Farm produce consumed in addition to the above:—

17 acres of mangold wurzel, 840 tons.
6 acres of swedes, 90 tons.
8 acres of rye and winter oats, fed off.
4 acres of winter tares, fed off.
13 acres of spring tares, fed off.
6 acres of clover hay, 10 tons.
20 acres of clover, after feed.
5 acres of poor pasture.

79 acres.

The foregoing account shows a charge of £87 3*s.* 7*d.* for the manure, to which must be added the cost of cultivation and charges on 84 acres of green and root crops, which cannot be estimated at much less than £336, making a total charge against the future productions of the farm of upwards of £400. In ordinary seasons about £100 might be taken from this, because there was a diminution for depreciated prices of stock to that extent between the valuation of 1848 and 1849. On the other hand, the interest for capital invested would be an additional charge of £50.

I should observe that I have been very fortunate in the management of my live stock, my losses from disease for the year being under £10.

Now, is this stock account a satisfactory or unsatisfactory one? Let us see. We have 56 acres of green crops fed off with corn and linseed, therefore sufficiently manured for the rotation; and we have 23 acres of root lands to manure. But what have we to pay for besides the £87 3*s.* 7*d.* lost in feeding out corn, &c.? Let us see.

	Tons.
700 quarters of barley, beans, peas, linseed, &c. (five quarters to the ton)	140
80 acres wheat-straw	100
12 acres pea and bean-straw	18
Straw purchased	35
Hay purchased	19
Hay home-grown	15
Bran and pollard, about	15
Dry tons	342
Mangold-wurzel and swedes	430
Tons	772

Besides the ashes of 80 tons of coals used by engine, and the blood, &c., of hundreds of pigs, &c. I am not calculator enough to say what quantity of manure this should produce, but judging from the quantity I have carted, it is not less than 1,200 tons, or carts, besides a considerable quantity of liquid, not a hogshead of which has been allowed to run to waste. However, it is quite clear that the essence of 700 quarters of corn, and other good things, will *tell* for years to come. It is only those who have witnessed the durable effects of good unwashed manure on tenacious and deeply-cultivated soils, who can appreciate its value. I do not believe I could purchase and cart an equal quantity and quality of manure for £600. For instance, my neighbours pay £17 to £20 a freight for London dung or sweepings, which is 6*s.* to 7*s.* a ton, without carting. I need hardly say that my land is in condition to carry out good crops, and no doubt will continue to be so, although naturally miserably poor, and although I crop half of it every year with wheat.

It appears by my statement that, after deducting the cost of live stock bought, the actual money value of meat made and sold during the year was £710. Now, I was curious to know how much per cent. of this was realised by my bullocks, sheep, and pigs. I easily ascertained it as follows:—

BULLOCKS.

Valuation, 1848	£249	Valuation, 1849	£157
Bought, 1849, none.		Sold, 1849	129
			286
	£249		249
		Increase	£37

SHEEP.

Valuation, 1848	£153	Valuation, 1849	£195
Bought, 1849	179	Sold, 1849	232
			427
	£332		332
		Increase	£95

PIGS.

Valuation, 1848	£218	Valuation, 1849	£247
Bought, 1849	128	Sold, 1849	676
			923
	£346		346
		Increase	£577

So that, in fact,—

£346 in pigs produced over and above their cost			£577
£332 in sheep	ditto	ditto	95
£249 in bullocks	ditto	ditto	37
			709
Wool from sheep			24
			£733

A pretty serious comparison of investment, but a true one. If my £581 capital, instead of being in sheep and bullocks, had been in pigs, it would have made a very enormous difference in my favour. Of course we cannot all keep pigs, but whence does this great discrepancy arise? The sheep and bullocks ate up nearly all my root and green crops, hay, &c., and in addition a large quantity of meal, &c. The pigs had only corn-meal, with a few roots. The breeding sows, pollard, corn, and roots. I breed nearly all my pigs. The sheep were folded during the summer, but in winter on Mr. Huxtable's boards, where I mean for the future to keep them entirely, as I can find it makes all the difference in their progression. (By the bye, sheep on boards want shearing much earlier than in the open fields, or they will not do well in close quarters. They must also have water.) I assume that pigs, sheep, and bullocks all ate in proportion to their weight and value, as they were not stinted. We know there was a ruinous depression in bullocks, and a considerable reduction in sheep. I see a great deal of my pork was sold at *5d.* and *5½d.* per lb. during summer. All my pigs and breeding sows are kept close confined in the yards summer and winter, and I will take especial care henceforth that my other animals shall not have much exercise.

In conclusion, I am satisfied there is nothing like plenty of stock. Bullocks, as I said before, are ungrateful fellows, and I do not wonder at it, for no gentleman eats shoulders or necks of beef, although they do of mutton. I am also quite satisfied that our root and green crops must be made secondary and subservient to the larger consumption of corn or cake. In fact, I sincerely believe, from my own practice, that Mr. Huxtable is right, both in keeping his animals without exercise, breeding them at home, and feeding them bountifully. I may, perhaps, some day trouble you with an account of my management of pigs.

My object in publishing the foregoing account, which is a faithful extract from my books, is to show the means I am adopting for bringing my land into a fertile state, and to elicit from others such information as may be useful. It is quite clear that the corn side of our farms, if charged merely with the expenses of the year, is satisfactory in its return; but when we cannot make the green and root crops pay their own expenses, the loss or difference is a heavy tax on the succeeding corn crops. I see in Mr. Hewitt Davis's farm accounts, published in the Royal Agricultural Society's *Journal* (vol. vii. part ii. page 532), he charges the loss on the turnip crop, fed off, at £6 9*s.* per acre, and on the green crop £1 9*s.* 6*d.* Whether by Mr. Huxtable's plan we shall succeed in reducing that loss remains to be proved—I am trying it. One thing is certain, that, as our liquid and solid manures are so costly to produce, the notorious national waste of them is a ruinous prodigality—scarcely an act of sanity, and certainly one of most miserable miscalculation. Landlords and tenants must really lay their heads together to remedy this defect.—*February*, 1850.

Cattle-feeding.—With reference to a past statement on this subject, I have been presented with the following valuation of the manure, on the principle deduced from the very extensive and elaborate experiments of Mr. Lawes; the computation will therefore stand thus:—

	Tons.		lbs.
Meal, bran, and pollard	155	= 347,200 at 3 per cent.	10,416
Straw	153	= 342,700 at ½ per cent.	1,714
Hay	34	= 87,160 at 1 per cent.	872
Mangold wurzel	340	= 761,600	2,253
		(5¾ lbs. of nitrogen per ton.)	
Swedes......................	90	= 191,600	382
		(4¼ lbs. per ton.)	
Carried forward			15,637

	lbs.
Brought forward	15,637
Green crops, and after-feed, 58 acres, estimated as dry at 1½ ton per acre .... 84 = 188,160 at 1 per cent.	1,882
Slaughtered stock, offal, and blood.. 10,000 at 10 per cent.	1,000
Left on the land the tops of mangold wurzel, 105 tons, at 13 per cent.	1,365
Tops of swedes, 30 tons, at 10 per cent.	300
Coal-ashes	—
	20,184 lbs.

20,184 lbs. of ammonia at 6*d*. will amount to £504 12*s*.; so that, on the moderate computation of the above, my prospective crops will have to be charged with this sum, to the credit of my cattle and green crops of 1849. But even allowing for a considerable loss by evaporation, or from other causes, there will remain an immense amount of carbonaceous and alkaline substances, and all the phosphate of lime which was not required in the animal economy. I think we may safely conclude that by proper management of stock, on an average of seasons, there is no cheaper way of maintaining or increasing the fertility of our soils than by a large consumption of purchased food, aided by the root and green crops of our farms, provided we economize the manure, which is rarely done. Every day's experience convinces me that the cooking and preparation of our straw, hay, meal (and possibly our roots), is essential to the profitable feeding our animals; but more of this hereafter.—*April* 18, 1850.

Oxen on Boarded Floors.—My Warnes's boxes, 8 feet by 9 feet, contain comfortably a pair of bullocks, weighing, when fat, from 40 to 50 score. Four of the boxes are now covered with planks 2½ feet wide, 2 inches thick, with an open space of 2½ inches between each plank. Six other boxes, with 2-inch openings and 3-inch planks. As soon as the bullocks were transferred to their new stage, they seemed quite astounded; their performance was pitiable and ludicrous. The sense of danger and insecurity was very apparent, and they seemed afraid to move. Still their appetite did not fail them; all their excrement, solid as well as liquid, passed readily through the openings into what was formerly their bed. But, would they lie down? Certainly not. For twenty-four hours they resolutely maintained their standing, one only excepted. I then spread a light forkful or network of straw under them, and in a few minutes they were all comfortably at rest. The straw soon worked through the openings, and now for the last fortnight they repose comfortably on the bare boards. The bullocks on these open floors are cleaner than those on the straw, although the former are never swept. The heavy pressure forces the liquid to the surface through the layers of our long, glassy, reedy wheat-straw, and keeps the animals wet. It probably is not so with soft barley or oat-straw. When the open boards are first tried, there is nothing pleasing to the grazier's eye, especially when compared with the unlimited supply of the ordinary straw sheds. The edges of the board are new and sharp, and the frequent lifting of the foot indicates fear and discomfort. In lying down and rising up, the sharp edges probably give pain, but in two or three weeks all this passes off, the edges get smooth, and you will find your animals lying in various and easy positions. The 2-inch openings and 3-inch laths I prefer to the $2\frac{1}{2}$ openings and $2\frac{1}{2}$ laths. The former are easier to the animal's feet; and, besides, although the foot is 4 inches wide, the hoof is wedge-shaped from front to back. For calves, I find $1\frac{1}{2}$-inch openings answer well.

I attach great importance to these open floors; they will enable us to keep almost any quantity of stock. The manure requires no turning or fermenting, there is no expense of littering or frequent removal, and no loss of ammonia by fermentation. The comfort is great in every respect. Some of my pigs and sheep have been six weeks over my liquid manure-tank without the slightest symptom of ill health, although I feared it when I made the trial. Gypsum is strewn on the boards every morning. Burned earth is an essential auxiliary to boarded floors; although I burned 1800 cubic yards last year, unfortunately I did not reserve enough to carry me through the winter. Next season I shall slightly thatch a few of the heaps, to keep them dry, ready for absorbing the winter's supply of manure in the boarded boxes. Gypsum is another necessary appendage to this system. A little sprinkled every morning on the boards is highly necessary and beneficial; about a peck to ten bullocks. Every manger should have a large lump of rock-salt, and a water-trough always supplied; the animals will not drink more than is proper for them. The same remark applies to pigs and sheep: with horses, a little discretion is required, should they come in over-heated.

The following instance of the effect of salt is interesting. Six store bullocks, from marshes and straw-yard, were purchased and placed in three boxes. The manger of one box contained a large lump of salt. The other two boxes, being just finished, had none. The boys who attended them observed that the two which had salt ate freely, while the other four scarcely would look at their new food under confinement. I observed that the two having access to salt were constantly licking it.—We are using cabbage as well as roots. Now I do protest against giving fattening animals roots or green food, enough to make them purge. The state of their dung must be our guide. When about the consistence of thick batter, having a certain appearance of cohesion, we are right; but when it falls in a weak splashing condition, indicating diarrhœa, the animal cannot thrive, any more than ourselves under similar circumstances. I have great difficulty in restraining my worthy old bailiff in this matter; the old custom hereabout being to cram them and scour them with an unlimited supply of "green wittles." A very moderate quantity of cabbage is sufficient, and we seldom exceed one bushel of roots daily to each bullock. The remaining food consists of fine-cut straw and hay chaff sprinkled with barley and bean meal, and soaked crushed linseed soup poured over it. If there is a disposition to scour, the roots or green food are withheld for a day or two. It frequently happens that confinement and good living cause the newly-purchased animals to rub excessively. We immediately, in such cases, administer a pound of Epsom or Glauber salts in about a quart of water. This is repeated, if required, in a few days. This allays the excessive heat and irritation of the skin. If an animal looks dull and does not feed well, the dose of salts is administered. Very poor animals are sometimes lousy; wash well with tobacco-water, to remove it. We find no inconvenience from having two horned bullocks in one box; although one will probably be the master bullock, we never can discern any advantage in its condition. This is because both have enough food; were they scantily supplied, this system would not do. It is very necessary to question your stockman daily as to the condition and health of the animals, as they are apt to forget to tell you if an animal shows any deviation from his healthy habits.

Animals arriving from a long journey should have their feet well washed out with strong salt and water, with a ready access to water, and a lump of salt to lick. A dose of salts tends to remove their feverish symptoms. In conclusion, where six to ten sacks of meal are used daily, I consider a steam-engine indispensable, especially as there is in addition so much chaff-cutting, pumping, linseed-crushing, and thrashing. The mere convenience of its sack-tackle is considerable.

N.B.—I mentioned before that the thickness of the yellow deal is two inches. There should be no knots in it, or the weight of the oxen might break it. If slated roofs are too warm in summer, they have the advantage of transmitting heat in spring and autumn, when it is a desideratum.—*March*, 1850.

Thin Seeding.—The success of very thin sowing is dependent on a great many "ifs." If your land is in a warm, dry, early, southern or eastern district; if you sow early; if your cultivation is garden-like in depth, manure, and cleanliness; if every grain is carefully inserted and covered beyond the ken of birds; if you have no attack of wireworm and slug; if your land is not so light that the roots of your wheat get frozen in winter; if it is drained, and the seed does not swell and burst in a wet season; if each grain is perfect and unbroken, and if your general harvest time is the third or fourth week in July; if all these "ifs" can be satisfactorily answered, there is no doubt about the propriety and advantage of very thin seeding.

I know a striking instance of this, in the case of Mr. Piper, of Colne, in Essex, who every year grows wheat on the same land, never ploughs it, but hoes it perfectly clean, and applies soot. He dibbles 1½ peck per acre, and averages, I think, 5½ to 6 quarters per acre per annum. He farms profitably. When I saw this crop five years ago, it was far too thick, with an enormous quantity of straw. Mr. Piper was here yesterday, and told me his wheat was promising again to be an extraordinary crop.

I am quite sure that six pecks per acre is the utmost quantity we dare sow. On naturally rich soils, or where an extra supply of manure is used, four pecks, or even less, are an ample supply. I merely sow that quantity which from experiment I have found best adapted to the poor plastic clays and barren sands of Tiptree Heath. Those who travel through the rich vegetable fen-lands must be grieved to see the ruinous effects of thick sowing. I remember, in passing to Norwich I saw the wheat crops twisted, matted, and laid, as though a troop of wild horses had madly frolicked in them.

The desideratum is to have a full standing crop, free from weeds, and not so dense as to exclude air and light: the absence of light causes the stem to be unhealthy and spongy, instead of having that beautiful coating of pure glass which the Almighty has so wisely destined to keep the plant erect and protect the circulation of its fluids. If I used 5 cwt. of guano, instead of 2 cwt., on my wheats, I should certainly diminish my seed by 2 to 3 pecks. When I dibble, I never exceed a bushel—the seed being properly deposited. The result of my experiments in seeding is that 1 bushel of wheat always produces on my land more than 2 bushels; but that 6 pecks produce the best result, therefore I adopt that which pays best. Mazagan beans and white peas both produced 2 quarters more per acre last year by thick than by thin sowing.

Flue Boilers to Steam-engines.—I dare say that I am not the first or only farmer who has been plagued with black smoke and a bad draught from one's engine chimney. As I have conquered the difficulty, I may now save some pains and penalties to others. In my humble opinion, 9 out of 10 who fit up engines are rather defaulters as to flues. You are assured that no sweeping is required—that the draught will keep all clean, and so forth: the consequence is, that you find the engine, that went off so freely when new and all the flues clear, gradually loses power, more stoking is required, and the neighbourhood is poisoned with smoke which ought to be flame. The vexation and waste of coal is immense. Now, I do assert that flues, especially in flue boilers—I mean those having a tunnel through the centre—should be set so that you can readily clean out, not only the brick flues, but that which passes through the boiler. On examining mine, by breaking through the brick-work, I found it almost choked by a fine heavy dust or sand from the coal or bricks, or both; I removed several barrow-loads. Surely such boilers should never be bricked up, without accessible doors to clean them out occasionally. The moment you see a dense volume of smoke issuing from a steam chimney, depend on it there is imperfect combustion and waste. I say, therefore, look to your flues and chimneys. When my man complained, "Sir, I cannot get the steam up!" "Well, are all your flues swept?" "Oh! yes." "Is the flue through the boiler swept?" "No, we can't get at that;" and yet it was nearly full of sandy grit. Perhaps some of your correspondents can enlarge upon this subject. Flues should almost encompass the boiler, provided you have a high dome to it, to prevent its priming, or spoiling the water.—An opening for cold air at the back of the bridge facilitates combustion. It is the want of draught caused by foul flues that causes the furnace-bars to melt or warp.—*Jan.* 14, 1851.

Steam-engines.—I have derived much advantage by the use of a cast-iron pan occupying the ash-pit, and filled with water. The falling embers and intense heat under the ash-pit convert the water into steam, which cools the under surface of the furnace-bars, and prevents their forming the coal into slag or clinkers. It also prevents the warping and burning of the bars, and economizes fuel and labour, besides facilitating the rapid generation of steam. When the coals fuse or run together, they form a solid mass over the vacancies between the bars, adhere to them, and stop the draught. It is then impossible to keep up the steam. Some idea of the coolness thus gained may be formed by the fact that from 100 to 200 gallons are thus evaporated daily, a pipe being always at hand to supply water when required. The abstraction of caloric thus permits a much denser volume of air in the ash-pit, and with it of course a much larger supply of oxygen to keep up combustion. In fact, without this arrangement, we cannot do the proper amount of work. It does away with much of the stoking or stirring, the reflection of the furnace in the water showing the brilliant and unobstructed state of the fire between the bars. The admission of cold air at the back of the furnace, and the facility of iron doors to clean out the flue boiler, gives us an ample supply of steam, without smoke, and a considerable diminution in the consumption of coal. A 6-horse steam-engine, working up to 8-horse power, with 90 revolutions per minute, requires a quick and ample generation of steam. We thrash and dress four quarters of mowed, long-strawed wheat per hour.—*March* 18, 1851.

Winter Tares.—I have always been successful in growing a very heavy crop of tares, simply by a heavy manuring of "pudding manure" from under my open boarded floors, applied on the wheat stubble, ploughed, rolled, drilled with two bushels of tares, and harrowed. It is a cleaning crop, for no weed or black grass has the slightest chance; it is completely overgrown by the tares, which are either mowed for consumption in the yards, or folded with sheep. The latter is to be preferred, the tares being mowed and placed outside round the fold-hurdles. I have very fine crops of green round turnips succeeding the tares; the tare stubble being scarified, harrowed, rolled, manured with "pudding," and once ploughed, the turnip-seed drilled with 3 cwt. superphosphate of lime and a few clay ashes. Although all the land was well manured, both for the tares and turnips, I can see an immense difference in the turnips where the tares were folded with rape cake. I think the system of seven or eight ploughings for turnips will soon be given up. An Essex friend told me, the other day, he had ploughed nine times for turnips, and still missed a plant, which did not at all surprise me. Every day convinces me that the plough, although a good machine for turning over the earth, is a most inefficient cultivator. I find Bentall's broadshare, followed by Coleman's or Ducie's drag or cultivator, is a fine preparation for the plough, which would otherwise, in strong clays, turn over certain long and solid blocks, which will be possibly unaltered in form for twelve months. The necessity for drainage in heavy lands intended for tares is too obvious to require comment. Eight years ago I sowed 2 bushels of seed tares per acre on a thirteen-acre undrained heavy-land field which I rented, and had the mortification to see them perish during the winter, being a loss of—

	£	s.	d.
Seed, at 12*s*. per bushel	1	4	0
Ploughing, harrowing, and rolling	0	8	0
Half a year's rent, &c.	0	15	0
	£2	7	0

I then, as a tenant, drained the land 4 feet deep and 30 feet apart, with 1-inch pipes, at a cost of £3. 2*s*. 6*d*. per acre. We hear no more now of such losses and failures. It is ruin to farm such lands undrained, although I consider drainage a landlord's affair,—charging the tenant an interest.—*October* 13, 1851.

Clipping Farm-horses and Bullocks.—Having done this the last five years, I can confirm its utility, and even necessity, by my experience. If you doubt it, try it on one of a pair of plough-horses, and in less than a week your horsemen, however prejudiced, will beg to have the other clipped. I assume, of course, that the farm-horses have a comfortable ventilated stable to lie in at nights, the same as our nag-horses. Is it not strange that a farmer cannot consider the same principle applicable to both classes of animals? Where is there so much vigour, condition, and activity as in the London horses? which are all comfortably ensconced at night, their hay and straw cut, their oats bruised, and their water "chilled." I find it a good plan to clip my farm-horses piecemeal, my man taking a slice off each daily—the change is less sudden. The same remark applies to bullocks. They certainly go on faster without their great coats, which were never intended for warm boxes or stalls, but Nature's open fields. Besides, I apprehend the hair requires daily nourishment, as much in proportion as any other portion of the body. The horses, instead of remaining wet all night, are dry in a few minutes.—*November* 4, 1857.

Why do we make Dung-heaps?—Merely to rot and carbonize the straw. This is an expensive process, involving much labour, cartage, and waste, which would be avoided by having covered yards, and allowing heavy animals to consolidate the manure whilst undergoing gradual carbonization and decomposition.

When we fold sheep on land, we consider it sufficiently manured, and do not regret the absence of carbonized straw. I hope the time will come when straw will be better appreciated and used as food.—*December*, 1851.

Will Animals Pay for Purchased Food?—I reply, decidedly not, even with the very best management. I mean, if you leave out of the calculation the manure they leave; but if you desire to restore or maintain fertility, no doubt feeding animals is the cheapest mode of obtaining manure; especially, if the crops can be consumed on the land, without the cost of removal and recartage of the manure.

Having, as shown by my balance-sheet, made much meat from purchased food, I am enabled to draw exact conclusions on this subject, and I find that my calculations correspond with those of other authorities.

According to my calculations, it takes to make one pound of butcher's meat (beef or mutton),—

	Price of food.	Value of meat.
8 to 9 lbs. linseed oil-cake to make 1 lb. net...	7*d*. to 9*d*.	4½*d*. to 6*d*.
45 lbs. of hay, £3. 15*s*. per ton..............	1*s*. to 1*d*. 3*d*.	
160 lbs. of swedes, 10*s*. per ton..............	8*d*. to 9*d*.	
8 to 9 lbs. of beans or barley, 30*s*. per quarter.	6*d*. to 7*d*.	
8 to 9 lbs. of rape-cake, £5 per ton..........	4¾*d*.	

I forgot to mention, that it takes one-seventh less to make a pound of pork; because, when we sell a pig, we sell its skin at the same price, whereas the skin of a bullock or sheep is sold as offal, and it weighs 12½ to 15 per cent. of the whole net weight. It takes about seven pounds of barley-meal to make one pound of pork, net dead weight.

Mutton always sells as an average fifteen per cent. higher than beef, and is therefore more profitable to raise; besides, there is less offal. A friend of mine, a close calculator, who on 1,500 acres does not keep a bullock, says, "Those who keep many bullocks will never want to make a will." I think he is right.

These calculations always show the impolicy of grass lands as intended for hay for feeding purposes. The loss of ammonia in hay-making must be enormous. I never make any now.

The result of my experience in feeding is, that rape cake, at £5 per ton, is our cheapest food; but, no doubt, when generally used, its price will approximate more closely to that of linseed cake, and thus diminish the advantage; although less palatable than linseed cake, it contains equal properties.

When a farm has arrived at a certain state of fertility, it would be unwise to continue largely the purchase of artificial foods.

Does Guano Pay?—This depends upon the condition of the soil. On poor exhausted soils it is a ready and cheap mode of restoring their fertility. I used it extensively when I first began farming, and when applied to the grain crops at the rate of two to three hundredweight per acre it paid well; but *now* it has lost favour with my bailiff—which is easily accounted for, my land being at present so well filled with manure, nitrogen or ammonia, that we can grow an ample crop without it. When the land only yielded two to two and a half quarters of wheat per acre, it was grateful for guano; but now, with a produce of five quarters, there is no necessity for its use.

After all, Mr. Lawes has clearly proved that where there is capital the cheapest way of obtaining ammoniacal and carbonaceous manure is by feeding cattle. His paper on that subject in the Society's Journal (vol. viii. p. 59), is well worthy of an attentive perusal.

I except bones and superphosphate of lime from these remarks, for we can always purchase them cheaper than by feeding.

A most important question arises upon the propriety and advantage of *the retention of the blood and offal of our animals*, and their application to the soil.

Forking.—Having forked 24 acres 10 inches deep, and placed the land in ridges, having a basis of about 4 feet, at £1. 1*s*. 8*d*. per acre, I have since forked the furrows 10 inches deeper, throwing it on the ridges, at least as much as will remain there. The cost of this is 1*d*. per rod, or 13*s*. 4*d*. per acre; so that half my land is dug 20 inches deep, and the remainder 10 inches. The forks continue to give great satisfaction, my men stating that if put in straight and level, they will resist their full "prizing" powers, as they call them. I wonder the makers of these forks do not advertise them in the papers, stating the price and where to be had in various parts of the country and in London. It would save me an immense deal of trouble and writing. Some of my correspondents say, "We can't get the forking done so cheap." Let them try it; unfortunately I cannot employ half the applicants I have for work at this price.—*Feb*. 4, 1852.

Drainage and Deep Cultivation.—When it rains very heavily, you will find me walking my fields and examining the drains and water-courses. We had heavy rains from the 11th to the 14th inst. On the 13th, 14th, and 15th drains discharged abundantly from all my wheat lands; whilst on similar soils, ridged up by the fork, and on other land ploughed 12 inches deep with six horses, not a drain discharged, nor was any water seen between the ridges. The remark applied equally to land drained 5 feet deep, 28 feet apart; and also to land drained 12 feet apart, and 2 feet 8 inches deep. No drains discharged from the young clovers. Late on the day of the 15th there was a trifling discharge from both the young clovers and ploughed and dug lands. The whole of these lands were alike in quality, a tenacious plastic clay. The conclusions I drew from the apparent discrepancy was, that very deep cultivation permits an enormous evaporation even during winter, for you may see the steaming vapour as it rises from the fallowed ground. I apprehend, then, that it is wise to deeply ridge up our heavy land before winter, to promote evaporation; and that in the spring we should keep the surface fine, to retain the moisture. In our dry eastern counties, those who plough their heavy lands often in the spring frequently miss their plant of roots. A gardener who digs his ground deep before winter, does not re-dig it three or four times in the spring. The young clovers, I suppose, evaporate much moisture by their leaves, and are thus well suited to our heavy lands. Tares do the same. There could be little evaporation from the finely-harrowed young wheats, or the drains would not have discharged so immediately and abundantly. I am a confirmed deep-drainer. As I pondered over the streaming drains and flowing ditches, I sorrowed for those who, from want of means or inclination, were deprived of these benefits. Their basin will be full to the brim, and Sol's cheering beams will, instead of vivifying mother earth, be wasted in converting the stagnant water into steam.—*January* 27, 1852.

Hedgerow Timber.—I rent 40 acres of land adjoining my own, on which are a number of small elm-trees, varying from 6 to 12 inches in diameter, and worth from 2*s*. 6*d*. to 7*s*. 6*d*. each. An arrangement has been made with the trustees to take them down at a valuation. One of the fields was, during winter, ploughed 12 inches deep; and whilst forking the furrows 10 inches below that, I was surprised to see the forkers embarrassed by roots the size of an ordinary cart-whip; so, stepping the distance to the small trees before mentioned, it was found to be 32 full yards! My men told me the roots extended very much further into the field. It is worthy of remark, that these roots ramified in every direction below the cultivated soil; and I found, in another of these fields, that they searched the soil to a very considerable depth, passing under an open ditch in order to take the lion's share from the growing crop. It strikes me that landlords generally cannot be aware of the insidious and extensive damage done by these comparatively worthless stems. By a rule-of-three sum, if an elm worth only 3*s*. 6*d*. to 5*s*. extends its roots 35 yards, how far are we to look for those of more gigantic proportions.

Although a strenuous advocate, on common-sense principles, for the abolition of trees in hedgerows (such timber is generally defective), I by no means recommend the general denudation of a country. Elegant and well-cultivated plantations should break the force and divert the current of the pitiless storm. Trees should never be seen in fences, for you cannot have a perfect fence under a tree.—A Devonshire clergyman who visited my farm last week, showed me in his note-book the size of his fields, varying from half an acre to three acres! Free-trade in corn will remedy this. It is clearly impossible that occupiers of such small enclosures can maintain a home, or foreign competition, with other more open districts. This dry spring affords a fine opportunity for estimating the extent of damage done by roots of hedgerow timber and by fences. Bright yellow discolorations in the growing crops, having a wide base and extending into the fields with acute angles, indicate fearfully the greedy capillarities of the gigantic and costly intruders. It is hopeless, as a matter of calculation, to compete with Nature's vast forests, whose carbon and ammonia, as Liebig truly says, are furnished by air and by moisture.—*May* 11, 1852.

Deodorization of Manure.—[In reply to " A Sufferer," complaining of the injurious effects to health which Mr. Mechi's system of irrigation, if generally carried out, would produce.]—" A Sufferer," does not reflect. Horses, pigs, and other animals will die. What becomes of them now? Farmers will make dung-heaps and spread them all over the country. In this district, when the fields are spratted or " five-fingered," you may smell them for miles. Merchants will import 200,000 tons of birds'-dung annually, to be stored in our towns and to scent our country. Is all this to be stopped, or is it to be preferred to the subterranean, unsmelt transmission of liquefied manure, which, when it reaches its destination, rushes from the pipes, and at once sinks into the earth, the only natural deodorizer? Experience has taught me that carboys of acid by the dozen, and gypsum by tons, are vain attempts at deodorizing, and this is confirmed by the highest authority—the Government Board of Health. Your correspondent may wonder that sheep and cows, having a choice of grass, will feed on that which twelve hours previously has been saturated by the much-dreaded liquid; but so it is, and cows have fine noses. Every country bumpkin knows that earth will at once deodorize carrion, an oniony knife, or other offensive smell; and but for this all-wise provision, our overcrowded grave-yards would long since have pestiferized our cities and destroyed their populations. We may be more nice than wise, and, as your recent editorial article remarked on the Irish report, the smelling gases are not often the most poisonous.—*October*, 1852.

Cut Straw Chaff.—I have 10 wheat-stacks and a barn full; the whole, or nearly the whole, will be consumed by the animals, which being upon boarded floors require no litter. The straw is cut about 3-16ths of an inch long, and becomes split at the same time, It is thus remarkably fine. The long straws are sifted from it, It is carried to three coppers of 150 gallons each, and there moistened with linseed soup; about 20 lbs. of crushed linseed, macerated 24 hours, is sufficient for 40 year-olds off. The waste steam from the engine passes around and under these cast-iron pans, and the mass is given hot to the animals the ensuing morning. One ounce of salt to each animal is mixed with the chaff. When opened, the mass of chaff smells like brewing. Formerly, my horsekeepers praised oat straw, but now, if they have anything but wheat-straw chaff, they grumble sadly at the change; it is such "hearty" stuff, they say. If hay is cut very fine, straw chaff should be mixed with it, to prevent its "balling" on the stomach. By intermixing cut mangold with straw chaff, it prevents scouring or looseness. When farmers use steam-power more generally, we shall not see straw wasted as it now is. Great is the outcry amongst my folks if we happen to be out of chaff. They say the animals won't do so well, give them what they will. Sheep do well on our heavy wet clays in the daytime, coming in to open boarded floors at night to eat rape-cake, and, if they choose it, cut straw. It is lying down at night on cold wet clays that does not suit sheep, and produces fever in their feet. On our principle we never have any foot complaints. We find a mixture of straw chaff with cut succulent green food most advantageous. It prevents its being "physic" instead of food.—*November* 8, 1852.

Irrigation.—[A writer in the *Essex Herald* had been taking Mr. Mechi to task for his proceedings in connection with this subject. The character of his strictures may be judged of by the following reply to them.]—There is no consolation for *Pro Bono Publico*. The mangold crop is what O'Connell called "a great fact." They were carted (and that's a comfort) before this wet weather set in, and there actually were from 60 to 80 carts per acre. As to the lugubrious tale about poisoning water, and agricultural labourers' delicate stomachs, 'tis evident that poor *Pro Bono* has been sadly gulled by some wicked wag. 'Tis rich, too, to consider that a labourer who probably stands for weeks turning over and intermixing a rank and reeking dunghill, should at half a mile distant be "struck comical" by the mere sniff or whiff of the same substance in a liquefied form. But no! 'tis not the smell—'tis the novelty that offends our old friends of the old school; anything new they can't endure, but I can't help it—I must fulfil my destiny; I must carry into my agricultural pursuits the same sentiments of common calculation and common sense, and the same disdain for antiquated prejudices, as marked my ordinary business career. I feel that it will make *Pro Bono* unhappy to know that all my people on the farm are particularly healthy and remarkably hearty feeders. The very youth who holds the jet actually said yesterday, whilst demanding an increase of wages, "This somehow makes me feel wonderful hungry, and though I eat *five* 4-lb. loaves a week, I could manage another if I had the wages." But *I* don't wonder at our excellent sanitary condition, when I find medical men inhaling ammonia as an antidote to infection when they return from fever cases and other dire diseases; poisons are acids—as well explained by Liebig, and well understood by our intelligent medical practitioners; and the bites of adders are counteracted by ammoniacal vapours and solutions, as the most powerful alkaline neutralizer. By the bye, the story of flavouring the brook a mile below me arose from an odd circumstance, strongly condemnatory of the old dunghill system. About two years ago, in an evil moment, I was induced to make a real old-fashioned dunghill, of rich pig and other "muck," and placed it on a very stiff clay headland, ready for the field. Well, I stupidly forgot that the field had been deep-drained. Of course our heavy-land friends would say, it was of no use draining such stiff clays. Well, down came some heavy rains, and up came a report from some good neighbours a mile below me, that their tea no longer tasted of hyson or souchong. It seemed odd enough; but, on inspection, we found that the old-fashioned dung-heap had percolated through the drains, across a 6-acre field, and changed the water a mile below. If, after this, any farmer places any reliance in well-washed dung-heaps, or disbelieves the evidences of percolation, I shall have "no hope in the agricultural future."—*November* 5, 1852.

Acreage Consumed by Farm-horses.—I am firm in my conviction that one farm-horse consumes the produce of 6 average acres of arable land. If you admit that the cost of a farm-horse for his weekly keep is 10*s*. or £26 per annum, the case is at once proved; for M'Culloch, Porter, and Spackman do not allow more for the average gross produce of 1 acre in England and Wales than I have stated; and M. Lavergne, in his recent able and comprehensive volume on "British Agriculture" (translated by a Scottish farmer), estimates the gross produce at 200 francs per hectare (2½ English acres), or £3. 12*s*. per English acre. This corresponds very nearly with my own estimate made a few years since in a paper I read before the Society of Arts. A farm-horse would thus clear 7 acres instead of 6½, which was my calculation. I will not go into the question whether 72*s*. per acre gross produce is creditable to British agriculture in the nineteenth century, although I have a strong opinion about it.—*December*, 1854.

Reaping-machines.—Our farming friends may now safely give up the scythe, the sickle, and the bagging-hook, except in a few cases of closely laid crops. For three years I have used Hussey's reaper (made by Garrett and Son); and although great improvements have since been made, it is economical in time and money as compared with manual labour. I completed a very heavy harvest on the 7th of September, with my regular labourers only, and might have done so earlier, but wanted my horses for ploughing, so that the men had to cut 11 acres by hand. The early harvesting has enabled me to scarify all my bean and corn stubbles, and plough my land for tares, although I only keep five horses on 170 acres, all arable. I will give my agricultural friends a hint how to render the reaping-machines most acceptable to the labourers. In my case I let 9 acres (nearly all wheat) to each man to cut, cart, and stack, within the month for £5. 5s. (about 11s. 6d. per acre). I then lent them the reaper, and during the whole harvest I have never heard a complaint of a bolt, screw, or nut being out of order, whereas, under other circumstances, it never gave satisfaction. Practically six men could scarcely bind out of its way; indeed, had we cut the full width, it would have required eight binders, which I could not spare. Six binders can always bind as much as twelve to fourteen reapers could cut; therefore the machine, with three horses and three men, did as much cutting as twelve to fourteen reapers. My land is in 7 feet stetches, with intermediate furrows: therefore not so favourable to the machine as level land. The time is fast coming when even little farmers will avail themselves of machinery. It was grievous to see a week or ten days' time lost in harvest by my neighbours as compared with myself, and yet, in addition to this precious time, at greater cost of money expenditure. The difference of centralized buildings, ready access, and the use of Hannam's carts instead of waggons, are agricultural economies that are gradually forcing themselves on the farmers' minds. I wish some of my agricultural friends would believe that I farm at less cost per quarter than they do; it would be a great help to their pockets. It is quite painful to see how much the harvest is delayed in many districts of this and other counties by undrained land, great hedgerows, timber-trees, and worthless pollards, to say nothing of the superabundance of weediness, and absence of the horse-hoe. Surely landlord and tenant must consider corn worth growing at present prices.—*September*, 1855.

Steam-engine Furnaces.—In this, as in most other matters, inquiry and experience lead us to the conclusion that there is much room for improvement, and that our present system is sadly defective. I always felt dissatisfied with volumes of smoke, red-hot furnace-doors, and frequent stoking; but until I had read Mr. William's able treatise "On the Combustion of Coal," I knew not how to remedy these evils. Since I adopted his talented and common-sense suggestions all is *couleur de rose*—a bright gas fire, no smoke, cool furnace-door and ash-pit, diminished stoking, and greatly increased steam. I give the following dimensions of my arrangements:—

Boiler 10 feet long, 3 feet diameter; flue through the centre

18-inch diameter. Furnace 4 feet long, 2 feet wide (exclusive of dead plate); the furnace-bars 33 inches below the extreme curve of the boiler, The bridge, a straight one, 7 inches below the extreme curve of the boiler.

Consequently I have about 30 cubic feet of space in my furnace for the proper admixture and combustion of the gases; and I have an area of bridge surface equal to 30 superficial inches to every square foot of fire-grate. These spaces are more than double what I used to have under the old system. My furnace-door is pierced with ⅛-inch holes, and by a plate equally pierced behind the bridge I have the power of admitting atmospheric air above the fuel according to the power required. The consequence of all this is a flame varying from 20 to 30 feet in length filling the centre flue and side flues according to my requirements. The importance of having flame instead of smoke must be obvious, seeing that flame has 3,000 degrees of heat, whereas smoke is barely warm. I found that the ordinary opening in the flue at the end of the boiler put out the flame in its attempt to curve up into the centre flue; but I more than doubled the aperture, since which it not only sweeps through the centre of the boiler but illuminates the side flues. My boiler is kept full to within 8 inches of the top. Having a dome, it does not prime; and, with high pressure and rapidly generated steam, the old proportion of one-third steam room is quite unnecessary. Instead of being, as I was originally, short of power, I can make my power anything I choose up to 12-horse (or 72 gallons evaporated per hour), the original calculation being a deficient 6-horse. The fact is, in most furnaces there is not room enough for the proper expansion and admixture of gases; hence, in their attempt to expand we have heated doors, and other inconvenient evidences of the misapplication of heat. I need hardly say that I have convenient trap-doors at each end of the flues, so as to be able to remove any grit or soot in a few minutes—clear flues are indispensable. My remarks will hold good for ordinary coppers, which should always have holes drilled in the furnace-doors, the furnace-bars being at least 2 feet below the copper—much more if a very large one. The greatest heat from a candle is at an inch above the flame. The flame will smoke if a solid body is pressed upon it, or rather into it.—*February*, 1856.

Boydell's Traction Steam-engine.—I devoted two days last week to the examination of the operation of this machine as a locomotive and tractive power, and have come to the conclusion that it is "a great success." This success is owing to the endless and wide railway attached to the circumference of the wheels, which gives a fulcrum for the lever, and a bearing sufficiently wide to carry a great weight on soft ground, without imbedding in the soil. Hence the avoidance of friction and clogging: we might illustrate this by a sportsman on the mud-oozes, whose feet would sink in and thus render his power unavailable; but by attaching to his feet, wide pieces of board, the pressure is diminished to a bearing condition. Thus, in the case of Mr. Boydell's machine, although it weighed nine tons, its impress was scarcely perceptible where a horse's foot left a deep indentation. This is a most important desideratum, seeing that weight in a traction-engine is indispensable. We can form some idea of the value of this implement when we reflect that a common portable agricultural thrashing-engine, which only weighs three tons, requires two horses to draw it on the common road, while two more are required to draw the thrashing-machine. Mr. Boydell's engine walked from Camden Town to Acton, taking in tow its four-wheel waggon, with coals, and four heavy iron ploughs, and water enough for four hours' work. When on the soft turnip-field (after a night's rain) it drew after it ploughs, scarifier, &c., with perfect ease, and then walked home again to Camden Town. It can ascend an acclivity of one in three, which is nearly walking up stairs, our stairs being one in two. It can back, advance, or stop instantaneously, the pinion being shifted from the cogs to the driving wheel; and the power thus suddenly released is carried off by a separate fly-wheel, which may be used for driving thrashing-machines, mill-stones, or other purposes. In fact, instead of a farmer sending for and sending back a 6-horse-power engine and thrashing-machine, requiring in each trip six horses, this machine will move itself anywhere—draw the corn to market, bring home manure, and do the cultivation and work of the farm. I hope a company will be formed for its development, Mr. Boydell having expended nearly £10,000 in accomplishing his object. A full description of it is given in the *Mark Lane Express* of the 7th instant. It may briefly be described as a horizontal engine mounted on wheels, with a man to steer in front and the engineer behind. The two cylinders were 6½ by 10, worked at 60 lbs. per inch, with a quick movement, and estimated at 16-horse power. 20 lbs. of steam was required to keep the machine moving, the other 40 lbs. for traction. Messrs. Boydell and Glazier's works are at Camden Works, Camden Road. The machine can turn as easily as a common waggon, and does not mind a deep furrow or a side hill. It will evidently require a sort of railway buffer spring at starting, to avoid breaking the chains which attach it to its load.—*April* 10, 1856,

Quantity of Iron used Annually on a Farm.—Including my pumps, machinery, steam-engine, &c., I have about 12 tons of iron on my farm, and 55 tons of iron pipe for irrigation. Allowing the whole to wear out in 33 years or 3 per cent. per annum, the weight of iron consumed per acre per annum on my farm of 170 acres would be 28 lbs. per acre. In France on the best-managed farms the estimate is 16 lbs. per acre. I annex, by permission, Messrs. Garrett and Sons' estimate:—

Implements containing iron in use on a farm consisting of 200 acres of mixed soil; land of average quality, farmed on progressive principles.

Implements.	Quantity of iron contained.			Quantity of iron worn out per annum.		
	cwt.	qrs.	lbs.	cwt.	qrs.	lbs.
4 four-wheeled waggons	22	0	0			
6 carts	12	0	0	1	0	0
1 light market-cart	3	0	0			
1 wheelbarrow	0	1	8			
5 ploughs	7½	0	0	3	0	0
5 carriages for do.	0	1	12			
1 set heavy harrows	3½	0	0			
1 do. medium do.	3	0	0			
1 do. light do.	1½	0	0	0	2	0
1 do. very light do.	½	0	0			
2 carriages for do.	0	1	0			
1 drag-harrow	7	0	0	0	0	14
1 scarifier	10	0	0	0	1	0
3 iron rolls	26	0	0	0	1	0
1 corn-drill	6	0	0			
1 seed and manure-drill	6	0	0			
1 harrow for small seeds	0	1	0	0	2	0
1 Chambers' distributor	7	0	0			
1 patent horse-hoe	5	0	0			
1 Hussey's reaping-machine	5	0	0	0	1	0
1 six-horse-power portable steam-engine	50	0	0	2	0	0
1 six-horse-power do. thrashing-machine	25	0	0	4	0	0
1 dressing-machine	0	1	12	0	0	7
1 smut-machine	0	1	0	0	0	4
1 haymaking-machine	8	0	0	0	1	0
1 drag-rake	5	0	0			
1 weighing-machine with weights	3	0	0	0	0	7
1 barley-drilling machine	0	1	12	0	0	4
1 chaff-cutter	4½	0	0	0	0	14
1 turnip-cutter	1	0	0	0	0	7
1 hand-power root-pulper	1	2	0	0	0	7
1 cake-crusher	1	0	0	0	0	4
1 mill for crushing food for stock	4	0	0	0	0	4
8 rick-stands	64	0	0	0	0	14
0 iron hurdles	190	0	0	2	2	0
3 round iron bins	5	0	0	0	0	7
6 pig-troughs	5	0	0			
Sundries						
25 forks (various)						
6 scappitts						
20 pair traces	6	2	0		2	0
4 hand-hoes						
3 corn-shovels						
6 turnip-cleaning knives						
Tools, &c.						
Bolts, nails, and miscellaneous iron	..			5	0	0
	430	2	16	20	3	9

Being 2,333 lbs. or 11½ lbs. per acre actual wear, independent of the original supply.—*May*, 1856.

Forking cheaper than Ploughing.—In one field three strong horses are drawing the first plough to the full extent of their power at a slow pace, followed by another plough without the breast drawn by two horses. The extreme depth thus attained is only 8½ inches. The land is for mangolds next year. In another field four men are digging with five-tined steel forks, the depth averaging 11 inches. For this they received £2 per acre, or *3d.* per rod, and earn *2s. 6d.* per day. This is also for mangolds. Comparing the quality of the work in each field and the cost, the five horses and two ploughmen only doing three roods per day, the balance of advantage is evidently in favour of the digging. The consolidation by horses, the glazed surface caused by the plough sole, the long tenacious unbroken furrow slices, and the many times trodden headlands, contrast wofully with the broken, lightly lying, and well-mixed earth left by the diggers. The land looks different when torn up and crumbled with the fork, the ploughed field having a squeezed, glossy, and more tenacious appearance. It is easy to imagine what a gain there is to drainage by the rough unequal bottom under the fork. On one of these fields I had, after clover once hayed and once fed, 6¾ quarters of red wheat per acre in 1856, and 7 quarters of rivett wheat in 1857; total 13¾ quarters in two years on a plastic yellow clay. So much for drainage, cultivation and manure. I find that my oats yield over 11 quarters per acre.—1858.

Rape-cake, Old and New.—My sheep and bullocks were eating old rape-cake, which being exhausted, they were supplied with some recently made; not a mouthful of this would they touch, but after packing it away for six weeks the same animals took it readily. The bullocks consume 5 to 6 lbs. per day. My usual allowance to sheep is 1 to 1½ lb. Fat sheep will eat more than lean ones.—1858.

Draining.—I wish it to be distinctly understood that I am still a believer in deep drainage, although I feel that in certain soils it is essentially necessary to accommodate the distance between the drains to the quality of the soil. In my remarks at the London Farmers' Club lately, I stated that my original drains (my drains were filled ten inches with gravel and stones, and a 2-inch pipe placed on the top, but not for the purpose of carrying water, which all passes amongst the stones) at twelve feet distance, kept the land more dry and workable in winter and spring than the deeper drains at wider intervals; but it does not at all follow that the deeper drains at the same intervals might not produce an equal or even better effect if filled up in the same way as my shallow drains. I believe we have all something to learn yet about drainage. I consider that my old original idea of area of porosity in the drain is an important consideration, or, in other words, that a large pipe (irrespective of its water-carrying power) would more effectually dry the soil than a small one. Some recent facts have come to my knowledge which convince me that the mere cutting the drain down to the depth at which the pipe is placed, tends to aërate and dry the soil immediately over it, so much so that in the month of March or April I can see, at a distance of 500 yards or more, every drain in my fields by the dried surface immediately over it, which dry surface gradually extends until the darker or moister space between the drains becomes uniform in dryness and colour with that immediately over the drain. From this I infer that the evaporation as well as percolation is greatest where the earth has been deeply disturbed to insert the pipe; if so, it teaches us the value of very deep culture. I attribute the drying more to evaporation than to percolation, because the appearances I have mentioned take place long after the drain has ceased running. This drying is more apparent and striking where the drains have been filled with pipes and stones than where a small 1-inch pipe alone has been used. It is a great mistake to suppose that water immediately descends. Let fall a drop of water on blotting paper, cloth, or any porous substance, and it spreads laterally by capillarity, and in this way would naturally reach the drain horizontally until the whole substratum to the bottom of the drain was saturated. If my observation is correct, it explains the advantage of proximate drains in those dense soils which absorb water slowly and transmit it with difficulty. My irrigation teaches me that in dry summer weather the fissures in clays readily pass my sewage to the deep drains in the most dense tile-earths, say to 1-inch pipes at 5 feet deep, and 50 feet from drain to drain, the pipes running full stream with the coloured fluid; but still those soils so drained, in winter and spring, work less friably than where my drains are at 12 feet apart, 32 inches deep, and filled with stones and pipe. The effect of aëration to the roots of plants is unmistakable. Dig a trench 5 feet deep, and place a line of large pipes at the bottom, and then plant your trees on the surface, and you will find them quite outgrow others not having this advantage. Gardeners know quite well that ventilation under a vine border has great value, and I believe from observation that the mere placing of pipes in the soil, though no water should pass through them, would improve the crops. I was assured of this fact by a gentleman from Devonshire, who has seen two considerable instances at different periods. There can be no doubt that in certain soils shallow drains are ruinous and ineffective, as they fail to withdraw water; and, as a general rule, deep drains place at the disposal of the roots of plants so many more thousand tons of earth per acre, that they must always command our preference. Besides, the more complete filtration of the essences of our manures through a deeper soil, commends depth of drainage to our practice—1858.

Irrigation with Sewage.—It may be interesting to agriculturists to know that I continue my irrigation with much success and without any difficulty. I confine it principally to the

Italian rye-grass, pasture, and green crops. Not to irrigate the former, is to have no second crop; and the latter become by irrigation of rich and fattening quality. I find it unnecessary to irrigate the cereal and pulse crops, because the rye-grass land and clover leas, when broken up, yield by their fertility large crops of every kind. The ordinary pasture which was once infertile now grows us abundant hay, and we are enabled to feed it up to the 12th May. The after-crop is also rendered by irrigation very productive. As my fat cattle are now sold, I use a sack of guano daily in the tank; and this, with the house sewage and other matters, adds fertility to the water which runs from my great spring. As we shower on the land about 80 to 100 gallons per minute, the necessity of an ample water-supply is very apparent. We find it desirable to do only about two acres per diem—each acre, therefore, receives about 25,000 gallons in five hours. This is equal to about 1 inch rain-fall, or 100 tons per acre. I find, practically, that the more I put on, the more I grow. 'Tis quite clear that all rapidly growing plants demand much moisture; and if we expect repeated growths without repeated rain-fall, or its equivalent irrigation, we shall be disappointed. We have long ceased to find any practical difficulty in the manipulation of my irrigation scheme, which seems perfect in all its parts. The agitation of the solid matter with the liquid, and the prevention of its sedimentation, is admirably effected by the movable air-blast, which at a depth of 1 to 12 feet below the surface boils up constantly the whole mass, and prevents the soiled matter from being drawn into one great mass round the suction-bulb, as described in a former number of your journal. All attempts at effecting such a result by machinery would be comparatively inoperative and costly. 4-horse power effects all my irrigation, or about two-thirds of the power that I use to drive a pair of 4-feet 4-inch millstones. Our gutta-percha tubing, which I have used several years, requires a little patching occasionally, which is done easily by my own labourers. The corrugated joints are sometimes broken by the pressure, being thinner than the other parts. The pump valves and seats require occasionally *re*-turning to preserve their level and water-tight action. Water-work engineers are obliged to be very particular about this. I have several times tried to substitute prepared canvas for the gutta-percha tubing; but it always bursts under the pressure. The comfort and cleanliness of our jets, when applied to the drains in and about the house, are very considerable, flushing and scouring away any offensive matter; and if you happen to have a hundred fat hogs in hot weather on boarded floors, they may all be clean washed by it (and stimulated to feed) in five or ten minutes. The agitation of matter in our tank is so perfect that no strength is left in the refuse, so effectually is all decomposed soluble substance removed. A calm review of my seven years' experience in irrigation enables me to reflect on the suicidal waste of manure occurring in this great food-requiring Queendom. In one case, guano-buying farmers see their most valuable manure solutions washed down the brooks by the water from their untroughed farmeries. In the other, our landed proprietors and farmers see with apathy rivers of the best guano flowing from our cities to be wasted (would nature permit it) in our rivers and seas. My only consolation is the conviction that, long after I am dead and gone, future generations will be more wise and calculating. Already the nuisance of concentrated offensiveness has compelled attention to the subject; and our sanitary reformers will rejoice that in sheer praiseworthy efforts to promote health they have compelled a large increase in the quantity and quality of our national nutrition. The mechanical difficulties are insignificant, but the mental obstruction of doubt and disbelief is prodigious. Our sewage, like our great fen drainage, can only be accomplished by commissions and acts of parliament, ruling the obstinate or ignorant minority by the intelligent and willing majority. It is necessary to guard against the blunder of disproportion, for if your pump cylinders draw more water than the pipes will convey, your machinery must inevitably break. This was originally the error at Rugby, and then wiseacres declared sewage irrigation a failure. The omission of ample air-vessels would also cause the machinery to be destroyed. Without air vessels a jet cannot be obtained. Any irrigator who feels a difficulty will readily be permitted to inspect my operations. I think I mentioned before, that the only way to prevent the nuisance of offensive smells from my great tank, is to introduce into the dome a jet of waste steam, which is a perfect deodorizer. I ought to mention that there is no difficulty in growing a fine wheat crop after two years rye-grass, provided you plough in 5 cwt. of rape-cake per acre. This kills all the wireworms. I have a splendid wheat crop so treated. Do not sow too thickly.—*June* 7, 1858.

Reaping - machines. — As reaping-machines are now coming into more general use, and as they are causing considerable anxiety to those who do not understand the use of them, I venture to trust you with my experience in the matter, having cut my wheat with one for seven years. During the last five years the machine has not cost me 10*s.* for repairs. The machine is one of Hussey's, made by Messrs. Garrett of Leiston — and I well remember that those gentlemen requested me to return it, desiring to give satisfaction, and fearing from the number returned to them that they might lose customers. My men, however, were too good judges to part with such a friend, and although for the first year or two their want of practice caused them a little trouble, the last five years the reaper has done its work perfectly, whether the crop of wheat was partially laid, or stood erect; and they are of opinion that, after all, Hussey's machine is the strongest and most advantageous to them. They say that by dropping their deep steel-toothed rake on the corn when sufficient has fallen over on to the floor of the machine, they have the heavy sheaf in the exact shape for binding. There is no scattering, and consequently no gathering. In this respect they agree with Mr. H. Hammond, of Norfolk; and I think they are right. Of course much depends on circumstances. As I always get up my harvest by my regular labourers, we only cut a moderate width with the reaper, so that five men by great exertion bind out of its way. Probably, with a large staff of extra hands, it may be more desirable to use M'Cormick's with Burgess and Key's screws to throw off the corn, even at the cost of a little extra gathering. The great secret is to take care that the knives and the parts they work in do not get choked; this is prevented by the observation and activity of the man sitting on the machine, who, the moment he *hears* a slight dulness in the sound, exerts himself to raise up and bring over the straw that leans forward, and which causes the choking: the knives, when working freely, jingle or ring clearly. If the *first* attempt at choking is not immediately attended to, the jamming of a mass causes stoppage or breakage. When the machine meets the laid corn, the man who sits on it raises the corn with the smooth end of his stick actively applied; when the machine follows the laid corn, the man brings the straw to the reaper by a simple bent wire curved like a reaping-hook attached to a light stick. The cutting knife is sharpened every day by means of a three-sided file, which gives it a serrated edge. Another very important point is, that where the land is in stetch and furrow, the wheels should always run on the stetch, and not one wheel in the furrow and the other on the stetch. If there are deep water-furrows, as on the numerous undrained stiff clays, the machine should be eased gently over them, and not be bumped and strained by sudden and violent shocks. Hence the discrepant opinions amongst farmers as to the value of the machine. A light-land farmer with level land will find no difficulty, whilst the undrained heavy-land farmer and his men are terribly plagued, and occasionally return the machine in disgust. If you really mean to succeed, lend your machine to the men. I always did so. Their own self-interest soon taught them to take care and keep it in good working order.—*August*, 1858.

Thick or Thin Sowing?—Fifteen years of experience are worth something, or at all events ought to be of some value. Does the quantity of seed sown regulate the quantity of corn to be produced? Most decidedly not. As a general rule, the larger quantity of seed sown produces the smallest result, because it implies a poor or ill-cultivated soil, having no power to compel the plant to tiller. It would be absurd to lay down an arbitrary rule of quantity for all sorts and climates; but we may take these general rules as a safe guide:—

That the quantity of seed must be diminished in proportion as the natural or artificial fertility of the soil is increased.

That in such soils the sowing of too much seed produces a rank and close vegetation, prematurely developed, laid early, apt to be mildewed, and ruinously unproductive in quality and quantity.

The extreme illustration of this is afforded by the bunches grown from masses of seed dropped from the drill, or accumulated by mice.

That time is gained, or early harvesting is promoted by two causes—a highly manured, drained, and fertile soil, or by a large quantity of seed. In the latter case prematurity is attained at a sacrifice of quantity. If I were asked, whether I would sow thick to produce an early harvest, or whether I would sow thin and earlier to produce the same result, I would most decidedly prefer the latter mode.

Experience has taught many farmers that if they will continue to sow the same quantity of seed as they used to do when they farmed less highly, they must sow later to avoid a prematurely laid crop.

If every farmer had tried (as I have done) for a series of years, on a moderate space, the comparative results of given quantities sown at stated periods, each man would have arrived at a suitable quantity adapted to his own climate, soil, and circumstances.

My frequent intercourse with farmers from every county and every clime enables me to appreciate the enormous errors and discrepancies in regard to quantity of seed sown; and also convinces me of the want of uniform action and profitable knowledge amongst British agriculturists on this subject.

Several of my wheat-fields this year are estimated at six to seven quarters per acre. I needly hardly say that the straw is like reeds, and abundant in quantity. This is from a bushel of seed drilled per acre. Now, when some of my Welsh or foreign friends see this, they naturally suppose I have sown as much seed as they do, and wonder that my crop stands so stiff under such heavy ears. They seem quite amazed that one bushel of wheat or two bushels of oats should produce such results as six quarters of wheat and eleven quarters of oats per English acre.

I ought to be equally surprised when I hear of their sowing three bushels of wheat, and four to seven bushels of oats, to produce miserable results of two and a half to three quarters of wheat and five or six quarters of oats.

I have said that high manuring renders a small quantity of seed absolutely necessary. I ought to add, that every weed should be extirpated, and the whole of the soil placed at the sole use of the growing crop. But how stands the fact on the majority of farms in this kingdom? A fierce competition goes on between the thickly-sown grain crop and a powerful natural crop of hungry weeds, the latter too often consuming that which ought to have been the nutriment of the former, thereby reducing it in quantity and quality, to the serious injury of the farmer. This is no highly-coloured picture. If I travel by the flying train in the month of May, I can, even so, perceive this blot upon English farming in every direction; a painful remainder of agricultural neglect and miscalculation.

How few know the use of Garrett's horse-hoe! For fifteen years my wheat and other crops have benefited by this. The farm labourers know well the value of clean hoeing, and can predict the failure or success of the crop accordingly.

Why a farmer should deem it necessary to hoe his turnips, and not his corn, is to me a mystery. The same principle applies equally to both. The amount abstracted annually from the farmers' pockets by the growth of weeds is something enormous in the aggregate.

The effect of extra manuring on the proportion of seed was strikingly exemplified in a distant wheat-field of mine, sloping towards my bedroom. On one portion of that field, forming a square and then an oblong, my sheep had been folded twelve hours longer than on the rest of the field. In every stage of the growth of the corn that extra folding was shown as distinctly as if coloured on a map. The crop was thicker and more early laid, and more frothy at harvest. Strictly speaking, three pecks, instead of one bushel, of seed would have been the proper quantity for that portion. I am still of opinion that land can never be too rich for wheat, provided the quantity sown is adapted to the circumstances of the field.

I have formerly stated that on my land I have found that two bushels of seed-wheat, as compared with one bushel, reduce the yield by a sum equal to the rent of the land.

Mr. Hewitt Davis is entitled to great credit for what he did practically in proving the advantages of thin sowing, combined with deep and clean cultivation.

In dealing with such an enormous area as the cereal crop of the United Kingdom, the waste of seed forms an aggregate item of national importance.

I never found any farmer who complained of my not having straw enough; on the contrary, thick sowers have admitted that the quantity was much larger than their own.

On light chalky soil, or limestone rock, especially at high elevations, as in Gloucestershire, I have known thick and early sowing practised, because by covering the ground early it protected the roots from frost. We know quite well that, whilst the leaf of wheat suffers little from frost, the plant when root-frozen is destroyed. Under such circumstances it might be advantageous to thin out the wheat by hoeing in the spring. In light loose sands the wheat root is apt to suffer unless sown early.

I trust that these remarks may lead to a due consideration of the question.—*August*, 1858.

Some thin-sowing experiments of mine were recorded in the Royal Agricultural Society's Journal, vol. vii. page 37, 1846. Those experiments have been confirmed by two years' experience. I assume that everybody drills or dibbles—there is no dependence on broadcasting.

Tenant's Capital required per Acre with High Farming.—If you find a farm already drained and improved, your rent will be high; but your capital need not be so great as though you had to make the necessary amendments.

It would need to be as follows:—

	Per acre.		
In-coming valuation for tillages, hay, and manure......	£3	0	0
Live stock....................................	5	0	0
Farm-horses....................................	1	10	0
Steam-engine	2	0	0
Farm implements	1	0	0
Purchased food for stock....................................	1	0	0
Twelve-months' rent, rates, tithes, &c....................	2	0	0
One year's labour	2	0	0
One year's housekeeping....................................	1	0	0
	£18	10	0

Supposing you enter at Michaelmas, your crop of corn will not be ready for sale until the September following; and it will, in fact, take nearly the whole twelve months for its gradual realization. It is this slow return that makes farming notoriously a less money-making business than trade, commerce, or manufactures.

Besides, as a general rule, it is more of a ready-money business, and you have not the advantage of purchasing on credit.

A great deal of land is hired with a capital of less than £5. per acre. We cannot, therefore, wonder at the non-development of progress in agriculture.

Poor lands, with a low in-coming valuation, will find more bidders than highly-farmed lands, because there are more poor tenants than rich ones. On such soils the valuation might be,—

	£	s.	d.
In-coming tillages, manure, &c.	1	10	0
Live stock....................................	1	0	0
Farm-horses (cheap ones)	1	0	0
Farm-implements	0	10	0
Twelve months' rent, rates, tithes, &c..................	1	8	0
Twelve months' labour	1	10	0
Twelve months' housekeeping	0	10	0
	£7	8	0

I assume in this case the utmost economy. The farmer himself following the plough, and thus economizing labour. The scale of house-keeping expenses would also be the medium between the labourer and high farmer.

There is a large class of most industrious and intelligent men, who begin with very small means, but by getting a little loan, and some credit in their purchases, tradesmen's bills, &c., manage to "get the fore horse by the head," and thus ultimately become rich and extensive farmers. In their early career their style of dressing and living is of the most economical character, probably not £50 per annum for house expenses. I have a great respect for such a class; their natural talent and industry are the parents of capital.

High-pressure Steam.—The time is coming when we shall better understand the great advantage of using steam at higher pressure than is now in use. I believe 140 lbs. per inch to be as safe as 14 lbs., provided the strength and diameter of the boilers be proportionate.

To those who doubt this, I would recommend a perusal of Dr. Alban's treatise (published by Weale, Holborn); also Craddock's lectures on the same subject.

As compression is costly, it follows that expansion must be gain. The 14 lbs. opposed by the atmosphere is formidable at 30 lbs. pressure, but comparatively unimportant at 140.

I find that the express engine which conveys me to Essex is worked at 110 lbs.; the steam cut off at 1-inch, expansion forcing the piston the other 23 inches, the cylinder being 24-inch. The engine-driver of the Great Northern express train told me that he worked at 140 lbs. per inch. I recently visited Mr. Collinson Hall's mill, at Prince's Gate, near Romford, and was much gratified by the great economy with which his engine was worked. At 120 lbs. pressure per inch he works three pair of millstones and other machinery at a cost of only 4 cwt. of coals per day of twelve hours. His boilers are made of the best Low Moor iron, $\frac{3}{4}$-inch thick. The lower boiler is about 3 feet diameter, with the fire in its centre, on the Cornish principle, having 7 inches of water around the fire-flue. Over this boiler, and connected with it, is another boiler of multitubular construction, with steam space above the tubes.

To use his own words, "The heat passing through the lower boiler flue, strikes a quantity of fire-bricks, which direct the heat to the tubular boiler above. The heat, having passed through these 32 tubes 10 feet long, is much spent, and then passes round the external surface of the two boilers and *steam-chest* before it can reach the chimney."

He also says, "The true mode of arriving at cheap steam-power—press high, expand it. Slow fires, and as little draught as will continue the work and hold the steam up to the working pressure, plenty of boiler-room, and well protected by fire-bricks and good walls, to prevent the escape of heat."

I feel convinced that a moderate degree of heat around the steam-chest is one cause of his great economy, steam being readily expanded by heat or condensed by cold. It is for this reason that portable engine makers place the cylinder on the flue or boiler.

The time will come when the Royal Agricultural Society

must abolish their limit of pressure, at present only 45 lbs. per inch.

A reference to Armstrong on boilers, will teach the proper proportions of heating surface, water-space, and fire-grate; and thus prevent many of those unprofitable discrepancies and mistakes which are too frequently made for want of proper knowledge.

The question of combustion will be best understood by the study of Williams's admirable book on combustion.

How to Farm Profitably with Little Capital.—I have noticed a very money-getting farmer in my neighbourhood, who never keeps any live stock, except a couple of cows, and who never buys any feeding stuffs or manures. He grows no root crops (except an acre or two for his cows); he makes no long fallow.

He keeps his land clean and fertile by ploughing in green crops, which require no hoeing or labour, and only one ploughing. I know he makes money, for he often purchases land; and if it is out of order, his first crop is green winter tares, ploughed in and followed by buck-wheat or mustard, also ploughed in green. It is surprising how soon this system destroys all the weeds, and leaves the land clean and fertile.

If when he first takes the land it is much exhausted, he then does sprinkle a little guano on, to start the first green crop. By this system his expenditure is confined to rent, rates, tithes, and taxes, horse labour, and a very moderate amount of manual labour. There is no investment in live stock, food, manures, casualties, or attendance and housing of cattle. Such a man would require very little shelter or buildings. It is far cheaper than the long-fallow system. He generally sows strong growing green crops, which will *master* or overcome the weeds.

It is the opinion of some knowing hands, that this farmer manages to get better profits than his neighbours who adopt the ordinary system.

The weakest part of this system appears to be in the disposal of the straw. On inquiry, I find that he has much difficulty in getting it trodden down or rotted. It would certainly pay him much better to steam it as straw-chaff, with a little rape-cake, for a few bullocks, or for his horses, so as to economize his hay and improve his manure-heap. Occasionally, if his horses are not otherwise wanted, he makes a half-fallow after his tares before he sows mustard or rape.

If this system of farming were generally adopted, there would not be much meat or manure produced. It appears to me only justifiable where there is a scarcity of capital or a deficiency of farm-buildings.

The Difficult Question in Agriculture is, how to get the best return for your straw, your root, and your green crops. My own practice has convinced me that this can best be done by *consuming much of the straw* whilst feeding the root and green crops. This cannot be effected without steaming or cooking the straw, cut up, of course, into fine chaff, and mixed with other materials (as well illustrated by Mr. Horsfall), and given warm to the animal.

When dry-straw chaff is given, the animals will not consume enough, but linger after the roots. When the straw chaff is steamed with about 3 lbs. of rape-cake, ¾ lb. of malt-combs, and ¾ lb. of bran, they fill themselves well, lie down, and are comparatively indifferent about roots. The cost of this is trivial, for where steam-power is used, the waste steam circulating amongst and under the coppers will keep the food hot. This gives a good opportunity of testing the qualities of rape-cake; for when dissolved with the straw chaff, the smell of mustard or other improper admixtures is strongly perceptible. These remarks apply as well to sheep as to bullocks. I observe that when the cooked straw chaff is put into the manger very hot they do not object to it; but, like ourselves, just give it time to be eatably cool.

Small or Large Farms.—I should be sorry to see our small farms abolished. A landlord with farms of various sizes, from fifty acres upwards, is more independent, and more secure of tenants, than where all the holdings are large. He has in the former case a larger area to select from, more adapted to the varying demands of capital. A clay farm of 100 acres, well-drained open fields, and with a covered yard to cost £400, and a moderate house worth £300, would almost always command a respectable tenant at a rental of 30*s*. per acre. Generally speaking, such farms have no proper convenience for stock, are undrained, and the fields small and shaded by hedgerows and timber. Such farms are much dearer at 20*s*. per acre than that which I have quoted at 30*s*. per acre. You seldom find a tenant disposed to quit such an improved farm, because it is profitable to him. Not so with the unimproved farm. There are men, who work at the plough themselves, content to take a fifty-acre having the advantages I named—say:

Drained open field.
House to cost £150.
Covered yard to cost £150.

A couple of coppers to cook the straw chaff for their cattle are indispensably necessary.

How to get rid of Twitch, or Couch-grass.—In our eastern counties, with dry summers, this is an easy task. Deep and frequent cross-ploughing, and then when the clods are dried through, crosskilling, crab-harrowing, and scarifying, will expose and dry up every particle of this annoying weed. A good heavy crop of this weed will, when perished, make good food for the succeeding crop.

With undrained heavy land, numerous small fields, and great banks or fences, it is almost impossible to get rid of couch-grass. It naturally spreads towards the ploughed land; the ploughman cuts it up, and the harrows spread it gradually all over the field, because it will shoot from every joint. Our plan is to watch after harvest, and fork out and carry off any patch that is seen in the stubble, and especially near a ditch or fence, to avoid its extension to the fields.

Water furrows on undrained lands, are productive of this pest to agriculture; I have known as much as 30 cart-loads an acre carted from a 40-acre field in Herefordshire, and then far too much left behind. In Lincolnshire I have seen immense stacks piled for the purpose of making paper; but I hear the speculation was, from some unexpected cause, unsuccessful.

Wherever patches exist they should be forked up and well shaken out from the earth, and removed entirely from the field. Hoeing is of no use for twitch, or couch-grass. It is astonishing how much land in England is tied together and injured by this weed.

Other deep-rooted weeds are easily mastered by deep cultivation and a well-cleaned root crop.

Sparred Floors for Live Stock.—Several years' experience in this matter confirm my favourable opinion of its utility and profit. On a poor, exhausted farm, producing little straw, it becomes almost an imperative necessity. In my case, my farm now producing so much straw, I am compelled to limit my sparred-floor feeding. For all animals it has proved itself by far the most sanitary process. However closely packed may be your animals, they always get a circulation of air around them. In hot weather, it is absolutely essential to the well-doing of fattening hogs. For sheep, during winter, it is admirably adapted. You will never have lung disease amongst cattle so placed, provided they have ordinary ventilation. Poultry, rabbits, &c., thrive well upon sparred floors. For using with irrigation, the manure below the floors is especially available.—*October*, 1850.

A poor Heavy-land Farm of 100 Acres.—10 to 12 acres would be occupied by fences, ditches, roads, waste, buildings, &c.; 16 acres (at least) consumed by the 4 horses; 20 acres in fallow, producing no crop; leaving about 52 acres to produce crops for sale or for use of live stock.

Rent, rates, tithes, and taxes are paid upon the full landlord's measure of 100 acres; so that they form a large acreable charge on the available acres.

A considerable portion of the growing crops is impoverished by the roots of hedges and hedge-row timber, which extend many yards into the field, and take the lion's share of the manure and cultivation. The numerous headlands suffer by the trampling of horses. I have in no way overrated these calculations. On all farms the roads, ditches, homestead, and fences, occupy a good deal of ground.

The above farm would probably not produce a gross available average return of more than £350 on 100 acres; and it is only men who work hard themselves, and live like a labourer, who can "make ends meet" on a farm so circumstanced.

Local Customs should not be despised.—Climate and soil are very various, and influence the cropping and management.

Amongst the hills in Cumberland and Westmoreland, turnips in August will be up to one's knee, and grass long and luxuriant; whilst in Essex the young turnip is scarcely visible or much eaten by the fly; the pastures dry and drab-coloured.

The latter is a cereal district, and you may leave your corn on the swathe with impunity, making your stacks very large. No such liberties must be taken in the former ease.

Farmers who are transposed to opposite climes and soils must succumb to circumstances, and alter their system, otherwise they will inevitably fail, as I have too frequently witnessed.

An Irishman or Scotchman must give up his hopes of great green and turnip crops, when he migrates to the southern clay, and turn his attention to mangold wurzel. Swedes sown in May would be frizzled in September. They can only thrive when the nights get lengthy and where the soil is friable.

Our weeds in the South are easily destroyed; not so in humid and Western districts.

Pigs pay better than Sheep or Bullocks.—A quarter of foreign barley, in meal, which costs, with grinding, 30*s*., will yield, in pork at 6*d*. per lb., about 27*s*. to 30*s*. The cost of preparing it and placing it before the animals will be 4*d*.

The cost of preparing five tons of mangold for a similar purpose will be at least 5*s*., the return in meat being the same.

The offal or waste from a well-fattened hog will be about 25 per cent. The offal or waste from a sheep will be 45 per cent. From a bullock somewhat less.

A fat hog will put on from 5*s*. to 8*s*. per week. A sheep seldom increases 1*s*. per week.

Nine times out of ten you can buy your lean hogs at 6*d*. per lb., net dead weight. Your lean sheep generally cost you 8*d*. to 9*d*. per lb.; of course the pork market is more limited than the mutton market, and may be more readily overdone.—*October*, 1858.

The Four-course Rotation considered.—A reference to the cost and average return of each crop will show clearly which are the most directly profitable; but, then, if we grew all corn, and sold that corn at market, we should have nothing left to make manure with, except the straw of our cereals; and thus, of course the land would become impoverished. But if we grow or purchase food enough, cereal or other, to make ten score of meat per acre (net dead weight) over the whole farm, there is no fear of its diminishing in fertility, because the large quantity of meat so fattened would produce ample manure for the crops.

The difficulty of growing repeated crops of cereals arises from two causes: first, the inadequacy of soluble silica to glaze the straw; and, secondly, the difficulty in cultivating and cleansing the soil.

The Rev. Samuel Smith has solved this problem by his admirable practice.

I do not consider the four-course system the most profitable for very high and clean farming; but would recommend the growth of oats or barley after wheat on such portions of the soil as are over-luxuriant.

If the land will, in such cases, produce seven quarters of barley, or eleven quarters of oats per imperial acre, there is evidently no exhaustion by such farming.

A disproportionate quantity of ground occupied by green and root crops is unprofitable.

I have on my poor farm often grown six to seven quarters of rivett wheat, after a heavy crop of red wheat.

The great secret is, to grow an immense root crop on a very small area.

It is the opinion of many good farmers that the four-course system, with very high farming, is unprofitable.—*October*, 1858.

Grubbing Woods and Earth-burning.—I have seen great mistakes in this respect, especially in stiff clays. When the timber and underwood have been cleared off, it is customary to let the job of trenching the ground, and removing all roots, &c., to the depth of 18 inches. The cost of this (with average day-wages of 10*s*. to 11*s*. per week) may be as much as 1*s*. 6*d*. or 2*s*. per rod, *i. e.* £12 or more per acre. The roots, &c., are given in.

Now, I consider it to be a great mistake to allow these roots, &c., to be taken off the land. They should be stacked, ready for igniting clay fires during the following summer. You would thus be enabled to burn probably from 300 tons to 400 tons per acre, two-thirds of which would be available for the adjoining lands.

My experience of earth-burning is most satisfactory, and, in one case especially, instructive and profitable to the agriculturist.

A poor, yellow, tenacious tile-earth clay field opposite my residence, had been laid down two years with fine grasses. The bad, natural grasses grew up, choked them, and no stock could thrive on it then. The field, although drained, was like bird-lime in winter, and cast-iron in summer.

Having robbed the field of 250 cubic yards per acre of its top soil, I felt sure that my neighbours would reproach me with having ruined the field, so I cautiously left half an acre of the original grass undisturbed, unburned, and unrobbed. Twelve years have elapsed, it is still pasture; but to this day I have been unable by any means to make the unburned and unrobbed half-acre equal to the other portion. The grasses are coarse and of inferior quality. This is a most encouraging fact for earth-burners.

Professor Voelcker has recently elucidated and explained the advantages of clay-burning, to which I might add the advantage of calcining, and thus rendering more available an immense quantity of silica, for the stones in the clay are completely pulverized by the fierce action of heat.

I have observed the tendency of burned earth to sink down into and amalgamate with the subsoil, thereby facilitating its aëration. It also causes heavy lands to work easier, and in every way is a most cheap and effective way of permanently increasing the fertility of the soil.

I believe the advantage arises principally from the improved mechanical condition of the soil, which admits a more free circulation of air and water.

Our poor exhausted pastures on clay lands, if ploughed and burned, would furnish abundant cereal and other crops: this I have proved on my farm.—*October*, 1858.

Burned Clay.—I am highly impressed with the value and profit of burned clay. Every farmer knows that the yellow-ochrey subsoil of stiff undrained clays, free from calcareous matter, but full of iron rust, is, when first exhumed, poisonous to plants. Burn it into brickdust, and it at once becomes food instead of poison. You entirely change its chemical and physical condition.

You might roll the original wet birdlime-like clod into a ball, place it on your mantlepiece and it would become as hard as a cannon-ball and shine as if varnished; but when reduced by heat to brickdust, its tenacity and induration are for ever departed. Every portion of it becomes readily accessible to air, water, and manure. It is attractive, absorbent, and filtrative, instead of being, as formerly, sullenly unalterable and repulsive. The seeds or germs of evil weeds which it contained are rendered, by calcination, food for other plants.

I have rejoiced to see in my great clay fires stones of every sort and size shattered and reduced to siliceous, alkaline, and phosphate dust, delightfully available to the growing cereals, which, by the chemistry of nature, make the glass of their straw and the phosphates of their grain from these now available materials.

I have reflected how many centuries it would take, of aëration and weathering, to separate those obstinate aggregations, which *fire* renders available in a few hours! and every farmer knows how much more manure and cultivation is required to render the yellow subsoil profitable.

I feel very strongly on this subject. It is one of the keystones of heavy-clay profit. I have burned many thousand loads of brickdust ashes, but I ought to have burned more. There is no fear of exhaustion. With plenty of this clay under your five inches of ploughed soil, you have an abundant mine of wealth. Those passive, and therefore useless, treasures which Dr. Daubeny so ably discovered, are rendered active and profitable by burning.

I look upon our clay subsoil as a doctor's shop full of chemicals. If you doubt it, dig up some subsoil yellow clay, shut it up in a drawer for a few months, and when you open that drawer it will remind you nasally of Apothecaries' Hall—by the various smells of its chemical compounds.

We are too apt to forget that, for thousands of years millions of reptiles, worms, and insects, have lived and died and decomposed in our soils. For thousands of years the feathered tribes, carnivorous or omnivorous, have used our earth as their feeding-ground, their dung-heap, and their grave. Time has dissolved their elements and the elements of their food, and the inorganics have been washed deep into the subsoil. The same may be said of our primeval vegetation.

There is something very encouraging in the durability of burnt clay brickdust. It sinks gradually down into the obstinate subsoil, and mixes with it in minute granules, rendering it more permeable and more accessible to the roots of our crops. Fifteen years of practical experience have enabled me to come to these conclusions.

When I first entered on my farm, the high-shouldered green lanes rendered fences of little protection. I burned the sides to a considerable depth, and carted the ashes on my fields, thus leaving the lands convex and self-drained.

The cost of a ton of Peruvian guano, £12, would produce you 480 loads, or cubic yards, of burned clay-ashes—a permanent improvement for four acres of soil.

How to improve Heavy Land cheaply where the Landlord's and Tenant's Capital is limited.—I rent 45 acres of very stiff clay land adjoining my own, at £1 per acre. There are no buildings upon it, and it was undrained, and consequently unprofitable to farm. Not being then sure of a renewal of the lease, I determined on improving it as cheaply as I could, trusting to the remaining eight years of the lease for remuneration.

There being a good fall, I drained one field 50 feet apart, 5 feet deep, with 1-inch pipes, at the following cost:—

	£	s.	d.
54 rods of drains cut, and pipes laid in at 6*d*. per rod....	1	7	0
1000 pipes at 13*s*. per 1000	0	13	0
Total per acre	£2	0	0

I then double-ploughed the land; the leading plough with four horses, the second plough having five horses, bringing up immense clods of yellow tenacious pernicious clay. These clods, when dry, were collected and burned into brickdust ashes at a cost of 6*d*. per cartload of 27 bushels. About 10 loads of chalk per acre were also applied. Ever since this was done—

eleven years ago,—the drains discharge well during winter rains. In the spring the land does not *appear* to be so well drained as on my own land, where the drains are much closer, but, notwithstanding, I always have had good crops since I drained and deeply ploughed it. Last year I had 6 quarters of beans per acre—and this year the wheat crop is estimated at 7 quarters per acre, the straw superabundant and like reeds. The average of my wheat crops upon this field has not been less than 5 quarters per acre—and other crops in proportion. It requires no conjuror to show that such an operation has been highly remunerative.

The other three fields were drained at a somewhat greater cost, at 24 feet and 40 feet apart, with equally satisfactory results. The deep, wide, and cheap drains thus pay well.

The crops I grow on such soil are wheat, mangolds, or tares, oats, clover, wheat, beans and wheat, and a proportion of winter tares, fed off in May and June by sheep, each eating 1 lb. of rape-cake per day; the land is then laid up for oats the ensuing spring, and last year I had 11 quarters of oats per acre.

If I take oats after mangolds, I apply 2 cwt. of guano per acre for the oats.

The red clover is taken once in eight years; the first growth mowed for hay, and sold. The second growth, when fairly on the head,* consumed by sheep, eating 1 lb. per head per diem of old rape-cake. The following crop of wheat is a very strong one, and therefore I take a second crop of bearded rivett wheat, which (having 2 cwt. of guano sown with it) usually produces 6 to 7 quarters per acre. After the two crops of wheat, the land is well manured with farm-yard manure, ploughed in before winter by two ploughs, one following in the track of the other, and in the spring 2 cwt. of guano and 2 cwt. of salt, scarified in, and a crop of mangold taken, followed next spring by oats, guanoed. Sometimes the wheat is followed by beans, and then wheat again, before a root crop.

Sometimes, to vary the crop, we take white clover and trefoil, and feed it all the year with sheep, eating 1 lb. of cake per day. You may then take wheat, beans and wheat. If you can sell your beans to your pigs or sheep at 10 per cent. loss, it is a *great gain;* but, as a general rule, for sheep, rape-cake is cheaper than beans, and the manureal results more enriching to the soil.—*October*, 1858.

Questions.—Were I about to hire a farm, I should do something more than merely look at it. Having satisfied myself that my capital would be fully equal to the undertaking, these would be the questions I should ask:—

1. Is it drained naturally or artificially, and what is it in geological formation?

* It is a great mistake to keep red clover fed down close. By preventing the surface development you thereby prevent the formation and full growth of the roots, which subsequently are food for the wheat which follows.

2. Has it been farmed according to rotation, or by a continuation of corn crops?
3. Is there sufficient accommodation for stock, and proper housing for the farmer and labourers?
4. Are the fields small, the hedgerows excessive, and is there a large number of hedgerow trees?
5. Is the landlord a great game preserver?
6. Has it ever been subsoiled or deeply cultivated?
7. What is the probable in-coming valuation per acre?
8. What is the rent, poor-rates, tithes and other taxes, per acre?

Before I hired a farm I would take with me a labourer and dig a hole in every field, to the depth of 2 or 3 feet, that I might know the character of the subsoil, for herein lies the prospect of your success or failure.

The agricultural pie-crust, or ploughed soil, to the depth of 5 inches, always looks pleasant enough and dark, but inside the pie you will too often find a most miserable contrast, inconceivably at variance with the deceptive surface which has been so long cultivated and aërated. There is nothing more instructive than the contents of a 5-feet drain cut through a field. Mere contents, when exposed to daylight, appeal forcibly to agricultural common sense with reproachful truth. It is in that 5 feet of subterraneity that you must look for your agricultural profit or loss; and yet I have seen many farms hired without a spadeful of earth being moved or examined; and I have seen many farmers, in a very brief period, leave farms so hired, minus their capital.

If I wished to form an opinion of a farm by its outside appearance, I should examine it in March, before the ground was covered with vegetation; again in the middle of May, to see whether the crops were "going to Halsted Fair;" and again in the end of July, just before harvest, when the corn and root crops would speak in eloquent language of their condition and feelings.

A man of judgment and capital may often hire some naturally good soil at a low rate, because the preceding tenant, from various causes, has preferred growing weeds to corn, and the landlord may have neither judgment, desire, nor capital for improvement. A dilapidated farm, however good, naturally gets a bad name, and is often to be hired cheap by a man who will, by improvement, develop its powers.

I would rather take a farm after a bad farmer, who *took little from the land*, owing to a large growth of neglected weeds. Here you have an abundance of unexhausted material which only requires conversion and availability.

It is often found, too, that men take farms and miscalculate the cost of improvements. When their capital is all expended they are obliged to make a sacrifice and leave, instead of being able to remain and reap the reward of those improvements.

Over-trading in farming is as inevitably ruinous as it is in trade. Too much land and too little capital ends in failure.

Beware of Valuations.—Knowing farmers, who are going out, will work you a nice bit for fallows ploughed no end of times, whilst every scrap of rubbish that can be worked into a dung-heap and carted on these fallows will be called manure. If you are in a position to do so, offer a given sum, and thus test the probable claim before you hire.

Cattle and Cow-feeding.—On this subject I would strongly advise a perusal of two admirable papers by Mr. Horsfall, in vols. xvii. and xviii. of the *Journal* of the Royal Agricultural Society of England. The practical and scientific facts there disclosed will enable you to render stock feeding a more profitable operation than that in general practice. The important fact that his feeding-houses are kept at a temperature of 60° during winter must not be overlooked.

Lois-Weedon Culture.—To the Rev. S. Smith we owe a great debt of gratitude: he has practically demonstated that which Daubeney and Liebig have theoretically indicated—that our earth is full of passive or unavailed-of treasures, which become active and profitable by deep and frequent cultivation, and that by thus bringing the celestial and terrestrial elements in contact, a profitable agricultural fruition must necessarily result. I have had the pleasure of witnessing Mr. Smith's practice, and can testify to its success and advantage. Every one should peruse this little useful work. He may be said to have developed the theory and sentiments of that great master in culture, Jethro Tull.

Equable Temperature for Stock.—I am convinced by observation that one cause of lung complaint in bullocks or heaves in pigs is a sudden change of temperature. I occasionally kept some spare bullocks in a barn; once a month, when we threshed, the wind blew through it, and in consequence my bullocks never prospered. Pigs that lie on horse-dung or heated manure, and then walk in the ordinary air, will almost certainly get heaves or lung disease. Non-ventilation and a putrescent atmosphere will produce many diseases amongst live stock, and amongst human beings too.

Exhaustion of Farming.—I have said elsewhere that the four-course system is not the most profitable with very high farming. Take care, however, to permit no exhaustion. The moment your fields show the slightest diminution of power, take a green or root crop, well manured, and feed it on the land with linseed-cake, rape-cake, or corn. On a clay farm I should consider there was feebleness unless we got 5 quarters of wheat, 10 to 11 quarters of oats, 5 quarters of beans, and 30 tons of mangold per acre, with abundant clover and other things in proportion. You may always regulate fertility by the quantity of stock kept; although sometimes when stock and food are very dear, it may be cheaper to use artificial manures. Deep cultivation is an essentiality. I assume that no farmer will allow of any weeds. You cannot have a great crop of any sort unless it has undivided possession of the soil.

Thick Sowing and Poor Farming: National Loss caused thereby.—Taking Mr. Caird's statistics for our authority, one-ninth of the produce of our grain crops is used for seed, thus proving that our seed only multiplies nine times. Now, on my farm the increase is 40 for one in wheat and oats, and proportionately in other things. Surely this is strong evidence of the necessity for improvement. The economy would be, in seed alone (assuming that my quantity was used and my produce attained), nearly two millions of quarters, and the increase to produce from fifteen to twenty millions of quarters. I fear that much seed is wasted by continuing the old broadcast system instead of using the drill and horse-hoe. Of course I would only recommend my own quantity of seed on similar soils and under similar treatment. There can, however, be no doubt that we sow generally a great deal too much seed.

Guano.—On a poor exhausted farm nothing pays so well as guano; it acts immediately, and thus produces a larger quantity of straw and food to make manure for the future. When first I took my farm, every sprinkle of it showed its effect; now, however, it is only occasionally needed, and its effect is not so very perceptible. For distant fields it is economical, by saving much cartage of farm-yard manure. Its effects in the conservatory, and on fruits as well as on flowers, are surprising. I apply it, mixed with chilled water, at the rate of 1 oz. to a gallon, or somewhat less; too much would cripple the roots. I always buy the best Peruvian guano. I agree with Baron Liebig, that purely ammoniacal manures enable a bad farmer, who sells all off and keeps no stock, to impoverish his soil by an exhaustion of the terrestrial ingredients necessary for the crop.

Threshing-Machines.—Experience has taught us a lesson in this matter. Twelve years ago I used feeding-rollers, on the Scotch principle; then we dispensed with them, and drove at greater velocity; now I have put in Goocher's patent beaters and concave, which are found practically to prevent breaking of the corn, although they are like enormous cross-cut files, with the roughest possible surfaces; in fact, the two rough surfaces of the concave and beaters look just as if they must grind the corn, whilst, on the contrary, it is found that the chaff is all sufficiently rubbed, and the corn comes away undamaged. With these concaves and beaters it is not necessary to drive with extreme velocity, nor is it needful to set the beaters so close to the concave as on the old plan. I ought to have the new patent shakers, but content myself at present with the old circular rakes.

Should we consume our Straw, or tread it under

foot? or should we consume our Green Crops carefully, or tread them down wastefully, and plough them in?—I have tried both plans extensively, and have come to decided conclusions on the subject. If I had a doubt about it, that doubt was effectually removed by an attentive perusal of the facts so admirably collected, registered, and tested, chemically and physically, by Mr. Horsfall, in his excellent paper on "Dairy Management," in the *Royal Agricultural Society's Journal*, vol. xviii., p. 150. By this paper we may be assured that all agricultural produce pays better to consume than to plough in unconsumed. It is shown unmistakably that straw has quality and value as a feeding material, if properly prepared. Therefore it is as unreasonable to tread it under foot as to tread in bean-meal, oil-cake, or other substances. The question of bedding is settled by the sparred floors. The cost of preparing the straw for food, where steam is used, forms no impediment to its profitable use as food. A ton of straw may, by steam-power, be cut up into ¼-inch lengths for less than 3*s*. per ton; by hand-labour it would cost 6*s*. per ton. The steaming would cost very little; but, even supposing the cost of boiling or steaming was 3*s*. per ton, still there would be a manifest advantage in feeding out, and there would be a saving in dung-heaps or carting, in comparison with the ordinary process. Mr. Horsfall says, "In wheat-straw, for which I pay 35*s*. per ton, I obtain ⅔ lb. of oil, besides 32 lbs. of starch, or (the starch reduced as oil), 18⅔ lbs. for 1*s*. 2½*d*., available for the production of fat, or for respiration. I know no other material from which I can derive, by purchase, an equal amount of this element of food at so low a price." Mr. Horsfall can afford to give 35*s*. for a ton of wheat-straw, or 40*s*. a ton for bean-straw, to use as food, with a good profit; but if he purchased it merely for the purpose of manure, it would not be worth more to him than 9*s*. 7*d*. per ton.

For several years I steamed nearly all my straw for my animals, horses included, and was enabled to keep a very large number. Owing to a change of bailiff and alterations in my buildings, rendered necessary by my increased family, I partially reverted for a couple of years to the old system of straw for bedding: I soon found that I could not keep half as much stock, and the whole affair was far less satisfactory. The same remark applies to green food as to straw; any cost of preparing and cutting up is far more than compensated by the advantageous conversion of the food by the animals which consume it. A very successful farmer of my acquaintance, who keeps more than 1,500 sheep, puts down his horse-power in the field, and cuts up all his green crops into about ⅛-inch length, mixing a little meal with it. I understood him to say that a man and boy, with the horse, will cut up enough for 300 sheep daily. In wet weather, or when the food is too succulent, he mixed a little straw with it.

If it were right as a principle to plough in farm produce rather than consume it, we ought to plough in our oil-cake, bean and barley-meal, and hay, instead of giving it to the animals; but Mr. Horsfall has shown unmistakably that, in the case of albuminous matter, it is worth twenty times more as food than as manure, and the same remark applies in degree to straw and other feeding-stuffs. Feeders generally would derive much advantage from a perusal of Mr. Horsfall's excellent paper. The consumption of straw will, of course, necessitate a larger amount of capital in live stock, sparred floors, and buildings. Mr. M'Culloch, of Auckness, obtains a better result from his stock by mixing his food with cut straw in boiling water, as described by Mr. James Caird. For the future I shall avoid sowing rape-cake in the soil, except where there is wireworm. Mr. Horsfall's experiments confirm my long-continued practice of using rape-cake as food for animals. By cooking the straw, &c., we procure animal heat cheaper from coal than from food.

WHY DO WE WASTE OUR STRAW, SO VALUABLE FOR FEEDING PURPOSES? HOW MUCH SHOULD IT BE WORTH PER ACRE?

This is a vital question for agriculture. For many years I have been gradually more and more convinced that straw has a considerable value for feeding purposes, for which alone it should be used, in order to extract from it the largest profit.

It is true that, when I have propounded this notion in the presence of practical farmers, their shouts of laughter have testified to their disbelief; and I have smiled at their prejudice and miscalculation, in conscious conviction that they would gradually have to surrender at discretion.

The quantity of wheat-straw removed from an acre of well-farmed clay, where the average is 5 qrs. per acre, would be 2 tons per acre. Science has shown us that, ploughed in and considered as *manure*, its worth is but 9s. 4d. per ton; while, used as *food*, it will, if properly prepared, realize a value of 40s. per ton. Now, what farmer would knowingly throw away £2 to £3 per acre, in so economic a business as farming? and yet, this is literally being done over millions of acres.

If it be denied that straw has a greater value as food than as manure, it would, by parity of reasoning, be desirable to compare the manurial and feeding values of oil-cake, barley, beans, peas, hay, and roots.

Whilst my farming friends ridicule my dislike to ploughing in straw, they would stand aghast at my proposing to them to plough in their barley-meal, linseed-cake, or other feeding material. But I can see no difference: the folly or error is in each case equal, and the loss comparatively as great.

Whence does this singular disbelief arise? Simply because the straw, in an unprepared condition, is not in an available condition as food.

I purpose to give a practical illustration of this question, by a statement of my own proceedings; but every one who would understand the question in its most comprehensive view should *study* Mr. Horsfall's admirable papers on dairy management, in the Society's *Journal*. The whole feeding question may be considered as greatly developed by those papers.

The question of converting both our straw and our roots more advantageously than we now do, is a true breeches-pocket question for the British farmer; nor are the public less interested in the more abundant supply of meat which would naturally follow the more economic use of our straw and roots.

The general appearance of thriving animals is unmistakable. If, after feeding, they lie down contentedly, free from restlessness, all goes on well. Such is the case with my 10 young shorthorn bullocks, of Irish breed, about 30 months old, which were bought in at £9 each.

They consume daily—

	s.	*d.*
216 gallons cut wheat-straw		
6 do. rape-cake..	2	6
3 do. malt-combs..	0	4½
5 do. bran	0	5
Moistened by		
20 gallons of hot water (bean straw requires twice the quantity)...........................		
300 lbs. of mangel-wurzel..............................	1	4

In round numbers, they cost at the rate of 3s. 6d. per week, independent of the wheat-straw. If I valued the wheat-straw at 40s. per ton, it would add 2s. 6d. to their weekly cost. The roots I value at 10s. per ton. The animals are in a fattening and growing condition, and evidently are advancing remuneratively. This we can judge of by their appearance, as I have not, like Mr. Horsfall, a weighing-machine for cattle. Nothing tests the value or force of food so soon as milking-cows. I strictly adhere to Mr. Horsfall's proportions of food for mine; and the result is an ample supply of milk, and an *increase in condition*.

The food for each cow is as follows, daily:—20 lbs. straw chaff; 8 lbs. of hay; 5 lbs. rape-cake; 2 lbs. bean-meal; ¾ lb. of bran; ¾ lb. malt-combs; 35 lbs. mangel or swedes. Cost (without straw), 7s. 7d. per week.

The whole question may be said to hinge upon the condition in which the food is administered. It must be *moist* and *warm;* and the animals must have proper warmth and shelter. As a general rule, this is not the case throughout the kingdom: hence much food is wasted or misapplied. Were I to give my bullocks the same quantity of cut straw in a dry state, they would not eat one-half of it; and, besides, they would be restless and dissatisfied. This I know from experience.

I will now describe my mode of preparation, and then calculate the cost.

I do not use the ordinary close steaming apparatus, but a number of cast-iron pans, or coppers, each capable of containing 250 gallons. These are set in brick-work, with a four-inch space around them, each space connected with the adjoining one by a six-inch earthen pipe.

Into these spaces, and around these coppers, circulates a portion of the *waste steam* from the engine, after having passed through the cylinder.

I should state that a close vessel of water, connected with the supply tank, is kept in a nearly boiling state by the waste steam, before it passes around the coppers, and a vertical four-inch pipe takes away the steam after it has passed around the coppers; so that so long as the steam-engine is at work, the steam flows around the coppers, after heating the close vessel of water, and then passes into the atmosphere.

The coppers are all sunk into the earth, so as to stand level with the floor. By this means, when an extra supply of food is required, it may be piled up in a mound, and kept hot for two or three days.

The straw chaff, *cut fine* and sifted, is thrown dry into the copper, twenty-seven gallons at a time, and then the proportion of malt-combs, bran, and rape-cake strewed over it; then a pail of hot water (drawn from the hot-water vessel close at hand) is thrown over it, and it is all incorporated by mixing with a steel fork, and *well trodden down;* then another twenty-seven gallons of chaff, with the other materials and hot water; another mixing and another treading down, until the copper is full and solid: and if extra quantities are required, it may be continued in the same way above and around the coppers, but it must be *moist and solid* (if too wet the animals will not eat it). The larger the mass, the longer it remains hot.

Practically, we find we can in winter manage if our engine only goes twice a week; but as a general rule we work it for grinding, irrigating, thrashing, &c., more often than that. The mass of subterranean brick-work absorbs the heat from the waste steam, and holds it for several days.

The heat so obtained costs you nothing, for it would be wasted in the atmosphere.

I think the time will come when farmers will turn it to several useful purposes.

Animals will eat rape-cake abundantly, when so mixed and dissolved, but not when dry.

This is an admirable food, and it should be administered, more or less, through the whole year.

I should say that our roots are cut either by a Gardner or Bentall, and mixed in the manger with the warm steamed chaff.

There will be no blowing, griping, or scouring, with food so prepared, and the animals eat it as hot as they can bear it.

In my earlier career I reared first forty and then fifty calves, and sold them as fat bullocks, so treated, never having been off the boarded floors for two-and-a-half years, and never having had straw under them.

The ten bullocks I am now feeding are on sparred floors.

The cost of cutting a ton of straw into chaff, one-fourth of an inch long, may be taken at 3s. to 4s. The trials of chaff-cutters, as reported by the judges in the *Royal Agricultural Society's Journal*, shows that 112 lbs. or more of hay could be cut in three minutes by steam power. It would be well, however, to double that time or cost, because we know on such occasions that everything is in "competing order," which could not be expected on a farm. Therefore, 2s. a ton for hay, or 4s. per ton for straw, would be a liberal cutting-up allowance by steam power.

If we are to consume all our bean, barley, wheat, and oat straw, we must keep our animals on sparred floors, or on burned clay, and we must invest more capital in animals, and shall make much more meat per acre. If a ton of straw will make 40 lbs. of meat, and if two tons of straw are grown per acre on our cereal and pulse crops, it would be four score of meat per acre over the whole of the cereals and pulse.

Oh! but where is your manure to come from, if you *eat* your straw?

Why your animal, by this mode of feeding, consumes 560 lbs. of rape-cake with every ton of straw. This is better than littering the yards by cartloads in wet weather, to sop up the water, and save some of the liquid manure which would otherwise be washed away by rain from untroughed roofs.

But what feeding property is there in straw?

A good deal of hilarity was excited at our London Farmers' Club the other day, by my stating that every 100 lbs. of wheat straw, contained the equivalent of 15 lbs of oil. Since then, I find I have understated the case, and that really each 100 lbs. of straw contain—see Morton's admirable Cyclopædia, vol. ii, page 1153 (Voelcker's analysis)—seventy-two per cent.! of muscle fat and heat-producing substances, of which twenty-seven per cent. are soluble in potash, and thirty-five per cent. insoluble.

The soluble fattening substances are equal to 18½ lbs. of oil in each 100 lbs. of straw.

In conclusion, I would recommend every feeder of stock to *study* Mr. Horsfall's papers in vol. xvii., page 260, and vol. xviii., page 150 of the *Royal Agricultural Society's Journal*. They will enlighten his mind, dispel his prejudices, and increase his profit.

If by his system of feeding 14 lbs per week of meat and 3 lbs. of internal fat can be gained by each full-sized animal (and I am sure this can be done as an average), I know of no other system which will exceed it in result, or equal it in economy.

The consumption of straw, in the way here suggested, would produce a very great increase of meat, manure, and corn.

If supplies of this warm food were conveyed to sheep in our fields, in cold and miserable weather, many losses would be avoided, and our turnips would make more mutton.

In order to provoke a discussion and examination of this subject, I send this communication to several papers, and shall probably enlarge upon it in some future papers.

Feb. 28*th*, 1859.

By Mr. Horsfall's mode of feeding you may get the manure without cost, and a handsome price for your straw and roots.

The following *facts*, deduced from Mr. Horsfall's paper, will show that 1,000 lbs. of swedish turnips, or 100 lbs. dry are worth 1s. 9¾d. *as manure*, whilst

	s.	*d.*
100 lbs. of hay are worth	1	2¼
100 lbs. of straw	0	5
100 lbs. of bean-meal	2	6
100 lbs. of oil-cake	3	1¾
100 lbs. of Indian meal	1	1¾
100 lbs. of locust beans	0	5

Here is an instructive and interesting comparison with a vengeance! A ton of swedish turnips are worth, *as manure*, 4s. per ton, or nearly half the manurial value of a ton of straw or locust beans.

Oil-cake or rape-cake are worth, *as manure*, £3 3s. per ton.

Sub-Irrigation combined with Subterranean Drainage.—Referring to Mr. Scott's letter annexed, it is easy to appreciate the advantage of the system. The grass having by its roots drained the soil of its moisture, you saturate the land to its surface by admitting water from the river, and stopping the drains. This done, turn the taps, and permit the water to flow away, leaving in the soil as much moisture as it chooses to retain by capillarity. This operation repeated as required, is an admirable and very profitable mode of aërating the subsoil, and stimulating an abundant vegetation. It should never be forgotten that aëration by filtration and capillarity is one of the most profitable advantages resulting from drainage and irrigation.

"18, Parliament-street,
"London, *July* 18*th*, 1859.

"Dear Sir,—I have drained and sub-irrigated a hundred acres of meadow land belonging to Squire Pread, of Tyringham Hall, near Wolverton Station, and am to let on the water to-morrow evening and on Wednesday, and if you know any one interested in such a work, I shall be happy to show it to them in operation. The meadows are two feet under the surface of the river Ouse, from which we irrigate; and as the land is drained from four to five feet deep, we have a pressure of irrigating water of upwards of six feet. The work has cost under £6 an acre, and has added £2 per acre per annum to the value of the land. It is all regulated by taps and keys and sluices, the same as the New River water supply to houses.

"I am, dear Sir, yours respectfully,

"I. J. MECHI, Esq." "THOMAS SCOTT."

ON THE ADVANTAGES OF STEAM IN AGRICULTURE—HOW FAR THEY HAVE BEEN AVAILED OF.

READ BEFORE THE CENTRAL FARMERS' CLUB, LONDON, *May*, 1859.—I purpose, first, to review the general benefits conferred by steam, to estimate the extent of its use in our manufactures, locomotion, and mercantile marine, and to see in what relation, in this respect, agriculture stands to the other industrial occupations of the kingdom. I shall also glance at the progress of steam culture, recognize with gratitude the merits of its early pioneers, and indulge in an opinion of what our use of it in culture ought to be, and ultimately will be. I shall also consider the question of fixed or portable engines, the value of steam for irrigation and drainage, on what sized farms an engine will pay, and add some practical hints about steam-engines and boilers.

Nine years ago I addressed a rural audience on this subject with the following introduction, which so exactly represents my present feeling that I repeat it:—

"Steam—mighty steam! The term suggests a thousand pleasing and profitable reflections; that marvellous and almost invisible power which brooks no opposition—which never tires. Scouring the plains, piercing the hills, threading the valleys, and ploughing the wide ocean; mastering, with indignant ease, time and space, wind, water, and seasons. The varieties of its power may well amaze us: here it is wielding the ponderous hammer that gives shape and consistence to gigantic metallic masses; there it weaves the gossamer web, or twists the slender fibre; it plunges the hardy miner deep into the bowels of mother earth, and raises from her lap her mineral and metallic treasures—these glow and flow with liquid meltings at its powerful blast; here it is printing bank notes, there it is coining golden sovereigns; to-day it is preparing food and clothing for the body, to-morrow it feasts the mind, spreading far and wide, in countless numbers, the broad-sheets of intelligence. Instruments of death and of preservation alike acknowledge its power.

"What a comprehensive word is this said *steam*. It means peace, progression, civilization, education, abundance, and cheapness; it is the death-blow to monopoly and privation. Ignorance and prejudice shrink away at its approach; the iron barrier of separation is broken by it; the interposition of time, of distance, or of poverty no longer wounds the tender affections; it increases alike our political power as a nation and our morality, for the increase of physical comfort must, in a Christian community like blessed England, predispose to moral good. But if this all-pervading power clothes the body with elegance and cheapness, and stores the mind with knowledge and intelligence, can agriculture alone escape its influence? Impossible. It must and will feed, as well as clothe, the people cheaply. The landlord or the farmer who saves his time and his money by the concentrated power and speed of a hundred horses on the rail, or five hundred on the ocean, must draw comparisons and conclusions adverse and disparaging to our present slow and crawling system of agricultural mechanics. The general application of steam in agriculture involves a thorough change and reformation of our farming system. It is a question of more capital and less land, both for landlord and tenant. It is a question of a compensation for unexhausted improvements, or an ample protection of tenure by lease; and it is a question of public registration and easy transfer of landed property. It will compel a more accurate observance of the laws of mechanics, and will sharpen the intellects of the agricultural labouring community. In a word, the employment of steam-power in agriculture will compel or induce a larger employment of labour and production of food. Drainage, deeper cultivation, open fields, good roads, better buildings, more live stock, and less weeds, must and will be the concomitants of agricultural steam-power; for steam-power means amendment and progression. It would be a curious statistic could we accurately know the number of horses that would be required to produce a power equivalent to that now in action by our fixed, locomotive, and marine engines. I apprehend that, if the whole surface of England were sown with oats and cropped with grass for hay, there would not be enough to feed the requisite number of horses; and if there were food enough we must have whole towns of stables, streets of harness-makers, and squares of farriers and veterinary surgeons.

"Well, then, but for steam, the happy inhabitants of merry England could not and would not have those luxuries, comforts, or necessaries which they now enjoy. Honour to that departed philosopher whose sagacity and perception, under Divine Providence, applied the bubbling resistance of our tea-kettles to the most noble and useful purposes of humanity."

My Opinion of British Agriculture.—While the agricultural community is congratulating itself on its rapid progress, and while our talented friend Monsieur de la Tréhonnais is holding us up to his countrymen in France as models of agricultural progress, your humble servant is lamenting our agricultural backwardness and imperfection. This discrepancy of sentiment may be readily accounted for. They compare the present with the past. With them the extensive background of non-improvement throws up in pleasant relief the bright spots of progress. With them the exceptions excuse the rule. With me they do but condemn it, and point to its amendment. We may admit that much of our light and self-drained land is very much improved, and in many districts very highly farmed; but that extensive portion of our island called cold, stiff, tenacious clay, fifteen-sixteenths of which are still undrained, is to my certain knowledge in a most unsatisfactory and unprofitable condition, as regards the interests of landlord, tenant, and the country at large.

Now it is, in my opinion, precisely these soils which, when improved, are the most dependable for a result, containing, as they do, an undeveloped treasure of ammoniacal and phosphatic fertility. Those gifts have not yet been availed of, and it is steam cultivation alone, after drainage, that can place those subterranean treasures at our disposal. My observation of the present cultivation of our stiff clays would give an average depth of about four to five inches—all below this may be considered an unknown and unimproved territory. It is true that, after drainage, the filtration or percolation of water and manure will gradually and certainly aërate and improve the subsoil, but the process is too slow for these quick-moving times.

You want rapidly to dry these dead and saturated masses by atmospheric exposure. The dense and closely-packed mass of infinitesimal granules must be separated by pulverization, so that the millions of almost imperceptible fibres may introduce themselves without difficulty to the hitherto unapproachable but fertilizing ingredients of the subsoil.

Liebig, and our other great chemical lights, have proved to us that every breath of air that passes over newly-exposed clay abstracts from it its moisture, and in exchange blesses it with ammoniacal and fertilizing gases.

As you follow the steam cultivator on a dry day instantaneous exhalations strike your nostrils, and convince you that the earth is a great apothecary's shop, full of chemical compounds. The rough and lightly-laid fallow absorbs the fructifying sunbeams, and imparts to the air in contact with it an expansive heat, which causes it to rise in wavy playfulness in its struggle through the superincumbent but colder atmosphere.

The rusty-looking iron of our so-called poor clay subsoils, makes greedy claim upon the passing ammonia. A volume might be written by our chemists upon the advantages of evaporation, percolation, dews, frosts, fogs, and sunshine.

Jethro Tull was the prince of cultivators, but the want of

artificial drainage defeated all his calculations. The Rev. Mr. Smith, of Lois Weedon, is the great Jethro Tull of the present day. Fifteen years ago I was convinced that on our stiff yellow clays' cultivation was more important than manure; acting on that conviction, after I had drained my land, I broke it up with three horses, six other horses following in the same track, with Smith of Deanston's great subsoil plough. Our labourers called it a little earthquake, and my crops have never forgotten it; but for all that, I saw how costly was horse-power when deep cultivation was attempted, and how necessary it was that we should apply steam to get a yard deep of cultivation instead of ten or twelve inches.

Agricultural Doubts about Steam.—I confess I was very much astonished that our progressive friend, Mr. R. Smith, in his recent lecture to this club on agricultural progress, should describe steam culture as "yet a venture." I consider steam cultivation an accomplished fact; profitably accomplished, and therefore practically attained.

It is impossible to deny with truthfulness that both Mr. Fowler's and Mr. Smith's plans are practically proven and sealed with the stamp of superiority over horse-power, both in cost and effect, by the award and medal of the Royal Agricultural Society of England. From my own observation of both these plans, I am sure it will pay to use them.

Had I not my fixed steam-engine, I should at once adopt the practice, although my land has all been already very deeply disturbed, but I suppose I must hire a portable engine. As

A Proof of the Advantages of Steam Cultivation, let me mention the following fact:—At my great gathering in July, 1856, Mr. Fowler's steam-plough, with the subsoiler attached, cultivated two stitches of clover lea, being part of a field on which wheat was to be sown in October. Although that field had been formerly subsoiled, and forked by manual labour, Fowler's subsoil brought up and exposed to view some undisturbed nasty ochrey and rusty subsoil. Some of our agricultural friends would shrug their shoulders and say nothing would grow on it; but mark the result. In October or November the wheat was duly drilled over the whole field; as soon as it came up, and in every stage of its growth, those two stitches shewed their superiority. After harvest, the field was all manured and dug with the fork, and produced a fine crop of mangel in 1858. It is now (April 1859) in wheat again, and in this early stage of growth, the two stitches—steam-ploughed in 1856—still shew a superiority! My men called my attention to this only on a recent occasion.

But who can seriously doubt the benefits of deep cultivation on strong clays after drainage? After the recent showers, I could see the deeply-moved soil, over drains, shewing light-coloured and dry, whilst the intermediate spaces were dark and damp.

It was *deep cultivation* that did this, producing facile aëration, powerful capillarity, and rapid evaporation.

It proves that a yard or four feet deep of cultivation is not a bit too deep; and when I remember that at my friend Dixon's, near Witham, a parsnip was pulled up whose roots were thirteen feet six inches long, and then broke off, I seriously believe that we have no present idea as to what depth of cultivation and drainage we shall ultimately arrive with steam power.

Why did that parsnip go so deep? Because the earth had all been moved to the depth of fourteen feet. It had been a brick-earth pit, filled up with soil from the adjoining land, when it was necessary to open a new pit; air and water had circulated freely to the depth of fourteen feet. It is not what an operation costs, but what profit it pays, that must guide us. The shilling flail is superseded by one that costs £300, as a matter of economy and profit. Who is to say that we shall not have scarifiers or grubbers whose tines will gradually go four, five, or six feet deep, drawn by a 100-horse power engine? Am I visionary in anticipating such a result? Is it more astounding than Fowler's draining plough, drawing, as it were by magic, its lines of pipes, like ropes of sausages, deep into the bowels of the most obstinate clays? And here I should consider myself ungrateful indeed did I not record my admiration of, and gratitude to, that spirited and far-seeing man, who has devoted his fortune and his mind to the successful realization of what agriculture once considered a romantic and chimerical idea.

If my anticipations are to be realized, let our shallow drainers deepen their ideas and spare their pockets.

Our present Plans of Steam Cultivation.—My public position, as an agriculturist, brings me to many an anxious and intelligent inventor, whose sleepless mind is worn and absorbed by the great one idea, and who languishes for the wherewithal to develop and give a practical bearing to his thoughts. I often feel, as I listen to the anxious and confidential communication, how much must be done and suffered ere the practical public will avail of, and pay for the inventor's genius. We ought to feel grateful to those who I know have devoted their money and time to the improvements in machinery.

It is not my intention to make invidious comparisons between the various means for steam culture. Let each one consult the judges' decision, as given in the last number of the *Royal Agricultural Society's Journal*. Let him spend a little time and money in watching the practical operations which are now so extensively going on, to which access is so liberally granted, and which are so accurately described by the various agricultural publications of the day. Years ago I ventured to predict that we should soon have forty different modes of steam cultivation. Such an idea is rapidly approaching realization. We have now—

1. Fowler's Draining and Trenching Ploughs.
2. Smith's Scarifiers.
3. Williams's ditto.
4. Boydell's Traction Engine.
5. Bray's ditto.
6. Romaine's Cultivator.
7. Fisken's Plough.
8. Rickett's Archimedean Cultivator.
9. Halkett's Railway System of Steam Culture.

And I know of others which are yet to meet the public eye.

I rejoice in the pungent and gladiatorial rivalry on this subject which fills the columns of our agricultural newspapers.

The steam-press is developing steam cultivation—drawing the attention of even the lag-behinds of agriculture, and making them progress in spite of their prejudices.

I have no fear but that each claimant for public steam favour will meet his reward according to his merits. Agriculture is a fine open field of comparison, if people will but look at it.

I recently saw Mr. Smith's Steam Cultivator (made by Messrs. Howard) at work on a farm of stiff soil in Hertfordshire. Its work appeared to me simple and perfect. It was smashing up or grubbing the land four-and-a-half to five inches deep at the cost of one shilling an acre for coals, two-shillings-and-sixpence an acre for manual labour, and something for the wear and tear of the steam-engine and steel-wire rope, &c. The rope was much smaller than one's little finger, say nine-sixteenths of an inch diameter. I have often heard heavy land farmers say that they should like to have horses without feet; this is actually the case with steam, which cultivates without pressure or consolidation.

Halkett's Guideway Steam Cultivator.—I cannot pass by, in silence, Mr. Halkett's noble efforts to effect the operations of the farm on a grand scale by an entirely novel process. Having witnessed the operation, I was struck with the simplicity and unerring accuracy of the work done, as well as by the application of the whole power of the engine without rope, and with a mere fractional friction. Every one who heard Mr. Halkett's paper read before the Society of Arts must have retired with a conviction that the subject was worthy of the most profound consideration, and of a fair national trial on a large scale.

Who is to do this and find the means is another question. I have never yet heard any one dispute Mr. Halkett's calculations. When I see that 240 tons weight can be drawn on a railway, at a speed of twenty miles an hour, a whole mile for two-pennyworth of coal, I feel that the whole question hinges on the calculation of what sum would be sufficient interest for wear and tear, and first cost of his proposed railway. I exhibit a photograph of the machine in operation, performing various farm labours.

If our unduly costly railways pay the shareholders an interest equal to consols, and yet take us as cheaply as the old coach, saving three-fourths of our time, is it so utopian to imagine that similar causes should produce equal effects in agriculture?

Is not time, in horse and manual labour, as much money as time on the rail?

By-the-bye I have just heard that Boydell's traction-engine is drawing coals into Manchester, from a colliery, at one penny per ton per mile, on the high road. It always surprised me that railway buffers and springs were not attached to the machine when it had to draw ploughs or scarifiers. But for these buffers and springs, our railway engines would be breaking their chains, and doing much mischief by sudden concussion.

I hear that as much as £10,000 has been expended on Romaine's cultivator since I lent my aid to its introduction. The inventor is still sanguine of success, judging from its operations in Yorkshire, but a large expenditure is yet required for its full development; it is intended, I believe, to fit it with Boydell's wheels, or something on the same principle. I deeply regret Mr. Boydell's severe indisposition, arising from his anxious and unwearied exertions about his traction engine.

I have received the following from Mr. Hall, who has used Fowler's plough for some time. It will be seen that he works at very high pressure:—

"NAVESTOCK, ESSEX, *April* 26th, 1859.

"DEAR SIR,—I find in practice that my portable engine, working at three hundred and twenty lbs. pressure, consumes eight hundred and fifty pounds of coal, worth eight shillings and sixpence, per each day's work of ten hours, while drawing Fowler's four-furrow plough, by the wire-rope system; and six acres is a fair day's work at present, and which requires three men and two boys, and one horse for water.

"This same engine was worked with Boydell's wheels as a direct traction, drawing Fowler's (same) ploughs. To work ten hours, and plough six acres, she required eleven to twelve hundred pounds of coal.

"She therefore consumed about a quarter of her fuel, to propel herself, besides the damage done to the land by her wheels, which was fatal to that principle for cultivation—but to be enabled to proceed into any field, without horses, is a most valuable acquisition.

"My fixed engine, working at one hundred and twenty lbs. pressure, consumes five hundred-weight of coal in twelve hours, driving one pair of barley-stones, grinding eight bushels per hour; and two pairs of wheat-stones, grinding four bushels per hour each.—I remain, Sir, yours very truly.

"COLLINSON HALL."

"P.S. We worked this engine at two hundred pounds pressure, and then four hundred weight of coal performed the same quantity of work as the five hundred weight at one hundred and twenty pounds now does.

"Since the mill was burned down, in 1845, I have thought it prudent to reduce the pressure."

We must not forget

The Pioneers of Steam Culture.—Years since I had the privilege of inspecting Lord Willoughby D'Eresby's steam-ploughing in Lincolnshire, worked by the "California," a portable steam-engine exhibited in the Crystal Palace of 1851, one of the most perfect and powerful portable engines I ever saw. Again, we are much indebted to the Marquis of Tweeddale for the Yester steam-ploughing, which ought to have convinced the agricultural world long ago not to be afraid of exposing a heavy subsoil to atmospheric influences.

Then, Mr. Usher, of Edinburgh, has strong claims on our thanks and sympathy, when we consider the large sums he expended on producing his steam cultivator.

Experimenting is no joke. I believe that to perfectionate these implements has cost the inventors a fortune of many thousands.

Comparative Value of Horse and Steam-power.—We are much indebted to Mr. John C. Morton for his able paper on the cost of horse-power in the Royal Agricultural Society's last journal, but, if I had any doubt before, that paper has convinced me that horse-power is at least from 50 to 100 per cent. dearer than steam, where the latter can be brought to bear. If manufacturers were asked even to make the comparison, they would ridicule the idea, and tell you that but for steam you could be neither clothed, housed, nor fed. What a manufacturer wants and uses is "power"—cheap, untiring power,—and is this not exactly what the agricultural cultivator requires?

Now, you can never get combined or continued power with horses in any number. When first the Mole Plough was tried on a stiff clay in Essex, before the introduction of the capstan, upwards of 30 horses were attached to it, and a very Babel of confusion ensued. In their struggling attempts at uniform draught, the outsiders compressed those in the centre until a cloud of steam arose from the excited and oppressed animals. Compare this with the tranquil grandeur of a twenty, fifty, or five-hundred horse-power engine.

In comparing horses with steam, we could only allow a horse to work full collar, *without intermission or rest*, for four-and-a-half hours—that would be an ample day's work, and it would cost 2s., because a large well-fed draught-horse cannot be kept for less than £30 per annum.

Let us see what my own steam horse costs working ten clear hours per day, full collar; and my engine is not of the latest improvement, having been in use ten years. The exact measure of one strong horse-power in steam is the evaporation of six gallons, or sixty pounds of water per hour. My own engine evaporates fifty-four gallons per hour, and, therefore, gives nine-horse power, working ten hours per day, which is equal to eighteen real horses working five hours per day.

	£	s.	d.
I burn half a ton of dust coal, at 9s.	0	4	6
Cartage	0	1	6
	0	6	0

Horse-power would cost £1 7s.

One labourer, at 2s. per day, manages my engine, feeds it, and cleans it.

How much more would it cost to attend on eighteen horses?

I could enlarge upon this comparison *in extenso*, but in these days it is only in agriculture that such a question would be entertained, and I must say I feel humiliated that my friend Morton, in his recent excellent paper, has taken so favourable a view of the endurance and availability of horse-power as compared with steam.

In the great Cornish pumping-engines, which are considered as the most economic in combustion, coal being dear there, three pounds of coal per hour will produce one horse-power, so that assuming that four hours' *incessant* work would exhaust a horse for twenty-four hours, twelve pounds of coal, costing five farthings (or twenty shillings per ton), would do as much work as a horse which costs 2s. This is no exaggeration,—even the common portable agricultural engines, which are far less economical in fuel than the fixed condensing engines, will, when in perfect order, produce a day's work equal to one-horse power for twenty-four pounds of coal, or twopence half-penny. The trials of these engines by the Royal Agricultural Society, as reported by the judges, shew a consumption of about five pounds of coal per horse-power per hour.

A very respectable miller assured me that he once, for a wager, ground two hundred quarters of corn with fourteen shillings and sixpence worth of coal, which would be under twopence per quarter, or about one farthing per bushel; and I know that with the common Cornish boiler, and non-condensing high-pressure engines, the ordinary fuel for grinding is only one penny per bushel.

How the increased population of this country could be fed had we to depend on wind, water, or horses, is beyond my comprehension.

We see, in fact, that almost everywhere a steam-engine is attached to the wind or water-mill, and, in addition, we have great steam mills at many of the railway stations.

Considering that a vast number of steam-engines are worked

night and day, it may be fairly estimated that one-horse power worked twenty-four hours, is equal to the labour of six real horses for the same period.

Take an Atlantic steamer that steams unceasingly night and day, and suppose her power to be one thousand steam horses, you would require six thousand real horses to do the work!!

To imagine what space so many animals would require, their food, water, attendants, bedding, harness, and shoeing, seems an impossible absurdity; and yet, practically, when a farmer uses a horse where he might use steam, he is in an equally ludicrous and unprofitable embarrassment.

This brings me to the conclusion:—

On how small a Farm will a Steam-engine pay, and what has a Steam-engine to do on a Farm?— When I speak of the general application of steam-power in agriculture, I assume an improved and profitable condition of agriculture, very different from that which unfortunately generally exists; but let me take a well-regulated and well-drained farm of two hundred acres or less, making five score of meat per acre (I make more than ten score, the labourer makes thirty-two score), there will be plenty to do to grind corn, crush oats, break rape-cake, cut and steam chaff, thresh and dress corn, pump water, and, if opportunity offers, work irrigation pumps, and, if you add to this the cultivation of the soil, an eight-horse power engine will not have many holidays. It is a great convenience to your neighbours to send in their corn to you to be ground. I find that in this way the money I receive in grinding for others pays for all my coals, so that my engine only costs the wear and tear and attendance, and still does all my work, irrigation included. Since harvest I have ground more than three hundred quarters of corn for my pigs.

When your engine rests it eats nothing.

I find that by treading down the chaff, cake, &c., when steamed, and thus preventing the access of air, it will keep sweet and hot for a week or more, according to the bulk of the mass, and the animals like it better.

On a farm of two hundred acres there ought to be at least two hundred tons of straw, to cut into chaff, and to be steamed by the waste steam from the engine. The time will come when we shall warm our bullock-sheds with steam in cold weather, as the manufacturers warm their mills, and in summer it would pay well to drive a circulation of air by a fanner through the cattle-houses, and not a fly will be seen there, nor any disease. There is no doubt that during summer much beef could be, and should be, made by bullocks comfortably warm, but untormented by flies, or excess of sunshine; but then all this implies a manufacturing adaptation of means to an end, which will involve a system of intelligent reconstruction in our farmeries.

All this will come when our doubled or tripled population

will demand twice or three times the amount of meat now produced on our little island.

Steam on small Farms.—There is no reason why small farmers should be deprived of the benefits of steam cultivation, —already some spirited individuals in our district, who are owners of nearly a score of steam-engines, execute the thrashing, and Fowler's plough-draining, over an extensive district, at a fixed price per acre, and I know that they are about to carry out steam cultivation on the same terms.

Gain in time and opportunity by Steam-culture. —Although, irrespective of the above consideration, steam is much cheaper than horse-power, the question of cost becomes insignificant in comparison with opportunity. Nothing can illustrate this better than the words of Mr. Smith, of Woolston, in one of his recent letters on the use of his steam cultivator. He says, "I have shown that two hundred and twenty-five acres of heavy clay require the work of an eight-horse power engine forty-five days. I find from practice it would require thirty-five horses to perform this work in the same time, *i. e.* five horses for three hundred and fifteen days, the whole of a year; this, of course, does not include what can be done by the apparatus in the spring and summer." In other words, as a farmer of two hundred and twenty-five acres would only have eight or nine horses, three-fourths of his stubble-land would be unbroken during the forty-five fine days of August, September, and October. It is only the chemist of agriculture who can sufficiently appreciate the enormity of this loss of aëration, evaporation, filtration, and consequent fructification. If the consolidation of stiff clays in damp weather by pressure renders them infertile by the exclusion of air, which I practically know to be the fact, the opposite of this, by steam cultivation in dry weather, must be a great gain.

Mr. Smith's comparison of horse and steam power confirms my own calculation, that four hours of *unremitting* draught, without a rest, is an ample day's work for a horse. In the midland counties, where the barbarous practice of four horses in a line and two drivers still exists, the ceremony of turning at the headlands, and the alternate coaxing and threatening to get the horses into working condition, consumes no end of time.

Even in our own well-ploughed pair-horse county I have, on a fine May tranquil morning, been highly amused by the colloquy, if I may so term it, between a pair of knowing fat horses and a good-natured but indignant ploughman, as the ejaculations of "Boxer and Wiolet," "worree," and "Hike, come hither," came ringing on the morning air, the horses taking especial care to reserve their effort to pull for the ploughman's last burst of indignant excitement, sometimes accompanied by a small clod. Stern, untiring steam, will destroy much of the poetry of agriculture, and give it a Manchester character.

The great Economy of Steam-power is proved by the judges' report of comparative trials at the Chester Show :—

Hay cut into chaff	128 lbs. in 3 minutes.
Roots cut for sheep	314 " "
Do. for bullocks	620 " "
Do. for do.	1,278 " "
Roots pulped	490 " "
Thick oil-cake broken	165 " "
Corn winnowed	761 " "
Corn dressed	400 " "
Wheat thrashed and dressed	200 sheaves in 13 minutes.
Barley thrashed and dressed	100 " 5 "

I know that such results as these could not be obtained by ordinary farm labourers, because in these trials the machines and men are "well up to the mark," every energy strained to the utmost, and the engines in first-rate order; but even making an allowance for these circumstances, steam is, indeed, a wonderful economy.

Every farmer ought to study the judges' reports in the *Royal Agricultural Society's Journal.*

The trials of steam cultivation are as follows :—

Fowler ploughed six inches by nine (equal to three-horse work), one acre per hour at a cost of 9*s.* 2*d.* per acre; and Trench ploughed an acre twelve inches deep and fourteen inches wide, at 18*s.* 4*d.* per acre. The gain over horse-power in the latter case was enormous, as I know practically.

Messrs. Howard, of Bedfords' Smiths' Steam Cultivator for the two operations of cultivating and cross-cultivating, or smashing up to the depth of from six to seven inches, gave a charge of 14*s.* per acre, which was considerably cheaper than horse-power. I have reason to believe that both these implements have since been working even more effectively and economically on ordinary heavy land farms.

On our railways, 240 tons can be carried one mile for two pennyworth of coal, and three minutes' time of the stoker, guard, and engine-driver.

Compare this with horses on the common road at 7*d.* per ton per mile! which would amount to £7.

Drainage and Irrigation effected by Steam.—The great fen district of the Bedford Level, once a swamp of 200,000 acres, owes its value and fertility to a steam-power of some 1,200 horses, which, distributed at intervals towards the coast, works enormous pumps or wheels, which, creating an artificial fall, by raising the water, cause an outfall for the drainage. Some of these engines throw up 120 tons per minute.

Again, the great Whittlesea Mere, a sort of inland sea, is now a garden of cultivation, having been pumped dry by Appold's steam-pumps, such as we saw at the Exhibition of 1851. These lands, like the great Bedford Level, are preserved from inundation by steam-power always acting or ready to act.

I have to thank Mr. Laurance for the following communication:—

"Elton, Oundle, 19*th April*, 1859.

"Sir,—I beg to acknowledge the receipt of your letter of the 15th.

"The Appold pump, at Whittlesea Mere, drains upwards of five thousand acres of low land, exclusive of the water-shed from the high lands, which will include four or five hundred acres.

"The engine, pump, and buildings, including extensive piling for foundations, cost £2,500. (The drains and ditches are not included in this sum).

"The cost of the first three years' working and repairs—1851 to 1854—averaged one shilling per acre. In 1852, the newly-formed banks broke, and one thousand acres of land were inundated. This had to be pumped out, and the average of the cost was raised by this circumstance.

1855	....	6*d.* per acre.
1856	....	8*d.* ,,
1857	....	10*d.* ,,
1858	....	8*d.* ,,

This includes coals, repairs of engine, engine-man's wages, oil, &c., &c.

"The quantity of water raised six feet high is 16,000 gallons per minute. The lowest lift is four feet six inches, the highest ten feet. The engine works now about three days a week, and runs four or five hours per diem, not consecutively, but at intervals, the supply of water not being sufficiently rapid for the discharge by the centrifugal pump.

"There is no publication containing these facts. You are welcome to them,—I am, Sir, your obedient servant,

"John Laurance."

This is an instructive communication. If we add to the 1*s.* per acre, 5*s.* or 6*s.* for annual interest of the drainage, we have the average value of one bushel of wheat as the charge for converting a lake into a fertile field ! ! !

Messrs. Easton and Amos are now making Appold's pumps for the West Indies, capable of throwing or raising 30,000 gallons of water per minute ! I mention this to shew that you must bring your minds to the consideration of artificial drainage combined with irrigation for even your stiff clays.

The drainage of the country, by wells for steam-engines, by large water-supply for your towns, by railway tunnels and cuttings, by the removal of trees and fences, and, above all, by the evaporation of a great and deep arable culture, are causing you a diminished rain-fall, which may, in time, render irrigation by steam a necessity for your grass-lands and root-crops. I know of much sea-walled land, now in a state of nature, that might be profitably improved by steam drainage and irrigation.

It must not be forgotten that much of the manure placed in our land finds its way in solution to our rivers and brooks, and that what we look upon as pure water contains the most valuable elements of our manures. Hence the value of mere water for irrigation; and I am astonished that Professor Voelcker, in his paper on Sewage Irrigation, in the last number of the *Royal Agricultural Society's Journal*, attaches no value to 50,000 gallons of water per acre, or a rain-fall of more than two inches. As a farmer said to me the other day, "If you can't get water, you can't get grass;" and he was quite right.

Saving of Food by Steam-culture.—A diminution of one-third or more of our horse-power would set free for the food of man a vast extent of our soil. If the horses of agriculture consume the produce of one-fifth of its available area, it follows that something like 2,500,000 of acres would be gained for food for the population. Spackman estimates the farm horses at 1,500,000—in my opinion far too large an estimate, seeing, on arable farms, that we have only one horse to twenty-five acres.

Every hundred acres of arable land require four horses, and each horse consumes the produce of five acres, or the food of seven men.

I consider that steam for cultivation, grinding, thrashing, chaff-cutting, pumping, &c., would economize two-fifths of the horse-power of the farm.

Warmth of Soil gained by deep Steam Cultivation.—We all know that heat and moisture are the two elements of decomposition and of rapid growth, as shewn in tropical countries. Deep and loose cultivation tends to this result. Possibly the action of light may also be important. One cause of the rapid growth of market garden vegetation is depth of cultivation, combined with the subterranean heat of decomposing town manure, and wherever there is heat moisture is attracted.

The necessity for a more perfect cultivation is obvious,—even on a fallow you may pick up small hard knobs or clods, which, on breaking into fragments, exhibit a little treasure of unexplored and unavailed-of territory, confirming the great Jethro Tull's principle of infinitesimality in cultivation.

I have great faith in Croskill's clod-crusher, in very dry weather, for unlocking obstinate clods. Might not that heavy tool be drawn by steam? It would only require guide-wheels, &c.

Town Sewage applied by Steam.—I have so often enlarged upon the vital importance to this country of sewage-irrigation from our towns, that I will only say to my brother-farmers—Consider the value of a daily folding on the land of twenty-eight millions of well-fed human beings (or sheep), and add to this all the animal deposits in our towns, and various other waste products, and you may then fairly estimate how much you lose by permitting these treasures to flow away to the sea. Let it be "willed" by agriculture, and the engineering difficulties will vanish.

Thirteen-fourteenths of the excrement of human beings and

animals are the urine; so that it is in a condition to flow away, even without the addition of water.

Watford, Rugby, and other towns, will bear witness to the facility with which this operation may be effected, but it must be done by steam-power; and that is why I mention it in this paper.

The question will very soon force itself to a solution, for, in spite of filtration, the fluid from our Board of Health works poisons our rivers in summer. That solution must inevitably be a filtration through an agricultural soil, from which the nastiness of our towns and cities will re-appear in the more acceptable form of food for their inhabitants. The great privy question must be talked about and dealt with, in spite of our delicate sensibility.

The question of the application of the sewage of our towns to agricultural fertilization is one that is gradually forcing itself upon public attention, and is dependent on the use of steam. The very fact of a large water-supply to our towns will compel its application to the soil, or your rivers will become sewers. There are no cesspools now from which it may be taken in carts to the land.

The Board of Health at Croydon are in a complete fix in Chancery on this question.

The anglers on the pellucid river Wandle will not receive it, and the landowners are bringing their action because they will not have their land fertilized by it, however agreeable and profitable it may be to the tenants; where, then, is it to go? When I stood over the tanks at Croydon, into which flowed the nastiness of 28,000 people, and reflected on that estuary which is to pour into the Thames, at one point, the abominations of 2,800,000 living beings, besides that of tens of thousands of animals, I almost trembled for the result. Take this Croydon affair as an example of the facility and cheapness with which irrigation may be effected by steam-power.

A single engine, consuming fifteen shillings-worth of coals every twenty-four hours, raises one million gallons of water, and then forces it through a twelve-inch pipe to a tank a mile distant, and 150 feet above the engine.

Now it is quite clear that about the same power and the same size pipe would re-distribute subterraneously to certain hydrants on the fields, the said quantity of water when *enriched* with all the good things of Croydon.

Agriculture compared with Manufactures.—Spackman, in his "Occupations of the People," estimates the agricultural interest in land and tenants' capital for the United Kingdom as £2,000,000,000, or twenty-five times as large as the manufacturing interest, which he estimates at £78,000,000. Although I think this is exaggerated, there can be no doubt that agriculture is by far the largest interest in the kingdom. But is it the most intelligent and unprejudiced? I think not. If

I were to test this comparatively, I should estimate it by the amount of steam-power which it employs relatively to the other great producing interests of the country.

Let us see how the matter stands. So far as I am able to obtain approximate estimates,—

	Horse-power.
Manufactures employ 150,000 steam-engines of an average power of 20 horses	3,000,000
Railway locomotives, 7,550, 100-horse power	755,000
Marine engines, 2,000, of 100-horse power	200,000
Our armed steam navy, 450 ships	100,000
Agriculture, only 6,000, 8-horse power	48,000

Now, if Mr. Spackman is right, agriculture should employ millions of horse-power, instead of only 48,000.

In these days I take the use of steam to be the measure of progression, intelligence, and profit.

What is there in agriculture so complicated or difficult that steam could not master?

I saw in Manchester, the other day, two 18-horse power engines, which cost a thousand pounds, employed entirely in packing bales, and working the hoists or lifts which carried the men and cotton goods from floor to floor. The hydraulic squeeze, given by steam-power, caused a bale to be packed in three minutes, which, by manual labour, used to require fifteen minutes.

Time, surely, is money, as much in agriculture as in any other industrial occupation.

Taking the average of farms at the ordinary depth of cultivation, the number of steam-engines required would be enormous for cultivation alone; but if our clays are (as they ought to be) moved to a depth of two or three feet, then, indeed, great will be the requirement of steam power.

As our ordinary depth of cultivation is under five inches, and as our little island is sea-girt, tripling or quadrupling our depth of cultivation would be equal to an immense extension of territory, without additional rent, tithes, or taxes. At present, in our stiff undrained clays, all below five inches is a *terra incognita*, unseen and unavailed of, as is shewn by the "going off" of the crops in April and May.

Steam Estimates.—In estimating the probable amount of steam-power, used generally in our various industrial manufacturing and commercial operations, I have to tender my thanks to my official and other friends for the kindness with which they have placed statistical facts at my disposal, and for the information which they have otherwise afforded to me.

I have been assured that in a circle of twenty miles, in and around Manchester, there are 50,000 steam-engines—if so, agriculture owes a deep debt of gratitude to Manchester, which I hope she will repay by similar means.

I find that every fifty miles of passenger railway employs forty locomotives. The number of miles travelled on our railways, in 1857, was over seventy-four millions; the average consumption of coke, 34 lbs. per mile. A very great economy has lately been effected by the use of coal: the furnace door is left open, and the air rushing in, strikes against a deflecting-plate, which throws it on the surface of the fire, and causes perfect combustion without smoke. This is a hint which might be availed of in our agricultural portable engines. The air has much the effect of being blown on the coals by a bellows. Flame gives much more heat than red-hot coke.

Conclusion.—Apologising for the length of these remarks, I hope you will think with me, that I have proved that steam is not only an advantage but a necessity for agriculture, and that it has not been sufficiently availed of. A great responsibility attaches in this matter to those in high places who have large estates. We know, especially where there is only annual tenure, that the landowner is much looked up to by his tenantry, and that there is somewhat of a patriarchal character in their relations. So long as that exists, a heavy responsibility rests with the lord of the soil; his example and encouragement are required, and almost demanded in this matter of steam.

It may be necessary for men to exercise a gentle despotism in the removal of prejudices, which are often very strong in agriculture.

How all this may be done is easily explained by a reference to the late great Mr. Coke, of Norfolk, who converted a poor tenantry, and a miserable estate, into the opposites of farming wealth and greatly increased rentals.

We have modern examples of this, such as Lord Lonsdale, the Duke of Bedford, and many others, who combine investment, improvement, and encouragement, with honour, profit, and progression to themselves, to their tenantry, and to their country. There is plenty of room for such examples to be followed in our, at present, half-farmed country.

The mere value of steam to agriculture, in the sawing and preparing of the timber of an estate is considerable, and I remember to have been delighted thirteen years ago with the workshops and machinery of the Duke of Bedford, at Woburn, whose farmeries, cottages, and hedge-rows are a standing censure on the general agricultural non-improvement of this kingdom.

In conclusion, agriculture has been, in the matter of steam, backward, miscalculating, and ungrateful.

The statistical comparisons which I have made are humiliating for British agriculture, and, when I say agriculture, I mean landlord as well as tenant, for property has its duties as well as its rights. When I see that landlord, tenant, and labourer are indebted to steam manufacture for cheapness and abundance in almost every necessary they possess, both mental and physical, I do consider that common gratitude should induce them to adopt similar means to feed abundantly and cheaply the enlightened manufacturing population to whom they are indebted for those benefits.

My agricultural friends may think me somewhat severe in these my observations, but they are our best friends who tell us of our faults, and I only enforce what I practise, and practise profitably too. I shall therefore hope to receive their forgiveness for this my contribution to their agricultural literature. Pleased, indeed, should I be to see agriculture so perfect that "Othello's occupation would be gone."

I have annexed a few of my practical observations and convictions about Steam-Engines, for the information of those who will take the trouble to read them.

They are as follows:—

Fixed or Portable Engines.—There can be no doubt that fixed engines are more economical and durable than portable engines. I have had one in use ten years, and it is nearly as good as the first day I had it. There is much less wear and tear in a fixed engine than in a portable one. Bringing home the corn in the sheaf, at harvest-time, in Hannam's carts, is quite as economical as stacking and thrashing in the field, and afterwards bringing home the loose straw, chaff, &c. But, if we cultivate by steam, we *must* have portable engines; and, then when used for stiff work at the homestead, they should be fixed in a strong frame or support to prevent oscillation. Every thing connected with steam-power should be firm, steady, and free from trembling movement. So important is this considered in our manufacturing districts, that their buildings are most substantial. For Mr. Salt's 500-horse power engine at Bradford, 1,200 tons of stone, bolted and fixed as one mass, were required as a foundation to hold the monster firmly. Our old agricultural buildings would be racked to pieces by steam-power.

It would do farmers good to see the unerring movement of our manufacturing machinery, all smooth and steady. A well-finished engine is almost as finished as the works of a watch, and as far as possible should be kept free from dust, grit, or rust. This is the case in our manufacturing districts, where the engine has a room to itself, as clean as a drawing-room.

Farmers who use steam ought to know something about it, and I would recommend their adopting Messrs. Ransome's instructions, ably given in the last number of the *Royal Agricultural Society's Journal*, which every farmer of 150 acres would find a profit in subscribing to.

Mr. Williams's plan of avoiding smoke is worthy of inspection, and may be seen at Messrs. Redpath & Co.'s foundry, near the Stepney station. A five-pound note will save much waste and nuisance, and give increased power.

Mr. Fairbairn's test of safe boiler-pressures is as follows: he says—"The following table, deduced from my own experiments, exhibits the safe working-pressure and the bursting-pressure of boilers of different diameters, calculated for an external shell of a thickness of $\frac{3}{8}$ths of an inch.

Diameter of Boiler.	Working Pressure.	Bursting Pressure.
ft. in.	lbs.	lbs.
3 0	118	708¼
3 6	101	607
4 0	88½	531
4 6	78¾	472
5 0	70¾	425
5 6	64¾	386¼
6 0	59	354
6 6	54¼	326¾
7 0	50½	303½
7 6	47	283¼
8 0	44	265¾
8 6	41½	250

"Taking from the above table the strength of a boiler 7 feet in diameter, we find its bursting-pressure to be 303 lbs. per square inch."

There are certain practical matters in relation to fixed engines which are worth knowing. I therefore consulted the following books with much advantage:—"Armstrong on Boilers," "Williams on Combustion;" I have also "Dr. Alban on High-pressure Steam," and "Craddock's Lectures on the Steam-engine."

This information and my own observation have induced me to come to the following practical conclusions upon certain points connected with fixed steam-engines not multitubular:—

Furnace.—That there should be one square foot of fire-grate for every horse-power.

That the fire-bars should be at least two feet below the boiler-bottom.

That the space above the bridge should be equal in area to thirty square inches for every foot of fire-grate.

That the flues in every part, and the opening into the chimney, should have an area of thirty square inches for every foot of fire-grate.

That the furnace-plate and fire-door should be pierced with thirty half-inch holes for every foot of fire-grate, a deflecting-plate being placed in the furnace.

That the boiler should have at least nine feet of heating surface to every foot of fire-grate.

That there should be very little stoking and no smoking.

That it would repay well to read "Wye Williams on Combustion," "Dr. Alban on High-pressure," and "Armstrong on

Boilers," all published by Weale, High Holborn; also "Craddock's Chemistry of the Steam-engine," by Simpkin and Marshall.

That locomotive or multitubular boilers generate steam quickly, but are difficult to clean, and soon wear out.

That Cornish boilers are less safe for high pressure than flue-boilers, unless very carefully supplied with water; but if kept filled with water, and the steam taken from another boiler or vessel attached to and above them, as in Mr. Collinson Hall's plan, then I consider the Cornish boiler perfectly safe and most economical.

That flue-boilers, having a length of three times their diameter, are simple, durable, and safe.

That we should have Sylvester's trap-doors at each end of the centre and every other flue, so as to cleanse them when required.

That rushing air, like rushing water, will travel quickest through a smooth, clean flue, free from sharp angles or rough obstructions.

Mr. Fairbairn has recently discovered that, in long thirty-feet flue-boilers, the flue is of only one-third the strength of the outside shell, although of the same substance. His remedy is simple and effective. This deficiency of flue strength does not exist in boilers under ten feet in length. He says—

"If we take a boiler of the ordinary construction, thirty feet long, and seven feet in diameter, with one or more flues, three feet or three feet six inches in diameter, we find that the cylindrical external shell is from three to four times stronger in its powers of resistance to the force tending to burst it, than the flues are to resist the same force tending to collapse them. This being the case in boilers of ordinary construction, it is not surprising that so many fatal accidents should have occurred from the collapse of the internal flues, followed immediately by the explosion and rupture of the outer shell. To remedy such evils, and to place the security of vessels, so important to the community, upon a more certain basis, it is essential that every part should be of uniform strength to resist the forces brought to bear upon it. The equalization of the powers of resistance is the more important, as the increased strength of the outer shell is absolutely of no value, so long as the internal flues remain, as at present, liable to be destroyed by collapse, at a pressure of only one-third of that required to burst the envelope which surrounds them."

That feed-pumps should have a vertical action, with a wide piston and short slow stroke, experience having taught me the inconvenience of a long thin piston and rapid horizontal motion. Perreaux's vulcanized India-rubber valves are infallible.

That it is desirable to have a supply of water well heated by the waste steam passing around it before pumping it into the boiler.

That all bearings for rapidly revolving shafts should be very wide, so as to diminish friction by pressure, and admit of lubrication.

That great care should be taken not to bind the shafting by over-screwing the brasses.

That all riggers should be turned perfectly smooth, so as to make the driving straps bind on them, by excluding air.

That all bearings should be well supported and free from the least vibration, and that shaftings should never be long enough or thin enough to whip when at work. It is this which causes driving-straps to come off.

That the foundation of your engine should be solid and sufficient. I think I read that Mr. Salt's great engine at Saltaire, Bradford, required 1,200 tons of stone for its foundation.

That our manufacturers in Manchester, Leeds, &c., evince their appreciation of the necessity for extreme accuracy in their machinery, by the ponderosity of their buildings.

That our tumble-down farmeries are often unfit for the vigorous attachments of mighty steam.

That great mistakes are made by bricklayers, engineers, and others, in the erection of engines, flues, and setting boilers. See "Armstrong on Boilers," and "Williams on Combustion."

That it is very desirable one should know something practically about the matter in which we are so much interested—practically, so as to detect or prevent erroneous operations.

That your boiler should always be of two or more horse-power than your engine, and that both should be well master of their work.

That the absence of glass water-gauges and the mere use of steam-cocks, too common in many of our manufactories, is a dangerous and costly neglect, often resulting in accident, or in the burning of the boiler plates, and interruption of the works.

That all high-pressure engines should have a Bourdon steam-gauge, and also a mercurial steam-gauge.

I am a believer in Craddock's theory of explosions, and also in Dr. Alban's proposition, that there is much less ebullition with high-pressure than with low-pressure steam, the steam bubbles being infinitely smaller by greater compression.

That we owe a debt of gratitude to Mr. Wye Williams, who has taught us to prevent smoke and economize fuel, and who has also enlightened us on the circulation of water in steam-boilers.

That the steam-chamber, or steam portion of the boiler, should be enveloped in a heat greater than its own temperature, but not sufficient to make the boiler-plates of too high a temperature.

That excessive heat in the ash-pit, red-hot fire-doors and furnace-plates, and over-heated fire-bars, indicate either the absence of a sufficient supply of air to the upper portion of the fuel, or inadequate draught or flue-room.

That multitubular boilers have their joints loosened by too intense heat passing inside the tubes. That such boilers, when attached to, and above, a Cornish boiler (as in Mr. Hall's case), do not suffer injury, but utilize the heat which passes through them.

The advantages of high pressure, great expansion, and rapid movement of the slide, are fully availed of in the locomotive; there the pressure is often 140 lbs. per inch; the steam cut off at 1-24th of the stroke, and the stroke or slide movements very quick.

The effect of all this is admirably explained by Dr. Alban. The rapid and almost continued exit of the steam causes a vacuum in the exhaust-pipe, and thus relieves the piston of a large portion of the pressure of the atmosphere, whilst the gain from expansion, at 140 lbs. pressure per inch is very large, as shewn in Craddock's tables. It must be borne in mind that compression of steam costs us nothing more than the expense of a somewhat stouter boiler. It costs no more fuel to produce steam at high pressure than in an ordinary open copper; (*vide* Armstrong). When travelling on the Great Northern by express, the engine-driver told me he worked his engine at 140 lbs. pressure per inch.

The most economical management I know of with high-pressure steam, not condensed, is that practised by Mr. Collinson Hall, of Prince's-gate, Romford. He works three pairs of mill-stones at a cost of five shillings per day for coals. This may be considered equal to eighteen horse-power, or thirty-six horses per diem. His pressure is 120 lbs. per inch, worked expansively.

The peculiarity is having a multitubular boiler fixed above, and attached to, a Cornish boiler, the heat passing through and then around both boilers, including also the steam space. I very much admire the economy and safety of the arrangement, the Cornish boiler being always full of water.

In fact, Mr. Hall's success is partly owing to his superheating the steam in his upper boiler. As superheating steam dries it, a portion of moist steam is admitted from the boiler at every third stroke, to act as a lubricator. No doubt you are aware that this principle is being acted upon extensively by the Peninsular and Oriental Steam Navigation Company, who hope to save some 30 per cent. on the £700,000 which they pay annually for coals; the subject is well worthy the attention of agriculturists. Some years ago, the American government caused a commissioner to report on the suggestions of Mr. Frost, an Englishman, on super-heated steam, and confirmed his views of its economy.

We all know that a very slight degree of cold diminishes the expansion and pressure of steam, and it is easy to comprehend that the opposite of this increases its power; practically I have acted on this principle for some time, by allowing my last flue to encircle the steam space of my boiler; a heat of 650 degrees has no injurious effect in this respect. No doubt it was this consideration that caused Mr. Hornsby to place his cylinder in his boiler; and I think Messrs. Tuxford placed theirs in the smoke-box. A fearful loss of power is often occasioned by exposing a long supply steam-pipe to atmospheric influence.

Cornish boilers are dangerous for high-pressure, if the upper surface of the internal flue is uncovered or only slightly covered by water. The danger is at starting, when the water rises over the red-hot portion of the flue; it is like plunging a red-hot mass of iron into water.

Many a new good *Cornish* boiler has been ruined by the stoker raking out a red-hot fire, and thus suddenly exposing the boiler to a full blast of cold air from the open door. The sudden and unequal contraction starts the rivets, and makes the boiler leak.

I have been told that the admission of cold air through the furnace-doors, on Williams's plan, is apt to affect *Cornish* boilers. Probably a deflecting plate would prevent this.

All sudden and violent changes of temperature are injurious to boilers.

Steam Cultivation.—Since reading my paper on this subject to the London Farmers' Club, I have witnessed the trials of steam-ploughs and cultivators at the Royal Agricultural Show, Warwick. Those trials have still further confirmed me in my opinion that steam cultivation is a practical and profitable operation; pregnant with benefits to the cultivator and owner of stiff cold clays.

Experience has taught me that the causes of their supposed infertility are consolidation and the absence of atmospheric influence. After drainage and aëration by deep and frequent tillage, which can, by steam, be cheaply and quickly effected, they will, I feel convinced, command a preference over the lighter soils; especially for wheat, beans, oats, tares, clover, and mangel wurtzel. By Fowler's drainage and steam-ploughs such soils may be at once rendered profitable, at a comparatively small cost. I know a case where the parties letting out Fowler's draining plough, drained a field of fourteen acres for less than £20. The subsoil being a stiff chalky clay required no pipes, but merely a plug or wedge drain, made by the mole of the plough, at the depth of three feet from the surface, at seventeen feet intervals. The steam cultivator and subsoil plough following this, would at once render the land available for improved and remunerative crops, affording an ample profit on the investment.

Animals in July, August, and September—the Fly Season.—The amount of fat taken off our animals during this period of irritation and excitement is a considerable loss. This is easily remedied by a punkah or large fan-wheel moved by a strap from the steam-engine; not a fly will remain in the cooling draught. It is a great mistake to force air through small holes at much cost. It should be a large wheel with a slow motion requiring little power.

I always lime-wash my slated roofs, the heat is thus reflected and the roof kept cool. It will not wash off, but is removed in winter by frost.

Londoners should use it to keep their attics cool, and thus discourage the breeding of bugs.

In winter our bullock-sheds should be warmed like our green-houses or cotton factories, by steam or warm water.

Burned Clay as Bedding substituted for Straw.— A successful farming friend of mine has used, for many years, burned clay under his sheep. They are of course under cover during winter. One barrow-load daily to every twenty sheep is the right quantity. The clay is burned into brick dust, during summer, and thatched near the homestead to keep it dry. As 13-14ths of the sheeps' manure are urine, it is easy to understand what a fine effect this manure has when drilled for turnips or other crops.

Sheep never get sore feet on this burned clay.

It is particularly healthy for them or any other animals, and enables you to consume your straw as food.

By summer burning you may have a load of twenty-seven bushels of burned clay for six-pence. It answers admirably for aërating and improving stiff clays.

WHAT DOES IT COST TO KEEP A HAMPSHIRE DOWN EWE FOR TWELVE MONTHS, INCLUDING THE KEEP OF HER LAMB UNTIL SOLD AS A STOCK LAMB IN JUNE OR JULY?

Mr. Bond, in his very useful paper read before the London Farmers' Club, estimates it at 5d. per week., or 21s. 8d. per annum, charging the food at cost price. Having an impression that the cost is greater than this, I should be glad to see some of your correspondents' estimates. The cost price of mangel in our county would be about 7s. 6d. per ton, or 2d. per bushel; swedes with us would cost 10s. per ton at least. Would it be safe to reckon on less than half the cost of a fattening sheep as the proper charge? Ewes are great consumers when giving milk, to which must be added the food of the lamb; and the cross of the Cotswold, quoted by Mr. Bond, would produce a large consuming lamb. Mr. Lawes, in his valuable papers on Sheep Feeding (Society's *Journal*, vols. x., xii., and xiii.), shows the weekly cost of fattening a Hampshire Down sheep to be—

	s.	*d.*
8 lbs. oil-cake, at 1¼*d.* per lb.	0	10
7 lbs. clover-hay, at 0½*d.* per lb.	0	3½
106 lbs. swedes, at 5*d.* per 112lbs., or 8*s.* 4*d.* per ton	0	4¾
	1	6¼

for a period of six months, under favourable circumstances of shelter. This accords with my own experience. After paying for the purchased food (clover-hay and oil-cake), nothing was left to pay for the swedes, attendance, and shelter. Mr. Bond estimates the keep of the sheep and lamb during the three spring months at 9d. per head per week. Is this enough? Would not such an animal, with her large cross-bred lamb, consume as much as a fattening sheep? Again, during the three summer months the estimate is 6d. per head for the ewe with her lamb. How does this contrast with Mr. Lawes's 1s. 6d. per week? My object is merely to elicit truth and a sound basis, because Mr. Bond's statement of profit beyond the manure would be entirely annihilated if the ewe cost 7½d. per week instead of 5d. We know that stock ewes are excellent scavengers on a farm, but they are large consumers. I hope Mr. Bond will be kind enough to tell us how many acres of produce are consumed annually by the 300 ewes and their lambs; and what is the rent and quality of the land. A neighbour of mine told me that 70 fattening sheep, having 1 lb. of cake per day, consumed 36 acres of his produce. He thought 100 ewes would require the produce of 50 acres at least. On this calculation Mr. Bond's flock would require 250 acres; at his estimate of annual cost, 21s. 8d. each, the return upon this 250 acres would be but £542. I do not agree with Mr. Bond about two-years clover. I find that my first mowing of clover for hay sells for about £8 per acre; I then allow the second crop to grow fully, and feed it with sheep eating 1 lb. of rape-cake per day. This gives me a heavy crop of red wheat, succeeded by five or six quarters of Rivett wheat. On my farm of 170 acres I grow 50 acres of wheat annually, and 50 acres of oats, barley, and beans. I presume, from Mr. Bond's statement, that on his 800 acres of land he only grows 150 acres of wheat. In these times we must produce much corn as well as meat. Two-years clover leas are not likely to do this, nor are poor pastures. Breeding lambs and fattening them for the butcher would produce more corn than selling them as lean stock. Mr. Bond's paper having appeared in many publications, I have also distributed these remarks with a view to an elucidation of the subject.

Note.—If the sale of, and profit on, the lambs or sheep sold is not as much as the *market* price of the food that they have consumed, there will be a charge against the manure equal to the difference or deficiency. This is the proper way to estimate the cost of the manure.

Feb. 7, 1859.

Farm Residences—their Influence on the choice and character of a Tenant.—My abundant intercourse with the agricultural community enables me to form a correct opinion on the matter of farm residences. Many a good improving tenant, with ample means, has said to me—"Your south-country farms are apparently cheap, as to rental, but the farm buildings, and especially the farm houses, are totally unfit for men of capital and intelligence; and however willing I may be to improve the land on a sufficient tenure, it is not at all to be expected that I should erect a farm house and farm buildings on the land of another." Therefore landlords so situated must be content with a humble and uncapitalled tenantry, with all their unsatisfactory results. Good farm buildings would cost £7 per acre, and a sufficient farm residence could not be erected under £5 per acre. A fixed steam-engine, with all necessary thrashing and other machinery, would involve an outlay of about £2 10*s*. to £3 per acre. Of course, all that is properly done by a landlord should command a sufficient additional rental.

Encouragement to Improvers.—In 1846 I transferred to my neighbour, in exchange, about two acres of land which I had drained and forked deeply in 1843. This year, 1859, the crop on these two acres and my neighbour's adjoining land (all in the same field, and drilled the same day), is barley. In every stage of the growth of that barley, the two acres transferred thirteen years ago shew a decided superiority, have ripened earlier, promise a larger crop, and which is of a quality worth several shillings per quarter more than the adjoining unimproved land. In fact, every year, in almost every crop, this advantage has been visible during the thirteen years since it left my hands. Surely such results ought to convince the doubtful of the monetary benefits conferred by drainage and improvement of our soil.

Parish Roads, as at present managed, deserve our censure. There are, no doubt, exceptions; but, as a general rule, they are terribly mismanaged. If good roads, like our public ones, are profitable by economizing horse labour, and by sparing the wear and tear of our vehicles, it follows that the bumpkin-like condition of our parish roads must be wasteful and unprofitable. Many a creaking vehicle finds its untimely crisis by concussion with an unbroken and projecting knob; and many a broken knee to tired and leg-weary horses results from the same cause. But can all this be wondered at? Each farmer has his annual turn at road-mending as surveyor, and the ideas vary as much as the colours of the rainbow. One considers it economy to "shoot down" a most heterogeneous mass of "picked" stones and flints, varying in size from a cricket ball; and, slightly spreading them, they are left for ever after to Dame Providence. Calculating horses having established a foothold and wheel-rut on this objectionable mass, take especial care "the self-same track to trace again," thus raising sundry shoulders, which effectually dam in the falling rain, stagnating, saturating, and softening the road. It really appears as if the example of our well-managed high-roads is entirely lost upon our local road-menders, whose greatest recommendation with the parishioners is that they won't spend money; or, who are "put on," that they may have an opportunity of making or mending some road to their own farm. I know of several hills in my neighbourhood where no end of money has been wasted in attempting to make a good road. No provision is made for letting the water off on each side of the road at intervals from the top downwards; but it is allowed to accumulate to a little torrent, and thus scour away the road itself at its declivity.

On a hilly road "convexity" ought to be imperative; but too often "concavity" is paramount; so that I know of a great many broken knees this summer by treading on loose, large, unbroken stones, from which the bedding has been washed away.

Now, by breaking all large or round stones, raking them into the centre or ruts, so as to make the horses change their walk, and thus wear the road evenly, taking care it is sufficiently convex to shoot the water to the sides, you will have an even and economic road.

Sometimes a drain and pipe carried under the road may effect a proper diversion of the water; and in all cases the ground of the road should be subdrained, where there is no natural filtration. After a heavy rain or high wind I have sent a man to crush, with a sledge hammer, sundry projecting unbroken stones standing above the level of the road, just high enough to catch the toe of a leg-weary horse. It pays to break all round stones of any size; and no one should be allowed to sweep the grit off the roads to make mortar.

Aug., 1859.

How Bullocks can be made to pay?—Although I once found bullocks unprofitable, I can now, by rigidly adhering to the practice of Mr. Horsfall, as described elsewhere, make them pay for their food, and leave me the manure free of cost—except the straw.

Sparred Floors.—*August*, 1859.—Experience has proved these to be profitable in every way. If you divide a lot of sheep or bullocks, the butcher will go first to those on sparred-floors—their sanitary condition is superior, the expense of attendance less, and no straw is required for bedding.

The Miseries of a Public Improver.—The amount of personal labour arising from my public position in agriculture is not slight. Every inventor believes that I can develope his scheme, and find money for its introduction. I must answer a thousand questions about every agricultural practice. Introductions without number demand my civilities. Every new manure-maker wishes me to experiment with, and certify as to the merits of his compound. Large, also, is the supply of foreign seeds, and strong the claim of new machinists. Still, so far as time will permit, there is a great advantage in being able to acquire knowledge from many new and intelligent sources, and charming friendships have arisen from my agricultural pursuits.

The consciousness of having been of some service to one's fellow-creatures is a great set-off against trouble and anxiety. The recollection that the two American reapers were first tried on my farm, in 1851, is a pleasing *souvenir*. *Then* they were wondered at; *now* Messrs. Burgess and Key alone are preparing to make *fifteen hundred* for use in 1859. The inspection of Garrett and Sons' horse-hoe, and various implements, by foreign visitors, has, I know, led to many purchases for foreign parts. My operations in sewage irrigation have also facilitated or induced the economy of town sewage. On the whole, therefore, I have reason to be gratified and grateful.

In concluding this volume, I have not done with British agriculture. While I admire the progress that has been already made, I feel that it is but a tithe of that which is to come. I shall therefore continue, as opportunity offers, to stimulate agricultural advance, with a view to the national profit and honour.

APPENDIX.

Having always contended that Agriculture may be dealt with on the same principles as Commerce, I make no apology for appending to this work the following Lecture on the Principles which ensure Success in Trade.

ON THE PRINCIPLES WHICH ENSURE SUCCESS IN TRADE.*

Value of Confidence.—Every effect has its cause: of course there is such a thing as chance, or luck, which you may illustrate by a prize in a lottery, or a £10,000 legacy from some one from whom you never expected a shilling; but these are exceptions—not the rule. Now, if we were about to erect a house, a wise man would take care to place it on a sound and solid foundation—the higher and larger, the wider should be the basis. In my early career I remember asking myself this question:—Why do customers change or transfer their favours? Not because they are satisfied, but because they have lost confidence. The remark applies equally to the merchant, manufacturer, shipowner, or trader. I do not, however, intend in this paper, to enter upon the causes of commercial success or failure, although, from having passed the first eleven years of my career in the service of an eminent mercantile firm, I have my opinions upon that subject. There is no tie so strong in worldly matters as self-interest; therefore, if you act with integrity to your customers, if you have the ability to obtain and place before them the article they require, with the necessary accompaniments of civility, attention, and good feeling, you win their confidence and connection. What an important word is that said *confidence;* it reminds me of the compound multiplication of the horse-shoe nails. Let me illustrate it. How frequently have I observed, in my early career, at my counter, the eager and buoyant schoolboy buying his first shilling penknife. "Is it a good one, Mr. Mechi?"—"Yes; I'll exchange it if it does not suit you." Ah! that penknife, it pleased him. He grows to the bearded youth: he must have razors—he remembers the penknife. He falls in love—'tis natural to fall in love—a work-box for his intended. He gets married—'tis natural to get married—he must have cutlery, and marriageable accompaniments. So, you see, the good penknife won his confidence. We have his friends, all his friends' friends, as a compound multiplication of continuous recommendation. I have always found it advantageous to treat my customers with the utmost latitude of liberality in regard to their exchanging, or even by returning the money for any article not approved. In fact, I say to them, "Do here as you would in your own house; please yourself if you can." Thus liberality begets liberality. I have seldom found it abused—except occasionally by a churl who is neither satisfied with himself nor anybody else. A rigid and prompt attention to jobs, or small matters, is very essential, and too often neglected; and yet customers are as often offended by these neglects as by more important ones. Now, this confidence is a very pleasing and profitable conclusion to arrive at; but, before we

---

* A Lecture delivered at Crosby Hall, Bishopsgate Street, London—1856.

attain it, let us see what has to be done. I will briefly pass in review, and dispose of the young man who stays out late at night, who gets up late in the morning, who waits on Providence, with his hands in his pockets, hoping for customers: his windows uncleaned, his shop-frontage unswept, his wares undusted, and his general personal appearance in harmony with his other mismanagement; his orders procrastinated, and his business (his customers' wants and wishes) made, in fact, subservient to his ease or to his pleasures. His time of performance will be short—if dependent on credit, *very* short. Anxious and observant creditors grow nervous and pressing—the fall of the curtain is illustrated by an auctioneer's sale-paper, and we shall see on the shutters, in dark and significant characters,—"THIS SHOP TO LET." His unfortunate servants and dependents, if he has any, are launched on the wide sea of competition, possibly infected by his bad example—he himself, sunk one important degree in the scale of social degradation. 'Tis a painful picture, I have too frequently seen it; I pray you, avoid it. Well, as I said before, in establishing a new business, remember that you are on your trial. In first transactions you will be closely watched, and not easily forgiven. Confidence is a plant of slow and careful growth; but when you have the confidence of the public, again remember it may be lost. If, in full reliance on this confidence, you relax in those sound principles which obtained it, you must expect a retributive re-action. Your old friends, your customers, will complain, and perhaps hope and believe the first offence arises from accident; but they will never forgive you for a second abandonment of just principles. In order fully to succeed, you must be a perfect judge of your business. I mean, you must have taste as to a pleasing form and pattern, a rigid observance of quality and finish, an acute perception of price, and a conviction that high prices diminish demand, whilst moderate charges increase it.

The Accumulation of old Stock (a fearful term) ruins many a tradesman. His taste and judgment are inferior to those of his customers; they reject the untempting, though oft tendered, and consequently, old-fashioned or deteriorated article. A great evil attends this. The buyer is disappointed; he purchases from a more able and successful contemporary, who probably secures his custom in perpetuity. Before I leave the old-stock question (and we must all occasionally have a little), remember to watch a hanging article; it may be much approved, but appear too dear in the public view. If you are assured of this, reduce the price at once either to or below cost price, and avoid the pattern for the future. Every wise man will take stock of his goods at least once a year; he will value them, if well bought and in good saleable order, at cost price; but if old or unsaleable stock, the value at which they could be then bought should be then taken to exhibit the real state of his affairs.

I once knew an ironmonger who considered he had a large surplus, but failed. On an examination of his stock, it was found principally to consist of goods purchased years before at prices far above those of the day. He always took stock at its *first* cost, and endeavoured to sell accordingly. His trade diminished, and he became poor *in fact*, though solvent *in figures*. The ordering of stock, and its classifications, are matters seriously affecting your success; I have known a good many young tradesmen with brilliant prospects ruined by want of a proper system. If you have a reputation for integrity and industry, competing manufacturers will be most pressing and bland in persuading you that everything they have is most saleable. Each one will urge his suit, hoping to exclude his competitor. Here is your great danger. Young beginners are apt, naturally enough, to be too sanguine and hopeful: but remember (until you have ascertained your average weekly or monthly sale) to err on the safe side by ordering too little rather than too much—you can always add to them when necessary. When the period of payment comes round, the syren and soft voice of persuasive eloquence will be exchanged for the stern tone of threat or remonstrance; if, finding yourself over-stocked, you are unprepared for payment, the suppliers will say—"Sir, it was *your* duty to know what you wanted, ours was to endeavour to vend our manufactures." As I consider this part of the question a vital one, perhaps you will excuse my enlarging upon it in detail, by stating the result of my practice and experience; and here again I must impress a rigid attention to booking every article sold, its sort, its price, the weekly, monthly, and annual amount of your takings—and comparing them with the sales of the same periods in past years. These are the bases for your stock calculations. If your business is an uniform one, the amount of your orders should be the amount of your sales, minus the profit. The limitation of a monthly amount will be a useful check—and you should have a book in which you will enter the articles ordered, their prices, and carry out the amount as correctly as if you had sold the goods on credit—this will form a check on the invoice when it comes in, and you will see also, in good time, whether your supplier has accidentally or intentionally sent you in more or different articles than you ordered, which some are apt to do.

But suppose you are satisfied about the amount you should order, the next and equally important consideration is the classification of your stock. The public are very good judges of what suits them, and generally leave you an abundance of what they don't want. It may be either in quality or price. Let me illustrate it. Supposing my usual stock of work-boxes to be £500. Before I ordered or manufactured, I should take stock of those in hand in classified columns of *prices* as well as styles and qualities. Because if I did not, it might happen that I had three times as many as were necessary at £10 each, and yet lose and offend several customers who wanted them at £5 each. Still I might have my usual amount invested in work-boxes, but it was neglectfully and improperly classified. I speak of these matters from experience. A wise tradesman will endeavour to allot his capital in fixed amounts to the various branches of his trade, with a view to his own convenience and the wants and wishes of his customers, and this is no easy affair in an extensive trade, particularly where there are frequent changes of fashion. Take especial care never to be short of the running or every-day article.

Attraction by Display.—Experience has taught me, that with all articles of luxury or taste, it is good policy to devote a considerable portion of your capital to plate-glass and elegant cases. However beautiful a young lady may be, she must be seen to be appreciated. I have, therefore, as far as possible, discarded drawers and boxes, and substituted the visible for the invisible. Thus, whilst you are busily engaged, your customer's eye may be attracted by some object which presents itself to view, whereas, if immured in a drawer, no such pleasing result could take place.

All counters should be of plate-glass. When money was of great value to me, I began with so many feet of glass counter, and carefully noted how many things were sold, merely owing to their being visible and attractive.

The result was unmistakably in favour of the operation, which I have since carried out to its utmost limits.

Again, with shop-fronts; the absence of little panes and crossed bars is most conducive to success and attraction.

I am now nearly fifty-four years of age, during twenty-nine years of which I have conducted my Leadenhall Street business. Before that, the first ten years of my servitude was as clerk in an eminent mercantile firm. At that early period, as I walked every morning from the west-end to the city, I was forcibly struck with what was then the almost only elegant shop-front in London, I mean that of Mr. Everington, on Ludgate Hill, which then, as now, was resplendent with plate-glass and looking-glass. That shop-front made a deep impression on my mind, and educed a series of calculations most conducive to my success.

In fact, a philosophic stroll through London will present to the acute observer ample materials for estimating the probable failure or success of many shopkeepers.

Cleanliness.—Above all things, in our dirty city, is cleanliness. It will pay you, in a fancy business, to wash down your front once a month, and re-paint the whole outside once a year, which is my practice. Of course the outside, so far as it can be reached, must be washed down every morning—the windows cleaned every day. Some of our drapers' shops are good examples in this way. It need hardly be said that the personal appearance of the shopkeeper and his shopmen should harmonise with the other arrangements.

If it were possible to know the thousand and one influences that predispose customers, they would form a very interesting volume.

Supposing that, as I have recently done in a new establishment, you expend £5,000 in fittings and ornamentations; you should charge 10 per cent. per annum (or £500) to your trade expense account before you take your net profit. Thus the outlay will be all repaid within ten years. You thus estimate these assets each year at a reduction of 10 per cent.

A nice discretion is required in selecting your stock, adapted to the rank, condition in life, and means of your customers. Let this be a golden rule, to take care that everything is good of its sort. In illustration, many a shilling penknife is ruined because a farthing is saved in the steel of the blade. This is bad economy; 'tis in your power to stimulate and improve art by encouragement, whereas a constant nibbling at prices, with a view to cheapness, has often a reverse tendency. Beware of over-trading; it has ruined thousands, from the humble shopkeeper to the greatest merchant. However large your capital, if you over-trade you are lost. For either by over-stocking, or by giving undue and unlimited credit, embarrassment must overtake you—credit is capital if properly used. I would recommend any young man, depending in part on credit, to open his accounts with houses of character and capital, and, at all times, it is highly desirable to transact business only with honourable, straightforward people. The relation of business to capital must depend very much on the nature of the business and the period of return. In my own ready-money business I find that each hundred pounds taken weekly requires a capital or stock at cost price to the extent of £2,500 to £3,000, and that the capital is turned over twice in the year. A man may be ruined by having too much business; that is, a business disproportioned to his capital. In business as in farming, the concentration of capital rather than its diffusion is desirable. For instance, on a well-stocked shop the rent may be diminished one-half in comparison with a half-stocked shop or farm. If you give long credits, and have not a large capital, you must, to be safe, take longer credits than you give. In all trades, particularly if extensive, take stock annually at least, with an account of all you owe, and all owing to you, keeping a separate account of your personal or private expenditure, and bear in mind that, without being miserly, 'tis consistent with comfort and independence to spend rather less than you get. Whilst it is your duty to be punctual in your own payments, 'tis equally sound policy to collect at regular and stated periods the debts owing to you. Accounts do not improve by keeping, and no honest man will object to pay when called upon, when in his power. Remember that this is a world of vicissitudes and changes, and that a good debt now, may, by force of circumstances, be worthless three months hence.

Finance Department.—A perspective and prospective arrangement of your financial affairs is quite as requisite to you as the Chancellor of the Exchequer's Budget is to the nation. You will, therefore, have a diary (Letts' is a good one), and divide each month into weeks, entering carefully your acceptances and various responsibilities, such as rent, wages, &c. &c., and on the other side your probable weekly receipts. It is very desirable not to take too sanguine a view of the in-comings, but rather to leave a margin for casualties or disappointments, which must occasionally take place. If you are known to be honest, frugal, and industrious, and deal with respectable firms, you can generally make the time for your acceptances tally with your returns. It is best to be on the safe side. When you become a man of capital, you may purchase for cash, and take the extra discount then allowed.

Fire Assurance.—I should hardly venture to allude to the propriety of insuring against fire, but that the statistics of fire-offices show too plainly that a vast proportion of property in this kingdom is uninsured.

Not to insure is neither honest to yourself or to your creditors.

Collection of Accounts.—There is nothing which causes greater loss to a tradesman than an arrearage of book-keeping, and a neglect of regularly collecting accounts.

Cost what it may, make it therefore an inflexible rule to have your books posted up daily, and your quarterly or other accounts sent out at the exact period. Then comes the difficulty of collection. You may have to call twenty times or more ere you meet with your debtor; so, do not depend on the casual use of one of your shopmen, but devote a specific time and person to the collection, even if you pay a commission. It may be a good policy to do so, taking care to employ an honest regular man. Having collected your accounts, take care to enter them as paid. Nothing gives more offence to a customer than an application for a paid account.

If you have doubtful or bad debts, transfer them to a separate book, and don't estimate them in your assets.

Painful as it may appear, still it is true that the hard and rigid exacter of the settlement of accounts gets best paid. The good-natured or too-easy creditor generally comes off second-best.

If your business is done on credit, take care to diffuse your accounts, and not have too many eggs in one basket. Taking people as you find them, there is an excellent average of honesty and capability, and a small percentage of loss; but there is a desire with the worthless to get largely into debt. Therefore follow the rule of average practised by the fire and life insurance offices, who will never exceed a given sum upon any risk, however tempting. This rule will hold good in almost every business.

"Order is Nature's first law," disorder an infringement of it. A place for everything, and everything in its place, tends greatly to the economy of time, which is, in fact, money. Unless you have a fixed and permanent residence, properly numbered for each class of articles, you will be frequently ordering that which you really don't require, and of course occasionally lose the sale of what you have misplaced. If I sometimes pounce on the weak points of agriculture, I must also say that I cannot help seeing many sad mistakes in trade. I wonder how many thousand pounds'-worth of time is daily wasted in England by tradesmen running or sending about for change? It is a rule in my establishment to provide every morning a permanent sum in sovereigns, half-sovereigns, five-shilling-pieces, half-crown-pieces, shillings, sixpences, fourpenny-pieces, pence, and half-pence, all classified in divisional bowls, so that the cashier can give change with the smallest possible detention, either to himself or the customer. It saves much breathless haste, delay and disappointment.

Knowledge of Languages.—During my early days no such institutions as these existed for the acquirement of knowledge. Fortunately for me, a kind and foreseeing parent enabled me, by a residence abroad, to gain a knowledge of the French and Italian languages. That knowledge has, I assure you, been very pleasing and beneficial to me; and I strongly recommend you to avail yourselves of the opportunity presented by this excellent institution to acquire the continental languages.

Advertising.—Allow me to say a few words on the subject of advertising, because I think there is a false delicacy amongst some people on this matter. In my opinion advertising is a legitimate means of making known the wants and wishes of both buyers and sellers; whether they be for an estate worth half-a-million of money, or for a pair of "Mechi's best razors." It is merely making an extension of your shop-front in the newspapers; whether the article be seen there or in the window, in both cases its qualities remain to be tested. It never can answer to advertise a bad article. By advertising a good one, you extend your connection, which might otherwise be limited by the number and class of people who happened to pass your door, and their connections. For my own part, my spirit likes a wide range; and I remember once receiving an order through the Hudson's Bay Company, from poor Mr. Simpson, in his Polar expedition, whilst almost at the same time I was supplying a missionary from the Sandwich Islands.

Having devoted the last ten years to agricultural pursuits, I have been occasionally asked, "How do you feel comfortable away from your business?" I reply, "I receive daily the following statement of my affairs from my old and faithful servants." I quote it; it may be useful in similar cases.

"Date—Goods ordered—Goods brought in—Farm account—Private account—Goods paid for—Trade expenses—Amount taken this year—Amount taken last year—Cash in hand—Banker's balance—Letters from—Persons absent."

The choice of your servants or dependents is a matter of serious consequence to your welfare. Conduct, character, and capability, are essentials; but it will require an observant discrimination to detect and apply their leading or excelling characteristics. You will select method and regularity in your bookkeeper; decision, observance, and discretion in your buyer; a bland urbanity, with persuasion, in your seller. Whilst you exact from the members of your establishment a rigid observance of order, propriety, and decorum, treat them with that kindness and esteem which their good conduct so justly merits; encourage a feeling of manly self-dependence, and promote their comforts and amusements. In former times, when there were few or no literary institutions, the members of my establishment contributed to a book-fund—founded, of course, on some donations from myself. Even now I consider it my duty to provide them daily with the leading journal of Europe, that their hours of refreshment may be brightened by the beams of intelligence. A reciprocal good feeling cannot be too much encouraged. An occasional contribution to a festive and rational meeting forms a happy relief to the cares and anxieties of their daily occupation.

The Necessity for Recreation.—The very term recreation is expressive of the wear and exhaustion caused by incessant application. In the early years of my career, with a very limited capital and a desire to grasp at better things, my anxieties and application were intense and overpowering, and produced that mental exhaustion which is most unfavourable to success. In those days there were no railways, steam-boats, or ready means of getting quick and cheap transit; I therefore ventured to keep my horse and gig, and found that one hour's escape from the impure air and excitement of the city was a most profitable restorative.

With this impression strong on my mind, I have never had any doubts about the benefits of early closing, or an occasional half-holiday.

When you have made money, you will find that **every man has his hobby.** Mine was to improve the landed property which I had bought. The discussion of the principles of that improvement involved me in a very tornado of opposition, but at the same time introduced me into most agreeable and intellectual society. Things have settled down now, and we all seem to be agriculturally agreed that the people of this country have a powerful gastronomy, which must be attended to, and that we must, by improved means and increased capital, compel mother earth to give up to us her most ample treasures.

Some dangers, however, beset a public man—for such I suppose I may in some degree now consider myself. Scarcely a day passes without some appeal, some tempting offer by sanguine patentees, who only want *you* to bring out their inventions, or some offer of a directorate which is to make one's fortune. Happy is it if you are enabled to encase yourself in the armour of content and moderation.

In conclusion, if the Almighty has blessed you with talents and with success, remember that those precious gifts entail upon you the moral responsibility of a stewardship, that you may administer of your superfluity with kind feeling and discrimination to your needy, sick, or less fortunate fellow-creatures.

INDEX.

CPSIA information can be obtained
at www.ICGtesting.com
Printed in the USA
LVHW102013060123
736479LV00002B/300

9 783375 129088